Hearts and Aces

Book Seven of the Kelsey's Burden Series

KAYLIE HUNTER

This book is a work of fiction. All names, characters, places, businesses, incidents, etc., are the imagination of the author, and any resemblance to actual persons or otherwise is coincidental.

Copyright 2019 by Kaylie Hunter
All rights reserved.

Cover design by Selfpubbookcovers.com/riafritz

BOOKS BY KAYLIE

<u>Kelsey's Burden Series</u>
Layered Lies
Past Haunts
Friends and Foes
Blood and Tears
Love and Rage
Day and Night
Hearts and Aces

<u>Standalone Novels</u>
Slightly Off-Balance
Diamond's Edge

For a complete, up-to-date list of novels, visit
www.BooksByKaylie.com

Dedication

To my mom:

Thank you for having my back as I leapt, weaved, and ducked into the publishing world. Your support made all the difference.

Love Always...
Your favorite child

Chapter One

We all agreed our suspect was the thief; now we had to prove it. Our client, the owner of a chain of jewelry stores, was paying us top dollar to catch the bad guy. So I sat alone, hours after everyone else went to bed, monitoring the operation from my dining room table while Bridget and Trigger were in Delaware ready to pounce if our guy made his move.

Someone unlocking the front door pulled my attention away from my computer and I glanced at the clock. Three in the morning. I stood and stretched before going to the kitchen to fill another coffee cup. "Good morning, Tyler," I said without turning around.

"How'd you know it was me?" he asked, relocking the door and taking the cup.

"Who else is insane enough to still be up?"

"Some of the guards at Silver Aces haven't gone to bed yet, although they're hammered so I'm not sure it counts."

"Dumbasses. If they don't slow down they'll be hospitalized for alcohol poisoning before the weekend gets here." I returned to the table, nodding at a chair for Tyler to join me. "Why are you patrolling tonight?"

Tyler was a prospect for the Devil's Players, a local motorcycle club I had befriended years ago. When I realized he had good instincts, I hired him to keep an eye on the family, the retail store where most of the family worked, and our three houses. I also gave him the freedom to set his own hours. Some weeks, he worked only a few hours, just checking in periodically. Other weeks, he practically lived on our back deck, guarding the house like a sentry.

I looked up at Tyler when he remained silent. "Well, out with it. Is there a problem I'm not aware of?"

"None," he said, shaking his head.

Tyler and I both looked toward the front of the house, hearing a car approaching. We pulled our Glocks. Tyler slid out the back door into the dark. I moved to the front door, stepping outside with my gun aimed toward the truck that pulled into the driveway. The driver turned on the interior light as he parked. Ryan, one of the security guards at Silver Aces, waited in the truck with his hands up as he looked calmly back at me.

I called out to Tyler, "All good. It's Ryan!"

Tyler came around the corner of the garage, holstering his weapon. I tucked mine back into my holster as Ryan escorted a woman from the truck to the house.

"Figured someone would be up," Ryan said as I held the door open for the woman. Tyler followed them in, relocking the door behind us.

"Did you just get into town?" I asked him.

A multitude of guards were expected this weekend for a tournament of sorts. Carl had built a fighting machine, The Circle of Hell, and the guys wanted to compete against each other. The competition was originally scheduled last month, but between Lisa banning Donovan from competing until his fractured arm healed and Nicholas' birthday party last weekend, requiring everyone to pitch in to control two dozen nine-year olds, the guys had agreed to postpone. Unfortunately, postponing only gave the guys more time to plan an even bigger tournament which now included other events.

"No," Ryan answered, raising an eyebrow at the woman with him.

Ryan wasn't much of a talker. While his blondish-brown hair, loose-fitting jeans, and sun-kissed skin suggested an all-American facade, the way he moved and spoke screamed badass street fighter. More recently, I'd learned that Ryan possessed a knack for explosives and enjoyed playing with things that go boom.

The woman stood there watching us as she fidgeted. Her light blond hair bounced around her shoulders as she looked back and forth between Ryan and me. Her right hand twisted the material of her bright flowery dress. "Reel said I might be welcome to use your kitchen as long as I don't make too much noise."

"Reel?" Tyler asked.

"Disregard," Ryan growled, glancing down at the woman.

"I'm Kelsey Harrison. Are you a client?" I asked the woman, more than a little confused.

She giggled, looking up at Ryan. "No. I'm his wife, Tweedle-Dee."

"Or you can call her *Deanna*, like normal people," Ryan said, sighing.

She reached over and pinched him. "Behave." She stepped past Ryan, setting her purse on the kitchen counter and taking off her jacket. Looking about the kitchen, she began opening cupboards. "I hope you don't mind. I promise to be quiet, but I'm a baker and when I get nervous, I like to bake. Reel's apartment—"

"*Ryan*," Ryan corrected her.

"Right. Ryan's apartment doesn't have a kitchen."

"I have a mini fridge and a toaster oven. That's all I need. It's just a room to crash in from time to time."

She rolled her eyes before continuing, "If I would've known, we could've booked a hotel room."

"A hotel room with a full-size kitchen?" Tyler asked.

She pulled a bag of flour out of the cupboard. "Not necessary. I've been known to take over the kitchens in hotels. As long as I'm out of the way for their dinner rush, I've never had an issue."

Ryan rubbed a hand across his forehead, seeming to attempt to rub the stress lines away. I looked at Tyler who had an eyebrow raised as he watched Tweedle-Dee pull bowls and preheat the oven like she owned the place.

My laptop beeped. I jogged over to hit the icon for the incoming call. "I'm here, Bridget."

"Trigger just texted me that our guy is on the move. Figured you'd want to know."

"Are you in position?"

Tyler, Ryan, and Ryan's wife moved over to the dining room table and looked over my shoulder.

"Holy, hell. Is that you, Tweedle?" Bridget asked.

"Bridget! I was so excited to come visit for the tournament. I'm baking at Ms. Harrison's house. Can you come over?"

"Kind of busy at the moment, but if all goes well in the next twenty minutes I'll be home for the weekend festivities."

"What are you working on?" Tweedle asked.

"Babe," Ryan said, shaking his head. "They're in the middle of an op. Let Kelsey and Bridget work." He wrapped an arm around her, pulling her back from the laptop so I could sit in front of the screen.

"It's all good, Ryan, but I do need to focus," Bridget said before looking at me. "I'm turning on the body cam."

The screen went black, then bluish-grey. Tyler reached past me and adjusted the settings to brighten the images.

"I've got visual. What's the plan?" I asked.

"There are three points of entry: front door, back door, and an oversized ventilation duct on the roof. He'll enter through the roof. I'm on the next roof over."

"What if you're wrong?"

"I've got cops down the road ready to move in, but I'm not wrong."

"We know he's armed. I don't want you taking any risks."

"No worries. Trigger and I rigged the ventilation shaft. When he goes in, he'll drop down about ten feet, coming face-to-face with the night vision camera I installed earlier and the new security bars that will prevent him from getting into the store. Before he has a chance to backtrack I'll drop the top hatch, trapping him inside. If he doesn't want to die of starvation in there, he'll have to turn himself in peacefully. Hang on. Trigger's texting."

I picked up my phone and read the text that he sent both of us: *Suspect parked two blocks away. Moving in by foot. I'm disabling the car as a backup plan.*

Bridget texted back: *Ye of little faith. When are you going to learn, grasshopper? My plans don't fail.*

Ryan and Tyler laughed, reading over my shoulder.

"Should I call Bones?" Ryan asked.

"No!" Bridget, Tyler, Tweedle, and I answered together.

I looked up at Tweedle, and she winked at me.

Tweedle patted Ryan's arm. "Reel, Bones would just worry. Let Bridget do her thing."

"Fine." Ryan ran a hand through his hair, pulling at it. "But call me Ryan here. We talked about this." He wrapped his other arm around her as they leaned closer to the monitor.

Bridget tapped twice on her earpiece, getting my attention without speaking.

"I see him, Bridget. North fire escape. Man, he's quick."

"And quiet." Ryan nodded. "We can hear cars in the distance, but he just climbed an old two-story fire escape without making any noise. That isn't easy."

"It helps that he's only five foot two inches and weighs less than a buck twenty." I handed Ryan the file on the suspect.

"Aww," Tweedle said. "He's just a little guy."

"Who's suspected of killing two people and robbing seventeen jewelry stores," Ryan said as he dropped the file back on the table. "This guy likes knives, Bridget. Keep your distance when you move in to trap him."

Bridget tapped twice on her earpiece. With his back facing Bridget, the suspect soundlessly removed the top cover of the ventilation shaft. On her body cam we watched Bridget creep toward the other roof. As soon as he dropped into the shaft, she leapt the short distance between roofs, running to the nearby air conditioner. She dragged a metal grate out of hiding and dropped it over the hole. Standing on the edge of the grate, she kept it weighted while she pulled a battery-operated wrench from her utility belt and bolted the grate down.

A hand flashed out between the bars, swiping a knife toward Bridget's foot. She managed to jump clear of the knife, and when it swiped out again she stomped on his wrist, pinning it to the rooftop so she could peel the knife from his hand.

"He's likely to have a gun, Bridget," I reminded her.

She stepped back out of the perp's view and called the cops.

"That's it? It's all over?" Ryan asked.

I high fived with Tyler. "That's it. Game over."

Bridget squealed in excitement. We watched her body cam bop side to side.

"What's she doing?" Tweedle asked, pointing to the monitor.

Tyler laughed. "Her victory dance."

"What's the pay on a job like this?" Ryan asked.

"This was a reward gig," I said. "The company posted a three-hundred grand reward to whoever caught the thief terrorizing their jewelry stores."

"Shit," Tweedle cursed. "I'm in the wrong business."

Ryan shook his head at her before turning back to me. "How long did this op run?"

"Start to finish, three and a half days, including our research time. Bridget and Trigger didn't fly out until yesterday."

"Damn. Nice profit."

"Be sure to mention that to Donovan. He told me the investigations unit would never be as profitable as the rescue and security work."

"Calvary is here," Bridget said over the computer. "I'll leave the video running through the arrest, but you can go to bed now, Mom."

"Call me Mom again, and you'll be working retail, Bridget."

"Sorry, boss. Won't happen again," she said as she chuckled.

"Trigger, you good?"

"All set, Kelsey. We'll collect a check and head home in a few hours."

"Signing off. Good job, team."

Tyler reached over and signed out of the video chat and com systems.

"I'd better start baking," Tweedle said, returning to the kitchen. "Any requests?"

"Apple pie," Tyler said. "Kelsey has a bushel of apples in the garage, but hasn't had a chance to make pies yet."

Tweedle gave Ryan a look that he had no trouble interpreting. Without hesitating, he walked out to the garage. Tyler retrieved the coffee pot and filled our cups. After returning with the bushel basket, Ryan set it on a barstool and joined Tyler and me.

I pointed toward the hallway. "You can nap on one of the couches in the family room."

Ryan shook his head. "I'm good. Used to it," he said glancing over at Tweedle with a smirk.

"Tyler?" I asked.

"No. I'm going to finish this coffee then do another patrol."

"What's got you spooked? And don't tell me nothing."

"Nothing's wrong. I swear it. The tournament at Silver Aces is bringing in a lot of new faces is all. There's a lot of people I don't know, coming and going. It's making me edgy."

"They're all guards, handpicked and hired by Donovan or Grady."

"I don't know them," Tyler said as he stared directly at me. "There's at least thirty guys already here and another forty coming for the weekend. I can't tell the good guys from the bad guys. You're the one who taught me not to trust anyone until my gut told me they were trustworthy."

Ryan nodded. "He's got a point. We could pull a couple of guys to run patrols."

"That still leaves Tyler working with guards he doesn't know or trust. And Donovan, Bones, and Grady need a break this weekend."

"I talked to the Players," Tyler said. "The guys are willing to work security this weekend, if you're willing to pay for the extra payroll."

"I am. Keep the focus on the kids and the houses, though. Anything on this side of the highway will be protected by Devil's Players. Anything on the other side will be monitored by Silver Aces. If you need more labor, call Renato with the Demon Slayers."

"Sounds good," Tyler said.

Grady walked into the dining room, looking from the clock, to me, to Tyler, to Ryan, and then to Tweedle who was mixing something in a large bowl. He shook his head as he took a drink of my coffee. He was wearing running shorts, socks, and running shoes. His chest was bare, showing off his sculpted muscles dusted with a fine layer of blond hair. My eyes wandered his body. When I looked back to his face, I found him grinning at me.

"Ever heard of a shirt?" Ryan asked.

Looking into the kitchen, I saw Tweedle's cheeks were red as she quickly looked away.

Grady winked at me before turning to Ryan. "I'm heading downstairs to work out. You want in?"

Ryan nodded before walking over to Tweedle. He wrapped his hands around her waist as she looked up at him with a bright smile. "I'll be in the basement. *Do not leave this house without me.*"

"Where would I go?"

"With you, I never know," he said before he kissed her forehead and turned toward the stairs.

Grady leaned over the back of my chair. "You need to sleep for a couple of hours."

"I'm heading that way. Wake me after your workout? I've got a busy morning scheduled."

As a way of answering, he smacked a kiss to my lips before strutting toward the basement stairway. I admired his ass until he was out of view.

"I'm out," Tyler said. "I'll text you if I need you." Tyler left through the living room sliding door.

"Tweedle? You need anything before I go to bed?"

"I'm all set. Looking forward to some quiet baking. The trip here was a nightmare."

"Why? What happened?"

"First, I tripped on that horizontal escalator thingy at the airport."

"The auto-walk? Were you hurt?"

She shook her head. "Just embarrassed. After I tripped, my skirt caught in the track which then started to suck up the material as it dragged me across the room. By the time Reel—I mean *Ryan*—ripped away the material to free me, everyone had a full view of my ample backside, and he was pissed."

"Not at you, I'm sure." I stood and carried my cup over to the breakfast bar. "Likely he was mad because everyone could see the bits and pieces, that in his mind, only he gets to see."

"Maybe. He calmed down after a woman donated a baby blanket and safety pins to rig up a skirt. Our luggage had already been checked with security. But I was embarrassed the whole trip because several of Ryan's coworkers were there, all flying in together. That wasn't how I planned on introducing myself. That's why, even hours later, I feel the need to bake."

"Well, bake away. We have a stocked pantry in the basement, so if you run out of flour or anything else, just holler down the stairs to the guys and they'll bring you whatever you need. If we are out of something, there's always someone willing to run to the store."

"Mom?" Nicholas called from the end of the hallway.

"It's still nighttime, Nick," I said, heading down the hall. "Back to bed. Come on." I guided him back into his bedroom and into his bed. Sitting beside him, I pulled the blanket up and tucked it around him as his eyes drifted closed again. "Sweet dreams," I whispered in his ear before kissing his forehead and sneaking back out of his bedroom.

Tweedle silently waved at me from the kitchen. I nodded before entering my bedroom. My bed seemed to be calling my name and with every step, my brain shut down. I wasn't awake long enough to register if my head even landed atop a pillow.

Chapter Two

I sensed Grady sliding into bed beside me and felt his heated damp skin snuggle against mine. I turned my head into his chest without opening my eyes. One of his arms moved between my shoulders with his hand reaching into my hair. The other hand slid down my body, parting my legs.

Before I could moan, he pulled my head back by my hair and covered my mouth with his. His tongue searched and swirled as his fingers danced within my panties.

Breaking the kiss, Grady whispered, "We have to be quiet. The house is full of people, but I locked the door."

I looked up at him as I wrapped a leg around his hip. "I can be quiet."

~*~*~

"Hmm," I hummed into Grady's chest. "That was a nice way to start the day."

Grady chuckled beneath me. "I vote we call in sick and stay in bed."

"And the kids?"

"It's after nine o'clock already. They're in the classroom with Beth. Tweedle fed them. Anne made them get dressed and brush their teeth. And Donovan drove them over."

Beth had been employed as the kids' teacher for a little over a month now. The kids loved her, and she was good at challenging them educationally and socially.

"Beth's going to have her hands full. With all the visitors, the kids will be distracted."

"Tweedle didn't make Beth's job easier by fueling the kids with sugar. We had a disagreement about apple pie being breakfast appropriate."

"Oh my goodness, that sounds so good," I said, rolling out of Grady's arm and pulling him with me. "Let's hurry and shower. I'm hungry."

Grady's hand wrapped around my waist as we stepped into the bathroom. "Me too. But not for pie."

~*~*~

"Well, someone got laid," Katie said as Grady and I entered the dining room thirty minutes later.

"Jealous?" I asked as I sat to the left of the end chair.

"Ladies, behave. Or else..." Hattie scolded, setting cups of coffee in front of both Grady and me.

"Good morning, Hattie," I said, grinning up at her.

"Good morning, sunshine," she said, smiling over at me.

"Did you fly in with Wild Card?" Grady asked.

"Yes, and Reggie. Pops and Jackson stayed in Texas to manage the ranches."

"Reggie's here?" I asked. "Where?"

"He's sleeping in the dorms," Wild Card answered from the living room couch. "How come you don't get that excited when I visit?" He was stretched out on the couch, shirtless, with Hattie's afghan covering his midsection. His bare legs were exposed, crossed at the ankles with his feet propped up on the arm of the couch.

"You better not be naked under that blanket. That's my favorite blanket."

"You used to like it when I got naked."

"Neither of you are going to like it when I launch your ass through the living room window," Grady said to Wild Card.

"Hattie, Grady's being mean," Wild Card said as he rolled over and closed his eyes.

I was relieved to see he was wearing shorts. And, yes, ex-husband or not, I looked, which earned me a glare from Grady.

Hattie giggled as she returned the pot to the kitchen. It was then that I noticed the breakfast bar was covered in baked goods.

"Tweedle, why are you still baking?" I asked.

"I just finished the last of the pies, and then I'll take a break as the breads rise."

Bones and Ryan entered through the garage, both carrying two brown bags each of groceries. Tweedle started pulling ingredients before they could even set the bags down.

"You're making homemade bread?"

"I already made apple-cinnamon bread for Bones, banana bread for Katie, and blueberry French bread for Lisa. Now I'm making sour dough, French, and ciabatta breads for sandwiches later. Do you think two dozen loaves will be enough?"

I turned to Grady and raised an eyebrow.

"Tweedle, you're going to get me in trouble," Grady said. "I told the girls they wouldn't have to lift a finger to help this weekend. I have all the food being catered or slapped on a grill."

"But we're days away from the weekend, so unless Hattie wants her kitchen back, leave her be," Bones said. "Besides, she's less trouble when she's baking."

Tweedle glared at Bones, pulling the eggs from the top of the bag he was holding. Ryan took the bag from him and helped Tweedle take care of the groceries.

"I'm perfectly content," Hattie said, handing Bones a cup of coffee before she plated some muffins and carried them over to the table. "She even washes everything as she works. The kitchen's spotless."

Hattie sat next to me, and Bones sat across from me. Donovan entered through the front door and held a hand up for Hattie to remain sitting as he retrieved his own cup of coffee. Ryan started another pot, as Hattie sat beside me, smiling while she watched them.

"Bridget?" Bones asked me.

"She and Trigger should be on their way back," I answered, snagging a blueberry muffin. "The thief was arrested around three this morning."

"*You're kidding me*," Donovan said. "The reward for that bastard has been out for months."

"It takes a thief to catch a thief," Tweedle said, laughing from the kitchen. "I miss Bridget."

"She has a unique set of skills," I said, saluting my cup at Tweedle. "Kind of scary how knowledgeable she is at high end heists."

"It's a nice break from the sex traffickers and murderers you usually go after," Grady said, turning to me and winking.

"The thief also murdered two people," Ryan said as he put the milk in the refrigerator.

Bones glared at me from across the table.

I glared at Ryan. "I liked you better when you didn't talk."

The corner of Ryan's mouth turned up in a smirk.

My phone chirped, alerting me to a text message.

Tech: *Are we working today?*

I took a picture of all the baked goods on the breakfast bar and sent it to Tech as a reply.

Two minutes later, Tech walked through the garage entrance, heading straight for the breakfast bar. "This explains why Katie didn't come back to the apartment."

"I ate so much, we'll need a forklift to get me out of this chair," Katie said, rubbing her six-pack abdomen.

Tech carried his plate and a folder over to the table and handed me the folder. "I'd like Bridget and you to go over this later. Sounds like what you were looking for."

Ryan walked over, carrying three bowls of fruit. He handed a bowl to both Grady and me before he sat with the third. I smiled as I picked up a piece of cantaloupe with one hand and opened the file with the other. I smiled wider when I saw the million-dollar reward for another jewel thief. I closed the file when Donovan tried to look. If we could snare this guy, we'd win the bet with Donovan.

Tech smiled back at me.

"You promised Bridget would have this weekend off," Bones said, pointing at me.

"It's only Tuesday," I said, shrugging. "The weekend doesn't start until five on Friday. Plenty of time."

"Speaking of which," Donovan said as he read something on his phone. "I need a six-man team for a rescue and recovery in Mexico. Bus leaves in an hour." Donovan stood, snagged a piece of pineapple from my bowl and headed for the door.

Grady looked at me with a raised eyebrow.

"If you're not back in two days, Mr. Tanner, I'll come down there and kick your ass. This is your party—and you promised I didn't have to do anything."

Grady leaned over and kissed me before strutting down the hall. He'd been covering home base for too long, watching the kids as I took out-of-state jobs. He needed a mini adventure.

Ryan picked up his phone and texted someone. When he read the reply, he turned toward Tweedle. "Bridget said she's minutes away and can keep you out of trouble if I go with the guys."

She pursed her lips and squinted her eyes at him. "I don't need a babysitter."

"Babe, you fell on the luggage conveyor."

"I thought it was the auto-walk," I said.

"That happened at the first airport," Ryan said.

"*Snitch*," Tweedle said. "*Go*! But you have to be back in two days. And if you get hurt—"

"I know. I know. There'll be hell to pay," he said as he walked into the kitchen and kissed her.

"Aww," Katie said, sarcastically. "Look at the love birds. Who would've thought Ryan was such a romantic?"

Ryan glared at Katie before heading out the door.

I turned to look at Bones who was looking at the clock.

"If you're thinking of a quick *visit* with Bridget, keep it out of my garage. I'm tired of walking in on you guys."

Bones laughed, moving toward the garage. Before he got to the door, Bridget opened it. He grabbed her hand and propelled her back outside.

"A bit obvious," Tweedle said, giggling.

"They are a naughty bunch," Hattie said, nodding her agreement.

"Not me," Wild Card said, getting up from the couch and folding the blanket. "I'm just a lonely cowboy."

"*Please*," I said. "You have women strewn across the U.S."

"Except in Michigan," Wild Card said as he stretched his arms over his head, his chest and ab muscles pulling taunt. "What's wrong with the women here? I'm a catch."

"And what exactly do they get if they catch you?" Katie asked. "An STD?"

"You can inspect the product if you'd like," Wild Card said, leaning over Katie. "I assure you it's perfect in every way."

"I might not be able to win a fist fight against you, Wild Card," Tech said as he looked up from his plate of pastries. "However, I'm perfectly capable of wiping out your bank accounts, having you declared dead by the government, and then switching your records for someone on the top ten most wanted list."

Wild Card straightened and took a step away from Katie. "That won't be necessary. Message received." He moved toward the basement stairway. "I think I'll take that quick trip to Mexico."

"Sounds like a good plan," Tech said before turning back to his plate.

"That was kind of hot," Katie said, turning to Tech.

Tech glanced up at her. Standing, he took her hand in his and pulled her toward the garage door.

Tweedle giggled as they left. "Damn. Is sex the only thing people think about around here?"

Bridget walked in through the garage.

"That was quick," I said to Bridget, winking at Tweedle.

Bridget smirked. "Probably the first time Bones has been turned down. I'll make it up to him when he gets back."

"Sexual relationships should be private, ladies," Hattie said, shaking her head at us.

Bridget and I grinned at each other.

Hattie rolled her eyes before turning to Tweedle. "Do you mind if I plate up some cookies and muffins for Whiskey's construction crew? They're building the new houses down the road."

"Not at all," Tweedle answered. "I have a feeling I'm not done baking this week. I'll be nervous the entire time Reel is gone. Damn it, I mean Ryan."

"Are you going to tell us why you call him Reel?" I asked as I helped Hattie load a platter.

Bridget and Tweedle exchanged grins.

"His dad is—well *was*, until recently—the town drunk. He got Loretta knocked up the weekend he told his wife, now ex-wife, he was out fishing. Nine months later, Rod and Reel were born, though that wasn't their legal names."

I smiled a big smile. "*Nice*. How pissed would he be if I spread that story around so everyone starts calling him Reel?"

"About as pissed as you were when Reel intentionally threw you under the bus with Bones about Bridget capturing a murderer," Tweedle said, smiling as she plated another platter of cookies.

Hattie giggled. "I like her. She's spunky."

"Yeah. I think we'll get along just fine," I said as I gave Tweedle a fist bump.

"Just don't piss her off," Bridget said. "I've seen her sedate two grown men with her spiked cookies, then dress them up in Halloween costumes and drop them off in the middle of town square. She's not someone you want to cross."

Hattie and I looked back at Tweedle.

"I only did that once," she admitted, waving a spatula in the air to emphasize. "And they totally deserved it."

"As long as they deserved it, dear," Hattie said, nodding her approval.

Grady returned to the kitchen, clad in military camo and carrying a bulky duffle. Wild Card came up the stairs, dressed similarly with two more duffle bags.

"You got sniper rifles?" Wild Card asked.

Grady nodded. "You got night vision gear?"

Wild Card nodded toward the bag in his right hand. "Ladies," he said bowing his head before he walked out the garage door.

"Behave," Grady said to me before smacking his lips to mine. "I mean it."

"You have two days, Mr. Tanner," I warned.

"Yes, ma'am," he said, heading out the door.

"Ryan's always been the only badass I've known," Tweedle said. "Looks like he's just one of many around here."

"Oh, Ryan's still a badass even compared to the others," Bridget said. "You should've seen what he did with the stack of C4 they confiscated a couple weeks ago. Blew trees up from their roots right out of the ground."

"C4? As in explosives?" Tweedle asked, turning a little white.

"For the record, I wasn't the one who let that slip," I said, pointing at Bridget. "I was warned over and over again, never to mention Ryan's training if I met his wife."

"What else don't I know?" Tweedle asked as she pummeled a wad of bread dough.

"Probably best if we wait until they return safely from cartel country before we tell you the rest," Bridget said, taking a step away from the counter.

"Cartel country?" Tweedle asked.

"You did hear the part about them going to Mexico, right?" I asked.

"And you saw the camo and gear?" Hattie asked with a raised eyebrow.

Tweedle pouted, looking at each of us. "I had an image in my head that they'd be staying at a resort and saving a tourist."

"They might be saving a tourist," Bridget said, nodding.

"And they might even stay the night at one of the resorts before they fly back," Hattie agreed.

"Tweedle..." I said, looking between Bridget and Hattie. "Hattie and Bridget mean well, but they're lying to you. The guys will most likely be jumping out of a chopper in the middle of the jungle, hiking miles into some well-guarded compound, shooting the shit out of people, and high tailing their asses back out. I'd also place a wager that the trip will include Ryan blowing some shit up. You need to face the facts. Your husband does some dangerous shit. Once you can come to terms with it, you'll worry less."

"How do I know if he's any good at it? That he won't get hurt?"

"I've worked plenty of jobs with your husband," I said. "I can assure you; he knows his shit."

"The rest is faith, dear," Hattie said.

"I think this weekend will be good for you," Bridget said, stepping closer to rub Tweedle's shoulder. "It will give you a chance to see Ryan's soldier side."

"Or... She'll get to see him get his ass kicked in the Circle of Hell," I said, laughing. "Carl's still arguing that Franky's plastic sword is not as motivating as the lead pipe."

"I saw the video," Reggie said as he closed the sliding door on the back deck. "Carl's original design was *terrifying*." Reggie shuddered. "I still can't believe Donovan's only injury was a fractured arm after Meathead slammed him into the floor like that."

"You came!" I lunged at Reggie, my arms wrapping around his shoulders as he swung me around. "I missed you."

"Missed you too, sis," Reggie said, kissing my forehead before setting me back on my feet. "I'm glad Donovan postponed the tournament for a month so I could make the trip."

"That was all Lisa. She told Donovan that unless he wanted to be served with divorce papers, he couldn't fight in the Circle of Hell until the doctor cleared him."

"Damn," Reggie said. "She's got him by the balls."

"Language, Reggie," Hattie scolded, handing Reggie a cup of coffee. "This is a family-friendly home, and we're trying to clean up the conversations around here."

Reggie looked at me, grinning. "And how's that going?"

"I'll have you know that I'm adjusting just fine." I grinned, stretching my arms before flexing my muscles. We had installed a swear rule, where if an adult got caught swearing in front of the kids, they could sentence us to ten pushups. It took me about a week to get my swearing under control, but the hundreds of extra pushups were good for my biceps. "With the tournament this weekend, though, I'm worried Sara will slip back into bad habits. A couple of days of wall to wall off-duty guards and we'll be right back where we started."

"It's all good. Wayne was doing pushups when I left. Then he ordered the kids to return to their school room."

"They listened to him?"

Reggie snorted as he plated himself some muffins. "He told them he had no problem calling you and snitching on them. They skedaddled."

"Good, but I should get over there. I have some work to do." I turned to Bridget. "And a new thief to research."

"What's the reward?" Bridget asked.

"A million even."

Reggie whistled.

"I'll help Tweedle finish up her baking and then I'll bring her over," Hattie said. "You kids go beat Donovan on that wager."

Chapter Three

"Why didn't you go to Mexico?" I asked Reggie as we climbed the stairs at Headquarters.

"Because I'm as smart as I look," Reggie said. "Last trip to Mexico, I came back with a nasty rash and a million mosquito bites. If I stay here I get to eat and drink as much as I want and sleep in."

I entered the passcode to open the war room door. "If Grady comes home with a mysterious rash, he's sleeping on the couch." I placed my thumb on the second lock for a fingerprint scan. The panel turned green, and I shook my head at the over-zealous security update Carl installed last week.

Stepping aside, I let Reggie go first, then Bridget. I hadn't told Reggie about Bridget's redecorating of the war room, and he tapped his foot in front of him against the 3D mural on the floor where it appeared the floor plunged into a fiery lava pit below.

"Did I just walk inside a video game?" Reggie asked as he walked forward, examining the other 3D murals of robbers and monsters bursting into the room and the weapons mounted to the walls and ceilings. "This is rad."

"Nobody says rad anymore," Bridget said. "That died in the '80s."

"What would you call it then?"

"Bitchen," Tech said. Tech stood and walked over to my usual workstation, raising the section so I could stand while I worked. He had made some technology revisions to the stations which now had dual screens mounted to every other segment of the table. He was attempting to transition me to a paperless world, but it was a struggle. "I know you want to start the jewel thief file, but you have three other files to look at first. Two are consulting cases. The third is a potential client."

I sighed, passing the jewel thief file to Bridget. "Carl, can you help Bridget with any background work she needs?"

"Yes," Carl said as he hunched in closer to his screen.

I flashed my eyes from Bridget to Carl's monitors. She stepped behind him so she could see the screens. Her eyes widened when she saw what Carl was doing. "Carl, get out of those files and off their server before I tell Kelsey what agency you are hacking!"

Tech shook his head at Carl, then pointed to one of the file icons on my monitor. "First up, we have a case in Colorado. The county sheriff asked us to give them some feedback and see whether we can point their investigation in a new direction. Next is an FBI consulting case in Nevada. They want your basic profile workup. Donovan also asked for us to review five open stalker cases, but I warned him we're behind and might not get to them this week."

"What's the third file you mentioned then?"

Tech returned to his chair, checking his phone for messages as he answered. "A fifteen-year-old girl disappeared five years ago. Her parents want to hire us to find her."

"Tech, we've talked about the runaway cases."

"I know," Tech said, setting his phone down and looking back at me. "Just hear me out. The parents don't think she ran away."

"They never do," Bridget said.

Tech sighed. "I told them it was unlikely we'd take the case, but we'd review the file. They're willing to pay our hourly rate for your time."

"Can they afford to pay our rate?"

"I quoted them the amount, and they agreed."

"But can they *really* afford it, Tech? You're talking about desperate parents who would do anything to get their child back."

"I don't know. I've been too busy to run their background." He leaned his head back in his chair. "Between being your analyst and secretary, plus watching Carl and vetting everyone for Silver Aces Security, I'm a little behind."

"We have enough work we can hire some people, but where would we put them? I don't want our war room to be crammed full of administrators."

"I'll figure out the offices," Bridget said. "I'll talk to Donovan when he gets back."

"I know a guy who can do the background checks for the security side and who will work remotely. I'll talk to Donovan about him." Tech rubbed a hand across his forehead. "Then we'll only need a secretary to handle the incoming calls and emails. And the pile of paperwork that goes with it."

"Talk to Donovan, but I think you need an analyst for the investigation's side too. They can do the initial backgrounds and case workups, and then you can dive deeper on the cases we actually take."

"Combine the positions," Bridget said. "Hire someone who answers the phones *and* runs the initial backgrounds on the cases. I know someone who'd be perfect for the job."

"Who?" Tech and I both asked.

"Trainee Kemp. The guy booted from the trainee program for not disclosing that Henderson assaulted me. He's still in the area and job hunting."

"I do feel guilty that I hired you after I kicked both of you out of the trainee program."

"I knew you would." Bridget winked. "Plus, Kemp has a computer science background."

"Sold," Tech said. "Get him in here so I can talk to him about the position." Tech pointed to my monitor, silently ordering me to get to work, before he rolled his chair back to his own workstation.

I started flipping through the murder case in Colorado. A twenty-six-year old single mother was stabbed in the parking lot outside her apartment. No suspects. No witnesses. The woman's body was found two hours later, her purse and jewelry still on the scene. Her autopsy indicated that she bled out from a single stab wound that nicked her clavicle artery.

I read the background report on the victim. She worked as a waitress at a breakfast diner, and based on the official time of death, she would have been leaving her apartment to go to work. Her only possession was a 2005 Honda Civic. She had three hundred and change in her bank account. No known enemies.

I flipped to the photos of the crime scene. The woman's body was half propped against the rear tire, her purse inches away from her left hand. On the other monitor, I pulled up the contents of her purse. No phone. Her attacker likely grabbed it from her right hand while fleeing the scene.

"Did you try her phone?"

"It's not on. The sheriff has an alert set to track the phone if it's used."

"Can you get me a list of car thefts within a fifty-mile radius? Filter out newer models. We need to look for older cars, low technology."

"What are you thinking?"

"She's a single mother, struggling paycheck to paycheck. If she saw someone stealing her car, she'd likely try to stop them."

"Damn. And lose her life over a Civic?"

I shrugged. "Without her car, she'd have no transportation to get to work. It could've financially crippled her for years. And based on the position of the body, so close to the driver's door, my theory is possible. Now we just have to see if I'm right."

Bridget snorted but didn't look up from her computer monitor.

"I've got two cars that were stolen matching that description. One was two months ago. The other was the week before our victim was murdered."

An alert appeared at the bottom of my screen telling me Tech had sent a file. I clicked the alert and read the basic reports. I grabbed the phone and called the sheriff, explaining that I could continue searching, but I believed the crime was related to car thefts. Based on the cars being older models, he might be looking for someone who'd been out of the game, likely now released from prison. He agreed to saving his county a few bucks by running the research from there and said he'd let me know if he came up with anything. I hung up and compiled a report for him, emailing it directly to him.

"Who does the billing?" I asked Tech.

"I do," he said, sighing. "I tried to get Jerry to do it, but he said your notes and files were a mess and he couldn't make heads or tails of it. So... I keep a notepad going," he held up the notepad, "and send invoices when I get time."

The phone rang, and Tech answered it on speaker. It was the receptionist saying that Mr. Arthur Kemp was in the lobby. Tech let her know one of us would be right down.

"That was fast," I said.

"Did I forget to mention that I've been letting Kemp sleep on my couch?" Bridget said as she walked around the table and grabbed Tech's billing notepad. "I'll get him setup in Grady's office and have him start on these invoices."

"Shouldn't we describe the job and ask if he's interested first?" I asked.

"I've been texting with him. He already accepted the job and was willing to start today. He's bored."

Tech glanced up at me, waiting to see if I was going along with skipping the interview process. He had dark circles under his eyes, and I knew he was struggling to keep up with the workload. I shrugged, not caring that we weren't following the typical hiring process.

Tech nodded, completing our non-verbal conversation, before swiveling his chair in Bridget's direction. "Get him access to our main email account. There are over a hundred new emails I haven't opened yet."

"Done."

Bridget opened the door and James, president of the Devil's Players, stood on the other side with his hand in the air, ready to knock.

"Come on in, James," I called out to him. "I haven't seen you in a while."

"Been out of town the last few weeks," he said as he looked around the room. "This room is crazy. No wonder Tech never works at the clubhouse anymore."

"It's definitely got a vibe. Were you looking for Tech? Or for me?"

"You. Tyler scheduled some guys to work patrols, and I wanted to check in with you about the security assignments."

I raised an eyebrow at James. Tech laughed and excused himself to take some files to Grady's office. Reggie stopped playing a game on his phone and threw his arms over his head, interlacing his fingers to watch. Carl smiled broadly as his head swiveled between James and me.

"Tyler's in charge of personal security for my family," I reminded James.

"Tyler's just a prospect. As president, I'm in charge."

"No. Tyler is my employee. He can choose to hire club members, but he does so as my employee. We contract the club for crowd control on Saturdays. That's club business. The everyday protection of my family is overseen by Tyler."

"But Tyler is a prospect for the Devil's Players."

"So what? Is Whiskey's contracting company also managed by you? Or what about Chops' service repair garage?"

"No, those are their businesses," James said, sighing. "Look, maybe it would be best if I talk to Grady or Donovan about this."

"They're out of town at the moment, but please do speak to them. I'd like to know what they say when you tell them that anything that Tech and Tyler do as employees is club business. In fact, give me advance notice, so we can video record the event."

"That's not what I said," James insisted. "Tyler's only a prospect. He's not a full member, yet."

"And shame on you for that. That kid has proved himself for almost two years. Vote him in already."

"Don't tell me how to run *my* club!" James yelled.

"Why not? You're telling me how to manage *my security team!*"

We glared at each other for nearly two full minutes before James stormed out of the room. Carl giggled before turning his attention back to his computer. Reggie rolled his eyes before returning to his game.

I closed the electronic file for the murder case and clicked the icon on the FBI consulting case. It detailed a string of fraud cases in Nevada. The FBI was asking for a profile on their perp. Their cases typically had piles of research already completed, but they lacked enough profilers. I had established a quick-glance service through Special Agent in Charge Jack Tebbs and word was rapidly spreading to other offices. Tech offered the same rate to other law enforcement offices for the quick-glance service, or they could choose the hourly rate if we agreed to take on their case. Most took the quick-glance, just needing a second set of eyes to point their investigation in a new direction.

I was halfway through the profile when Bridget and Tech returned. Two minutes after that, the door opened and Hattie and Tweedle entered. Tweedle walked forward, admiring the wall displays. Her eyes flickered briefly to the floor as she was stepping onto the mural where it appeared the concrete dropped into flames. Startled, she threw herself backward, tripped over Tech's chair, and fell into one of the spare chairs. The chair flew, with her in it, into the back wall, slamming into the wall with enough force to cause the wall hangings to shake. I leapt forward, pinning the archaic battle axe to the wall as it swung toward her head. Tweedle slowly tipped her head back and looked up. When she saw the giant axe only inches away, she gulped.

"Let's not tell Ryan about this," Bridget said, giggling, from the other side of the room.

I raised an eyebrow at Bridget as I lifted the axe and handed it to Tech.

Bridget unsuccessfully tried to hide her smile. "I'll find someone to better secure the wall ornaments." She walked out, bursting out laughing as the door closed behind her.

"How are the new houses coming along?" I asked Hattie.

"Splendid, dear. They started framing the exterior walls on the first floor of Katie's house."

Tweedle exhaled deeply, looking down at the floor while she continued to sit in Tech's chair.

Hattie giggled, shaking her head. "There was, however, a minor mishap involving a nail gun and Tweedle's dress."

"It's the third dress I've destroyed in less than twenty-four hours," Tweedle said as she held out the side of the dress that had a perfectly round nail hole.

"Clothes are never a problem around here," I said, grabbing my phone and taking a picture of Tweedle. "I'm beginning to wonder, though, whether Ryan had the right idea keeping you safely tucked away in our kitchen."

I sent the picture to Alex, and he texted back a thumbs up.

The door opened and Nicholas and Sara entered, both running over to hug me.

"What are you two doing out of the classroom?"

"They both have dentist appointments," Hattie said. "I was able to change their appointments for during my visit."

"Are you sure? I can try pushing my cases."

"Nonsense. I already know that Sara's teeth are perfect and Nicholas will have two more cavities. I have the praise and shame-on-you faces already prepared."

Nicholas and Sara both laughed at Hattie.

"Cavities, huh?" I asked, crossing my arms and looking down at Nicholas with my serious parent face. "Do we need to babysit you while you brush your teeth?"

"I brush them every morning," he said.

"What about at night? You tell me you brush them before bed too. Are you fibbing?"

He shrugged his shoulders and looked up at me innocently. When I couldn't hide the smirk, he smiled his toothy grin and ran toward Hattie. "Bye, Mom."

Hattie raised an eyebrow at me as the kids pulled her out the door. "We'll have to work on your shame-on-you face, Kelsey."

"I'll get right on that," I said before turning to Tweedle. "I'm not sure whether it's safe for you to be in the war room until the weapons are properly secured."

"She knows Wayne," Tech said. "I'll text him and ask if she can hang out with him while we work."

"Is that okay with you?" I asked Tweedle.

"I feel like I'm in everyone's way."

"Nonsense. If you know Wayne, you know there's nothing he likes better than flirting with a pretty girl."

"That's an understatement," Beth said from the doorway. "Alverez turned him down for a date again. He's on the prowl for his next victim."

"He's not bothering you, is he?"

"No. I made it clear I wasn't available."

"Lied, huh?"

"Stretched the truth a bit." She shrugged, grinning. "My dog Storm does tend to get jealous."

"Well, watch out for my ex-husband. He's visiting from Texas, and you're his type."

"What type is that?" Beth asked.

"Gorgeous," Bridget answered as she walked back into the war room. "Goat's coming over this afternoon to secure the weapons so we don't have another mishap."

"Well, I'm off," Beth said. "Unless you have anything I can help with?"

"Bored again?" I asked.

"I need a hobby," Beth admitted. "I've been going stir crazy in my apartment."

"Stick around. You can help Carl and me with this case," Bridget said, nodding toward her side of the table.

"I'm not sure I can handle the gore."

"Jewel and art thief," I said. "No gore. So far, the thief hasn't hurt anyone in any of the burglaries. We'd like to catch him before his perfect record changes."

"A modern mystery," Beth said, walking toward Bridget. "Sounds intriguing."

I turned back to the profile I was writing.

Chapter Four

After finishing and sending the profile, I emailed our general mailbox asking for the extension office in Nevada to be billed for a quick-glance service. I also provided a few case details to add to the invoice. I received a reply email from Kemp that the invoice would be sent by the end of the day.

I closed the files, saving them by date and case number in an electronic folder before opening the third case. The runaway case. The case happened a little more than five years ago, and the fifteen-year-old girl would now be twenty-one. She would've reached out by now if she was still alive.

I hated these types of cases. They were depressing and often there was nothing I could do to help. Since Tech had promised I would look, though, I had no choice.

Sighing, I started with the parents' statements. Allie Jacobs argued with her parents about her curfew before leaving to go to her best friend's house. According to her friend though, she never showed. Her friend lived less than a mile away, and Allie had taken her bike. Neither the bike, nor Allie, were ever seen again. "Damn it, Tech."

Tech turned his chair to face me. "I know. I get why you hate these cases, but something is off about this one." He stood and walked over with his laptop. "Look at this." Tech clicked a few screens and a satellite map of the neighborhood came up. "This is farm country USA. Only fifteen houses exist between her home and her friend's house. Also, there are only two roads that intersect her road. Limited traffic and the houses are set back a good distance from the road. Anyone could have stopped Allie, and no one would have seen anything. This isn't a city neighborhood where a street kid turns to the wrong person for help. This is a small community."

"You're thinking kidnapping, but maybe she never planned on going to her friend's house. She was a teenager. She could've gone anywhere."

"Not likely," Tech said, expanding the map. "There's nothing else around unless she decided to ride her bike five miles into town."

"An older friend could have picked her up. A secret boyfriend."

"Her best friend confirmed that she wasn't secretly seeing anyone, and they didn't have any friends that could drive yet. Plus, she would have stashed her bike somewhere, but it was never found."

"Your theory is that one of the neighbors was involved? That's a lot of background checks to dig through."

"Which is why I asked Kemp to start pulling the backgrounds for all of the rest of the residents within a two-mile radius."

"We'll need to go deeper than that. A friend or a relative could have visited anyone living in the neighborhood."

"I'm working on the family's background now, diving deep. Allie would've been more likely to go quietly with someone she knew, whether that was a neighbor or someone close to her own family."

I raised an eyebrow at Tech. He usually didn't push for cases this hard. "This case got to you, didn't it?"

He shrugged. "I can't explain it. I don't know why this one feels more important. My gut is telling me we need to look closer." He grabbed some documents from the printer, handing them to me. "I'm willing to cover the cost. You were right. The family's broke. They've dumped everything they have into finding their daughter."

I sighed, looking up at the ceiling. "We'll take it pro bono, but no promises."

Tech threw an arm over my shoulder. "Thanks. I owe you one."

"Don't thank me yet. You'll likely have to research your ass off. And for what? There's no hope that this girl is alive. You know that, right?"

Tech nodded as he moved back to his workstation. "But we can stop whoever did this from ever touching another young girl."

"Don't get sucked in," Bridget said to Beth from their side of the table. "Stay focused on our case."

"Their case sounds more important."

"It is, but it's the type of case that will break your heart whether they solve it or not."

Bridget tapped on Beth's monitor, and Beth rolled her chair closer to her screen.

I called the police department in charge of the disappearance case. The detective on the case was happy to help after he verified my references. He emailed me his case files, including his notes. "Tech, as you and Kemp run the backgrounds, flag anyone who has a truck or SUV. If she was picked up, they took her bike with them. It was an adult-sized ten speed."

"They could've strapped it into a car trunk."

"Someone would've noticed and remembered. No. It's more likely to be a truck or large SUV."

"Her dad drives a truck."

"Wasn't the dad. He wouldn't have put a second, then a third, mortgage on their house if he had killed her." I picked up my phone and texted Trigger, asking if he could go back on the road. He replied that he was available and was only minutes away from Headquarters. Next, I called Wayne and asked if there was a seasoned guard available. He said he'd check with Jerry.

"You want me to pack a bag?" Bridget asked.

"No. I'll have Tech send Trigger with a body cam, and we'll watch the interviews remotely."

"Why do you need one of Ace's guards?" Tech asked.

"Because Trigger's not seasoned enough. If we do manage to find this guy, Trigger might decide to put a bullet in his head."

Bridget snorted. "Which is exactly why you should send him alone."

Beth nodded. "I'm liking that plan."

I rolled my eyes as someone knocked on the door.

Tech half stood, stretching to open it. Casey Pritchard walked in.

I nodded a greeting. "Casey, it's good to see you. I didn't know you were back at work."

"Laurie kicked me out for a few days. Said I was smothering her."

"How's she doing?"

Laurie's real name was McKenzie Griffith. We'd recently rescued her from her psycho ex-husband.

"Good. For the first time in years, she doesn't have to watch over her shoulder. I never got a chance to thank you for your help. When Wayne said you needed someone for a case, I figured this was the best way to repay the favor."

"Not necessary, but I could use someone to accompany Trigger to Indiana. I'd go myself, but I don't want to leave Nick while Grady's out of town."

"What's the mission?"

"Cold case of a missing teenager. Tech's theory is someone picked her and her bike up along the side of the road and drove away. We'll need the neighbors interviewed, and boots on the ground to follow any leads."

"Kelsey wants you to live-stream the interviews," Tech said. "I'll get the equipment ready."

"I'll pack and meet up with Trigger." Casey turned to leave as Trigger was entering.

"Trigger, good timing," I said. "I'm having Casey accompany you to Indiana so you don't do anything stupid. *Understood*?"

Trigger laughed but didn't say anything as he followed Casey out the door.

Tech smiled wickedly at me. "You really think Casey can keep Trigger from doing something crazy?"

I shook my head. "It's a coin toss."

Tech laughed as he left to get the equipment ready.

"This is much more entertaining than geometry lessons," Beth said, grinning.

Bridget tapped Beth's monitor again.

"Right. Focus, Beth," she said to herself.

I needed to take notes on the suspects, so I printed the summary page of everyone Tech had researched so far with a vehicle large enough to transport the bike. On each, I made notes of questions to ask and any details from their files that stood out like employment, family structure, or hobbies. I had ten suspects to interview within the first hour alone. And those were just the ones who lived close. Anyone visiting the area could've been involved.

The case application listed the names and numbers for friends and family members. Allie's best friend Kristyn was listed with a current phone number and a current address in Indianapolis. Though she was likely at work, I opted to call, anyway.

"Hello?" someone answered.

"Hi, is this Kristyn?"

"It is. May I ask who's calling?" She seemed annoyed, and I heard people talking in the background.

"My name is Kelsey Harrison. I work as an investigator for Silver Aces Security in Michigan. I've been hired—"

"Please don't tell me you're another private eye out to steal the Jacobs' money. They've been through enough. The case went cold years ago, and despite how I wish differently, Allie's dead."

"First of all, I know the Jacobs can't afford our services. I offered to look at the case pro bono. Second of all, tell me why you're convinced she's dead."

"It's been five years," she said, exhaling slowly. "I'm sorry. I don't mean to sound so cold, but I work in the city with runaways. I know what the odds are."

"You're right, and I agree. It still doesn't hurt, though, for me to take a look at the case. So can you tell me about the day she disappeared?"

"She didn't show. I'm not sure what else I can say. When I called her cell phone, she didn't answer. I called several times over the next hour before calling her mother to see if maybe she was grounded again."

"Was that normal? Did her parents ground her a lot? Take away her phone?"

"Not any more often than mine did," she said, laughing humorlessly. "Our parents were best friends. Any one of our four parents could ground us or take away privileges. Since Allie and I were the only kids who lived in that neighborhood, we were always together when we got into trouble."

"What about the fight she had with her parents about curfew?"

"About curfew? I heard they argued, but Allie wouldn't have run away if it was about our curfew. That was a game."

"What do you mean?"

"As I said, our parents were best friends. If I had a nine o'clock curfew, so did Allie. But we knew if either of us could get it extended, then the other's parents would extend theirs. We'd both been harping on our parents for days to get the time changed. The night before she disappeared, we joked about how stubborn they were being."

"Was that the last time you spoke to her?"

"I called her the next morning to tell her I was riding with my mom into town to buy a new backpack."

"What time was that?"

"I'm not sure. I was a teenager, so likely midmorning. We agreed to meet at my house at noon, but when I got home, she wasn't there."

"And you were home on time? Before noon?"

"No, actually. We were running late. I remember whining to my mom, but she said Allie had a key."

I flipped through the detective's notes. "I don't see anything in the police file about you not being home."

"I don't think anyone ever asked. They asked me if I'd seen her, and I said no. The police searched the house and the property. They even looked into my dad, but he was driving semis back then and was somewhere out west."

I found the notes on Kristyn's father's alibi and circled the date stamp of a gas station surveillance photo.

"Was there anyone else who frequented your house or Allie's house? A family member? Friend of the family?"

"Wow, um, let me think. Allie's grandma visited a lot. Her mom's friend Patty was around every summer to help with the flower nursery that Allie's mom ran. My uncle had visited, but he left the night before to head back to Lafayette."

I took notes as I asked questions. "What about regular visitors of any of your neighbors? Can you think of anyone who was around enough that Allie would've felt comfortable talking to?"

"Well, we knew all the neighbors, but I can't say we knew their extended families. Except for Mrs. Carpenter's nephew, Blake. We'd talk to him when he was out mowing his aunt's yard. He was a few years older than us, but we both had schoolgirl crushes on him. He seemed interested in Allie too, but they never did anything more than talk. If you track him down, let me know if he still looks dreamy."

"You didn't stay in touch?"

"No. My family moved away a year after Allie disappeared. It was just too hard. I was flunking out of school, and my parents wanted me to stop dwelling on it."

"I'm sure that was difficult, but I think their decision was a good one."

"I still dwell on it. Hell, I volunteer at a runaway shelter and am going to school to become a social worker."

"But you're working with the living and not following a ghost."

"Maybe. Look, I have to get back to work. Did you need anything else?"

"Do you know Blake's last name?"

"Blake Foster."

"And what about your uncle? What's his name?"

"Milo Sprigston, but as I said, he left the night before."

"I might still reach out to him, just to see if he remembers anything. He might've noticed someone in the neighborhood during his visit. If you think of anyone else, call me. Day or night."

"I will. And sorry about getting so nasty with you when I answered. I really do want someone to figure out what happened."

"I know you do, and I'll do my best, but no promises."

We ended the call and I tossed a post-it note pad at Tech. "I need backgrounds on those two. One's Kristyn's uncle and the other was an older teenager who worked at one of the neighbor's houses."

Tech looked at the names and raised an eyebrow. He pressed the speaker button on the conference room phone and called Wayne.

"Yeah," Wayne answered.

"Doesn't a Blake Foster work for Aces?" Tech asked.

"Yeah. Matter of fact, he's standing next to me. He came in a few days early for the tournament this weekend."

"Is he from Indiana?" Tech asked.

"Yeah," Wayne answered.

"Is he in his early to mid-twenties?" I asked.

"How old are you, Blake?" Wayne asked. "Says he's twenty-three."

"I'll be down to talk to him," I said, nodding at the phone for Tech to hang up. When the light turned red, I gathered my phone and the file I'd started. "What do we know about Blake?"

"Not much. I'd just heard the name bounced around. Bones worked a couple of jobs with him. If memory serves, he was a cop in Indianapolis before taking a bullet to his knee." Tech walked over and opened the door.

"You don't have to go with me."

"If things turn ugly, I'll be there to yell at one of the other guys to help," Tech said, grinning ear to ear.

"We need to teach you to fight."

"These hands were made for computers, not fighting. If I break a finger, I can't run a keyboard."

"Good point."

Chapter Five

I turned toward the stairs and started down. I spotted Wayne next to a dark-haired hunk at the bottom of the stairs. "Conference room."

Wayne raised an eyebrow but moved into the main conference room on the first floor. Blake held the door open as Tech and I followed Wayne inside.

"What's going on, Kel?" Wayne asked, crossing his arms over his chest as he leaned against a wall.

"I'm working a case and Blake's name came up."

"Is this about Allie?" Blake asked, taking a step forward. His demeanor instantly changed from cautious to hopeful. "Please tell me you're working Allie's case."

I glanced over at Tech who shrugged while sitting in a chair and leaning back to stretch his legs.

"Why would you assume that? I could be referring to a case from when you were a police officer."

Blake shook his head. "I didn't have your same experience when I was a cop. I wrote traffic tickets for ten-hour shifts."

"How'd you acquire a bullet in the leg then?" Tech asked.

"Dumb luck. I pulled a guy over for speeding. Didn't know he was the same guy who robbed a liquor store six miles away until I was in the hospital's recovery room."

"What can you tell us about Allie Jacobs?" I asked.

"I'll give you everything I have. It's in my car." He started for the door.

"Wait," I said, raising my hand. "I summoned you into our conference room to question you about a case, and now you want to go to your car?"

"You can trust him, Kel," Wayne growled.

"Why? Because Donovan or Grady hired him?"

"I've worked with him. He's a straight shooter."

"Ted Bundy was everybody's friend. So what?"

"Wayne," Blake said, handing his keys over, "can you grab the file box from my SUV?"

Wayne glared at me, but took the keys and left. Blake pulled out a chair, sitting directly across the table from me.

"What was your relationship with Allie?"

"Friendly. Flirty," Blake said. "I liked her, but I was a few months shy of my eighteenth birthday. She was only fifteen. It still didn't stop me from mowing my aunt's front yard three times a week, though."

"What can you tell me about her?"

Blake smiled at the table as he thought about her. "She likes hip-hop music, hot fudge ice cream sundaes, and fixing cars with her dad. Her best friend's name is Kristyn. Her birthday is in November, and she's a night owl by nature."

"You talk as if she's alive," Tech said.

"It's weird, but I can't accept she's anything but alive. I mean, I'm not an idiot. It's been over five years. Some instinct keeps screaming at me not to give up looking for her, though."

"Damn. This box is heavy," Wayne said, carrying the box into the conference room and setting it on the table.

Blake stood and opened the box. "I've run backgrounds and interviews on almost everyone in that town." He started stacking the thick notebooks and files on the table. "I interviewed every man, woman, and child who lived on that street and the two cross streets. My old lieutenant said it was the obsession that kept me on traffic patrol. He was right, but don't tell him that, because he was an ass."

"Before we dig through this mess," I said, tapping my pencil on the table. "Were you at your aunt's the day Allie went missing?"

"No. I was at the army recruiter's office, enlisting. I found out later that night that Allie was missing. I have a file on myself too." He pulled a file from the middle and slid it toward me.

I passed it to Tech. "When was the last time you saw Allie?"

"The day before. I was at my aunt's when she and Kristyn were riding their bikes. They stopped to talk. Allie was excited that school was about to start the following week. She kept making a point that she'd be a sophomore. I kept reminding her that I graduated high school already. They left when my aunt called me in for lunch."

"Anything stand out about either of them? Did they seem scared or angry about anything?"

"Nothing. I've racked my brain a thousand times, but they both seemed their normal selves. I don't recall seeing or hearing anything out of the ordinary."

I nodded and pulled the stacks of files toward me. I sorted out the names I had scheduled for interviews and flipped through them. Blake had interviewed all of them and verified their alibis. "If you went into the service, how did you have time to do all this research?"

"For three years, I stayed alive so that when I got state-side again, I could find out what happened to her. I filled a notebook with everyone's names and addresses. I started working the case while I was in the police academy and continued during my off time."

"Anyone you haven't eliminated?" I asked as I closed another file.

"Everyone was cleared. It couldn't have been someone who lived there. I also checked for criminal records on anyone related to someone who lived on those roads. Nada."

"What about Kristyn's uncle?"

"I don't know who that is, but as I said, I didn't find *any* criminal relatives," Blake said, shaking his head.

"You didn't interview Milo Sprigston then?" Tech asked, standing.

"No. Who is he?"

"Probably no one," I said, nodding to Tech. "We'll check it out." I pulled my phone and texted Trigger to change direction and head toward Lafayette instead of Indianapolis. "Thanks for the help," I said to Blake. "I'd appreciate it if you left your files in here. They might be useful to us."

I started heading toward the door, but Blake stepped in my path. "Don't shut me out. Please. This case has haunted me."

I glanced over at Wayne. He had a worried expression as he watched Blake.

"Give Tech and me some time," I said to Blake. "I've only had the case for an hour. You've had it for five years. I'll let you know if we find anything."

Blake was about to argue, but Wayne put a hand on his shoulder and pulled him out of my path. I left the conference room and returned to the war room.

"Tech, I need everything you've got on Blake."

"He gave us his file. It shows he was in the army recruitment's office."

I looked at Tech. Bridget looked up at Tech. Beth looked up at Tech.

"Okay!" Tech answered our silent mocking. "It's probably not the best idea to use the evidence provided by the person who needs the alibi."

"You think?" I said before handing Carl the folder. "Carl, can you get access to the army's records and check Blake's application file? You don't need to get into their main system, just the recruiter's office."

"Is that a good idea?" Beth asked.

"One of us watches him to make sure he doesn't do anything like re-enlist Donovan," Bridget said as she walked over and watched over Carl's shoulder.

"That would be funny," Carl said, typing on his computer.

I pointed a finger at Carl. "I doubt you'll think it's funny when we turn *you* over to the army as punishment."

Only his eyes moved up to see if I was serious. His smile fell when he realized I was.

Reggie, who was playing a game again on his phone, sighed dramatically. "I'm bored."

"Good. Do you know Blake Foster?"

Reggie nodded. "I've met him. I know Wild Card has worked a few jobs with him."

"Go hang out with him. Make sure he doesn't do anything stupid."

"Stupid how?"

"Like drive to Indiana stupid."

"I can do that," Reggie said, pushing his chair away from the table.

I focused on the background research Tech was sending me for both Blake and Milo. After about twenty minutes, Blake seemed to check out. His military career was average, never trying to achieve greatness which made sense if he was anxious to return home. His career as a cop was short, barely over a year of service before he was shot. Donovan hired him around the time my family was hiding in Texas last year. Since it was before we had a formal training program, Donovan had kept him mostly assigned to two-man teams, working with the more seasoned guards. All his evaluations came back that he was doing a good job and took protection jobs seriously.

Milo, on the other hand, was an odd duck. He lived in a trailer on the backside of the forty acres his parents owned. Single. No children that were on record. And his longest stretch of employment had been as a ticket attendant at a movie theater. He'd lasted a year. "Find out why Milo's career as a movie theater attendant ended," I said to Tech while I continued reading.

"Already hacking their server," Tech said.

"Blake's alibi checks out," Bridget said. "Carl confirmed Blake was taking a comprehension test from eleven until about twelve-thirty."

"Blake's officially not a suspect then. Good to know." I nodded, turning to Tech. "What's taking so long?" I snapped my fingers for him to hurry up.

"Hold your horses. I've almost got it."

I entered Milo's address while I waited for Tech. Turning on the wall TV, the satellite image appeared in front of me. I spotted the parents' house and moved to the east to find the trailer where Milo lived. Zooming in closer, I was unimpressed with the garbage bags lining the outside of the trailer. Nor did the tires stacked in the driveway inspire me to move to the neighborhood.

"Does Milo have a truck or SUV?"

"No registered vehicles in his name," Tech answered, not looking up from his computer.

I zoomed out again and moved the screen back to the main house. "Well, look at that. How much do you want to bet that Milo borrows daddy's truck?"

Beth glanced up at the screen that showed two cars and a truck in the driveway. The truck was the oldest of the three vehicles. "You're having fun, aren't you?"

"There's a lot about this job that sucks—" I started to say.

"But when Kelsey is on the scent of a bad guy, this shit is a blast," Tech interrupted.

"If only Tech could get his hands on the termination file for our suspect..." I said.

"Got it," Tech said. "Weirding the girls out. That's exactly what the manager wrote. Milo was fired two weeks before Allie disappeared."

"Holy shit," Beth squealed. "You got him."

"Not so fast," Bridget said. "Finding a suspect isn't enough. Now she has to prove it was him. First to herself, then to the cops. And there's no guarantee that if she does prove he was involved, that we'll figure out what happened."

"That sucks," Beth said, her shoulders deflating. "You make it sound impossible."

"Not impossible," Bridget said. "She's just a long way from the finish line."

I pulled my phone and called Trigger.

"You're on speaker, Boss. And I'd like to request anyone other than Casey for future road trips. He won't let me change the radio, and he's a country music fan."

"Suck it up. What's your location?" I asked as Tech took over my computer and zoomed out. A blinking red dot appeared on the screen. "Never mind. Tech pulled up your GPS unit. Looks like you are about an hour from our mark."

"We have a mark? I thought we only had a list of people to interview?" Trigger asked.

"Things change. The mark is a single white male living in a trailer at the back of his parents' property. I'm going to have Tech send you the coordinates to a location on the far north of the property. Go in on foot to do recon first. This guy is reading as extremely odd and likely owns a shotgun."

"Doesn't everyone own a shotgun?" Casey asked.

Outside of the war room, loud clanging and thumping noises, followed by a brief scream, had me running toward the door. On the other side of the walkway, I leaned over the rail and looked down. Tweedle was laid out on the floor with a cut on her forehead and her skirt hiked up to her boobs. She scrambled to roll over and pull her skirt down.

"Wayne!" I yelled.

"I only took my eyes off her for a second, Kelsey! I swear," Wayne said as he ran over and helped Tweedle from the floor.

"Ryan is going to kick our asses when he sees all the bruises on her!"

"Looks like I brought over the clothes Alex gathered just in time," Lisa said as she crossed the gym, holding up two tote bags. "I'll get her cleaned and changed. Get back to work."

"Dress her in bubble wrap and strap her to a chair if you have to. Our lives depend on it." I walked back into the war room to find Tech, Bridget, and Beth laughing. Carl was hunched close to his computer. "Carl?"

Bridget jumped up and looked. "No, Carl. You can't order twenty pizzas."

"Actually, I'm getting hungry," I said.

"Me too," Tech said.

"*Hello?*" a voice from my phone yelled.

"Shit, sorry. Tweedle fell down the steps."

"Who's Tweedle?" Casey asked.

"Ryan's wife."

"Is she okay?"

"She'll live. But it was her third near-death experience since being left in our care."

"What were the first two?" Trigger asked.

"One involved a nail gun, and the other involved an ax, but I'll deny both happened if asked."

Casey whistled. "Okay. We've got the coordinates from Tech, and we're navigating that direction. It'll be an hour at least before we're there."

"Call us when you're ready. We'll be twiddling our thumbs until then."

"You got it, boss," Trigger said before disconnecting the call.

"Now what?" Beth asked.

"Now we work on something else until Trigger and Casey are ready for us."

"How can you focus on something else?"

"It's better than pacing for an hour," Tech said, laughing. "This is a daily occurrence for us, so you get used to it."

"What's next on the list that I can clear while we wait?" I asked Tech.

"Grab one of Donovan's stalker cases," Tech said, nodding to the stack of folders on the credenza. "I haven't looked at them yet, but we can start a workup."

I read the label on the side of the first folder: "Daphne Davenport."

"The movie star?" Beth asked.

"Hell, if I know," I said, shrugging. I couldn't remember the last time I watched a movie that didn't involve cartoon characters.

Chapter Six

"This chick can't be for real," I said, lowering my working station so I could give my aching feet a rest. I had been reviewing Daphne's file for the past forty-five minutes and my feet couldn't take any more.

"Wayne covered for Billy Hobbs last week so Billy could take a few days off," Tech said, leaning back in his chair to take a break. "Wayne said Daphne whined for three days that she wasn't safe without Billy at her side."

"I'm betting Wayne loved hearing that. Have I met Billy?"

"Don't think so. He usually works security for big events involving the rich and famous. His assignments don't cross paths with our investigation work. He was only assigned a stalker case because the other guys threatened to quit after spending one day with the client. Billy's used to the crap that comes with these hoity-toity clients, so he volunteered."

"The flowers delivered to Daphne could be coming from anyone."

"So?"

"What if she's sending them to herself?"

"Sending herself flowers with creepy messages?" Tech clicked his mouse a few times before reading from the screen, "*Your thighs glistened as you walked across the stage last night. It made me hard. I can't wait to have you.*"

"*Ooh*," Bridget said, bouncing in her chair. "She'd totally write something like that!"

"Especially after Michael broke up with her on the red carpet!" Beth said, nodding at Bridget. "She was so mad."

"Did you see her upper lip turn white because she was pressing her lips so tight?" Bridget asked Beth.

Beth nodded, grabbing Bridget's arm. "Did you read the article in *People Magazine*? A friend close to the source said she threw a vase at Michael's Porsche, smashing out the windshield."

"She has nice boobies," Carl said, turning in his chair as one of the TV monitors lit up with a red-carpet picture of Daphne in a barely-there dress. Her breasts were pouring out of both sides of a thin strip of material.

"Nice, Carl," Tech said, chuckling as he laced his fingers behind his head and admired the picture.

The door opened, and Wayne entered with a stack of pizza boxes. "What an ugly woman," Wayne said, shaking his head at the TV screen.

"She's beautiful," Tech said, glancing over his shoulder at Wayne.

"Not after you meet her," Wayne said, shuddering. "Ick."

"Is she faking the stalker?" I asked Wayne.

"No idea. I didn't stick around long enough to find out."

"You have to give us the dirt," Beth said, taking the top pizza box and opening it.

"Not much to tell," Wayne said as we grabbed a slice. "She's a bitch to everyone. Her own family would disowner her if they didn't all work for her. She checks her reflection in the mirror every ten minutes and raises hell if someone has something she wants. She made her sister strip out of a dress before an event and trade with her, because her sister's dress was nicer. Poor girl was in tears and skipped the event."

"Does she really have a tattoo of a bird on her ass?" Bridget asked.

"Yup." Wayne nodded. "A bluebird."

"How do you know?" I asked.

"She insists her bodyguards are present while she skinny dips in her pool. She says she worries her stalker might breach the property's security. I know when a girl likes to be watched, though, and that chick almost orgasmed in front of us."

"I knew it." I stood and tossed the file onto the far cabinet. "Daphne invented the whole thing."

"How do you know?" Tech asked.

"She's not actually scared. Someone with a crazy stalker isn't likely to go skinny dipping in an outdoor pool."

Bridget shrugged. "Everybody reacts differently."

"I agree, but not that differently. It's also not the only red flag I noticed."

"You want me to terminate her contract?" Wayne asked.

I shook my head. "I'm not willing to risk a client's safety over a hunch. No. I need to prove my theory first." I looked up at the monitor of Daphne on the red carpet. "Give Billy a call. Have him convince her to come to the tournament this weekend. Let's set the bitch up and see what happens."

"*Ooh*," Bridget squealed again. "This is going to be good."

Wayne laughed, heading toward the door. As he exited, the kids came tearing in around him and into the room. Wayne held the door open for Hattie before he left.

"Well?" I asked. "How'd it go at the dentist?"

"Good," Sara said, grinning.

I smiled at her before looking at Nicholas. He moved to sit by Carl. I raised an eyebrow and waited him out.

"I don't want to talk about it," he said, sighing dramatically.

"Well, I do," Hattie said, crossing her arms over her chest.

"How many cavities?" I asked.

"Three," Hattie said, holding three fingers up at Nicholas. "And one of them was an adult tooth."

Nicholas stared at the table.

"What do you think we should do about this, Nick?" I asked him.

He shrugged a shoulder, not looking at me.

"You can't let your teeth rot out."

"Yeah, man," Tech said. "Girls don't like guys with rotted teeth."

"I don't care what girls like," Nicholas said, shrugging again.

"You will eventually," I said, walking over and lifting his chin to look at me. "By then it will be too late. You'll look like some redneck with bad hygiene."

"What's hygiene?"

"Cleanliness."

"I'm clean."

"Your teeth aren't," Tech said. "Do you really want to be the guy with bad breath and black rotting teeth? You can also get digestive infections."

"Really?"

Tech turned to his laptop, typing rapidly against the keyboard before he stopped and pointed up at the screen behind Nicholas. The picture of Daphne was replaced by a close up of a man with black rotted teeth, a lip sore that looked like herpes, and puss-filled welts on his face that were likely from a meth habit. It was the extreme visual for a kid with just a few cavities. Nicholas paled, walking toward the door.

"Where are you going?" Hattie asked.

"I'm going to go brush my teeth again," he answered, opening the door and leaving.

Hattie patted Tech's shoulder. "That was perfect, Mr. Tech. Thank you."

"I do what I can," Tech said, laughing.

I sat back in my chair and looked at Hattie. "You look tired. Do you want me to take the kids off your hands?"

"I'm fine. Perhaps they're wearing me out, but I'm flying back to Texas next week so I'd like to spend as much time as I can with them until then."

"If it gets to be too much, holler. One of us can take over. Do you need an escort back to the house?"

She shook her head. "Tyler's waiting for us downstairs. I'll take one of the pizzas with us if no one minds. Saves me from having to cook."

"I think we're about done," I said, tossing the crust of my third slice onto a paper plate. "I'm stuffed." I stood and grabbed the bottom pizza boxes which hadn't been opened. "Want me to carry these downstairs for you?"

"If you could, dear," Hattie said. "The stairs are a bit steep."

"I'll take them," Bridget said, glancing up at the clock. "It's almost time for Casey to call back. Beth and Carl, let's grab Tweedle and go back to the house."

"We're being kicked out, aren't we?" Carl asked, pouting.

"Yup," Bridget said, pulling him along. "It's always best to have fewer witnesses."

Beth looked like she wanted to argue but followed Bridget.

I moved around the table and gathered the paper plates and napkins, throwing everything in the trash. Tech moved the partial box of pizza to his workstation and picked up another slice. He'd already eaten half a pizza himself.

My phone rang. Seeing it was Reggie, I answered, "What's up?"

"Well...," Reggie drawled out. "You know how I'm the cute, adorable one?"

"What did you do?" I asked as I walked out of the war room and looked around the gym.

"It didn't seem fair that Blake spent all those years looking for Allie and then he was locked out of the investigation."

"Reggie? Where the hell are you?"

"We booked an air taxi to fly to Indiana. Now we're in a car rental about ten minutes from Milo Sprigston's place."

"*Damn you, Reggie! What the hell is wrong with you!*"

I could hear Blake in the background. "*I told you she'd be pissed.*"

Reggie put a hand over the phone, but I could still hear him. "She'll calm down. She loves me."

"I can hear you, *idiot!*"

Wayne, Jerry, and a few other guys came running up the stairs. I motioned them into the war room. I put the phone on speaker before setting it on the table.

"What's the worst that could happen?" Reggie asked.

"Blake could lose his shit—*and kill the guy!*"

"Oh." There was a pause followed by Reggie whispering into the phone, "You think he'd do that?"

"Jesus, Reggie," Wayne said. "Kelsey's right; you're an idiot."

"I'm tracing Reggie's phone," Tech said. "Reggie, take the next left, then in two miles take a right. I've already texted Casey to wait until you get there. They're prepping for a reconnaissance mission."

"Sweet," Reggie said.

"I'm going to beat the snot out of you when I see you," I hissed toward the phone as I fisted my hands. "How the hell can you even afford an air taxi? They cost a small fortune."

"I might've put it on your charge card," Reggie admitted. "It was worth it, though. We got to Lafayette in less than an hour."

"You are paying the bill."

"But, sis, you're rich," Reggie said. "You won't even notice the money gone."

"*Not the point*! It wasn't your money to spend!"

"Now you're just being mean."

"Just get to the rendezvous point to meet up with Trigger and Casey. We'll discuss the rest later."

Wayne leaned over and disconnect the phone. "Blake's only worked protection duty, and Reggie, well," Wayne shrugged, "Reggie is Reggie. We don't let him go on ops without supervision."

"Red Dog to base," Casey's voice called over the conference room speaker.

"This is base. We hear you loud and clear, Red Dog," Tech said.

"What's the deal? Why are Reggie and Blake on their way?"

"The better question is, how many tranquilizer guns do you have?" I asked.

"Uh... Got two rifles, two handguns, and fifteen tranq cartridges."

"I was sort of kidding, but..." I looked over at Wayne to see what he thought of the idea.

"It would be safer," Wayne agreed, nodding. "Donovan put me in charge while he was out of the country. I'll back your decision."

"Are you two serious?" Casey asked. "You want me to shoot Reggie and Blake?"

"Affirmative, Red Dog," I said, grinning toward the phone. "Drop them into dreamland."

"Man... I don't think I can do that. What happens the next time I need one of them to cover my six?"

"I'll shoot them," Trigger said. "No problem. They know I work for Kelsey and have to follow her orders."

"You sure?" Casey asked him.

"Kelsey?" Trigger asked. "I need final confirmation. I see their SUV approaching. Are you ordering me to shoot them with tranquilizers?"

"Yes. Do it. Be sure to shoot them in the lower body, though. We don't want anyone losing an eye."

"Consider it done," Trigger said, sounding excited.

"Red Dog, turn on your body camera," Tech said as he laughed. "You too, Trigger."

The far left and center TV screens sparked to life. Casey and Trigger were standing behind their SUV with the hatch open. We watched on the center screen, labeled Red Dog's cam, as Reggie and Blake got out of their rental. As they started walking forward, Trigger stepped out from behind the SUV and shot a dart into Blake's leg. Reggie's eyes got large before he turned to run in the other direction. Trigger nailed him with a dart in the ass. Both men dropped to the ground.

"I can't believe that shit just happened," Casey said, laughing. "Now what?"

"Handcuff them in the backseat of one of the SUVs and get the keys for the rental."

As Trigger walked toward Reggie, he turned toward Casey with a huge smile on his face. This was the crazy shit I hired him to do. In Trigger's cam we watched Casey shake his head and laugh.

I picked up the remote and hit mute. "Tech? Do we have anything else on Milo? Any special training? Hunting skills?"

"Nothing we know of. Kemp's been sending everything he can find, but so far everything's come back odd but non-threatening. Milo only has twenty Facebook friends, most of which are family members, and his profile picture shows him fishing."

"Current employment?"

"Last paycheck was from a temp agency. Not sure if he's working today or not."

"Give me the number," Wayne said. "I'll call on my burner phone and ask if he's available to work today?"

Tech wrote the number down, and Wayne stepped out of the room. I unmuted the phone as Casey and Trigger finished loading Reggie and Blake in the back of the rental.

"Make sure Blake doesn't have handcuff keys on him. Reggie doesn't think that far ahead, but Blake might."

A minute later Trigger held a handcuff key in front of his body cam. "He had it taped to the inside of his belt."

After they closed the back door, Casey asked, "What now, base?"

Wayne stepped back into the war room and shook his head. He didn't have a location on Milo.

"You have a green light to proceed. Be aware, we do not know the location of the mark. He could be on the property. We also have no knowledge if he has dogs or guns."

"Do we know anything, base?" Casey asked, looking at Trigger's body camera.

"Kelsey," Trigger said before I could answer Casey. "What do you want to happen if we run into this guy?"

"I'd say it's fifty-fifty at this point that he's our guy so don't kill him. Secure him. Don't tranq him unless you have to. We'll want to ask him a few questions. I'm having Tech send his DMV photo to your phones. He's five foot eight inches, weighs three hundred and forty pounds, but it's mostly fat from what I can tell. As long as he doesn't shoot you or sit on you, you should be safe."

"Is this the norm when working these investigations?" Casey asked Trigger as they moved into the woods.

"Yup," Trigger said. "We go off script a lot. The only rule is that you do whatever the fuck Kelsey says, which could be just about anything."

"Lucky bastard," Casey mumbled before starting a slow jog to the south.

Chapter Seven

Ten minutes later, the trailer came into view on the body cams. They split up, circling the trailer in a wide radius.

"Hold your position," I ordered before muting the phone. "Tech, zoom in on Trigger's camera."

Tech zoomed in on what appeared to be a storm shelter, half concealed under trash bags on the back side of the trailer.

I nodded to Tech to return to normal view as I unmuted the conference phone. "Okay. You can continue."

Wayne leaned over and muted the phone again. "What was that?"

"Could be nothing," I said, shaking my head. The chill zipping down my back told me otherwise, though. I glanced at Tech who was watching me. I shook my head again before concentrating on the cameras.

"Perimeter is clear. Orders, base?" Casey asked.

I unmuted the speaker. "Proceed to the trailer. Two-man entry from the front. Be careful."

"Windows on the trailer are blacked out," Trigger whispered as they approached the front.

"There are a lot of reasons people black out windows." What I didn't say was that all the reasons I could think of were nefarious. Better to keep that to myself. "Stay focused, Trig."

Trigger moved up the porch steps to the left side, his hand on the door handle. Casey crouched toward the right of the door and nodded to Trigger when he was ready. Casey swept in first with Trigger following close behind him. Within five steps inside, they confirmed the trailer was empty.

"Trigger, close the door and stand ready in case our guy comes home. Casey, move to the front of the trailer and walk slowly toward the back so I can get a good view."

Casey moved to the front window, unclipping his body cam to hold it in the air and slowly scan the front section which consisted of a small couch under the window. The couch was old, but a tear along the arm had been neatly stitched. Turning, Casey walked a few steps, sweeping the camera from side to side. The trailer was at least four decades old, needing new flooring and cabinets, but appeared to be kept in spotless condition.

I shook my hands, my palms sweating. "Open a few cupboards and the fridge, Red Dog."

In the cabinets, the dishes were perfectly aligned. The canned food all faced with their labels forward in neat rows. The ancient avocado green refrigerator was bright white inside, filled with fresh food. Casey moved to the closet-sized bathroom, then to the curtained bedroom space at the far end of the trailer.

"You've got to be fucking kidding me," I whispered, feeling my stomach lurch as Casey swept the camera around the bedroom.

"What is it?" Casey asked.

On Trigger's cam we saw a flash of sunlight as the back door of the trailer opened. Trigger's body had been turned toward Casey as he stood guard at the front door. Hearing the noise, Trigger turned around and came face to face with Milo. They stood shocked, staring at each other in surprise. After a brief pause, Milo fled down the back stairs. Trigger tossed his tranq gun and threw himself off the porch at Milo, tackling him to the ground.

"*Start the clock*!" I yelled at Tech, slapping him on the shoulder.

The far-right TV screen lit up with a stopwatch. We watched Trigger snag both Milo's arms behind his back, whirling rope through them. He captured one of the legs, but it kept popping out of his hold. Finally, he secured it with a rope, then the other, before bundling all the appendages together with a center rope.

"*Time!*" Trigger said, jumping up and lifting his hands into the air as he panted to catch his breath.

"Three minutes, forty-two seconds. You've done better," Tech said.

We watched Trigger shrug on Casey's body cam. "He's a doughy bastard. Makes it harder."

Casey handed Trigger his tranq gun. "Why didn't you just shoot him?"

"That wasn't our order. Besides, I didn't want to have to wait around for him to wake up. This is the part where one of us asks him a few questions."

"Let's hold off on the interrogation," I said. "Casey, turn around and look behind you."

Casey turned—gun first. When he confirmed no one was behind him, he lowered his gun. "What is that?"

"I believe it's a cellar door or storm shelter." I wiped my sweaty hands on my jeans. "We need to know what's in there."

"What do you think is in there?" Casey asked.

I placed my palms flat on the table and closed my eyes.

"Kelsey?" Tech asked. "Tell me you're not thinking what I think you're thinking."

I sighed. "Fuck, I don't know."

"Fill me in here, guys," Casey said. "What's your best guess for what I'm going to find when I open these doors?"

"I think..." I looked at Tech. He nodded, encouraging me to answer. "...Allie Jacobs is in there."

"I thought she was dead," Casey said, taking a step back. "*You said* she was dead."

"Either I was wrong this morning, or I'm wrong now. I won't know until you open the door." I took a step away from the table and exhaled slowly. "There's trash dumped all over his property, but the inside of that trailer is *spotless*. And then there's the bedroom."

"What about the bedroom?" Casey asked.

"There was a floor bolt where a chain could be secured."

"Fuck," Casey said, making the sign of the cross before he started removing the trash bags that covered the cellar doors.

An old padlock hung from the latch. Trigger moved forward, picking the lock and tossing it into the grass. They both stood back a moment, mentally preparing themselves.

I watched them closely on the screens, reading their body language. "Guys, if she's in there, you might need to tranquilize her. She might not be stable."

Casey took a deep breath, nodding, before pulling the door open. The sun lit only as far as the last step. Everything beyond the stairs was pitch black. Trigger made to move forward.

"Wait," I ordered.

We all waited in silence until a bare foot shuffled into the light. Then another. Then with another step, Allie Jacobs stepped into view at the bottom of the stairs.

"Your parents sent us," Trigger said, keeping his tone low and holding out his hand, palm up. "Milo can't hurt you anymore."

She looked from Trigger to Casey, then back to Trigger. Tears started spilling as she climbed the stairs. At the top of the stairs, she cringed away from Trigger's offered hand. He stepped back, so she had room to step away from the cellar.

Something behind them startled Casey, and he spun around to face the woods.

Blake stood frozen, staring at Allie before one foot stumbled in front of the other, moving him across the open dirt yard. "*Allie!*"

Allie's body shook as she cried. "Blake?" She dove toward him when he was within reach, wrapping her arms tight around his neck.

Blake fell to his knees as he held her, smoothing her hair out of her face.

"Now what, boss?" Trigger asked, sounding bored.

"Disarm Blake before he decides to shoot Milo."

This time Casey didn't hesitate. He pulled Blake's Glock while Trigger leaned over to check for an ankle holster. None of us had anticipated Allie snagging Trigger's gun, though. Before they could stop her, she fired three rounds into a hogtied Milo.

Casey yanked the gun out of her hand, and Trigger ran over to pull the darts. Everyone was silent for about five seconds before we broke out laughing.

When I could stop laughing, I leaned closer to the phone. "Best if you untie Milo now, Trigger, and hide the ropes. We'll have to call this in to the local police."

Trigger snorted. "Sure thing, boss."

"Tech, call the parents and tell them the good news. I'll call the cops."

The first call to the police was short and easy. The return call from the sheriff himself wasn't as pleasant. He screamed in my ear for nearly twenty minutes about jurisdiction before I reminded him that without us, he wouldn't have a child abductor in custody. He then threatened to arrest Blake, Casey, and Trigger. I told him I'd be glad to reciprocate by calling the media and ensuring he wasn't re-elected as sheriff. Thankfully, he hung up on me. Trigger called ten minutes later and said they were released. Blake was driving to the hospital. Reggie was sleeping in the backseat on his way back to Michigan with Casey and Trigger.

I picked up my phone to call one more person.

"Hello," Kristyn answered.

"Kristyn, it's Kelsey Harrison. Are you still at work?"

"Yes, just wrapping up a few to-dos before I head to class. Did you have another question?"

"Can you sit? It's important."

Kristyn exhaled slowly. "I'm sitting, but give me a moment. I've been waiting for this call for five years."

"It's not what you think. She's alive. We found Allie. Your uncle was keeping her prisoner behind his trailer in an old cellar."

"*What?* How? Why?" she cried. "*I don't understand.*"

"Breathe, Kristyn," I said in a slow calm voice. "Slow your breathing down." I waited a moment before I heard her gasps for air retreat. "She's going to be okay. She's at St. Francis hospital in Lafayette, and her parents are already on their way. Blake Foster is also with her. He was part of the rescue team who found her."

"I can't believe this. I thought she was dead."

"We all did. I've been working these cases for a long time, and everything indicated she was dead." A laugh escaped me. "I'm sure as hell glad I was wrong."

"It's her? You're sure?"

"Hang on," I said, pausing to look at my phone and forward a picture. "You tell me. I just sent a photo."

There was a brief pause before Kristyn gasped, followed by shrieking. "*It's her! She's alive!* I have to go. I need to get to the hospital."

"Drive safe. She'll be there when you get there. Blake will stay with her until then. He'll protect her."

"Thank you," she said, crying as she hung up.

Hearing someone behind me, I turned to see Bridget and Beth.

"That must have felt good," Beth said, walking over and placing a hand on my shoulder.

"It did," I agreed. "It's not often we get a win like today."

"I'm taking the credit for this one," Tech said, leaning back in his chair and lacing his fingers behind his head. "You didn't want to even look at the case."

"You're right. It read on paper like a few others I haven't solved," I said, nodding toward the missing prostitute files. "The unsolved cases haunt me."

"That's not the ending this time, though." Bridget set a fabric tote on top of the table. "We brought you guys a celebratory present." She pulled a six pack of beer out of the tote.

"What if the case had turned sideways?" I asked.

"Then the beer would've gone well with the box of tissues." Bridget pulled a box of tissues from the tote and tossed the box at me. I caught the box, tossing it on top of the credenza.

Tech opened several beers, passing them around. "I'd say we did pretty good for a Tuesday afternoon. I'm all for quitting early."

I glanced at the clock, realizing it was only three, and sighed before taking a long drink of my beer. "You can call it a day. I'm too far behind."

"I figured you'd say that," Bridget said, pulling another six pack from the tote. "At least we won't be thirsty while we work."

Tech laughed. "What the hell. I'll keep going as long as I can drink."

"There's the spirit," I said, slugging him in the shoulder. "Bridget, where are we at on the jewel thief?"

"I'm in love. Don't tell Bones," Bridget said, sliding a file to me. "The bastard only robs people who deserve it. He or she steals their victim's most expensive piece of art or jewelry, usually during a social event, then he or she disappears."

"Who's offering the reward money?"

"Four of the victims pooled their money for the reward," Beth said. "They know each other. All four are members of a prestigious yacht club in California."

"Have any of the stolen items turned up on the black market?"

"Not that Carl could find," Bridget said, shaking her head.

"What's your theory?" I asked her.

Bridget smirked. "I find it strange that four of the nine victims know each other. Especially when two of the four have houses on the east coast, and the other two reside on the west coast."

"I have houses scattered across the country," I said. "I might even know one of the victims."

"You do, actually," Tech said.

"Who?"

"Mark Farlow."

I cycled the name through my brain a few times until the light bulb came on. "The creeper in South Carolina who was stalking that waitress?"

Tech nodded. "The charges never stuck. He was released, agreeing to stay away from the waitress. She filed a lawsuit, but I heard they settled out of court."

"She went through hell because of that guy. I hope she walked away with a fortune."

Bridget's eyes sparkled with humor. "Even if she didn't, he lost big time, that's for sure. The thief stole a Picasso painting valued at over twenty-two million."

"He would've had it insured. There's no big punishment for him in that."

"That's where it gets interesting," Beth said. "All the victims had lapses in their insurance coverage when the thefts occurred."

Tech and I glanced at each other before leaning forward in our chairs.

Bridget and Beth shared a conspiratorial grin before Bridget explained. "Apparently, each victim cancelled their insurance policies a few days before the robberies."

I whistled slowly. "Which they never did. Whoever our thief is, he didn't want them to collect the insurance claim."

"Exactly," Bridget said. "The big question is, how would the thief know their insurance information?"

"Same insurance company?" I asked.

Bridget shook her head. "Nope."

"Hacker?" Tech asked.

"Doubtful," Beth said. "The policies were all cancelled by letters sent in advance to the insurance companies. A hacker would've cancelled the policies electronically."

I tapped my pen against the table. "If my agent got a letter from me saying to cancel my coverage, he'd better damn well call me."

"Maybe the agents didn't know, since the policies were cancelled at the corporate offices," Bridget said.

"That's a theory we can check on," I said. "Until then, let's keep going. Are all the victims sex offenders of some kind?"

"No," Bridget said. "But they're all assholes. We have one stalker, four suspected rapists, two embezzlers, one murderer, and a fucking pedophile."

I could feel my eyebrows rise. "You can't be serious."

"Oh, I'm serious. The disgusting part is they're all rich enough to have wormed their way out of the charges."

"Or," Beth said, "they were sentenced to something ridiculous like a five-figure fine or house arrest."

"Even the pedophile?" Tech asked.

"Roaming free," Bridget said, nodding.

We were all quiet, thinking as we drank our beer.

There was a knock on the door, and Tech got up to answer it. On the other side of the door, Tyler stood grinning at us.

"Problem?" I asked.

"Nope," he said, shaking his head and walking into the room. "I couldn't remember the code to your war room, though. Between the houses and the store, I have too many security codes in my head." He helped himself to a beer and sat in the end chair. "I'm calling it a day. I've got two guys from Devil's Players and two guys from Demon Slayers monitoring your house."

"If you called in the Slayers, you must be screwing with James," I said, grinning.

Tyler shrugged, the corner of his lips turning up. "I thought it was time he understood security was my gig."

"Good for you."

"Why does everyone look so serious?" Tyler asked. "I heard you solved a cold case today."

"We did," Tech said. "Bridget and Beth just filled us in on their case. It's, uh, unusual."

"How so?"

"We're rooting for the bad guy," Beth said, laughing. "The people he's screwing with totally deserve it."

"Simple then," Tyler said. "Just don't solve the case."

"It's a million-dollar reward," Bridget said.

Tyler shook his head. "You can't look at it that way. We break the law all the time to capture the bad guys or protect our family and friends. We do it because we're on the right side. Stay on the right side. Find another case."

"I agree," I said, closing the file. "The reward money doesn't justify punishing the only person who is holding those asshats accountable for their actions."

"What about the bet with Donovan?" Tech asked.

"There's no actual prize other than bragging rights. If we don't beat him in profits this year, we'll take him down next year. I'm not willing to risk my morals to knock Donovan down a few pegs."

"The year's not over yet," Bridget said. "Let's find another case."

"Hang on," Tech said, typing on his computer. "Kemp's been organizing the case requests. I'll have him bring us a summary."

I rolled my eyes. "You could pick up the phone, or heaven forbid, walk down the hall to talk to him."

"Typing is faster," Tech said.

Tyler walked over and held the door open.

Kemp walked through it twenty seconds later, carrying a stack of papers and a large folder. "I have the case file list, along with summaries including locations, general backgrounds, and payment details," Kemp said, handing Tech several sheets of paper. "I also have the invoices to be billed. If you can review them," Kemp handed me a thick folder with at least fifty invoices, "I'll get them in the mail today."

"Damn. If our billing is this far behind maybe we can still beat Donovan this year."

"I couldn't have been that far behind," Tech said, shaking his head.

"Afraid so," Kemp said. "I reconciled the invoices against the prior payments, just to make sure we didn't double bill anyone."

"My bad," Tech said, laughing. "And look at this. There are nine other cases with payouts of over a quarter of a million."

"Let's get to work then," Tyler said.

"I thought you were going home," I said.

"James isn't the only one who needs to learn I work for *you*. Donovan's about to realize it, too."

"Go Team Kelsey!" Bridget said, standing to high five each of us.

"You're all crazy," Beth said as she pulled a laptop toward her. "But send me a file."

Kemp assigned files out electronically. He offered to help Tech research leads as needed.

"Bridget?" I asked.

"Yeah?" she answered, not looking up from her laptop.

"Now that we've agreed not to take the case, who's the thief?"

She glanced up at me. "You mean, *thieves*."

I raised an eyebrow.

"I connected five teenagers who are either family members or close friends of the families who were burglarized. My guess is they're throwing the art and jewels into the ocean. Never mess with a pissed off teenager."

"I'll remember that," I said, laughing as I turned back to the file of invoices.

Chapter Eight

We were two hours into research when Trigger walked into the war room. "We dumped Reggie in the gym. We didn't know what you wanted us to do with him."

I went out and looked over the rail to the gym below. Reggie was sprawled out on the plank floor, sound asleep. Returning to the war room, I grabbed a pile of permanent markers from the credenza before going back to the walkway and whistling. Several guards, including Wayne, jogged over. I tossed the markers down. "Do me a favor and teach Reggie a lesson."

The guys laughed as they uncapped the markers. I went back to the war room and saved my work. "It's time to call it a day. I need to get home before Nicholas starts calling me every five minutes."

"Whose night is it to cook?" Tech asked, standing and stretching.

"It was mine, but Hattie texted that she had it handled. Tweedle was helping her."

"I'm inviting myself to dinner," Beth said. "I was supposed to go grocery shopping today."

"You're learning," Bridget said, smirking at Beth. "And you're in luck. Hattie said tacos were on the menu tonight."

"Yum," Tech said, rubbing his stomach. "I haven't had tacos in ages."

I shook my head at Tech before looking back to Beth. "What about your dog, Storm?"

"I have time to take him to the park before I swing back."

"Bring him to the house. Nicholas has been begging me to get a dog, and I've been stalling. He can toss a ball for him in the field after dinner."

"You sure? He's a great dog, but he's a German Shepherd. He'll shed all over your carpet."

"As long as he doesn't pee on it, I'm good. Seriously, bring him over. I'll bet he's just as sick of your apartment as you are."

"Actually, I was going to ask if I could bring him a few times a week to school. He's trained and will stay on his dog bed while I teach."

"As long as he minds you, I'm fine with it."

~*~*~

After dinner, Nicholas and Sara played with Storm until we called them in to get ready for bed. Anne led Sara upstairs, and I nudged Nicholas down the hall and into the bathroom.

"I want to see you scrub those teeth, young man," I said, grinning at him in the mirror. "All of them. Not just the front ones."

"I will."

"I know you will, because I'm going to watch to make sure you do."

Nicholas watched me in the mirror as he coated his toothbrush with toothpaste. While he brushed, I exchanged his hand towel for a clean one. An empty roll hung on the toilet paper rack with a partial roll sitting on top of the sink. Nicholas giggled as I swapped the rolls.

"Don't forget to brush the roof of your mouth and tongue," I reminded him.

He rolled his eyes, but did as I asked. When he was done brushing, I stopped him from wiping his mouth on his sleeve and handed him a tissue. He laughed, wiping his mouth and tossing the tissue toward the trash before running into his bedroom. He had missed, though. I stood staring at the tissue lying on the floor. I knew I should call him back into the bathroom, but he was already putting on his pajamas. I decided it wasn't worth delaying bedtime and starting a fight.

After throwing the tissue away, I rinsed the spit from the sink, shaking my head. Nine-year-old boys were slobs. Turning the bathroom light off, I crossed the hall into Nicholas' room. He was already climbing into bed.

"Young man," I said, placing my hands on my hips. "You have a hamper for your dirty clothes."

"It's okay. Eloise picks them up when she cleans. She'll make my bed, too. It's kind of cool."

Based on a recommendation from Nightcrawler, I'd hired Eloise a few weeks back to clean the houses and Headquarters. She was shy and usually cleaned when the fewest number of people were around. Though we seldom saw her, we always knew she'd cleaned because she left everything in five-star condition.

"It's not Eloise's job to clean up after you."

"You hired her to clean. That is too her job."

"Nicholas, get out of bed *and pick up your clothes!*"

"Fine," he said, sighing dramatically as he threw the covers away from him and stood. He made a production of stomping around the room and throwing his clothes toward the hamper. Half of them missed. I stopped him from climbing back into bed and turned him back toward the hamper.

"You're in a bad mood." He stomped back, jamming the clothes deep into the hamper.

"When I see my son taking advantage of people, yes, it puts me in a bad mood."

"Can I go to bed now?" he asked, crossing his arms over his chest and glaring at me.

"You really want to play this game?"

He turned his glare toward the wall but didn't answer.

"Fine. To bed then." I waved a hand toward his bed and he stomped over, throwing himself in and turning his back toward me.

"I take it you don't want to read with me tonight?"

Silence.

"That's your choice. From now on though, you clean your own room. Which includes making your bed." I leaned over and kissed the top of his head. "And remember, I love you even when you're behaving like a spoiled snot."

I tousled his hair, but he jerked away from me. Sighing, I left the bedroom and closed the door behind me. Back in the dining room, I picked up my phone and called Eloise.

"Hello," Eloise answered in a quiet voice.

"Hi, Eloise. It's Kelsey. Sorry to call you after hours. Do you have a minute?"

"Did I do something wrong?"

"Not at all. I'm actually calling because you are doing too good of a job."

"I don't understand."

"My son. He's turning into a spoiled brat. I need you to stop cleaning his room for him."

"Sara's too!" Anne said, coming down the stairs.

"Anne's saying to stop cleaning Sara's, too. We need the kids to learn to take care of themselves."

"What about vacuuming? And dusting? And making the beds?" Eloise asked.

"They're old enough to make their own beds. If their rooms are clean, I don't mind you vacuuming the floor on occasion or washing the windows, but their clothes, toys, trash, bedding—that's their job."

"Okay. If you're sure."

"I'm very sure. And if you notice the kids leaving messes for you to clean up, let one of us know. We'll handle it."

"I don't want to get them in trouble. They're nice kids."

"But?"

"Nicholas needs to work on his aim when using the bathroom," she said, giggling. "And Sara spills pop in her room and lets it dry and get gummy."

"I'm pretty sure Anne isn't aware that Sara is drinking pop, let alone spilling it in her room. As for Nicholas' aiming habits, I'll ask one of the guys to have a talk with him. If that doesn't work, I'll have him start cleaning all the toilets until he learns."

"You are a good mom, Kelsey."

"I'm glad someone thinks so." We ended the call, and I laughed at Anne's scowl.

"Where is she getting pop?"

"Likely the basement refrigerator. We keep some down there for company and mixed drinks."

"Grr..." Anne walked back up the stairs.

I looked around the room. If Grady were home, he'd talk to Nicholas about the peeing thing. It certainly wasn't a conversation I wanted to have. I'd likely be farming out a few other conversations in the years to come, too.

Whiskey, Tech, and Tyler sat around the table, smirking at me.

"Who's willing?"

"I would, but I'll laugh the whole time," Tech admitted.

"I'll take this one," Tyler said, standing. "As a prospect for the club, I've cleaned enough toilets to explain why it's not cool."

My cell phone, still in my hand, rang. I answered it, seeing it was Grady. "Hey, sexy," I said, moving into the living room for privacy.

"Hey, beautiful. You sound like you're in a good mood."

"Not according to Nick."

Grady chuckled. "His opinion doesn't count. He's mad at me all the time these days."

"Well, consider it your lucky day. Tyler volunteered to talk to him about peeing all over the toilet. You'll owe Tyler a beer when you get back home."

"Small price to pay." Grady laughed quietly. "How was work?"

"Good. We found a young woman who had been held captive for the last five years."

"How is she?"

"Physically, she's fine. Mentally, she has a long road ahead of her, filled with years of counseling, but she's got a lot of people who love her. She'll be okay."

"Sounds like one hell of a win, babe."

"How about your mission?"

"Nothing we can't handle," he said.

There was something in his voice though. Not fear, but something. Worry? "What aren't you telling me?"

Grady was quiet for a long moment before he answered. "The rescue mission involves pissing off a very dangerous family. They're well connected, and not just in Mexico, but in the United States, too."

I nodded to myself. "You're worried about blowback."

"We all are. The last time we took on a job this serious, we didn't have families. That's changed. It's making us look at things differently."

"Who's the victim?"

"Our intel tells us that two women and a DEA agent are being held in one of the buildings on the compound."

"Can you get them out and stay whole?"

"The mission itself isn't a problem. We can go in tonight."

"Then do it."

"And if there *is* blowback?"

"It won't be the first time we've had bad guys at our doorstep. We'll keep the family safe. If we don't keep fighting for the victims, though, who will?"

Grady was quiet again.

"What do you need?"

"I need you to ramp up security. I'd also like to tell Nick goodnight."

"I'll talk to Tech, Tyler, and Wayne about security." I turned toward the dining room. Tyler had just returned and heard me say his name. Tech also looked up. "Hattie will take the phone to Nick so you can say goodnight."

Hattie nodded, walking over to me.

"I love you," Grady whispered.

"I love you, too, but I'm going to be really pissed if you don't get your ass home safely, Mr. Tanner."

Grady chuckled, but it didn't hold his usual carefree tone. "Yes, ma'am."

I handed the phone to Hattie, and she greeted Grady as she walked down the hall.

"What's wrong?" Katie asked.

Tweedle grabbed Bridget's hand. Bridget squeezed hers back just as tight.

"They're okay," I said, joining them back at the table. "The mission itself isn't the issue."

"Then what is?" Lisa asked, holding baby Abigail against her chest.

"The cartel has connections in the U.S. If they find out who rescued the prisoners, they'll come after all of us."

"You're rattled," Tyler said, laying a hand on my shoulder. "We've been down this road before—more than once. We can handle it. So why are you rattled?"

"I don't know." I ran a shaking hand through my hair. "It was something in Grady's voice. He sounded... *spooked*? Like he was expecting something bad to happen."

"Then we take precautions," Lisa said. "We go on red alert. We keep the kids close."

"Lisa's right," Anne said. "We don't cower. We don't back down."

"I'll alert the security team," Tyler said, heading toward the front door.

"I'll call my uncle and warn everyone at home to be on the lookout for trouble," Tweedle said, nodding.

"I'll call Headquarters," Wayne said.

"I'll call Haley and Kemp," Bridget said.

"Alex is on a date tonight, but I'll call him anyway," Lisa said.

"With who?" I asked Lisa.

"He wouldn't say, but I'll find out one way or another," Lisa said, winking as she handed Abigail off to

Beth. Beth's dog Storm sat up and sniffed Abigail, making her squeal and spit bubbles.

"Everyone needs to be moved to one of the houses. We can't have people scattered all over town and unprotected. That includes you, Beth. Either we cancel school for a couple of weeks, or you'll need to stay here."

"Storm will protect me."

"They'll shoot him," Whiskey said, shaking his head. "No. Kelsey's right. Either you stay away or you stay under our roof until we have this sorted."

"Where on earth would I sleep? This house is packed to the rafters."

"You'd be surprised how many people we can cram into the houses," Katie said.

"And Storm?"

"He's welcome, too," Katie assured her.

"Beth," I said, gaining her attention. "I need you to understand how dangerous this is. We are talking about a Mexican cartel. They're ruthless. If you stay, you could be putting yourself in danger."

"A month ago, I would've run," she admitted. "I've seen and heard enough since then, though, to understand the danger your family faces because you protect strangers. I'm in. I might not be a soldier or a profiler, but I know self-defense and I own a gun. If someone's coming after this family, I'll be one of the people they'll have to go through to get to those kids."

A single tear slipped past my guard. I couldn't believe how incredibly strong this woman in front of me was.

"Welcome to the family," Hattie said to Beth from the end of the hallway, nodding in approval. "Now, let's get to work, everyone. Katie, call the club and get the rest of the bunk beds out of storage. Tech and Whiskey, check the windows and doors and set the alarm. Carl, check to make sure your new heat sensors are working to monitor the woods. Bridget and Tweedle, make a grocery list. I'm calling Texas to warn them." Hattie handed me my phone as she started for the stairs. "And, sunshine, stop the waterworks. There'll be time for crying later."

"Yes, ma'am," I said, laughing as I wiped another tear away.

Chapter Nine

It was a long night. By nine we had warned everyone we could think of calling. Even the local police were on alert. By midnight, we had all the bunk beds put together and ready when needed. Beth was settled in the upstairs spare bedroom. Bridget, Haley, and Kemp were staying at Alex's house. Tweedle had moved into Lisa's house. James and Wayne agreed to stay at Lisa's house to protect them until Donovan and Ryan returned. Trigger, Nightcrawler, and Tyler had claimed bunk beds in the basement. Security patrols were doubled. The tunnels were opened to move people between the houses if needed. We were ready. Or at least, I was praying we were.

"You should get some sleep," Tyler said. "You barely slept last night."

"You only know that because you were up half the night too."

"You both need to go to bed," Wayne said, refilling his coffee cup in the kitchen before joining us at the dining room table. "There's no threat tonight. If there's blowback, it will be after the mission. Sleep while you can. I need you both to be ready in the days ahead."

"What wasn't Grady telling me, Wayne?" I asked. "I know him. He was holding something back."

Wayne watched me, reaching a hand out to grasp mine. "The DEA agent. He knows her. They used to be close. She's a bitch, but she's good at her job. Likely Grady's thinking that if they got to her, they can get to anyone."

"How was she taken?"

"That's the freakiest part. They took her from her home. Somehow they surprised her and had her across the border before anyone knew she was missing."

"Holy crap," Tyler said.

"What's her name?" I asked Wayne.

"Sebrina."

I remembered seeing the name on Grady's phone about a month ago. I thought she was an employee of Aces who I'd never met. "He still talks to her," I said, looking up at Wayne. "Are they still close?"

"Sometimes." Wayne nodded. "Sometimes they're friends. Sometimes they hate each other. They've been circling like that near as long as I can remember." Wayne took another drink of his coffee before sighing. "Sebrina's what they call a handful, and I'm not talking about her cleavage."

"He still loves her," I whispered.

"He's *afraid* for her," Wayne argued. "He doesn't know if she's still alive, and if she is, what they've done to her. And on top of that, he's afraid they'll come after you and the kids next."

I nodded, standing up and turning toward my bedroom.

"He loves *you*, Kelsey," Wayne called out. "Don't ever forget that."

"I know he loves me, Wayne," I answered, stopping to look back at him. "But we both know you can love more than one person."

I thought about Grady as I made my way down the hall. Was I jealous? I shook my head, closing my bedroom door behind me.

I understood still loving someone from your past. A part of me would always love Eric, may he rest in peace.

He was the truest of friends and had a generous soul. Another part of me would always love Wild Card, too. A woman couldn't wish for a better fake husband.

I had to admit, I'd never been in a situation where I had to save the life of one of my exes. I couldn't imagine the raw feelings that would surface in that scenario. If Wild Card were in danger, I'd risk everything to save him. I had no doubt. Just like I had no doubt that even though Grady would hate it, he'd understand. He'd support my decision, even if it hurt. That meant I had to be strong for Grady. I had to find a way to help him through this. He would do the same for me.

I slid my boots off, tossing them toward the closet. Opening my nightstand, I checked the clip on my Glock, setting it beside the lamp. I lay back on the bed, forcing myself to slow my breathing and close my eyes. It felt like an hour before I stopped hearing the ticking of the clock in the atrium.

~*~*~

I had been dreaming, but I couldn't remember about what. Everything in my mind faded and wisps of fog and blackness surrounded me. I stood, fully dressed, reaching a hand into the fog. It felt hot to the touch. More like steam.

"I've been here before," I said to myself, "but it was cold last time."

I stepped forward, the melting fog coating my skin like sweat.

Leaves rustled to my right as everything around me came to life. I was in a road. A woman sat slumped in a Jeep next to me. The heavy forest rustled again and three men carrying guns rushed out. The gun in my hands started firing in their direction as they started shooting back. My gun was still throwing bullets when a hot stabbing pain ripped through my right shoulder.

I screamed. I threw a hand over my mouth, stifling my own scream as I realized I was sitting up in bed, awake.

Wayne ran into my bedroom, turning on the light. I saw he had his handgun out as he searched the room. When he realized I was alone, he holstered his weapon and pulled me into his arms. "You're okay. It was just a dream."

I felt my tears running down the back of my throat. "Grady was shot," I whispered.

"He's fine. It was just a dream."

Gripping the sides of his face, I stared at him. "No, Wayne. Grady was shot! *I saw it.* I don't know what happened next."

Wayne stared back at me. "Fuck."

~*~*~

There wasn't a safe way to contact the guys. They'd have a satellite phone, but even if they had it turned on, it wasn't safe to call them. To distract them. My scream had woken the whole house, including Katie and Tech from their apartment above the garage. Hattie and Tech managed to convince the kids I'd had a nightmare and settled them back into bed. The adults knew, just by looking at me, that it was more than that.

Whiskey made a pot of coffee while Anne loaded a plate of leftover muffins. James escorted Lisa, Abigail, and Tweedle up the basement stairs. Both Lisa and Tweedle were shaking. Bridget and Tyler entered through the garage door.

"We heard you scream. What is it? What happened?" Lisa asked.

I sat at the dining room table and looked at Bridget first. "We need better soundproofing in the houses if I woke everyone at Alex's house."

"Couldn't sleep." Bridget joined me at the table. "I was patrolling with Tyler."

"We don't have the details, yet," Wayne said, helping Lisa into a chair. "Kelsey thinks Grady was shot."

"The voodoo witch thing?" Anne asked.

I nodded, watching my hands tremble.

"Voodoo?" James asked. "Have you all been smoking whacky weed?"

"You don't have to believe it, man," Wayne said. "I've seen Grady and Kelsey go through this shit too many times, though."

"What happened?" Tweedle asked, still standing near the basement doorway.

"Come sit down, dear," Hattie said, guiding her toward the table.

Everyone found a seat at either the oversized dining room table or one of the stools at the breakfast bar. Only Tyler remained standing, leaning against the wall between the dining room and kitchen. For a crowded room, it was quiet. They watched me, patiently waiting for me to explain.

"I don't know anything. Not really. I know Grady was shot in the shoulder. I don't know what happened after that."

"Do you know where they were?" Wayne asked.

I shook my head. "A woman was lying in the Jeep. I think it may have been Sebrina. I didn't see anyone else except the three men who were shooting at Grady."

"Tech?" Wayne said. "I need satellite images. I have the coordinates of the compound."

Tech grabbed his laptop off the credenza and booted it up, nodding.

"Uh, Kel?" Tyler said, holding a hand up to his ear com. "I hate to interrupt, but while they dig through maps or whatever, do you mind stepping outside? Nightcrawler's currently holding a shotgun on a vehicle of unknown visitors, threatening to blow their heads off."

I glanced up at the clock. It was four in the morning. "Katie, give me your gun. Mine is still in my bedroom."

"Locked and loaded," she said, handing hers over. "I'll get yours along with a holster."

Tyler stepped out the front door first, nodding for me to follow after he looked around. A dark sedan was stopped fifty yards from my driveway. Nightcrawler stood centered between the car's headlights with a shotgun aimed at the windshield.

"Baby girl," Pops yelled from the passenger side window, "call your dog off!"

"Let him through!" I yelled loud enough for the guards lurking in the shadows to hear.

Nightcrawler lowered the shotgun and stepped to the side to let the vehicle pass. The headlights were turned off as the vehicle pulled into the driveway. Not only had Pops come, but Jackson was driving.

I greeted Pops first, comforted by his strong arms holding me. I barely turned before Jackson lifted me into a tight hug. Tyler grabbed their overnight bags from the trunk.

"Who you calling a dog, old man," Nightcrawler said as he approached.

"Nightcrawler," I said, pointing my finger at him, "if you take one more step toward my Pops with that attitude, I'll shoot a kneecap off."

Nightcrawler smirked before walking into the blackness around the side of the garage.

"That's the name he goes by? Nightcrawler?" Jackson whispered. "Really?"

"Careful. He's not someone you want to piss off."

I heard an evil chuckle from somewhere in the darkness.

"Why are the lights on?" Pops asked, completely at ease.

"Let's head inside. It's not safe out here."

"Where's Reggie?" Jackson asked.

"Shit," I said, looking at Tyler. "Is he still sleeping on the gym floor?"

Tyler shrugged.

"Was he drunk?" Jackson asked, looking between Tyler and me.

I shook my head. "He was interfering with my case. I ordered Trigger to shoot him with a tranquilizer gun."

Jackson looked away, placing his fisted hands on his hips as he gritted his teeth in frustration.

Pops chuckled, steering me toward the front door. "Sounds about right." Pops opened the door, stepping back to let me enter first. "That boy's been a handful since the day he was born."

"I'm going to Headquarters to check on him," Jackson called out.

I waved a hand over my shoulder, indicating that I didn't care, before stepping inside.

"So? Why is everyone up this early?" Pops asked, walking in behind me.

"Pops!" Hattie said, running over to hug him. "I wasn't expecting you until late morning."

"Jackson chartered a plane. Three more men who work with Aces flew back with us."

"That's good," Wayne said from the dining room. "If we need to organize a rescue mission, I might need more men to run security here. Kelsey, come look at this satellite image."

I joined him and Tech at the table and looked over Tech's shoulder. They had satellite images of a large house surrounded by several outbuildings and what appeared to be a tall metal fence.

"Anything look familiar?"

"No. I could only see a dirt road and the forest. I didn't see any buildings."

"How wide was the road?" Wayne asked.

"Barely a car width wide. It was definitely a back road."

Tech zoomed out, but the forest was too thick to see anything for miles. Two small cities, distanced about the same radius from the guys' last known location, were possible options to the east.

"I can send two teams," Wayne said, looking up at me. "I can have them scout both cities."

"No." I stepped over to Tweedle and placed a hand on her shoulder. "This is the part where we have to have faith. Sending more men will only complicate their situation."

Tweedle wiped the tears from her cheeks. "Someone needs to run to the store. I need more flour. The best thing for me to do right now is to bake."

"I sent some guys to the store earlier," Tyler said. "We have enough flour to start a cookie factory."

Tweedle smiled at him as she moved into the kitchen. "Any requests?"

"Chocolate chip cookies!" Katie said.

"Brownies," Tech said.

"Lemon poppyseed muffins," Tyler said.

"Banana nut bread," Lisa said.

Tweedle looked at me with a raised eyebrow.

"I'm not picky. A distraction is a good idea, though. I brought home the Miami case files."

"You've gone through those files a million times," Tech said, glancing sideways at me. "I know Uncle Hank asked you to take a look, but let's focus on our backlogged cases first."

"*Fine*. Just give me a case to take my mind off things."

Tech and Bridget gathered our other laptops and started them up. Tech pointed me toward a file that Kemp had created for quick-glance service requests that had been emailed to us. I took the oldest request and started working.

Chapter Ten

Ten minutes later, Jackson entered through the front door, turning to Reggie who was behind him. "*No*! I don't want to hear it. I don't need to know what you did. I know you—and I know Kelsey. Whatever you did, it had to have been pretty bad for her to unleash that level of retribution."

"*Babe*, I swear I was in the right."

Jackson shook his head and looked at me. Everyone else was staring at Reggie, or more precisely, the artwork all over his face.

"Does he know yet?" I asked Jackson.

"Not yet. I need a drink. You?"

"No. You'll need to skip the booze, too. Stick to strong coffee. If we get the call the guys are in trouble, I'll need you to go to Mexico with me."

Pops stood and walked over to place his hands on the breakfast bar as he glared at Reggie. "What in Sam Hill did you do this time?"

"Nothing," Reggie said, walking around Pops and into the kitchen.

Pops pointed at Reggie. "Your forehead says otherwise!"

Reggie raised an eyebrow, then glanced at his reflection in the microwave. "*Shit!*"

"No," Katie said, walking over to read Reggie's forehead. "It says *idiot*." She looked back at me with a smirk.

"I like the picture of the little boy peeing on his left cheek," Tech said, dumping a pile of files on the table.

"The cat whiskers are cute," Tweedle said, grinning as she poured a bag of chocolate chips into a batch of cookie dough.

"It's part of the theme," Wayne said before taking a drink of his coffee. "Look at his chest."

Reggie opened his shirt which was still unbuttoned. The word *pussycat* was written in big block letters.

"It was a struggle to keep our art rated PG," Wayne said, chuckling. "We had to adapt so the kids wouldn't see something inappropriate."

"This will wash off, right?" Reggie asked.

I shrugged. "Eventually."

"I know better than to ask," Jackson said, shaking his head. "But what did he do?"

"Blake Foster is a young and barely trained guard of Aces who had an obsession with his long-lost missing teenage crush. Reggie was supposed to ensure Blake didn't leave Headquarters, but instead he flew him to Indiana on my dime. They arrived on scene right before the property was to be swept and our suspect questioned."

Jackson turned to face Reggie. "You're lucky she only had you tranquilized!"

"It wasn't fair. Poor Blake had been searching for Allie for years. You should have heard him."

"*He was too emotionally involved!*" Jackson stormed into the living room, rubbing a hand over his head. "Wayne, I want the expenses billed to Reggie. He'll cover the cost of the plane and anything else he spent."

"Now, let's not get carried away," Reggie said, walking over to hold Jackson's hand. "Kelsey can afford it." Reggie pouted at Jackson, batting his eyelashes dramatically.

With the catlike eyelashes and whiskers, even Jackson was having a hard time keeping a straight face.

"You're paying the money. I don't care if it empties your bank account."

"*Fine.*" Reggie stomped toward the basement stairs like a petulant child. "I'm going to shower downstairs."

Jackson turned to me. "Are you sure I can't drink?"

"The guys ran into trouble in Mexico," Wayne said. "We're waiting to hear from them."

Wayne filled Jackson in on what little we knew.

"How long has it been?" Jackson asked.

"Half an hour? Maybe a little longer," I said.

"I need a burner phone."

Katie went to the credenza and opened the bottom drawer. "Charged and ready."

Jackson called a number from memory. Based on the number of digits he'd entered I knew the call was out of the country. He spoke in rapid Spanish so I only understood a handful of words. *Wake. Trouble. Soon. Be Ready.*

"Care to enlighten the class?" Katie asked.

Jackson shrugged. "We have an acquaintance with medic training less than two hours from their last known location. I gave him a heads up that the team was on their way and to have them call home."

"Can this acquaintance be trusted?" I asked.

"Yes. He's ex-army. When he got out, he gave a big F-you to the government and moved to a quiet beach town in Mexico. He's helped us out a time or two. He might hate the U.S. government, but he's a soldier through and through, even if he spends all his time these days mixing margaritas."

"He's an alcoholic?" Tweedle asked.

"No," Jackson answered. "He's a bartender. Who are you?"

"Reel's wife."

"Who?"

"Reel and Ryan are the same person," I explained. "Back to the call. So, we should hear from them in an hour or two?"

Jackson nodded. "Once Shipwreck gets everyone patched up, he'll find them a boat. He has a few connections in the smuggling world."

I raised an eyebrow.

"Not human smuggling," Jackson said, shaking his head. "Mostly weed. Okay—a lot of weed. His only involvement in human smuggling is calling Donovan if he hears about a holding location for sex traffickers. Donovan calls Homeland Security. Shipwreck doesn't trust the government to call them himself."

"Am I the only one who wants to know why this guy's nickname is Shipwreck?" Katie asked.

"The locals named him by accident," Jackson said, sliding into the chair next to Katie. "A storm crashed his sailboat into the shore. They kept pointing and saying *naufragio*, the Spanish word for shipwreck. He didn't know Spanish and thought they meant him. It was months before someone translated what was being said. By then, the nickname had stuck."

"As fascinating as that story is," I said rolling my eyes, "If we're not going to hear back for an hour or two, some of you should go back to bed."

"No way," Anne said, pointing to the files. "Put us to work. None of us will be able to sleep anyway."

"You sure?" I asked, looking around.

Everyone nodded.

I turned to Tech, who was typing on his laptop. "What do we have that they can work on?"

"I have some minor cases that could be researched, but nothing heavy. Most of what we have in backlog requires your eyes."

"What about your Miami case?" Lisa asked. "The one Uncle Hank wants you to solve."

"A fresh set of eyes might be just what that case needs. Hang on," I said, leaving the table to retrieve hard copies of the files I had in my bedroom.

"What do we know?" Bridget asked when I returned and dumped the files on the table.

"Uncle Hank noticed a pattern of prostitutes disappearing in the upper west side of Miami. We know of eight, but there's talk on the street that the numbers are even higher. A lot of crimes against prostitutes are never reported."

"Isn't disappearing prostitutes pretty common?" Jackson asked.

"Sure, if they turn up dead or in a hospital, but these women dropped off the face of the planet."

"International sex trafficking?" Bridget asked.

"Likely," I said, nodding. "What's odd, though, is that Uncle Hank can't find anyone who knows anything about the disappearances. Not even someone who's too scared to talk."

"Did you reach out to Mickey?" Anne asked.

"He put out some feelers and got nada back. He's puzzled, too. He asked me to keep him in the loop."

"Someone's stupid enough to do business in Miami behind Mickey's back?" Jackson asked, laughing. "Total death wish."

"Who's Mickey?" Beth asked.

"Trouble," James answered. "He's a crime boss in Miami. He's friendly with Kelsey and Grady, but for us mere mortals, if you saw him walking down the sidewalk, you'd likely piss yourself."

James leaned back in his chair, extending an arm over the top of Beth's chair. Storm sat up and growled at James. James slowly pulled his arm back. Storm settled back on the floor, and I swear the dog snorted. Beth winked at me.

I shook my head. "Mickey lives in a world of violence, but I trust him."

"It doesn't matter if you trust him, if he can't help us find the women," Beth said.

"That's not our mission. It's likely the women are either dead or have already been transported to another country."

"What's our mission then?" Bridget asked, not looking up from one of the profiles she was reading.

"To find out how the women were taken unnoticed and, if possible, who is taking them. If we can answer either of those questions, we can stop more women from disappearing."

"What do we know?" Lisa asked.

"We know they weren't nabbed off the street. We'd have witnesses if they were. We know they had different pimps, worked different corners or hotels. We know they have different backgrounds, education levels, appearances, habits. What we don't know is what they have in common. I found two girls who lived in the same building, but so far, that's the only link between any of the victims I can find except, astonishingly enough, none of them were addicts."

"None of them?" Anne asked.

"None of them. No one could even claim they smoked cigarettes, let alone did any illegal drugs."

"I'm not up on my prostitute education," Beth said. "Why is that a big deal?"

Jackson leaned forward so he could see Beth at the other end of the table. "A lot of pimps hook their girls on drugs before forcing them to work the streets. Calculate in that most prostitutes start off as runaway teenagers from abusive homes, and you have a workforce nearly three-quarters of whom are addicts."

"The lack of drugs has to be a clue," Bridget said. "But to what?"

"I don't know. These women didn't have the education and background to work high-end establishments where they could be easily abducted. They were corner-level prostitutes. They had pimps. They had coworkers who kept an eye out for each other and talked about sketchy johns. I can't visualize how being drug-free would make them easier targets. From a trafficking standpoint, though, taking girls without addictions to heroin or oxi means higher profits."

Katie looked at me sideways, narrowing her eyes. "You're itching to go to Miami and talk to the hookers."

"I was planning on flying down Monday," I admitted. "Grady had agreed to watch Nick if I waited until after the tournament."

"You'll have to postpone your trip or send someone else," Wayne said. "With the cartel threat, we need you here."

"I know."

Anne grabbed a notebook and pen from the credenza. She started writing a list of some kind. I moved over to look over her shoulder.

"I can go," Bridget said.

"Wouldn't work," Jackson said. "Kelsey has street contacts in Miami. She's a local hero for taking Pasco down. It would take you months to gain that level of trust. And while you were building that trust, it's likely the perp would hear about you and have you snatched or killed."

Bridget paled, looking over at Jackson. "Never mind."

"What about Charlie?" Katie asked.

"*No!*" came from Pops, Jackson, Reggie, and me, simultaneously.

I chuckled at how protective my Texas family had become over Charlie. "Charlie has a cop vibe. She also doesn't have the street contacts I have from when I worked undercover. Besides, when I called her earlier to warn her, she said she was with Kierson in Atlanta. They were playing house together for the week to see how it went."

Hattie chuckled as she walked around the table refilling coffee cups. "That has disaster written all over it."

"You don't think she can settle into a relationship?"

"Charlie can't pretend to be someone she's not. She's not the stay-at-home wife type. She needs a job. She needs to be as busy as Kierson, or it won't work."

"With him flying all over the country for the FBI, it's not easy for them to find time to see each other."

"Doesn't matter, dear. Look at you and Grady. You rotate who stays and who goes. You tried the stay-at-home thing too, remember?"

I cringed, remembering the panic attacks I'd had trying to pretend to be someone I wasn't. Hattie was right. Charlie and I were alike in that way. We both needed to have something more in our lives. Maybe we were adrenaline junkies. Maybe we had a death wish. Maybe our childhoods robbed us of any chance to be normal.

As if reading my thoughts, Hattie sighed and patted my shoulder. "There's nothing wrong with either of you other than a stubborn streak of independence." She filled Anne's cup as she read her list over her shoulder. "What about doctors' appointments?"

"Good one," Anne said, writing it down.

"What are you doing?" Tech asked.

"She's writing a list of everyday places you might go," I answered for Anne. "Grocery store. Liquor store. Dry cleaners. The mall."

"Why?" Tyler asked.

Anne looked up from her long list to answer. "I figured if we have a list of places they might have gone, we might find out where they crossed paths with the perp." Anne's nose wrinkled as she smiled. "That's fun to say—*perp*. I feel all badass."

Tech looked confused. "None of them had bank accounts. We don't have a way to figure out which grocery store or which doctor they went to."

"Not electronically," I said. "They worked in a cash-based business, so we'll have to narrow the list geographically. These women didn't have cars. They would've stayed local for most of their needs."

Tech nodded. "I'll start with mapping their addresses and seeing what pops up near where they live."

"Add their business locations, too," Bridget said.

"Their business locations?" Tech said, grinning. "You mean the street corners they worked?"

"Where they sold their bodies, yes," she said, grinning back. "This one worked a dive hotel parking lot." She slid the file she'd been reading to Tech.

"Once you get their work and home locations entered, we can search for each business type on Anne's list," I said.

"I'll help Anne with her list," Bridget said. "Lisa and Beth can help Tech pull the addresses from the files."

I settled back into my chair and focused on the profile cases. I was itching to work the Miami case with everyone else, but Tech was right. I'd studied it for hours and made no headway. Hopefully, their fresh eyes would turn up a lead.

Chapter Eleven

I had moved to the floor, leaning against the wall with my laptop balanced on my thighs. My ass couldn't take sitting on the wooden dining room chair anymore. The thickly padded carpet below me now was a welcome relief to my tailbone. Everyone else was scattered between the dining room table, the breakfast bar, and the living room, working on the Miami case. Tech kept shaking his head at all the paper being passed around the rooms. So much for his paperless initiative.

The ringing of a cell phone caused me to startle, toppling my laptop to the carpet.

I looked up as Jackson grabbed the burner phone. "*Hola.*"

I stood, abandoning the laptop, as I watched Jackson's face for traces of concern.

"*Si.*" He paused, glancing up at me and nodding. "*Si. Senorita Kelsey. Si.*"

The room was quiet enough that we could hear the other person on the other end of the phone speaking rapidly in Spanish, but not clear enough to make out any of the words. The sound of gunfire was very clear though. I dropped to my knees as the phone went silent, disconnected on the other end.

"Shit," Jackson cursed, slamming the phone down. He turned to Wayne first. "Alert our contact with the Coast Guard to be ready just outside international waters for a pickup. Have them keep it quiet, though. The boys will need help getting back into the U.S."

Jackson walked over to me, lifting me up and settling me in a chair before he crouched in front of me. He lifted a hand and wiped the tears from my cheeks.

"Grady?"

"He's alive. Shipwreck patched him up enough to be moved again. Bones is the same blood type, so they did a direct blood transfusion. Grady was still groggy but conscious. Shipwreck was arranging for a boat when the call was interrupted."

"Interrupted by gunfire," Tweedle whispered, standing a few feet away, holding a plate of cookies.

She swayed to the side but was too far away for us to catch. Reggie lunged forward—grabbing the plate of cookies—as Tweedle fell. Bridget dove across the living room, catching Tweedle's upper body before it slammed against the floor.

I looked at Reggie, glaring.

"Oops," he said, grinning.

"Nice save, Reggie," Katie said as she stole the plate of cookies.

Tech stole a cookie from the plate. "Have to admit, the cookies were my first thought, too."

"No concern for the woman left in our care?" I asked.

"*Please*," Tech said before taking a bite. "Tweedle has fallen down the stairs, been shot with a nail gun, and was almost decapitated by a fricken battle axe. Fainting onto padded carpet is nowhere near threatening her nine lives."

"He has a point," Whiskey said, snagging a cookie. "On the other hand, gooey chocolate chip cookies would've been a bitch to clean out of the carpet."

"And wasteful. These are amazing," Lisa said, moaning as she took another bite of her cookie.

Katie rolled her eyes. "Like we wouldn't have eaten them even if they'd hit the floor. *Please*. What's a little dirt and dog hair?"

Jackson shook his head and with Pop's help, they moved Tweedle to the couch. Anne covered her with the afghan.

Bridget looked at her elbow. "I got rug burn diving across the carpet."

I couldn't help the smile that appeared on my face. "Have fun explaining that story to Bones."

Hattie choked on the drink of coffee she was taking. "Mind out of the gutter, sunshine."

We all tried to hide our grins.

"Looks less serious in here," Wayne said as he reentered the house from the garage. "What did I miss?"

"Not important," Jackson said, shaking his head. "Everything set?"

"Coast Guard is on alert. They have three ships nearby and will be monitoring their radar for small vessels moving at high speeds while being chased by bad guys."

"Good. We'll just have to wait until we hear from them again."

"How long will that be?" I asked. "And how are they going to make it to a boat when they're under attack?"

"Shipwreck will have a plan; he always does. He's not going to be happy about them leading the cartel to his house, though."

"I'll pay him restitution," I said, waving my hand in the air to indicate that it didn't matter. "How long until we hear from them again?"

"An hour, maybe. Two if they have to travel to a different marina."

"You're padding the time," Pops said. "What's your real expectation?"

Jackson exhaled slowly. "Half an hour. Shipwreck will have a boat close. The Coast Guard will be ready for them.

Donovan will know we're worried and will call back as soon as they're safe."

"I need that drink now," I said to Jackson.

"About time," Jackson said as he sighed, moving into the kitchen and opening the liquor cabinet above the refrigerator. He ignored the weak stuff, pulling a bottle of Jack from the cabinet and a handful of shot glasses. Returning to the table, he poured two shots, sliding one to me.

Reggie reached for the bottle, but I slapped his hand away. "Reggie, you're in charge of breakfast. The kids will be up soon. They'll need something more than cookies to eat."

Reggie stomped into the kitchen, slamming pans and food around as he pouted. Jackson rolled his eyes before clinking our glasses, and we downed our shots.

"Can I have one of those?" Tweedle asked, sitting up on the couch.

"I've never seen you drink," Bridget said, pouring a shot of whiskey. "This should be good."

"She's a disaster sober," Tyler said. "What happens when she's drunk?"

"We shall see," Bridget said as she walked over and handed the glass to Tweedle.

Tweedle took the shot glass and downed it. She flung herself from the couch, hissing, *"That burns!"*

"That's whiskey, baby," Whiskey said, chuckling. "It's not made for sissies."

Anne glanced over at Whiskey, rolling her eyes as she poured herself a shot and downed it.

Whiskey laughed, wrapping an arm around Anne's hips and pulling her onto his lap. "Too bad one of us needs to stay sober for the kids."

"Probably best if they don't wake to a house full of drunks," Hattie said, taking the bottle.

"We won't overdo it," Jackson said, snagging the bottle back. "Promise."

Hattie shook her head at Jackson but left the bottle and went to the kitchen to help Reggie with breakfast.

I glanced at the clock and pushed away from the table. "She's right. Kids will be up soon. I'm going to sneak a smoke break."

"I'll go with you," Beth said, snapping her fingers for Storm to follow.

Tyler glanced over at me, but I shook my head that we didn't need an escort. "We'll be fine. Sun's coming up. You should take a nap."

"Not until we hear the guys made it out."

I stopped to rest a hand on his forearm. "They'll make it, Tyler. Anything less than that and I'll rain fire down on the cartel's asses like they've never seen before."

~*~*~

I raised the overhead garage door, and we wandered into the driveway. The sun was drifting at a lazy pace into the eastern sky, casting enough light to see the main highway.

"Just me," Nightcrawler called out before he rounded the corner of the garage. "Smoke break?"

"Yup," I said, holding out my hand.

He pulled a pack and a lighter out, handing them to me. "Nicholas find your stash again?"

"Yup." I lit up, exhaling slowly. "Third pack this week to disappear. The damn kid is too smart."

Nightcrawler looked down at Storm as he tapped his leg, silently calling him over. Storm moved cautiously, stretching his nose toward Nightcrawler's hand to have a good sniff. Deciding he was safe enough, Storm closed the distance and leaned against Nightcrawler, earning a scratch behind his ears.

"Good boy," Nightcrawler said. "Go ahead and stretch your legs, big guy." Nightcrawler pointed to the side yard, and Storm moved into the grass to do his business.

"It's not like him to leave my side," Beth said.

"He must trust either Kelsey or me to keep you safe," Nightcrawler said.

"Must be your magic," I said to Nightcrawler. "He's stayed glued to her leg all night."

"What can I say? I'm good with dogs. People, not so much."

"Could have something to do with your appearance," Beth said, openly scanning Nightcrawler from head to toe.

Nightcrawler kept his head shaved bald, had tattoos covering half his body, and wore a cut—a sleeveless motorcycle jacket with his club's logo on it. Underneath the cut, he was shirtless with rippling muscles traveling down to his well-worn jeans and heavy leather belt.

His dark brown eyes narrowed at Beth. "Like what you see?"

She lifted one shoulder in a shrug. "I'm just saying it's a statement."

"What kind of statement?" I asked, grinning back at Beth.

"He reminds me of when Storm raises his hackles and growls at someone."

"Then it's the right kind of statement," Nightcrawler said before wandering into the side yard to join Storm.

"He's likely to pee on a tree, too," I whispered to Beth.

"Heard that," Nightcrawler said.

~*~*~

I was finishing my second cigarette when Katie yelled from the garage door. I grabbed Beth by the elbow, dragging her along as I ran.

"Sounds good," Jackson was saying on the phone. "You bet. See you soon."

"They're safe?" I asked, rushing into the dining room.

"They're with the Coast Guard, heading to Corpus Christi," Jackson nodded. "Sebrina and Grady are being taken to medical, but Donovan says they'll both be fine. Nothing that rest and fluids can't cure."

"When will they be home?" Tweedle asked, gripping the refrigerator door handle.

"Wild Card and Ryan will fly back with Shipwreck later this morning. Donovan and Bones are staying with Grady until he can travel."

Wayne stood and carried his coffee cup into the kitchen. "I'll call some guys in Texas to guard them so Bones and Donovan can get some sleep." Wayne walked toward the garage. "I'll also update the boys at Headquarters. Maybe everyone can get some sleep now."

Nicholas stumbled down the hall, half asleep. He continued walking until he slammed into me, wrapping his arms around my waist.

"Morning, sweetheart," I whispered, stroking his hair from his face.

"Why's everyone up so early?" he asked while yawning, eyes still closed.

"It's almost seven, silly," Beth said, steering him toward the breakfast bar. "It's time for breakfast."

Whiskey lifted Nicholas onto a barstool as Hattie slid a plate and silverware in front of him. She turned to me, linking an arm through mine and leading me down the hall into the family room. I looked up at her, confused.

"Now, sunshine," she said, holding my cheek in her hand. "Now you can cry. Let it out before it breaks you."

A sob broke in my throat that I didn't know I was holding. She wrapped her arms around me, hugging me against her. I clung to her as the dam broke. I felt myself being lifted and recognized Jackson's cologne as I leaned my forehead against his shoulder. I was cradled on his lap while he sat on the couch.

By the time I could clear the tears and steady my breathing, I realized I wasn't the only one crying. Tyler held Bridget as she cried. Pops held Tweedle. Lisa held Abigail, smothering her with kisses and dripping tears onto her as Katie kept a supportive arm wrapped around Lisa's waist.

"Everyone seemed so calm," I said, resting my head on Jackson's broad shoulder. "I didn't realize you were all pretending, too."

Katie wiped her cheeks dry. "We pushed through because that's what you needed, but those men are like brothers. They're family."

"Damn straight," Pops said as he rubbed Tweedle's back. "I'm proud of you girls, standing together like you did."

In the silence that followed, Tweedle hiccupped, making us all laugh.

Chapter Twelve

"Why's everybody crying?" Sara asked from the hallway.

Nicholas walked up behind Sara and grabbed her hand.

"Come here, you two," I said, sliding onto the couch beside Jackson as the kids ran over to climb up onto our laps. "Everything's okay. We had a scare, but the tears are happy tears. Grady hurt his arm at work, but him and your uncles will be home soon."

Nicholas watched me, trying to decide if I was lying.

"It's the *truth*. Promise." I smoothed his hair from his eyes.

"When will he be home?" Nicholas asked.

"The doctors want Grady to rest for a few days. He should be here before the weekend, though. Uncle Wild Card will be coming back with Ryan today."

"Uncle Bones and Uncle Donovan aren't coming home today?" Sara asked, looking at Bridget and Lisa.

"Not today," Lisa said. "They want to wait for Grady. They didn't want to leave him by himself since Kelsey can't be there."

"Why can't we go see him?" Nicholas asked as he laid his head on my shoulder.

"They might have made some bad guys mad. Which means the rest of the family stays here with our bodyguards until we know it's safe."

Sara looked from me to Jackson and then around the room. She studied everyone's faces. She turned back to me and nodded, climbing off Jackson's lap. "Okay. Can I have pancakes with chocolate chips for breakfast?"

"No," Anne said, walking into the room. "But if you eat your eggs and toast, I'll let you both have a cookie for dessert."

"Cool," Nicholas said, scrambling off my lap and dragging Sara by the hand down the hallway.

"Everyone done bawling like babies?" Anne asked with a smirk.

"You need a turn?" Whiskey asked as he laughed and wrapped his arms around her, pulling her back into his chest.

"I was thinking it's Kelsey's turn to watch the kids." She looked over her shoulder and up at Whiskey, wiggling her eyebrows. "You and I can sneak upstairs for some alone time."

"You have the best ideas, woman," he said as he pulled her toward the hall.

"Where do they get their energy?" Tweedle said between yawns.

Pops steered her into a club chair. She curled up and within seconds was snoring. The volume of her snoring got louder, then louder still. If I wasn't watching her, I'd swear she was a four-hundred-pound man.

Alex walked into the room wearing a bright purple silk suit. He looked at Tweedle with a puzzled expression. "What the hell's wrong with her?"

"One shot of alcohol," Bridget answered, tossing a blanket on top of Tweedle.

"Wow, Alex," I said, smirking at Alex's suit. "You're awfully *bright* this morning."

"Well, thank you, luv."

"Where do you even buy a purple suit?" Bridget asked.

"Amazon. They have everything. Want to see the matching underwear?"

"*No!*" everyone said at once.

Tweedle snorted in her sleep, then resumed her loud snoring.

"She's going to wake Abigail," Lisa said before dashing toward the hallway with Abigail cradled to her chest.

We all stood and followed after her.

"Alex, how was your date last night?" Katie asked.

"Short, thanks to Lisa calling and interrupting. We had to scramble to find our clothes before the Devil's Players showed up with the bunk beds."

"Did you at least feed your date or did the whole event happen in the bedroom?" I asked.

"Of course. I made your lasagna recipe. It turned out superb."

"Didn't Haley say she had lasagna for dinner last night?" Bridget asked.

Alex walked into the kitchen as Bridget and I settled onto barstools at the breakfast bar.

"Hmm," Alex said as he filled a travel cup of coffee. "I'm heading to the store. Carl's expecting a package to be delivered today if someone can sign for it." Alex glanced at Carl to ensure he wasn't paying attention before he slipped a note out of his pocket and handed it to Beth.

Beth read the note and passed it to me while shaking her head.

I read a list of what appeared to be chemicals and smirked. "I'll take care of it." I slid the note into my back pocket and then sent a text to Dave, both a friend and a local cop. Within seconds he texted me back a smiley face.

"I'd like to stay at the house today, if that's okay," Hattie said. "There's laundry to do, and I'll make lunch for everyone."

"That's fine," Tyler said. "I've got twenty-four-hour security running. Just don't leave the house without an escort. I'm going to crash in the basement for a few hours but wake me if you need me."

"And leave the cleaning and laundry for Eloise," I said to Hattie. "You should get some sleep, too. You've got dark circles under your eyes."

"Perhaps I'll take a nap as well," Hattie agreed. "I am feeling rather overdone."

Reggie returned, wearing a black turtleneck and a black beanie pulled down to mid-eyebrow. "I tried every soap in the house. Nothing will remove permanent marker."

I could think of several products that would remove the marker, but I wasn't in the sharing mood. "Is that my turtleneck?"

"You mean, was?" Alex mumbled as he walked out the garage door.

"I've never seen you wear a turtleneck, so I figured you wouldn't mind," Reggie said as he stretched the sleeves, trying to make them longer. The shirt fit so tightly you could see every rib bone, not to mention his pokey nipples.

I shook my head at Reggie before sliding off my stool. "I'm going to take a quick shower. Kids, you need to hurry up and get dressed. Your ride leaves in fifteen minutes."

I could hear the kids running as I dragged myself to my bedroom, closing the door behind me. I showered, dressed in comfortable clothes, and reemerged ten minutes later with my hair still wet.

"You're leaving the house, looking like that?" Reggie asked.

"Careful, babe," Jackson said, throwing an arm over Reggie's shoulders. "I won't protect you if you push her too far."

Beth jogged down the stairs, wrangling her hair into a clip.

"Did anyone explain that a fifteen-minute warning for the kids is closer to a half an hour for the adults?" I asked.

"No, but that makes me so happy," she said before jogging back up the stairs.

I walked out of the house, into the garage, and then out to the driveway as four motorcycles pulled in and parked. Renato, the president of the Demon Slayers, and some of his men got off their bikes. Eloise was a passenger on one of the middle bikes. Nightcrawler stepped out from around the corner of the garage.

I reached out a hand to Renato. "Sorry we're messing with everyone's schedule."

Renato shook my hand, not bothering to attempt one of those odd handshakes the men did with each other. "Glad to help. I'm taking day shift with a couple of guys while the night shift gets some sleep. Anything we need to know?"

"A package for Carl is expected today. I need a heads up when it arrives. Under no circumstances should it be left unattended, given to Carl, or left out in the sunlight."

"What's in the package?" Nightcrawler asked, his eyes narrowing as he watched me.

"No clue," I said, pulling the list out and handing it to him. "Beth read the list and said Carl shouldn't get it."

Nightcrawler whistled after reading the list silently. "I only know what two of these are, and definitely they should *not* be left out in the sunlight or given to Carl."

He handed the list to Renato who laughed as he read it. "I thought you had to be a chemist to get this shit."

"Carl *is* a chemist. And a biologist. A linguistics expert. A computer science engineer. And he has several other PhDs that are way above my understanding."

Nightcrawler rubbed his neck muscles as he glanced at Renato before he looked back at me. "You should know that some of these ingredients are used to make meth. Some of the others are used to make bombs."

"He likely wasn't planning on making either—intentionally, that is." I nodded a greeting to Eloise as she passed us on her way into the house. "Carl has no concept of dangerous. He's driven by curiosity which is why we secretly get texts whenever he charges anything. Usually we know a good week in advance when something is being shipped, but I'm guessing he used overnight delivery for this stuff."

"They'll ship some of this in a frozen nitrogen tank," Renato said. "I'll text you when it shows, but they might not let a biker sign for it."

"Hattie will be home. She can sign. If they require Carl's signature, then you can explain to the driver that Carl can't legally sign for anything."

"Got it. Anything else?"

"The guys ran into some trouble. Grady will need a few days to recover before he can come home. Same for a woman they rescued. Still no word whether the cartel identified anyone on the rescue mission. Until you hear otherwise, stay alert and expect anything and everything."

"Do you need to fly out to meet Grady?" Nightcrawler asked.

I shook my head. "We have a rule that if there's a threat to the family, one of us stays home with Nicholas. It's not always ideal, but we try to make it work."

"Makes sense," Renato said. "Besides, by the looks of those black bags under your eyes, you're not in the right condition to travel yet either."

"The whole family lost sleep last night, but I'll nap this afternoon." I rubbed a knot in my shoulder muscle. "I'm beyond tired."

We turned, hearing the front door open. Pops stepped out and walked over. "Nick and Sara are fighting again," Pops said, shaking his head. "I swear they quarrel worse than Reggie and Wild Card did at their ages."

I sighed as I moved back toward the house. "I can't decide if they fight like that because they're so much alike—or because they're complete opposites."

I started to jog when I heard the high-pitched yelling. As soon as I walked into the house, the kids and everyone else went silent.

"Brush your teeth—all of them!" I ordered, pointing to Nicholas. I turned to Sara. "Young lady, you need to go back upstairs and brush your hair! You look like a ragamuffin."

"What's a rag-a-muffin?" Sara asked as she stuffed her laptop into her backpack.

"An urchin."

"Huh?"

"Just go brush your hair, and be quick about it." I heard everyone laughing quietly as I walked down the hall to check on Nicholas. "Back teeth too! All of them!"

He glared at me in the mirror, but brushed his back molars. When he was done, I stopped him from wiping his mouth on his sleeve and also made him rinse the sink. By the time we left the bathroom he was stomping down the hall, arms crossed over his chest, and into the garage.

Hattie laughed as she passed me the car keys on my way out of the house. Sara scrambled to catch up, climbing in behind Nicholas into the back seat. Carl ran into the garage next, sliding in beside Sara before I closed the door.

I opened the back hatch and whistled. Storm ran around the outside corner of the garage and performed an eight-foot leap into the back of the SUV. I checked to make sure his tail was clear before closing the hatch. Beth slid into the passenger seat as I got behind the wheel. After I backed out of the drive, two motorcycles pulled ahead of the SUV to lead us.

The kids started to argue, and I slammed on the brakes, looking over my shoulder at them. Both of them pressed their lips together and looked downward.

"Beth, if the kids continue down this bickering path today, find me. I'll handle it. I don't pay you enough to listen to it."

"No problem," she said, glancing back at the kids, ensuring they heard her. "Is Carl with us today?"

"Carl, what do you think about hanging out with the guys? Maybe running the remote while they practice on the Circle of Hell?"

"That sounds fun."

I glanced over my shoulder at Carl. He had his face pressed to the passenger door's window and was making puffer-fish faces against the glass.

He paused his game to look over at me. "I should've worn my costume."

"What costume?" I asked as I focused on catching a break in traffic to cross the highway. The two lead bikes had already crossed.

"My superhero costume."

"When did you get a superhero costume?" I asked, making the turn onto the highway before turning a few yards later to the left into the Headquarters' drive.

"UPS delivered it yesterday. Alex helped me pick it out. He says I'll get a lot of bang for my buck with it."

"That kind of scares me," I mumbled.

Beth leaned around her seat to look at Carl who was sitting behind her. "You should wait until this weekend to wear it," Beth told him. "More people will be able to see it then."

"Okay."

With a quick glance in the mirror, I confirmed Carl had returned to slobbering on my SUV.

"I'm not sure you helped, Beth," I whispered.

"Who says that was my intention," she said, laughing quietly.

I pulled perpendicular to the front doors, with two motorcycles still in front of us and two more behind us. A dozen security guards walked out and flanked the SUV. One of the guys took the keys from me as I escorted Beth, Carl, and the kids inside.

Finding a hair scrunchy in my bag, I whipped Sara's now brushed but still wild hair up into a ponytail, kissing her cheek when I was done. She giggled and ran toward the stairs. Nicholas, still not speaking to me, stomped in the same direction.

"It's going to be a long ass day," I said to Beth.

She laughed and followed the kids.

"Trigger is here," Carl said, clapping his hands. "Can I hang out with him?"

"Sure. I don't have him scheduled for anything today."

As if hearing us from across the gym, Trigger looked over. Carl ran in his direction. I pointed to Trigger, then pointed two fingers at my eyes for the universal language of *watch*, then pointed at Carl. Trigger gave me a thumbs up before turning his attention to Carl.

I walked across the gym and up the stairs to the war room. Entering, I found Kemp and Tech moving the chairs to the other side of the room and Bridget setting up cots.

"What are we doing?"

Tech looked at me as he took a cot from Bridget and moved it to below the large windows. "Kemp's covering the phones while we sleep for a couple of hours. Then this afternoon, Bridget will relieve Beth and take the kids outside to play, so Beth can take a nap."

"What about work?"

"I'd wager you've slept less than five hours total over the last two days. The rest of us have slept only a few more hours than you. We're useless until we rest. We'd only be spinning in circles all day."

"Hattie sent pillows and blankets," Wayne said, entering the war room. "I'm crashing with you guys. The apartments seem too far from Headquarters until we know the red alert has been lifted."

"I felt the same about not being here with the kids," I agreed. "Let's prop the door open, though, so we can hear if something happens. And, Kemp, you'd better wake us if needed."

"Yes, ma'am."

"Don't call her ma'am. She hates it," Bridget said to Kemp as she removed a chain mace—an archaic weapon with a spiked steel ball at the end of a chain—from the wall. She carried the heavy steel contraption over to the war room door and used it as a door prop.

When she turned back around, I was smirking at her.

"What? It does the job."

I continued smirking at her.

"Fine. I'll let Goat know to install something more normal to use in the future."

Tech tossed a pillow at her. "Night, bitches." He threw himself on the cot under the far window, tucking himself in with a blanket.

I took the cot closest to the door and Wayne took the cot under the large window overlooking the gym. That left the cot next to the file cabinets for Bridget. Removing my gun harness, I unloaded my Glock and slid it under my cot. I set my phone on top of a wall shelf a few feet away. After curling up on the cot, I was asleep within seconds.

Chapter Thirteen

"Hey," was whispered near my ear as someone shook my shoulder. "Wake up, beautiful."

Opening my eyes, I found Wild Card crouched down beside me. "What time is it?"

"Almost noon. Kemp asked me to wake you. He said you threatened him if he didn't wake you with updates."

I nodded, sitting up and running my fingers through my hair. Wild Card reached under my cot and loaded my Glock. I strapped on my shoulder harness before sliding the Glock in place and snapping the strap to keep it secure. I nodded again to Wild Card, following him out and grabbing my phone from the shelf as we left.

A few minutes later I was still wiping the crud from my eyes as I sat in one of the guest chairs in Kemp's office. Really it was Grady's office, but we'd reassigned it to Kemp until we could figure out the office spaces. Grady never used it, so it didn't matter.

"What's up?" I asked Kemp.

"First, Wild Card and Ryan returned an hour ago. Wild Card told me not to wake you, though, so don't blame me for that."

Wild Card laughed, sitting in the chair beside me.

"Deal," I agreed, grinning at Wild Card.

"Donovan called. He's getting messages from the media asking for an interview on the Allie Jacobs investigation."

"Pass."

"Donovan wanted me to relay to you that it would be good PR for the firm."

"The investigations side doesn't need any PR. We're carrying a backlog of cases. If Donovan needs good press for his side of the business, he can tie on a cape and do something newsworthy to get noticed."

Kemp gulped, staring back at me. I think he even paled.

Wild Card laughed. "You don't need to repeat her word for word," he said to Kemp. "Just tell Donovan that Kelsey said no and to talk to her directly if he has a problem with it."

"I like that plan better," Kemp said, nodding. "I'm less likely to lose my head."

I rolled my eyes. "What else?"

Kemp didn't have a chance to answer before we heard a loud noise in the schoolroom. Wild Card bolted ahead of me down the hall and into the schoolroom. Beth stood near the far wall, keeping Sara between her and the wall. Storm stood guard in front of Beth, whining as he watched Nicholas who threw one of the kid's chairs into the chalkboard.

"Get Sara out of here!" I yelled at Beth as I ran directly at Nicholas.

In the short time it took to cross the room he turned, throwing a second chair at me. I blocked it, knocking it away with my forearm as I protected my face with my other arm. Wild Card, who had approached Nicholas more stealthily from behind, grabbed him and held him in a straightjacket hold, pinning his arms at his sides. Nicholas kicked and screamed, even snapped his teeth at Wild Card, trying to bite him. I stood frozen, not recognizing the level of rage that had overtaken my son.

"Kelsey! Get the boxing gear out!" Wild Card yelled. "Hurry!"

"What?" I asked in a stupor.

"On it," Wayne said from the doorway before he ran down the hall.

I watched Wild Card struggle to carry my thrashing and screaming son out of the room and down the hall. I followed, still trying to process what I was seeing.

I stopped at the top of the stairs, watching Wild Card carry him down where Wayne and another guard met them and strapped boxing gloves onto Nicholas' hands. As soon as Wild Card released Nicholas, he stepped a few feet away and slid punching mitts onto his own hands, barely in time before Nicholas's fists started flying his way.

"That's it," Wild Card said. "Let it out! Come on. Is that as hard as you can hit?"

Nicholas came close to punching Wild Card in the nuts but Wild Card jumped out of the way in time.

"Keep it clean, boy," Pops hollered as he walked toward them. "Hands up! Elbows in! Protect your body. That's it. Turn sideways and put your weight into it. That a boy. One, two, hit. One, two, hit."

"Keep it coming!" Wild Card said, blocking another right punch.

I watched in fear and awe as they kept talking to him. He was not only responding to them, but I could see the hostile energy dissipating as he threw each punch. I had heard they'd worked with him after he'd been rescued, teaching him how to control his anger. I'd never seen it firsthand, though. By the time I had returned to the ranches in Texas, Nicholas was running and playing with the neighbor kids.

Beth and Sara walked over and stood beside me.

"What happened?" I asked Beth.

"I don't know. His phone rang, and he said it was Grady. Sara was taking a test, so I asked him to step into the hall. When he returned a few minutes later, he threw the phone into the window. After that... it's a blur."

"He'll be okay, Aunt Kelsey," Sara said, wrapping an arm around my leg. "Uncle Wild Card will help him."

I turned toward the stairs, still watching Nicholas. Pops held up a hand, motioning for me to stop. He nodded to Wild Card, who was still dancing around the gym goading Nicholas to hit the punching pads. I turned away, walking back to Kemp's office and closing the door. I pulled my phone from my back pocket and called Grady.

"Kelsey," Grady answered.

"What happened? What did you say to Nicholas?"

"I tried to call you," Grady said with a heavy sigh. "Your ringer must've been turned off. When I couldn't reach you, I called Nicholas. I asked him to get you—"

"*Grady! What the hell did you say to Nicholas?*"

Silence.

"Tell me what the fuck happened!"

There was a long pause. "I told him I wasn't coming home."

"He already knew you'd be away for a few more days. I told him before school."

"No. Not for a few days," Grady said in a hushed low voice.

I fell rather than sat into the guest chair. "What are you saying?"

"After I'm released from the hospital, I'm going to Montana for a while. I have some things I need to think about."

"What things? And why the hell can't you think about them here?"

He sighed. "I'm not ready to talk about it."

It was my turn for a long pause as a million thoughts scrambled in my brain, trying to understand, until only one thought remained. "This is about *Sebrina*. Isn't it?"

"Partly," Grady admitted. "It's complicated."

"You owe me an explanation."

I could imagine him on the other end of the phone, shaking his head. "Sebrina and I have unfinished business. I'm sorry, but it's the truth. I don't know what our relationship is at the moment, but that's not the only thing I need to think about."

The pause returned. I'd had it with Grady's stalling.

"*What else*?!" I yelled into the phone. "What other shit do you need to go all the way to Montana to think so damn hard about?"

Grady growled before yelling back at me, "It's partially about us too! I'm living with my girlfriend who refuses to commit while I raise *her* kid. It's not the life I wanted! In fact—except for Nicholas—it's the *exact reason* I left Sebrina! I keep falling for women who aren't interested in settling down and raising a family with me."

"And you think the best way to handle the situation is by running away? Abandoning the little boy who sees you as a father figure?"

"*I'm not his father*! Don't you get that?"

The phone disconnected. I moved it away from my ear and stared down at the *Call Ended* message.

"What the hell just happened?" I asked myself. Nothing Grady had said made sense. I knew him. I knew how he thought. I knew how he felt about me. How much he cared about Nicholas. Even if he still had feelings for Sebrina, he wouldn't abandon us over the phone like this.

Looking at my phone again, I called Bones.

"I take it you talked to him?" Bones said when he answered.

"I need a favor."

Bones was silent on the other end.

"I need you to convince him to go to Pops' ranch."

"What good does that do?"

"That's not the favor. Once he's there, I need you to shoot him with Pops' tranq gun and drag his unconscious body back to Michigan."

Bones was quiet for about twenty seconds. "You're serious?"

"I know he's your friend, Bones, but I can't leave Nicholas right now. I need you to drag Grady back."

"He won't be released until tomorrow morning. I can get him to the ranch, convince him he needs to rest before traveling any further, but that's it. I can't shoot him with a tranq gun. He'd never speak to me again."

"Are you willing to at least help load his unconscious body onto a plane?"

Bones laughed. "Sure."

"I'll handle the rest then. Thanks."

"Chin up, Kel. If it makes you feel any better, I think you're doing the right thing."

We disconnected, and I went to the war room. Tech and Bridget were awake.

"What happened?" Tech asked.

"Grady says he's not coming home."

"What?" Bridget said.

"No way," Tech said, shaking his head. "Grady's solid. You two are indestructible."

"Well something just exploded the shit out of our relationship." I paced a few times before turning back to face them. "I need help if I have any chance of fixing this."

"What do you need?" Tech asked.

"Get with Katie. I need a handful of tranq cartridges for Pops' gun."

Tech nodded and picked up his cell phone.

"Bridget, get a hold of Pops and Trigger. I need them to fly down to the ranches today. Bones will take Grady to Pops' house tomorrow after he's released from the hospital. When they get there, I need Trigger to shoot him with the tranq gun. Bones refused to do it, but agreed to help transport him back to Michigan."

"Want me to go?" Bridget asked, placing her fists on her hips. "I'd be happy to shoot Grady—right in his rosy ass cheek."

"Not necessary. But if you could question Haley about a to-go sedative, I'd appreciate it. It would be an ugly situation if Grady were to wake mid-flight."

"What if that Sebrina chick is with him?" Tyler asked from the doorway.

My mind was spinning with so many variables I wasn't surprised he'd snuck up on me. "I don't know." I rubbed a hand across my forehead. "Shoot her, too? We can't leave her alone on the ranch if the cartel is still after her. She'll have to fly back with them so we can protect her here."

"Who's Sebrina?" Tech asked.

"His ex-girlfriend," Tyler answered for me. "The DEA agent they rescued in Mexico."

"And you want to bring her *here*?" Bridget asked.

I threw my hands into the air. "Maybe this whole fucking mess will make more sense that way. Because I sure as hell don't get it! I have no idea what's going on! He says he needs time to think shit out—well, I'll give him time! He can sleep in the fucking apartments for all I care!

I'll be damned, though, if he'll be running around unprotected while we figure this shit out."

"You sound a little crazy," Tech said, smirking.

"I feel a little crazy. I'm hearing myself talk about hiring people to *kidnap* my boyfriend and hold him *hostage*! I sound *insane*!"

"That's not the insane part," Bridget said, giggling.

"It's insane that we're all antsy to help," Tyler said, throwing his arm over my shoulders.

I looked at each of them as a slow grin formed to match theirs. I nodded to Tech to call Katie. Bridget was bouncing on her toes in excitement as she called Haley.

Chapter Fourteen

I walked across the field to where Wild Card sat in the grass, his arm wrapped around my son who sat beside him. Wild Card looked up, and I could see the confusion in his eyes. I sat in the grass in front of Nicholas, taking one of his fisted hands within both of mine.

"I know you're angry and confused. I am, too. I don't understand why Grady is saying the things he's saying."

"You talked to him?" Nicholas asked, lifting his tear-soaked face to look at me.

"I did. He told me he wasn't coming home. But do you know what?"

Nicholas shook his head. "What?"

"If he's going to leave us, I say he has to man up and do it face-to-face. What do you think?"

Nicholas nodded, wiping his nose on his sleeve. "But how?"

"Well," I said, exhaling a deep breath. "I hired some people to drug him, kidnap him, and deliver him to our doorstop. How does that sound?"

Nicholas and Wild Card stared at me. I smirked.

"Holy shit, you're serious?" Wild Card said.

Nicholas launched off the lawn and into my arms. "You rock, Mom."

"I'm glad you approve of your mother committing multiple felonies, but I can't promise he'll stay, Nick. We can't keep him prisoner forever. I'll do what I can, though."

Nicholas nodded into my shoulder. "If he decides to leave, will you stay home with me all the time?"

"How about *most* of the time?" I asked, shifting him to my lap so I could look at him.

"How much is that?"

Wild Card leaned forward to tousle Nicholas' hair. "I'll come hang out with you when your mom goes on longer trips. How's that sound?"

Nicholas sighed, but nodded.

"Now that that's settled," I paused to pepper kisses on Nicholas' forehead, "I have a job for the two of you."

"What?" Nicholas asked, wiping his nose on his sleeve again.

"Gross," I said, shaking my head.

Nicholas giggled. "What's my job?"

"Find Jerry and get the keys to one of the empty apartments. Then you and Wild Card have to move Grady's stuff and make sure the apartment is ready for him."

"He's not going to sleep in your room?" Nicholas asked as he climbed off my lap.

"Nope." I climbed off the ground and offered a hand to help Wild Card. "Grady dumped me over the phone from halfway across the country. He's in the *dog house*."

Nicholas laughed before running toward the back door of Headquarters.

Wild Card stepped closer and kissed my cheek. "You amaze me." He held my hand and led us back to the gym.

"I'm doing the right thing, aren't I?"

"Yes," he said, glancing over at me. "No matter how it ends, you and Nicholas deserve a face-to-face explanation from Grady. I also know from experience that Grady will regret today for the rest of his life."

"It's not the same as what happened to us," I said, quietly.

"You sure about that?"

I thought about it a moment, but the truth was I wasn't sure if it was the same or not, because I had no idea what was happening. "No. I'm not sure. That's why I need to get his ass back here to explain."

"Then fight for him, darlin'. Give it all you've got."

~*~*~

While Nicholas and Wild Card handled moving Grady's belongings, I made my way to the basement to find Carl. Trigger had texted me that he had left Carl in Benji's care. I knew who Benji was, one of the guards at Aces, but I didn't know him well enough to trust he'd keep a close enough eye on Carl.

I shouldn't have worried. Carl stood near the safety mats, jumping up and down while he clapped and watched the men practice in the Circle of Hell. Carl was damn proud of his newest invention, and the guards loved it just as much. Willy kicked out, and the room filled with sympathetic groans as their mate fell to his knees cupping himself. Benji hit the stop button on the controls and two other guards ran over to help the younger guard out of the circle. He'd need an ice pack.

"Kelsey, Kelsey, Kelsey!" Carl yelled as he ran over and hugged me. "Is it time for lunch?"

"You ate seven pancakes and three eggs for breakfast. You're hungry already?"

Carl smiled brightly, shifting his weight from one foot to another.

"Okay. Let's see if there's any food in the breakroom."

As we started to make our way back to the stairs, Benji hollered at us and jogged over. "Trigger assigned Carl to me. Made me swear I'd watch him or reassign him formally to the next person."

"Do I need to make a blood oath to take over protection duty?"

"Nah. Plain words will do just fine. Are you officially taking over or should I follow you guys?"

"I've got him. Thanks for being diligent, though."

Benji nodded and offered a fist bump to Carl. "Later, bro."

I started for the stairs again. "You made new friends today."

"Benji's fun. He's going to teach me to skateboard."

"You don't own a skateboard."

"I have enough money to buy one."

"What about knee and elbow pads and a safety helmet?"

"I don't have enough money for those. Maybe I can make them."

"As long as you're safe," I said, looping my arm through his at the top of the stairs and walking across the gym.

"Oh, good," Hattie said, walking out of the breakroom. "You brought Carl. I was looking for him. Sandwiches and soup are ready."

Carl turned into the breakroom without another word, his mind completely focused on the food.

Hattie grasped my elbow, steering me a few feet away from the doorway. "Pops said he's flying back to Texas for the night to help you with a project. Now Wild Card and Nicholas are moving Grady's belongings to the apartments." Her forehead was pinched with worry as she watched me. "Is everything okay?"

"I honestly don't know, but I have a plan."

"You always do, dear, but I'm still worried about you."

"I'm holding it together. I think it helps that Nicholas has to be my priority right now. My feelings are secondary to his."

"Anything I can do to help?"

"Spread the word to the family that I'm okay, but I'm not ready to be bombarded with questions."

"Understandable," she said, nodding. "You'd best get something to eat. Do you know where Sara is?"

"She's with Beth. Likely they're in the classroom. If you can watch Carl, I'll go get them."

Carl walked out of the breakroom with a plate piled six sandwiches high.

"Mr. Carl..." Hattie started to say as I laughed and walked toward the stairs.

In the classroom I found Beth and Sara sweeping up the mess that Nicholas had made.

"I called the glass contractor to fix the window," Beth said. "I'm sorry I didn't stop him before he caused so much damage."

"You did the right thing by getting yourself and Sara away."

"Is Nicholas okay?" Sara asked.

"Yup," I answered, sitting in her desk chair and pulling her in for a hug. "I'm sure he'll talk to you when he's ready. Everyone will need to be patient with him for a little while, though."

"What happened?"

"Grady told him he wasn't coming home."

"Why?"

"I don't know, little bug. We're going to find out, though, okay?"

She leaned into me, wrapping her arms around me.

I rubbed her back for a few minutes before kissing her forehead. "Enough sad stuff. I like it better when you're all smiles," I said, tickling her.

Sara giggled and squirmed out of my arms.

"Hattie brought lunch. You'd better get a plate before Carl eats it all."

Sara giggled again. "He says he's a growing boy."

"If Carl is going through a growth spurt, we have a problem. He's taller than most of us already."

"He's so skinny," Beth said, leaning the broom in the corner. "Where does all that food go?"

"Have you ever seen Carl sit still for more than five minutes? I would love to have that kind of energy."

Beth nodded before turning to Sara. "Go get lunch. I'll be down in a minute."

Sara raced from the room. I stood to pick up the larger broken pieces of the chair that was smashed.

Beth glanced at the door before turning to face me. "I don't want to sound uncaring, but I'm worried about Sara's safety around Nicholas."

"Understandable. Wild Card and I will watch him. He won't be returning to class until we know he's handling things better."

"That's for the best, I think. Nicholas trusts him. Trusts Wild Card, I mean."

"Wild Card and Pops helped Nicholas get through the worst of his anger after he was rescued. I wasn't around. I was out hunting the monster who threatened his future. Grady was laid up in bed from a gunshot wound." I walked over and picked up more broken chair parts. "Wild Card saw Nicholas needed an outlet and taught him how to box. Maybe boxing isn't the best approach from a parenting standpoint, but it helps Nick. As a person with a few of my own anger issues, I completely understand the need to hit something."

Beth smirked and looked at the windows. "You can smash the rest of the window. It has to be replaced, anyway."

"Sounds appealing, but then there'd be more glass to sweep. Let's get some lunch instead. Maybe I'll spar with one of the guys this afternoon."

"Any chance you'd be willing to teach me? I took a self-defense class, but I only learned a few moves."

"Those few moves usually are the only ones you need. Most of the time, the best defense is hurt your enemy quickly and run like hell. But, yes, if you have an interest in learning, Katie and I can both work with you. You're in luck, too, because we work out Wednesday nights in the basement gym at the house. I recommend you eat a light dinner tonight so you have less to puke up later."

"That's a unique advertising slogan." Beth held the door for me to carry the chair parts through as she followed with the trash bag.

"Don't worry. It's Katie's night to cook. We usually have to fight over the least burnt scraps of food."

When we reached the bottom of the stairs, two men met us and took the trash bag and the broken chair from us. Without speaking, they walked away toward the exit. My phone vibrated, and I pulled it out to read the text message. Wild Card was letting me know that Carl had a package. As I texted him back, Wayne walked over, eating a sandwich.

"Quietly warn the guys that something is about to happen in the next ten minutes. Make sure Carl doesn't hear."

Wayne nodded and meandered back in the direction he'd just left.

"Beth, can you stay close to Sara? Let her know I'm teaching Carl a lesson?"

Beth raised an eyebrow but walked toward the breakroom. I texted Dave.

~*~*~

Finding Carl, I nibbled on a ham and cheese sandwich as I waited. Ten minutes later, Wild Card entered the gym carrying a silver nitrogen tank. He spotted me and started walking our way. Carl saw him and set his plate on the floor before running over to Wild Card. Carl took the tank and started for the gym doors. Wild Card shook his head and continued to walk toward me.

Carl was almost to the door when ten cops entered, yelling "*Freeze!*"

Carl planted his feet to the floor, holding the silver tank to his chest with both arms crossed over it tightly. He glanced over his shoulder at me before dashing our way. I expected him to stop when he reached me, but instead he shoved the tank into Wild Card's arms and continued running toward the back exit, yelling "*Ahhhhhhhhh*" the entire way.

The cops, still standing near the gym entrance, chuckled for a minute before chasing after Carl. They were halfway across the gym when Carl exited the doors.

"Better hurry!" I called out. "He's a fast runner."

Several of the younger cops sped up, closing the distance. I walked toward the doors, still eating my sandwich. When I stepped outside the sight was comical. Four cops stood just outside the doors, panting heavily. The other six continued their pursuit. Carl was in the field zigging and zagging to stay out of their reach. He was almost to the trees by the time one of the cops dove and caught a leg in a firm enough grip to take Carl down. Another cop ran over and placed enough weight on Carl's shoulders to keep him safely in place while a third cop carefully handcuffed him.

Carl was crying and mumbling words I couldn't hear.

"He seems really upset," Wild Card said from beside me. "Think you should call this off, whatever this is?"

I turned to see he was still holding the nitrogen tank. "I was told the chemicals in that tank could be used to make a bomb. How upset do you think he'd be if he accidentally killed everyone?"

Wild Card looked down at the tank before walking over and setting it next to the building. "What's the plan?"

"Dave and Steve are going to walk Carl through the booking process, then lock him in a cell. I can pick him up in a few hours."

"You won't be able to keep a straight face. You should take someone with you."

"I'll go," Beth said from my other side. "This was brilliant."

Carl wailed like a three-year-old as they escorted him across the field to the front parking lot. I took another bite of my sandwich, not feeling an inkling of guilt.

"Hey, Kel," Dave said, walking up with Steve to join us. "Are Grady and Bones still coming to poker tonight?"

"No. They won't be back until tomorrow."

"Damn. We won't have enough guys."

"I'm down for some poker," Wild Card said, shrugging. "But we'll need to play either here or at Kelsey's house."

"Set it up," Steve said, shaking Wild Card's hand. "We'll bring the beer and the snacks."

"We need to get going," Dave said. "We have a whole good-cop, bad-cop skit to play out in the interrogation room."

"Just don't record anything he confesses," I said.

"Understood," Steve said. "Do we even want to know what's in that tank?"

"*No.*" Wild Card, Beth, and I said at the same time.

Dave and Steve looked over at the tank and took a step back.

"All right then," Steve said.

~*~*~

Beth went back inside to find Sara. Wild Card went to find Nicholas to finish moving Grady's things. I stood outside staring at the chemical tank, trying to figure out what to do with it.

Ryan walked out the back door and approached me, followed by a man I'd never seen before. "Wild Card sent me out. Said you might need me to get rid of something for you."

I pulled the list from my back pocket and handed it to him as I nodded to the tank. He read the list and the corner of his mouth ticked up slightly. It was the only change in his facial expression.

"I'll handle it," he said, slipping the paper into his front pocket. "You going to explain the new bruises on Tweedle?"

"It's up to her to tell you. You could've warned me that she's a walking disaster."

"What fun would that be?" he said, the corner of his mouth sliding up a millimeter higher. "This is Shipwreck.

Jerry said you had the keys to one of the apartments for him until we figure out his new housing."

Shipwreck was wearing Hawaiian-style swimming trunks, flip flops, and a flamingo-plastered short-sleeved shirt which was left unbuttoned until mid-chest.

"Hello, Senorita," Shipwreck purred, grasping my hand and kissing it.

"Uh, *Shipster*," Ryan said, scratching the back of his neck, "you might want to lay off the flirting. Most of the women around here will kick your ass for that shit. Kelsey included. Not to mention, she's Grady's old lady."

"Damn," Shipwreck said, dropping my hand like it was contaminated. "What the hell am I going to do around here then? No bar. No babes. No weed."

"Who says we don't have weed?" I asked.

The men's heads swiveled back to me.

I shrugged. "I took the liberty of having an apartment arranged for you. There are clothes in the closet, personal products in the bathroom, and I left a present for you in the nightstand drawer. Thanks for getting my boys out of Mexico. Room twelve is all yours." I handed him the keys and walked back into the gym.

Chapter Fifteen

I returned a few phone calls and emails while I waited for Dave and Steve to scare the bejeebers out of Carl. When I received the text that I could pick him up, I woke Beth from her mini nap. Sara was with Bridget, learning *Lock Picking 101*. I let them both know to call Tyler when they were ready to leave.

When Beth and I arrived at the police station Steve, wearing his serious cop face, escorted Carl to the main lobby. Dave and a few other cops were behind glass doors in the next room, laughing.

Wearing neon orange, hand cuffs, and ankle chains, Carl wailed as drool dripped from his lower lip. "*I'm sorry.*"

"You're in *big* trouble, Mr. Carl," Beth scolded as Steve used his keys to unlock the cuffs. "You're lucky Kelsey was able to get you released. If you pull something like this again—they'll likely lock you up for good."

"I didn't mean to break the law," he cried, looking between us. "I'll be good! I *prom-mm-mise!*"

"From now on, if you want chemicals for one of your experiments, *you tell me,*" Beth continued. "I'll decide if it's legal and safe."

"I will. I will," Carl said, sniffling and wiping his snot on his sleeve.

Ugh, I thought. *I'm so not doing Nicholas' or Carl's laundry ever again.*

My part of Carl's punishment was the silent treatment. I marched out ahead of them, leaving the precinct. Carl shuffled after me. Beth stayed close on Carl's heels, lecturing him the entire trip home.

~*~*~

Dinner consisted of burnt chicken, undercooked potatoes, and slimy green beans. We were all grateful for the chocolate cake Tweedle had prepared for dessert. The guys moved down the hall into the family room to prepare for their poker game. The kids ran off to play in the field with Storm while Nightcrawler, Tyler, and a half dozen other men guarded them. Carl went to the basement to use the tunnel to hide in his bedroom at Alex's house.

"Well, ladies," I said, putting the last of the dishes in the dishwasher. "Who's working out tonight?"

"Lisa and I want to work on your prostitute case," Anne said. "We had more ideas to add to the list."

"I can help them," Tech said. "I'm not in the mood to play poker."

"I feel guilty," I admitted. "It's my case. I should stay and help."

"Nonsense," Lisa said, shooing me off. "You deal with this stuff every day, but this is an escape for us. Go burn some calories."

"I'm still working out," Katie said, stretching her arms over her head.

"Me too," Bridget said. "I haven't had a good workout this week."

"Can I go, too?" Tweedle asked.

We all cringed.

"Just to watch," she added. "You can tie me to a chair if it makes you feel better."

Katie grinned at Tweedle before turning back to me. "We'll work out at Headquarters. We only have one mat in the basement, but the gym at Headquarters has three mats. Tweedle can practice coordination exercises while we spar."

I shrugged. "Give me a minute to change and to let Tyler know I'm relocating."

I changed into the camo leggings Grady had bought me, a sports bra, a loose tank top, and a pair of comfortable running shoes. Stepping onto the back deck, I motioned to Tyler that I—pointing to myself—would be at Headquarters, pointing across the highway. Tyler gestured a thumbs up before his eyes flickered back to the kids and their surroundings.

Heading outside, I met the girls who had also changed into workout clothes.

"Okay, Tweedle," Katie said, handing her a jump rope. "Your first task is to jump rope while we run a lap in the woodlands. Focus on the timing the jumps, not how fast you can jump."

Tweedle took the jump rope but looked a little nervous.

"Best if you practice in the grass," I said, pointing to the side yard. "Don't worry about damaging the lawn. I'd rather lose some grass than find you bleeding when we get back."

Ryan laughed from the front porch.

"Go play poker!" Tweedle yelled at him, fake glaring as she scowled.

"Yes, ma'am," Ryan said, trying to restrain his laugh as he sauntered back inside.

I nodded to the guard in the front yard to keep his eyes on Tweedle. He was one of the Devil's Players. He nodded back, scanning the area as he stood in parade rest position.

Beth, Katie, Bridget, and I crossed the side street and started jogging down the trail. By the time we looped back to the house, none of us were breathing heavy, including

Beth. Tweedle was still struggling to complete two consecutive jumps and her guard was silently laughing. I led our group back into the woods to make another loop. They groaned but followed.

After the second loop, we escorted Tweedle toward the highway. She tripped twice in the road, but with Bridget on one side and me on the other, we got her safely across without being hit by a car.

"That was interesting," Beth said, chuckling. "How can you be so coordinated with your hands and so out of touch with your feet?" she asked Tweedle.

"I was born this way," Tweedle said on a long sigh.

Beth turned, her back to Headquarters as she jogged in place. "Maybe we should get a soccer ball."

Tweedle tripped over an invisible object and landed on all fours in the grass.

"Better invest in safety pads first," Bridget laughed, helping Tweedle up.

"That reminds me," I said, turning to Beth. "Carl wants to learn skateboarding—"

Beth's eyes widened and her jaw dropped as she looked at something behind us. I turned, reaching for my gun, but my hand grasped air as three men jumped out of a van and pounced. Another batch of men leapt out after them.

"Run!" I yelled as I attacked the first man. I punched him in the throat, taking him down as another man grabbed me from behind. Reaching up and behind me, I locked his head with my arm as I squatted and pulled him forward. He landed hard but was already rolling out of range when I stomped my foot forward. Bridget was closest to me, kicking her assailant like her life depended on it. I could hear Katie grunting somewhere behind me as a third man leapt toward me. A sidekick to his family jewels, followed by a knee to the face, had him falling into the grass.

A gun being discharged caused both sides to freeze and look toward the van. A man stood holding Tweedle tightly with one hand while he used the other to point a gun at her head.

We slowly raised our hands in surrender. The men grabbed us by the biceps and shoved us toward the van.

"You were supposed to run," I said to Beth as I was pushed inside.

"Sorry. Fight or flight never kicked in. I sort of got stuck in the frozen phase," she said as she waited her turn to be loaded.

"We'll have to work on that," Katie said as she laughed at Beth.

The guard holding Katie roughly shoved her inside. She stumbled knees first onto the floor next to me.

"Careful, asshole," I yelled at him.

"It's fine, Kel," Katie said, adjusting her legs under her and placing her back against the van's inside wall. "I can handle it."

The man holding Tweedle moved into the van next, still holding a gun to her head. At least he was being gentle and not abrasive with her. Bridget was shoved in next, followed by her captor climbing inside.

The last man placed his foot on the van floor as he dragged Beth behind him.

In what appeared to be a mirage, Storm came out of nowhere, snarling and leaping on top of the man who held Beth. Beth fell backward into the grass as Storm dug his fangs into the man's shoulder. Storm and the man struggled, rolling several feet away from the van.

"*Run! Get Tyler!*" I yelled at Beth as the van door closed, leaving her behind.

~*~*~

The van sped down the highway for only a minute or two, moving toward the west, before it turned north, then east. I knew I wasn't the only one in the van tracking the turns and how long we traveled. By the time we stopped, I was guessing we were in the mostly deserted industrial area north of downtown. The aging, oversized buildings were no longer cost effective for manufacturing companies. A few closer to downtown were converted to lofts or offices, but the ones farther to the north were left to decay, surrounded by weed-filled, crumbling parking lots. Near twenty or thirty buildings, varying in sizes, occupied a five-block stretch. Taxpayers had wanted the buildings torn down but were unwilling to allocate their tax dollars toward the endeavor.

"No funny business," the man holding a gun to Tweedle said as the van door slid open.

"Whatever," Bridget said, stepping out of the van.

I carefully followed after Bridget. During our trip, they'd handcuffed our hands behind our backs. "You're American," I said, to the man holding the gun. "None of you have accents. You're either American, or you've been in the country a long time."

"What's your point?" the man with the gun asked.

"Why are you working for the cartel?"

"Pays well," one of the other men said as he dragged Katie out by her hair.

She landed on her ass on the asphalt. I went to move toward her but she gave me a quick jerk of her head to stay back. Frustrated, I stepped away and scanned the area as two other men helped Katie to her feet. We were parked next to what I believed was the old bread factory. I scanned the outer perimeter before I swept my eyes to the building. Down the lot, at the furthest end, I saw a head peek out from behind a loading dock ramp.

I shook my head slightly, and the head disappeared. The man hiding appeared to be homeless. Hopefully he wasn't one of the mentally ill individuals who graced the streets, but statistics weren't in our favor. Almost half the homeless were plagued with anxiety disorders, depression, bipolar disease, or schizophrenia. It was a complexity that the city faced every day.

"Move," my escort said, jerking my arm as he turned me toward the building.

"You know these places are filled with rats," I said, yanking my arm away.

"Good. Maybe I'll get to watch them chew off your toes." He shoved me hard in the back and through the doorway.

It took a minute for my eyes to adjust. It wasn't pitch black inside, but the lights were off and the windows were closer to the ceiling than they were to the floor and caked with years of dirt and grime. The floor was cement and cluttered with trash.

I chose my steps carefully as I was led across the factory to a corner room. The space had served as an office at some point. An old desk, covered in layers of dust, sat facing forward with a chair leaning to one side between the desk and a row of file cabinets along the back wall. I looked up at the windows, but they were too high to see through. The wall that held the office door had an observation window that started about waist high and ran the length of the wall from the corner to the door. I watched the others as they were dragged one at a time into the room.

Katie's disgust for the lack of cleanliness was apparent when she walked inside. "Can we at least get clean chairs to sit on?"

Her silent answer was to be thrown face first to the floor.

"How's that for comfort, bitch?" the man asked as he leaned over the top of her, hissing in her ear.

"You need to brush your teeth, dude," Katie said. "Your breath reeks. Did you have sauerkraut? Ugh. Gross."

"Mouthy bitch," he said as he slapped her across the back of the head and stood. He turned toward me, but I sat willingly before he did anything. Bridget and Tweedle followed my lead and sat as well.

A minute later the door slammed shut, but two of the men stayed outside the window.

"Now what?" Katie asked, shifting to the side with one leg extended to counterbalance her weight so she could to sit up.

I glanced over at Bridget. "How'd you do?"

"I got a pen," she shrugged.

"I got a small knife," I said. "I win."

"Not so fast," Katie said. "You think I was letting them throw me around for the fun of it?" She turned her back to us and dropped a small set of keys.

"You win," Bridget said as she scooted closer to Katie to snag the keys.

"Do I get a prize?" Katie asked.

"If there's a handcuff key on that ring, I'll buy you a hot fudge sundae," I said.

"Oh, there's a handcuff key all right," Bridget said, unlocking her cuffs.

I watched and alerted Bridget when the guards turned to glance in the window. She uncuffed Katie next. They kept their hands mostly behind their backs, securing both ends of the bracelets to one wrist so the cuff wouldn't make noise. There was a long wait while a guard moved to stand facing us until he finally turned his back again. Bridget unlocked Tweedle's cuffs.

"Why do you still have the jump rope?" Bridget asked Tweedle, tossing the rope next to me.

"Everything happened so quick, I never thought to drop it."

I was sitting furthest from the door, my back to the desk. Bridget slid the keys toward me right before one of the guards turned around to check on us. I shifted my leg on top of the keys to hide them.

"What's the plan?" Katie asked.

"You'll use the desk to climb on top of the filing cabinet and slip out the window. You and Bridget escort Tweedle out. We're four blocks northwest of a McDonalds. That's the safest location to stop and call for help."

"Where will you be?"

"Right here. Causing a distraction."

"Bad plan," Bridget said. "You can't take on seven guys alone."

"I don't have to. I only need to distract them long enough for the three of you to get away, then I'll surrender." I twisted my body, lifted my leg, and snagged the keys, before turning back into my original position. "They'll split into two teams, half staying to guard me and the others will leave to search for you guys."

"What if they just shoot you?" Tweedle asked.

"Doubtful. If they wanted us dead, they'd have shot us already."

Katie snorted. "That's what your inner profiler instincts are telling you? That it's *doubtful* they'll shoot you?"

"I'm thinking Kelsey's odds are better than ours," Bridget said as she studied the windows. "Even if we manage to get Tweedle out the window without getting caught, she's prone to injuries. If she hurts herself, no way will we make it four blocks before they catch us."

Tweedle tipped her head and looked up at the windows. "I'm not so good with climbing. Or running."

"*Shit.* Fine. Let's see." I scanned the room again. "How are you at hiding?" I asked Tweedle.

"I'm *spectacular* at hiding."

Chapter Sixteen

"Juan—" one of the men yelled from across the factory. "Move the van inside!"

The guard in front of the window walked away. The other guard glanced briefly at us over his shoulder before turning his back to us again.

"Tweedle, move behind the desk and hide under it."

She scurried on all fours past me. I grabbed her wrist and uncuffed the handcuffs, before nodding for her to continue.

"Bridget, shift to your left and sit where Tweedle had been sitting."

Bridget scooched over several feet.

"When the guard comes in, I'll take him down, but Bridget, I'll need you to jump up and open the window, then get back into place. We want them to think Tweedle escaped."

Tweedle giggled from behind the desk.

"Tweedle, your job is to stay absolutely silent and out of sight. Understood."

"Got it."

"Silent. I mean it."

"Yup."

I rolled my eyes, and Katie snorted.

"What's my job?" Katie asked.

"Trip the bastard if you can. Make him land toward me."

"No problem."

The guard glanced over his shoulder briefly, then turned back to the main room.

"Get ready," I whispered.

The guard stiffened, then turned his entire body toward the window, practically pressing his nose to the glass as he stared into the room, counting the number of bodies. When he realized there were only three of us, he grabbed the door handle and rushed inside.

Katie tripped him, successfully landing him face and hands first into my lap. I already had my hands on the jump rope, double layering the rope around his throat and rolling and twisting to the side as I tightened the noose. He thrashed for near two minutes before he passed out. Bridget tossed me a set of cuffs and I secured his hands.

Katie helped me drag him into the corner beneath the window where he'd be out of sight if anyone peered into the room. I searched the shelves and found a roll of packaging tape. It wasn't ideal, but it would work to keep him from being able to yell if he woke. I tossed the roll to Katie who caught it deftly, tore a section off, and pressed it firmly over his mouth. We all moved back to our positions, with our hands behind our backs.

"That went well," Katie said. "Now what?"

"That Juan guy will be back any minute," I answered as I looked up at the open window. A fresh breeze was blowing down on me. "He's armed. If we can take him down quietly, we'll have the advantage."

"There are two other armed men out there," Bridget said.

"Not to mention the other three men who aren't," Katie said.

"*Please*," I said, grinning. "As if badass bitches like us couldn't handle five to three odds. Hell, get a gun in my hand, and I'll take them down myself."

Bridget and Katie laughed.

Tweedle sneezed. "Sorry," she whispered.

"You're supposed to be *spectacular* at hiding, remember?" Bridget said, giggling.

"The wind is blowing the dust around back here."

"Quiet. I hear someone coming," I said.

Juan came barreling through the door and looked around. He spotted the open window and jumped on top of the desk. Before he had a chance to look outside Tweedle sneezed again. Katie dove across the floor to close the door as I stood, clasped my hands together, and swung my arms like a hunk of lumber against the back of his knees. The force threw his feet forward and his head and body weight backward. On his way down, he slammed his head on a filing cabinet before landing on top of Bridget.

"Nice," Bridget said, rolling his body off her.

"Hurry," I whispered, snagging his phone and gun before they dragged him to the corner and piled him on top of the other guy.

I called Tyler.

"Hello?"

"Greetings," I said, smiling. "I don't have much time. Were you planning a rescue mission any time soon?"

"Smartass. We just got a call from the mission. Some bum reported to Father Eric that Lady Kelsey was in trouble. Father Eric called your cellphone, and Anne answered it. We're five minutes from the factory."

"Bonus. I'm armed. It's currently two down and five to go."

"Save some for us if you can. Ryan's ready to rip someone's head off."

"Tell him Tweedle's fine. She's hiding behind a desk while we work."

"I don't think that will help much, but I'll relay the message."

Katie signaled someone was coming. "Gotta go. Chat later."

I hung up the phone and slid it behind my back.

"Where the fuck are Juan and Alejandro?" a man yelled as he approached the room. "I swear if they went out for a smoke, I'm going to kick their asses!"

We heard several men laughing as the door opened. The man looked around, and just like his predecessor, noticed the open window. He charged toward the desk.

Katie jumped up too early to close the door which caused the man to pull his gun and turn toward her. I stood, holding my newly acquired gun against his head.

Bridget stood up, slapping at the dust on her jeans before holding out her hand to him.

He sighed, handing his gun over to her. "Santiago won't stop coming after all of you until he has Sebrina back."

"Why does he want Sebrina?" I asked as I tossed a pair of cuffs to Bridget.

The man laughed. "He thinks they're soulmates."

"Seriously?"

He shrugged. "Personally, I think he's tested his own product a few too many times. Fried too many brain cells."

I looked over at Katie. "I can't wait to meet this woman. The obsession men have over her is ridiculous."

"Maybe she's a siren. You know, from Greek mythology, luring men into her trap."

Bridget secured the handcuffs on the man. "If she is, that's one hell of a skill to have for a DEA agent. It's more likely she's wild in bed."

I narrowed my eyes at Bridget.

"Shit, sorry. Didn't think that comment out with regard to her history with Grady."

I pulled the bad guy toward the door. "Katie, take the gun from Bridget. You're a better shot. Bridget, you take the knife I stole earlier. Tweedle, stay where you are until either one of us or Ryan comes to get you."

Her only reply was a sneeze.

I nodded to Katie, and she opened the door.

Pushing the man in front of me, we followed behind him. The other four men were in the middle of the room but turned when they saw us walk out.

"On your knees," I told the man in front of me.

He slid to his knees. Only one of the men in the middle of the room had a gun. He held it pointing our direction.

"Drop the gun," I ordered.

"If I don't? What then?"

I turned my weapon on him and fired, shooting the gun out of his hand. He cradled his injured hand as he cried out and dropped to his knees.

"As you can see, my shooting is *excelente*."

"Your Spanish accent could use some work, though," Katie said.

"I didn't think it was that bad," I said.

"It's better than mine, but not great," Katie said. "You should ask Jackson for help."

"I was learning some when I lived in Miami, but I've been out of practice. Maybe the kids and I should take a class."

"Nicholas already knows Spanish," Bridget said. "He just doesn't want you to know that he knows. He likes to eavesdrop as much as Sara does."

"Little shit," I muttered.

We continued to watch the men as we chatted. None of them had moved except the one on the floor who was rocking back and forth, crying over his injured hand.

"*Get on your fucking knees, assholes!*" Katie yelled.

The other three men dropped to their knees, hands on the back of their heads.

"Huh," Bridget said. "Since there's nothing for me to do, I guess I'll call the guys. We don't have enough handcuffs."

"I'm hungry," Katie said to me, motioning for the man in front of us to stand. After he stood, she nudged him toward the others. "What do you think we have at home to snack on?"

"We don't have any burnt chicken, that's for sure. Everything you cooked tonight went into the trash." Having walked to within a few feet of the other men, I motioned for our guy to get back on the floor. He nodded and mirrored the others' positions, placing his hands on his head as he sat.

"At least I try. Maybe I'll get better someday."

"Katie, someone has to sit there with a fire extinguisher when you cook. It's safer for everyone if you quit trying. Or maybe focus on foods that don't require the oven or the stove, like sandwiches."

"I've only set the kitchen on fire once!"

"If we're talking Hattie's kitchen, then true. Don't forget, though, the damage you inflicted on Dex's kitchen in Pittsburgh."

"That was Rebecca's fault."

"Rebecca set the bacon on fire. You poured water on a grease fire and burned the walls and cabinets."

"I wasn't actually *cooking* when the fire started. It doesn't count."

"I think that counts," one of the guys said.

"No one asked you," Katie said.

"Go make sure the other two are still out of it," I said to her. "Bridget only has a pocket knife."

"I helped train Bridget, remember? She doesn't even need the knife to take on those two twat-heads."

"Now, Katie."

"*Fine!*"

"You sound like my nine-year old."

A minute or two after Katie left, Bridget returned. "Tyler says Ryan's going to need to punch someone."

I looked at each of the men in front of me. When Ryan came slamming his way through the front door, I pointed to the big guy on the end. He was the one who had shoved Katie around. The guy looked over at me, then over his shoulder as Ryan came flying at him. He jumped up and started running across the room, screaming. He didn't stand a chance. Ryan was on him in a second, beating the living shit out of him. Tyler and two others ran over to pull Ryan off.

When they finally peeled him away, I watched Ryan pace for a few minutes before I told him to go help Tweedle out from behind the desk. He nodded and puffed his chest in that direction.

"Dead or in jail?" Nightcrawler asked, raising a gun to the back of one the men's heads.

"Not sure yet. Haven't decided. Watch these guys while I take this one outside for a chat."

"Sure. Don't take too long, though. I want in on that poker game."

"It's still going?" I asked as I jerked on my guy's arm to get him to stand again.

"Tyler kept the kidnapping situation quiet. He was fairly certain the guys who nabbed you weren't all that talented," Nightcrawler said, shrugging. "He told Wild Card we had to run an errand for you and assigned him to run security until we return."

"Perfect." I pushed my guy toward the door. "I don't have to worry about saying *we're fine* a hundred times tonight."

Shipwreck held the door open for me, and I kicked my guy down the four cement stairs. He slammed his shoulder and knee pretty hard into the asphalt when he got to the bottom.

"Shit," the guy complained.

"Quit being a baby," Shipwreck said, walking down the stairs helping the guy to his feet. He led the guy over to the van as he glanced back at me. "Best do whatever you're going to do behind the van so if someone drives by, they can't witness anything."

I shrugged, following behind them. The van's side door was open so I sat on the edge, holding the gun loosely in my hands. Shipwreck forced the guys to his knees in front of me.

"Tell me everything."

"Like what?"

"Like everything," I said, shrugging. "What do you know about Santiago? What do you know about Sebrina? What do you know about us?"

"Santiago is a crazy bastard."

"What's his reach in the U.S.?"

"He can get anywhere. He hires guys like me to do his dirty work, or he kidnaps someone in Mexico and holds them hostage until their relatives in America do his dirty work."

"He ever come himself? To the States?"

"I've only heard of him crossing the border on two occasions. Both times it was to see Sebrina."

"Why is he fixated on her?"

"I only know what I've heard. They say he told her that either she marries him or he'll kill her."

"That's one hell of a proposal."

"Why the hell would she marry the bastard?" Shipwreck asked. "She's a DEA agent."

"Rumor has it she was helping Santiago get drugs into the U.S., but something happened to one of the shipments."

"I'm so confused," I said, sighing. "Was she working undercover to take Santiago down? Or was she working behind the DEA's back for some extra income in the drug trade?"

The guy shrugged. "No one knows. Santiago knew she was DEA, but whether she was setting him up or betraying the DEA, I don't think he knows. I think that's why he's saying she has to marry him or die. It's driving him crazy, and he was nowhere near sane to start with."

"Shit." I looked up at Shipwreck. "She's supposed to come to Michigan with Grady tomorrow."

"Perfect. We can just ask her," Shipwreck said, smirking. "I'd like to know if she's the reason the bastards found my house. I'll ring her scrawny little neck for it. I had a sweet setup down there."

"I have some ideas about that but we can discuss them later." I turned back to the guy in front of me. "What else? Who other than Santiago do we have to worry about?"

"His brother Miguel. Miguel lets Santiago run the day to day, but he's the brains behind most of the operation.

He makes all the big decisions. He also sits on the boards of all their legal businesses in Mexico and America."

"They have companies in the U.S.?"

"Si."

"Do you know the names of those companies?"

"Nah. I'm not in that part of the business. I just handle some shipments from time to time. This was my first kidnapping."

"You suck at it. I'd stick to smuggling."

He nodded, casually. "No matter, I guess. I get the feeling you ladies would've taken us down even if we were pros."

"We're trained in combat and hostage rescue. You should've researched us before you made a move."

He shrugged.

"Do Santiago and Miguel have any other family?"

"Santiago has a daughter who doesn't speak to him. She goes to college at a university in Arizona. Miguel has two sons, both younger and still live at home."

"Their wives?"

"Beautiful but not too bright."

"Anyone else?"

"Not that I can think of."

"What's the family's surname?"

"You don't know?"

"I haven't bothered to research them yet. I've been busy."

"Remirez," Shipwreck answered. "Even I knew that one."

"What will Santiago do to you if he finds out you failed to kidnap and hold us?" I asked the man.

"Santiago doesn't let anyone live who disappoints him. Why do you think I don't care about telling you about the cartel?"

"I thought maybe you were just a chatty person."

"Nah. Normally I'm a handful of sentences a day kind of guy. But, hey, if you're going to go down, take the assholes with you, right?"

"Makes perfect sense to me."

"Now what?" Shipwreck asked.

"Load them in the van. We'll take them with us."

"You plan to let us live?" the man looked at me with surprise.

Shipwreck raised an eyebrow as well.

I looked back at Shipwreck and shrugged. "They didn't actually hurt us. As far as kidnappings go, this one was by far my favorite."

"It was a nice break from our normal Wednesday workout," Katie said, leading two of the men toward me.

Tyler and crew led the others over.

"Look, gentlemen, here's the deal. If I let you go, either Santiago kills you or you make another dumb attempt to come after us and my boys kill you. That doesn't sound like a good plan to me, so I have a counter offer. Would you consider signing a contract, agreeing to be held in our custody until this whole thing gets sorted? I can guarantee you cots, food, and dry shelter. I'll even promise the boys won't beat the shit out of you."

All seven men nodded in unison.

"I have no idea how to write a contract like that," Katie said, nudging her two guys toward the van.

"Maybe we'll find something on Google."

Tyler handed me a pack of cigarettes and a lighter, then finished loading the rest of the men in the van. "Where do you want them?"

"Alex's house. Basement storage," I answered before lighting a smoke.

"Did Goat get the floor bolts installed?"

"We'll find out when we get there. I'll warn Alex if you handle the rest."

"You got it, boss. I'll ride with the prisoners," he said before tossing his keys to Ryan and climbing into the back of the van.

"He's good," Ryan said, nodding toward Tyler.

"I know. Donovan's been trying to poach him, but I pay Tyler well. Both in salary and entertainment."

"Casey said it was fun working for you. Several of the guys are interested if you ever need us. Most of us like the thought of a few less rules."

"Most of you couldn't handle taking orders from a woman. Besides, I don't have a need to blow shit up."

Ryan looked sideways at Tweedle.

"I already know," she said. "I'm so over it already." She continued smacking at her sleeves and sweatpants to knock the dust off. "I need a shower."

Ryan looked back at me, narrowing his eyes. "What have you done to my wife?"

"It's not our fault," Katie said, turning toward the SUV. "You're the one who brought her to Michigan."

"Can we stop for condensed milk on the way back?" Tweedle asked, following Katie.

"We don't have any money, remember?" Katie said.

"I'll pay," Ryan said, following after them. "I'm not making five trips to the store tonight though, so you'd better make a list."

"Ooh, more chocolate chips," Tweedle said, climbing into the backseat.

"Okay," Shipwreck said. "I'm beginning to like it a little more around here."

"About that," I said as I tossed my cigarette to the ground and stepped on it. "I heard I owe you a bar. It's too late in the Fall season to start building, but if you can wait until spring, we could potentially work out a deal."

"What kind of bar?" he asked as he followed me to the SUV.

Chapter Seventeen

After calming Alex down about his basement storage room being converted into a private prison for the near future, Nightcrawler dropped off the eighth bad guy, the one with the shredded shoulder from Storm's teeth. Haley treated his shoulder, cleaning and stitching the wound, as Bridget and I unfolded the cots for the prisoners and passed out pillows and blankets. Alex was still complaining when I slipped into the main house.

Anne looked at me from head to toe, inspecting me for injuries, before leading Sara upstairs.

Beth laughed, releasing a long breath, and then rested her forehead on the dining room table.

"What's wrong with Beth?" Nicholas asked as I steered him to his bathroom.

"Tired. She was up half the night with us last night."

Nicholas must have bought my story because he filled his toothbrush with paste and began scrubbing his teeth. He waited for me to start to say something before he brushed his back molars, then his tongue and the roof of his mouth. I still had to stop him from wiping his mouth on his sleeve, but I felt like I was making progress.

In his bedroom I was happy to see his dirty clothes were in the hamper, and he was climbing into his bed.

"Are we reading tonight?" I asked.

He lay down, staring at the ceiling. "I don't feel like it."

"Want to talk?" I asked, lying next to him in the bed, sharing his pillow.

"Do you think Grady will stay?" he asked, turning on his side to face me.

"I don't know. I hope so."

"If he stays, how long will he be in the dog house?"

"That's a good question. How long do you think I should punish him?"

Nicholas squinted his eyes and furrowed his forehead as he thought about it. "When you punish me, it's always different. It depends if I meant to do something bad."

"Maybe we need to find out what's really going on before we figure out the punishment then."

Nicholas nodded before rolling onto his back. "What if he still leaves?"

"Then we'll both be sad, but we'll be together."

"Will Wild Card stay?"

"Maybe for a little while."

"Will he sleep in your room?"

I choked on a laugh and ended up sitting up and coughing up half a lung with Nicholas beating on my back. Wild Card opened the door and stood there watching us.

"You okay?" he asked with a crooked grin.

I nodded, still coughing.

"I'll get you a glass of water."

He disappeared down the hall. I had finally stopped coughing by the time he returned, but the cold water felt good on my throat.

"Someone going to explain?" Wild Card asked.

"No," I said, holding a finger up to Nicholas' mouth to stop him from answering. "Goodnight, my beautiful boy."

Nicholas giggled and curled up under the covers. "Night, Mom."

I leaned over and peppered his face with kisses as he pushed me away and buried his face under the blankets. Walking across the room, I shut the light off and was about to close the door when Nicholas called out.

"Mom? Can we get a dog?"

I thought about how Storm had saved Beth from being kidnapped. "Maybe. We'll discuss it tomorrow."

"*Yes!*" Nicholas whispered, rolling over to face the wall.

I walked down the hall, a smile spreading across my face.

"What?" Wild Card asked.

"Private joke. Where is everyone?"

"Tyler put me in charge of security, but he must've run into you because he was driving your SUV when he left. Hattie had a headache and went to bed early. Abigail was teething and cranky, so Lisa took her home. Alex is at home watching Carl. Beth's in the dining room. Jackson moved Reggie over to his apartment because he was afraid you'd kick Reggie's ass if he did one more stupid thing, and we all know it's a matter of time before Reggie does something stupid."

I smirked at Wild Card. I loved Reggie to death, but the man was hopeless.

"That leaves the guys who are split between our makeshift poker room and running security."

"I'm going to check on Hattie."

"Not until you explain the blood on your shirt," he said, snagging an arm around my waist to stop me.

I looked at my shirt and sure enough, a small spray of blood ran across the bottom. It must have been from when the one guy hit his head.

"Not my blood."

"I guessed that already based on the spray pattern. Should we be expecting the cops to show up? Do I need to call your lawyer?"

"We were kidnapped, but we escaped and imprisoned our kidnappers. I'm too tired to explain more than that.

Tyler is still at Alex's house if you want the gory details. Tell him I gave you the green light."

"Am I going to be pissed?"

I thought about it and shook my head. "Rather boring, really. Same ole, same ole."

"God, that's frightening," Beth said from the table. "I'm going to bed."

"Are you okay?" I asked. "I feel like you got more than you bargained for tonight."

Beth raised her arms in an *I'm not sure* gesture. "Next time, I'd rather be kidnapped. Sitting here worried about the rest of you was hard enough, but to pretend nothing was wrong was the worst."

"Welcome to my world. The kidnapping was actually kind of fun."

Beth laughed as she climbed the steps and turned the corner.

I turned to Wild Card. "I need to check on Hattie. Check in with Tyler." I climbed the stairs, turning toward Hattie's room and knocking on her door.

"Come in, sunshine," Hattie called out.

"I heard you have a headache. You okay?" I asked as I walked across the room.

Hattie was sitting in her favorite rocking chair, overlooking the window to the field.

"Nothing a cup of tea and an aspirin couldn't handle," she said as she took another sip from her tea cup. "What about you? Tyler left in a hurry earlier, reassigning security before he disappeared with a handful of men."

"We were sort of kidnapped, but not really. I even made it home in time to tuck Nicholas into bed, so it's all good."

"No one was hurt?"

"Katie's butt might have a bruise," I answered as I laughed. "She could've fared much worse if we would've sparred like we'd planned, though."

Hattie smiled as she turned her attention back to her tea. She had dark circles under her eyes, worrying me that she was overextended, but her skin was also pale and that worried me more.

"Are you sure you're okay?"

"Just a long day, dear. Nothing to fret over. If it's all right with you, I'm going to read a chapter or two and then go to bed."

"Relax then," I said, leaning over to kiss her forehead. "I'll handle breakfast in the morning. You should sleep in late."

She nodded, opening her book. "I might just do that."

~*~*~

Returning downstairs, I found the kitchen and dining room were empty. I could still hear the guys down the hall in the family room laughing as they played cards. I could also hear someone working out in the basement, and another someone snoring loudly. The kitchen and dining room, though, were oddly missing their normal buzz.

"Where is everyone?" Anne whispered from the stairs behind me. "This is so eerie."

"I was just thinking the same. Drink?"

"Yes, please. What are we drinking?"

"Something fruity, fabulous, and strong."

"My kind of drink."

"Point me to the liquor," Shipwreck said as he climbed the basement stairs, "and I'll make all your dreams come true."

I walked into the kitchen and opened the liquor cabinet and the cabinet with the glasses. Shipwreck pulled out various bottles.

"Shipwreck, this is Anne. Anne, this is Shipwreck. He helped the boys get out of Mexico but ended up homeless in the process."

"Not to mention, minus a bar," Shipwreck grumbled.

"Oh, quit pushing me for answers," I said, sighing. "I've had a long, busy day."

"You dropped a comment about building me a bar, then you changed the subject," Shipwreck said as he set two hurricane glasses on the breakfast bar and slid them to Anne and me.

"What? No garnishes?"

"I didn't see any fruit in the refrigerator."

"Bottom right drawer," Wild Card said from the top of the basement stairs. He continued walking past us and down the hall.

Anne jumped, startled by something. She pulled a phone out of her back pocket, giggling. "It's yours. You should check your messages, too. Damn thing has been vibrating every ten minutes."

"It always does." I checked the newest text message which was from Tyler telling me to close the blinds. I slid off my stool and walked over to the wall panel. Thanks to Tech and Carl's combined electronical know-how, I could push a button and close all the common area blinds.

As I slid back onto my barstool, I laughed at Anne. She was sucking down her drink at a rapid pace. "Slow down or the guys will have to carry you off to bed."

She wiggled her eyebrows. "Which guys?"

Wild Card chuckled as he walked back into the dining room. "Jack on the rocks, barkeep."

Wild Card tossed a t-shirt at me which I took as an order to change out of my blood-stained tank top. Since I was wearing a sports bra anyway, I slid the tank top off and the t-shirt on without leaving my barstool.

"What happened to your arm?" Anne asked, grabbing my wrist to look at my forearm.

I looked at my arm. The reddish welts had turned a lovely shade of purple. "Blocked a chair being launched at my head by a very angry little boy. Which reminds me," I turned to look at Wild Card as he settled on the stool next to me, "can you help me watch Nicholas the next couple of days? I don't want him back in class until we know he has his emotions under control. He could've hurt Sara or Beth today."

"Already planned on it," Wild Card said, nodding as he sipped the drink Shipwreck had made for him. "I'll stay as long as Nicholas needs me. Don't think for a minute though that Grady's not going to hear from me about that shit. That kid's been through enough. Grady fucked up."

"Agreed, but it won't help our cause if we all beat the shit out of Grady when he arrives."

"I've only caught bits and pieces of everything that happened today," Anne said, "but it was enough to make me want to punch at least three people."

"It's been a wild day." I picked up my drink, finally taking a sip. It was delicious. I took another long drink before setting it down.

"Well? Did I pass?" Shipwreck asked, grinning.

"You did. The bar's yours if you want it. We just have to work out the details."

"The country bar you were considering building?" Anne asked. "I thought you changed your mind on that."

"I did, and I didn't. It lost some appeal to me until Shipwreck's situation. I like the thought of having somewhere close by to drink rather than my dining room turning into a frat house every night, but I didn't want to run it."

"I'm not sure about the country bar theme," Shipwreck said, wrinkling his nose. "I'm no cowboy."

Shipwreck was still wearing a Hawaiian shirt and shorts.

"Everyone has been bugging me about building a pool somewhere. I was thinking we could combine the pool and the bar. We could build a big cabana-style building with a tiki bar on one end of the building and an indoor pool on the other."

"Now we're talking," Shipwreck said, laughing. "I can totally picture it. Ladies walking around in bikinis all year round."

"Before your brain goes to the dark-side, I'm also thinking the bar should be membership-only, not open to the public. It would be less profitable, but we could control security easier."

"I still need to make a living."

"Ha!" Anne said, sliding off her stool and running into the kitchen. She dug around in a cupboard until she found a short round vase. Placing it on the breakfast bar, she dug a twenty out of her pocket and dropped it inside the vase. Wild Card pulled his wallet and dropped a twenty as well.

Anne looked at me.

"I'm wearing yoga pants."

Wild Card rolled his eyes and dropped another twenty into the jar. "What Anne's trying to demonstrate is that everyone has healthy bank accounts. Your tips will be higher than what you're used to."

"I'd still pay you a percentage of the profits, too," I said.

Shipwreck looked at each of us. "What's the catch?"

"The catch is that the bar will be *your* headache. I don't have time to deal with it, and I'd likely have you report to my guy in Miami so he can keep an eye on things. He already looks over everything associated with alcohol or food sales for me. Katie keeps track of my retail businesses. Donovan keeps the ball rolling for my share of Ace's. And Bones' sister Rebecca manages all the national and international companies."

"How rich are you?"

"Very," Wild Card said, chuckling.

"Loaded," Anne said, grinning.

"What about this guy in Miami? What if I don't get along with him?"

"Not a problem," Wild Card said. "I'd be happy to accompany you and introduce you to Baker. He runs one of the most successful sex clubs in Miami."

"Hmm. What about starting a sex—" Shipwreck started to say.

"*No!*" the three of us answered at once.

Chapter Eighteen

I was up with the birds, but Tweedle still beat me to the kitchen. "You just don't stop, do you?" I asked as I looked over all the baked goods on display.

"I texted Ryan. He's coming over to move some of this to Headquarters. I'm out of counter space."

I filled a cup of coffee and poured the rest into an empty carafe, carrying it along with several coffee cups to the dining room table before returning to the kitchen to start breakfast. Tweedle stopped baking long enough to help me cook enough food for the masses.

Whiskey, Ryan, and the poker players were the first wave to eat, leaving afterward to take the excess baked goods to Headquarters. Katie, Anne, Sara, and Nicholas were part of the second wave before they scattered to get dressed and ready for the day. Alex, Carl, Haley, Bridget, and Lisa were part of the third wave, who were almost done eating.

"Please tell me that's everyone," Tweedle said as she wiped sweat from her forehead on a paper towel.

"We still need to feed the security crew and likely a few guys from Headquarters."

"I'll make more French toast."

"I'll help," Reggie said, coming in from the garage. "Sorry I'm late, sis," he said as he kissed my cheek on his way by.

"Are we going to have a good day or a bad day today, Reg?" I asked while looking at the red blotches on his forehead where he'd obviously tried to scrub the word *idiot* off his skin.

"Good," Jackson answered for him. "Reggie *promised me* he'd behave."

"At least I can count on one brother," I said as I wrapped an arm around Jackson. "Food's on the table. Dig in. Reggie, start taking plates of food out to the day shift guards. Not everyone was able to make it inside. I'm going to check on Hattie."

"She hasn't been down yet?" Jackson asked, scrunching his forehead.

"I told her last night I'd handle breakfast. She's wiped out. Too much going on the last couple of days."

He steered me into the living room by my elbow. "Pops is worried about her," he whispered.

"Why?"

He shook his head. "She's been tired. *A lot*. Says it's nothing."

I studied his face, reading the concern before turning my attention to the dining room. "Haley, can you give me a hand?"

"Sure. What do you need?" she asked as she walked over.

Haley was only a second-year medical student, but she also worked at the clinic with Doc.

"I need you to get a hold of Doc and have him do a house call," I whispered. "Hattie needs a physical. She had a headache last night and said she was tired. Jackson told me she's been tired a lot lately."

Haley looked up at the clock. "The clinic doesn't open until ten o'clock on Thursdays so Doc should be able to come right over. I'll get my medical bag."

"Meet me in Hattie's room," I said before returning to the kitchen and climbing the small private stairway to Hattie's room.

Knocking on the door, it was a minute or two before Hattie called for me to enter. When I walked in, she was still in bed and working her way to a sitting position.

"I must've been more tired than I thought," Hattie said, smiling at me. "Is it really almost seven-thirty?"

"No worries. Breakfast shift is almost over, and the kids are getting ready for school."

"I should get up."

"Nope. Stay in bed. We need to talk." I helped her lean forward and adjusted the pillows behind her so she could rest more comfortably. "Jackson ratted you out. Said you haven't been yourself lately."

Hattie sighed, but didn't say anything.

The dark circles under her eyes were even darker than they'd been the night before. Not only was her face pale, but she looked like she'd lost weight too. I mentally kicked myself for not noticing. "Doc's on his way over to do a complete physical."

"It's nothing a little sleep won't cure."

"You've tried sleeping. Didn't work. Now we try this." I sat on the side of the bed, laying my hand on top of hers. "You're too important to this family to ignore your health."

"I really don't think it's anything to worry about, sunshine."

"Then let Doc check you out and confirm it."

"Fine. I'll agree to a physical, but no fussing. You know how much I hate people fussing over me."

"Because that's your job?" Haley asked as she walked into the room.

I moved out of Haley's way as she pulled a blood pressure cuff out of her medical bag.

"Damn straight, Haley," Hattie said before looking at me. "You can leave, Kelsey. You promised to handle the breakfast shift and that includes the dirty dishes. I'm in good hands."

"I'll leave you in Haley's care—for now," I said, rolling my eyes before I exited through the private stairway.

At the bottom of the stairs I paused to take a few slow deep breaths. I didn't want the kids to see how worried I was. Nicholas, especially, couldn't handle any more stress.

Wild Card spotted me and climbed the few steps to fold me into his arms. "Jackson told me. She okay?" he asked in a whisper.

"I don't know. That's what scares me." I hugged him back a little tighter.

"Take a moment. I'll get Sara to school and take Nicholas with me to get him out of the house."

"What time are we expecting Grady?"

"Not for a few hours yet. Bones called and said they discharged Grady and they're on their way to Pops' house."

I nodded into his shoulder, taking another deep breath of his cologne as he rubbed my back. "Thank you, Cooper."

"It's been a long time since you called me Cooper. I missed it," he said as he pulled back enough to kiss my forehead before walking away.

I stayed in the stairway, hearing Tweedle ordering Jackson and Reggie around as they gathered food for the outdoor security team and for Headquarters. I sat on the steps, listening to Wild Card argue with the kids until they were ready, then escorting them and Beth out the door. Tweedle, Jackson, and Reggie left at the same time, and the house was suddenly quiet. I stepped out of my hiding place to find Lisa, Anne, and Alex waiting to speak to me, worry etched on their faces. "Doc should be here soon."

As if I summoned him, Doc walked through the front door with Tyler.

"Look at all these sad faces," Doc said in his normal cheerful voice. "Quit borrowing trouble. We'll sort this out." Doc climbed the main stairs, all business.

"How is she?" Tyler asked. "I noticed she was pale yesterday, but I thought she was tired."

"I thought the same. I should've known better," I admitted, throwing myself into a chair.

"Don't do that," Lisa said, sitting beside me. "You were the one who checked on her last night and again this morning."

"I'm staying at the house today," Alex said. "You have Grady to deal with later. We have plenty of people to cover my shift at the store."

"You don't have to," I said. "Wild Card said he'd watch Nicholas for me. I can work from home."

"She's *my* Hattie, too," Alex said, grabbing a clean plate from the cupboard. "I'll take her a breakfast and a cup of tea."

I looked at Alex's outfit and smirked. "She'll get a kick out of your outfit today."

Alex was wearing a pink skirt with a matching pink blazer, a white silk blouse, and on top of his head was a large white silk bonnet trimmed in pink flowers.

Alex winked as he filled a plate. "I was thinking of Hattie when I dressed this morning."

"You look ridiculous," Haley said as she stepped off the stairs and into the kitchen.

Alex laughed, pulled Haley into his body and kissed her. "That's the point, luv."

Haley stepped away, slapping his ass as he started up the stairs with the food.

"So… He's not—" Anne started to ask.

"Nope," Haley said as she grinned.

"Is he bi—" Lisa started to ask.

"Not even a little," Haley said.

"Then, why—" I started to say.

"Because it entertains the shit out of him," Haley said as she started to put away the leftovers. "Get off your duffs and help clean this mess."

"That little shit…" I muttered as I walked into the kitchen and filled the sink with fresh dishwater.

"Who else knows?" Lisa asked, laying Abigail in her playpen.

"Just Hattie as far as I know," Haley said. "She helps him find some of his more outrageous outfits."

"The princess dress he wore last week?" Anne asked, laughing.

"Yeah, Hattie found that at a flea market in Texas and had it shipped to him. He spent a small fortune on the matching shoes."

I glanced over at Haley. "How long have you and Alex been a couple?"

"Off and on for the last year. I told him I wouldn't get serious about our relationship until he admitted to everyone that he's heterosexual."

Anne pouted. "Is he going to start dressing normal now?"

Haley laughed. "No. The outfits don't bother me. In fact, I find them just as entertaining as you guys. I don't give a shit what he wears during the day as long as he's naked at night."

"Eww," I said, turning away. "I don't want to picture Alex naked."

"Why are we talking about Alex being naked?" Katie asked as she entered through the living room sliding door. "And why did he text me that he wasn't working today? And why is everyone still at home and not at the store?"

"Sit," I said, motioning to the table as I walked over.

"What's wrong?" Katie asked, watching me closely. "I mean besides everything I already know like the cartel, Grady being an ass, and Nicholas' meltdown."

"Something's wrong with Hattie," I said, grasping her hand. "Alex is staying at the house today with me to keep an eye on her. Doc's with her now."

Katie turned her eyes to the fruit bowl on the table, focusing her attention away. "Anything I can do?"

"Not right now. I'll keep you posted, though."

Katie nodded, but her eyes stayed on the fruit. "I need to open the store. The employees will be wondering where I am." Katie walked back through the living room, exiting through the slider.

"Shit," I said to myself as I stared at the back sliding door.

I felt a hand on my shoulder and looked up as Tech gently squeezed. "I'm going to work in my old office at the store today. I'll let Kemp know you're working from home."

"Take care of her, Tech."

"We all will," Anne said.

Tyler walked across the room and picked up Abigail, carrying her out to the garage. Lisa followed with the diaper bag, and Anne grabbed their purses and followed them. Tech left through the living room sliding door. I shook my head, scattering my thoughts before clearing the remaining dirty dishes from the dining room table.

Doc left, saying he'd have more information in a few days after the lab results came back. Until then, he said to keep Hattie off her feet, resting as much as she'd allow. Haley left shortly after Doc to meet him at the clinic. Bridget arrived with our laptops and a few files. Alex returned downstairs and said Hattie was napping. He was in the kitchen flipping through Hattie's cookbook trying to decide on something she'd like for lunch.

Bridget tapped a pen on the table in front of me, startling me.

"Shit, sorry. Were you saying something?"

"No. I just saw you'd drifted somewhere else. You can dissolve later, but I need you in the present right now. What are we doing about the cartel?"

"Damn. I forgot about them," I said as I ran a hand through my hair.

"I'd rather we figure out a plan before the next kidnapping."

I picked up my cell phone and called Kierson.

"I'm busy," he said as a way of answering.

"With work or my cousin?"

"She's your half-sister, remember? But I'm at work. We just caught a case."

"Can it wait? Your case that is."

Kierson paused and I could hear him moving and then a door closing. "What's wrong?"

"Everything."

"Can you be more specific?"

"Santiago Remirez."

"Not familiar with the name."

"The DEA knows him. He's a Mexican cartel dealer."

"Not my expertise, but I can put you in touch with Sebrina. Grady and Donovan know her."

"Word on the street is that Sebrina betrayed Santiago."

"What does that mean?"

"I have no idea. Until I do, I'm not willing to make her my source of information."

"I swear, you walk into more *shit piles* than a horse."

"Thanks. You going to help or not?"

"What do you already know?" Kierson growled.

"Three names: Santiago Remirez, Miguel Remirez, and the woman known as Sebrina who I'm told by all works for the DEA."

"That's it?"

"Pretty much. Santiago's daughter attends school at a university in Arizona, but she's not on speaking terms with her father. I can also get you the names of the eight guys who kidnapped me last night, but they're just hired muscle."

"How do you expect me to get information on a DEA agent?"

"Beats me. Figured you'd have an angle."

"I'm not that high up the food chain with the DOJ."

"Tebbs?"

"Special Agent in Charge, Jack Tebbs, wouldn't stick his neck on the line for me. He might for Maggie, though. She's going to get us all fired if she keeps acting as crazy as you."

"She and Tebbs are just messing with you. You make it too easy."

"It's called being a professional."

"You're grumpy."

"Your cousin... sister... or whatever she is to you, is *driving me crazy*. We got into a huge fight this morning about coffee creamer. And, *yes*, I said *coffee creamer*!"

"Charlie drinks her coffee black."

"*I know!*"

I laughed. "Hattie predicted that this little experiment of yours was a disaster."

"She thinks we'll split?" Kierson asked, sighing.

"That's not what Hattie said. She said that Charlie can't sit at home and play house. She's too much like me. She needs a project. Something to keep her busy."

"Like a hobby?"

"No—*like a job*. She's a *detective*, Agent Kierson, and a damn good one. Find her work or I will."

"Should I send her to Michigan? Help with the security there?"

"She'll never try living with you again if you do. Ask her instead to work from your house running the background research on the Remirez family."

"It's worth a try. Hell, I'd try anything at this point."

I heard my phone beep, indicating I had another call. "Someone's calling me. Stay in touch." I hung up, looked at the screen, and answered the call from Pops. "How's it going?"

Pops laughed. "Good. We just boarded the plane. Both Grady and Sebrina are sleeping. I tried to call Hattie, but she didn't answer. Is she close by?"

"She's sleeping. Alex turned her ringer off."

"Sleeping? It's mid-morning."

"Pops, I called Doc over. He's running some tests. We won't know anything for a few days, but Hattie has to take it easy until then."

"*Damn it.* Why didn't she tell me she still wasn't feeling well? She's so damn stubborn."

"You two make a good match."

"*Bah.* I should be there."

"Nothing you could do if you were. Alex and I are keeping a close eye on her. She's just going to have to adjust to being spoiled rotten for a few days."

Pops was quietly muttering under his breath. "I'm glad she's home. I know she loves Texas, but if she gets bad news, she'll handle it better with her kids there."

I nodded, though he couldn't hear me. Alex walked over and held my free hand.

"Give her a kiss for me, baby girl. I'll be there as quick as I can."

"Safe travels, Pops."

Chapter Nineteen

I tossed the phone on the table, causing Bridget to jump. "Sorry." I turned to look at Alex who was still holding my hand. "Now that I know you dress like that just to fuck with us, I have to tell you the hat looks ridiculous."

"Only the hat?" he asked, releasing my hand to sit at the table.

"You and Haley went public?" Bridget asked. "Damn."

"How'd you know?" Alex asked.

Bridget shook her head at Alex. "Haley's my best friend and roommate. I know everything."

The tea kettle whistled and Alex returned to the kitchen to fix Hattie a tray before disappearing upstairs.

I picked up my phone again, calling Mitch this time, Grady's brother.

"Is this a *save the date* phone call?" Mitch asked when he answered.

"More like *save your brother from getting his ass kicked* phone call. Your brother has lost his marbles."

Mitch was silent for a few seconds. "How crazy are we talking?"

"Does the name Sebrina mean anything to you?"

"Yeah, unfortunately," Mitch said, sighing. "Where is he?"

"I had him drugged and kidnapped. He's on his way back to Michigan, but he's going to be pissed when he wakes."

"And Sebrina?"

"She's on the plane too."

"*Shit! Why?* Why is she being shipped to Michigan?"

"Long story, but she needs our protection at the moment. Someone's trying to kill her."

"Let them," Mitch growled.

"You don't mean that."

"The hell I don't." Mitch made a growling noise that reminded me of Grady. "You're in over your head on this one, Kelsey, and I can't get there until sometime next week. There's a joint task force with the customs office that is gearing up for a takedown. I can't get away until the big arrest day, but I'll try to get Michigan as soon as my schedule clears. And, Kelsey?"

"Yeah?"

"Don't trust Sebrina."

"Wasn't planning on it."

"I mean... Don't let her in your house. Don't let her get close to the family. Don't take your eyes off her."

"I just invited the wolf into the hen house, didn't I?" I said, looking up at Bridget as I talked to Mitch.

"More like you just dropped the python into the mouse house. She's dangerous, and Grady can't see that side of her."

"Lovely. I'll handle it." I disconnected the call and called Tyler.

"Yo," Tyler answered.

"We need to move the nursery and schoolroom to the house while Sebrina's in town. Mitch says she's dangerous."

Bridget was watching me and picked up her phone to make a call.

"That means you'll have to explain to the kids what's wrong with Hattie," Tyler said.

"It will be fine. I'm one hell of a liar," I said before hanging up.

I went to the basement and asked a couple of guys who were working out to help me move boxes out of the old war room. The room was big enough to serve as the new classroom temporarily. Half an hour later, Beth, Sara, Nicholas, and Wild Card started moving books and other supplies into the room.

"Why are we moving?" Sara asked.

"I talked to Grady's brother, Mitch. He doesn't want the family around Sebrina. He's worried she's dangerous," I answered.

"Dangerous like Penny?"

"Might be. He didn't explain."

"Who's Penny?" Nicholas asked as he emptied a box of books onto a shelf.

"Bones' ex-wife," Sara said. "She used to work for Nola."

Nicholas turned to stare at Sara with large eyes.

"It's okay," Sara said, patting his arm. "Nola shot Penny in the head. She thought Penny was working with the FBI, but really Aunt Kelsey bugged her purse at a party."

Nicholas sighed. "Cool." He turned to finish moving the books.

"I hope they both get good paying jobs when they're adults," I said to Beth as we moved one of the eight-foot tables. "They're likely to spend a fortune on therapy."

Beth dropped her end of the table, laughing.

"Where are we putting the nursery?" Tyler asked, carrying Abigail into the room. "Also, does Lisa know we just moved her daughter?"

"I'll call Lisa. Was Dave's daughter in the nursery, too?"

"Nope. Dave's keeping Juliette away until the cartel stuff passes. He didn't want to make his family a target if someone followed him home after picking her up."

"Smart. If it's just Abby, then we can put her in my room."

"Got it. You think it's safe enough with all the windows?"

"I had bulletproof glass installed in the atrium when we installed it on the sliding doors."

"Always one step ahead of me," Tyler grumbled.

"I trust you to catch the things I miss, Tyler, and you excel at it. That's why we make a good team. Now, if you're not too busy with your pity party, can you help convert the atrium into a nursery?"

Abigail squealed, delighted. Tyler smirked and walked out with her.

I turned to move one of the boxes when Storm started barking. I stepped into the hallway to find Storm frantically scratching at the furnace room door.

"Get the kids upstairs! Lockdown!"

Several of the Devil's Players grabbed Beth and the kids, running for the stairs. Wild Card ran into the gym and activated the security alarm. Bridget or Alex would protect Hattie. I glanced back at Wild Card, confirming he'd also pulled his gun.

The second I opened the furnace room door, Storm took off at full speed down the tunnel leading to Donovan's house. I glanced briefly in the tunnel, seeing it was empty except for the dog, before following.

"If someone shoots, we're trapped with nowhere to duck and hide."

"No worries. I plan on shooting first," I called back as I neared the end of the tunnel.

"Let me go first," Wild Card said when I slowed to peek out.

He didn't give me much of an option as he stepped in front of me and into Donovan's basement family room. I stepped out behind him. Storm had run to the back corner of the room and stood with his thick fur hiked and teeth snarled in front of the closed closet door.

"Storm, release," I ordered, remembering some commands Beth had taught me. Storm took two steps back and stopped growing. "Heel."

The German Shepherd made a one-eighty turn and ran over to my side. His fur was still hackled, but he was silent, waiting for his next command.

"Stay."

Storm whined but stayed in place as I moved beside the door and raised my gun.

Wild Card moved in front of the closet; his gun aimed at chest height toward the door.

"We have three options," I called out. "One, I open the door and let Storm attack."

Storm barked twice.

"Two," Wild Card said, grinning at Storm, "I empty my entire clip through that cheap ass hollow closet door."

Storm growled.

I looked at Wild Card, and we shared a grin. "Or three, you surrender and come out with your hands in the air."

Storm whined and sat.

"I'm coming out," a man called. "Don't shoot."

One of the cartel men who'd kidnapped me the night before came out of the closet with his hands on his heads. One of the handcuffs swung freely from his wrist.

"Are you the only one in there?" I asked, holding a gun to his head.

"*Si. Si.* I left the others in the storage room."

"Move forward three steps and then right two steps," Wild Card ordered.

The man complied and while Wild Card secured his other handcuff, I swept the closet. It was empty except for some of Donovan's camo gear.

"Did Donovan store any weapons in here?" I asked.

"No. He has a safe. Lisa had a fit the last time he left a knife out."

"Abigail can't even crawl yet."

"Yes, she can." Wild Card said, laughing. "They just don't put her down long enough to let her."

"Seriously? She can crawl?" I grabbed the guy and jerked him toward the tunnel that led to Alex's house, nudging him with the barrel of my gun to move.

"She's pretty good at it too," Wild Card said as he followed us down the tunnel.

I heard a noise ahead and grabbed the guy in front of me to stop him.

"Who's out there?" I yelled down the tunnel.

"Shipwreck!" a voice called from Alex's house. "All clear on this end."

I nudged my guy again, and we exited the tunnel a minute later.

Shipwreck grabbed my guy and manhandled him into the storage room. "I heard the alarm and decided to check on the prisoners. How'd this one escape?"

"Don't know. You can ask him while I get a garbage bag." I walked down the hall and into the small basement kitchenette. Under the sink, I found a box of garbage bags. I grabbed two before returning to the storage room. "Strip," I said to the prisoners. "All of you."

"What?" one of the guys said.

"*You heard her!*" Shipwreck yelled. "*Strip! Now!*"

The men started to remove their shoes and socks, and I turned to Wild Card. "Can you call Tyler with the all clear?"

"Gladly," Wild Card said, looking at the prisoners as they started unbuttoning their pants. "I have no interest in watching to see what comes next."

The men in the room had removed their jeans and socks, but still had their shirts and undershorts on. "*Naked*, boys. Nothing but your birthday suits."

"We can't take off our shirts without the handcuffs being removed." Each had one wrist handcuffed to a six-foot chain which was bolted to the floor.

I reached into my boot and pulled a switchblade. Hitting the release, the blade snapped loudly. "Either you figure it out, or I will."

The men started tearing the seams of their shirts and stripping off their underwear. I put on a pair of elbow-length rubber gloves and emptied the shit buckets while Shipwreck gathered the clothes in the garbage bags and shook out pillows and blankets. After the buckets were emptied, we refilled jugs of water and left food in the room before locking the door.

"Did our escapee tell you how he freed himself?" I asked Shipwreck.

"He picked the handcuff lock with the spring from a pen he had on him, but it wasn't until the guy who dropped off breakfast this morning left the door unlocked that he was able to slip out."

"Damn it, Alex. I'll have Tyler change the lock so Alex doesn't have access." Walking into the family room, I motioned for Wild Card it was time to leave. "You were a lot of help," I said sarcastically to him as I threw my gloves into the trash.

"I would've voted to shoot them and bury their bodies. Much less work."

"Liar. You would've tied them up and left them at the warehouse for the rats."

"I wasn't aware rats were an option," Wild Card said, laughing. "Yes, that's what I would've done then."

"How do you guys know each other so well?" Shipwreck asked, leading the way down the tunnel back to the main house.

Wild Card chuckled. "Remember me telling you about the crazy stripper I married in Vegas?"

Shipwreck stopped in the middle of the tunnel, looking back at me from head to toe. "That was you?"

"Yeah. I was in a jam."

"Damn," Shipwreck said as he stepped into Donovan's basement and crossed the room. "That's messed up."

Storm sat patiently, waiting where I'd ordered him to stay. I tapped my leg twice, and he came over for a scratch behind the ear. "Good boy!" I pointed to the tunnel to the main house. "Go find Beth!"

Storm barked excitedly before racing down the tunnel, tail wagging.

"What's messed up? That Wild Card married a stripper or that I was stripping in Vegas?" I asked.

"Not a damn thing," Wild Card said a little louder than necessary as we started down the next tunnel.

I turned back and looked at him, raising an eyebrow.

"Move, woman. I'm ready for lunch."

"I'm not hungry, but I need some industrial soap and a shower after dumping those buckets. What did you guys feed the prisoners last night?"

"That was Wild Card's doing," Shipwreck said. "He dumped a package of ex-lax in their food."

"Why?"

"You said I couldn't *beat* the shit out of them," Wild Card explained.

Chapter Twenty

After my shower, I decided I needed to dress in full battle gear if I was going to survive the afternoon. I checked myself in the mirror and smirked. I was wearing a dark purple halter top, a form-fitted leather jacket, my favorite pair of ripped, well-worn jeans, and of course, my knee-high heeled boots. My hair was dried straight, accenting the dyed black and silver streaks that my friend Dallas had touched up last week. After some light eye shadow, thick mascara, and heavy eye-liner, I was ready. As Alex would say, I looked *bitchen*.

Entering the dining room, Tyler whistled.

"You're way too young, Mr. Tyler." I blew him a kiss before running up the stairs to Hattie's room, peeking in to see if she was sleeping.

"Come in, sunshine. I'm awake."

"How are you feeling?"

"Bored. Doc said I needed to take it easy, but he didn't order me to stay in bed all day."

I walked over to her closet and pulled some cotton pants and a soft sweater that I knew she liked. "Get dressed. I'll send Jackson upstairs to escort you down."

"Thank goodness. I thought you were going to argue with me, too," she said as she went into her private bathroom to change.

I left to find Jackson who was in the kitchen helping Reggie. "Can you escort Hattie downstairs? She wants to visit with everyone."

"Of course," he said, drying his hands on a towel before walking away.

"Cooper, can you bring Hattie's rocking chair downstairs?"

"On it."

"Everyone else, help me move the table further out into the room. We'll set Hattie's rocker at the far end so she has more room."

It took six of us to move the table. Bridget got the couch afghan. Alex fixed another cup of tea. Wild Card came down with the rocker.

"Aunt Kelsey, how come you sometimes call Wild Card: Cooper."

"Because that's his real name. Cooper Wesley."

"Was that his name when you were married to him?"

"That was always his name. If you're asking if I called him Wild Card when we were married, then yes, sometimes I did. I usually called him Cooper, though."

Hattie giggled as Jackson carried her down the stairs. "I can walk just fine."

"Not on my watch," Jackson said. "It's our turn to wait hand and foot on you."

"Nobody said anything about breaking your back, though."

"Are you challenging my manliness?"

"Oh, dear," Hattie said. "Kelsey?"

"Quit making her blush," I said, laughing. "It's not nice."

Sara tugged on my pant leg. "Does Hattie really just have the flu?"

"Hattie's going to be just fine, little bug," I said, tweaking her nose. "Sometimes when you're older, it takes longer to get over viruses."

"Is there anything I can do?"

"Yes. You can go finish your schoolwork so you can play a game with her later when she's feeling up to it."

"What about me?" Nicholas asked.

"Well, I bet the dishwasher needs to be emptied, and the trash taken out."

Nicholas ran into the kitchen.

"That was way too easy," I whispered to Hattie. "How come they don't jump into action when I'm sick?"

Hattie looked at me and seemed confused. "You've never been sick, have you?"

"She gets sick," Wild Card said as he set a plate of cheese and crackers on the table. "She just downs a handful of pills and keeps going."

"Or passes out," Reggie said, laughing at me. "Remember when you fell onto that table of tomatoes at the grocery store? They rolled everywhere."

"When was that?" Wild Card asked.

"I didn't pass out. It was just a dizzy spell," I said, turning to Reggie. "Can you cut some cantaloupe for Hattie? I'd do it, but I need to check my email." When Reggie turned away, I looked directly at Wild Card. "It was around the same time I craved apple pies. I only had the *one* dizzy spell. It wasn't a big deal." Wild Card knew I was talking about when we were married, just before the divorce when I realized I was pregnant but didn't tell him.

I'd had years to deal with the miscarriage, but I hadn't confessed to him until last year. The day I found out I was pregnant had been the same day he'd brought home divorce papers. I should've told him, but I didn't. I left instead and had the miscarriage the week after.

I'd kept too many secrets, not just the pregnancy. Our marriage never stood a chance. I hadn't wanted it to. Not while I searched for my son. And I didn't trust Wild Card, or anyone else, enough to tell them about Nicholas. I didn't expect Wild Card to ever fully forgive me. I wouldn't have forgiven him if the roles were reversed.

Wild Card's jaw was locked tight, either in anger or frustration, I couldn't tell which. He stared at the platter of cheese and crackers, not looking over at me. After a long, silent moment, he nodded before walking out the back door onto the deck.

"Why did Wild Card leave?" Reggie asked, stepping out of the kitchen to look toward the door.

"Fruit does sound good," Hattie said. "I haven't had much of an appetite today."

Reggie glanced at the door again but went to the kitchen to cut up the fruit.

Jackson walked over and kissed the top of my head before following Wild Card outside.

"What are we working on, sunshine?" Hattie asked.

I turned my attention away from the sliding door to see Hattie pointing at my laptop and files.

"Everything and nothing, it seems. I haven't gotten much done today."

"Charlie emailed the basics on the Remirez family," Bridget said. "I didn't see anything useful, but they're still digging. Maggie emailed that Jack Tebbs is trying to get a copy of the files the DEA has on Santiago, as well as whatever they're willing to share about Sebrina."

"Sebrina? Isn't that the name of Grady's ex-girlfriend?" Hattie asked.

"The same," Bridget answered. "Sebrina... uh... *Tanner*."

"What?" I said, standing and looking at Bridget.

"I wondered if she'd changed her name," Shipwreck said, laying his forehead on the table. "Is it cocktail hour yet?"

"Are they still married?" I asked Shipwreck.

"This is getting good," Reggie said as he set several bowls of fruit on the table. "Tell us all the juicy bits."

"They divorced years ago," Shipwreck said to me before rolling his eyes at Reggie.

"See?" Bridget said. "At least it's not as bad as when you found out Bones was still married to Penny."

"You dated Bones, *too*?" Shipwreck asked.

I leaned over the table, glared at Shipwreck and yelled, "*Are you calling me a slut?*"

Wild Card ran into the room, followed by Tyler and Jackson. "I'm not sure what's going on, but Kelsey, let's take a walk."

I turned to glare at Wild Card. "*I don't want to take a walk!*"

"Oh, shit, she's pissed," Bridget said, moving closer to Hattie.

Jackson picked up Nicholas who I'd forgotten was sitting at the breakfast bar. Jackson held him, ready to run if needed.

"*Fricken...*" I started to say. "*Son of a...*" I fisted my hands, stomping a foot to the floor. "*Snapping turtle!*"

Wild Card almost held a straight face as I allowed him to push me toward, then out, the back sliding door.

I crossed the deck, snaring the pack of cigarettes that were lying on top of the rail. It took me five tries, but I finally got the cigarette lit. I paced back and forth, glancing into the yard and seeing several security guards watching me.

"*Mind your own business!*" I yelled.

They all turned their backs to me and pretended to be scanning the field.

"Damn. I haven't seen you this mad since I filled your boots with horse shit."

"As I recall, I filled your bed with cow shit as payback."

"Didn't say I got the upper hand," he said, stepping away and holding his hands up in surrender. "Why are you so mad?"

"Sebrina *Tanner*!"

Wild Card sighed, rubbing a hand down his face. "Shit. I was hoping Grady would be back when you figured that out."

"Why didn't *you* tell me!"

"I couldn't."

"*Why*? Cat got your tongue?"

"Damn it, Kelsey! Don't you think I wanted to tell you? That it's been eating at me?" He stepped a few feet away, fists clenched. "It's hard enough figuring out what you and I are to each other. Add to that juggling my relationship with Nicholas while trying to keep my damn mouth shut about you and Grady as a romantic couple! Grady and I used to be friends—*and it's just one big clusterfuck*!"

"What do you mean, *used to be*? You're still friends," I snapped.

"Are we, Kelsey?" he asked, walking over and looking down at me. "How can Grady and I be friends? How does that work when we're both in love with the same woman?"

"No, you're not," I said, turning away from Wild Card.

Wild Card grabbed my shoulders roughly, forcing me to turn and face him. I felt his anger as he held me, barely controlling his tightened grip on my shoulders. I was confused by his reaction, and then I saw it. I saw the truth I'd been hiding from. It was probably always there, but I'd been running from it. Wild Card *was* still in love with me. "Cooper..."

"*Don't*! I'm not stupid. I know how you feel about Grady. I'll do what I can to help you fix this, *but don't expect me stay after he wins you back*!" He walked across the deck and down the stairs.

I stood there, watching him retreat until he rounded the corner of the garage. "This cannot be my life," I said to myself.

"If it helps, I don't think you're a slut," Shipwreck said from the other end of the deck.

I walked over and threw myself into one of the deck loungers. I was quiet for a few minutes. Shipwreck sat in the lounger next to me, waiting for me to speak. I put out my cigarette before turning to face him. "Sorry I blew up at you. Makes total sense if you did think I was a slut. Hell, maybe I'm an accidental slut."

"Bridget explained that you didn't know Bones and Wild Card were friends when you started things with Bones. She also said the relationship with Grady happened after a lot of heavy shit went down."

"I've really fucked up," I said, staring at the place where Wild Card had disappeared from view. "I didn't even realize..."

"You know now," he said, shrugging. "From what I've seen in the last twenty-four hours, I'm surprised you can even remember your own name. I also get the feeling that the last twenty-four hours barely register on your life's disaster scale."

"Are you saying I'm a magnet for trouble?"

"Nope. You know what you're doing. This problem with the cartel wasn't your problem, but you took it on because it involved someone you cared about. The mess with your son, you ran that like a boss. It hurt. It got dirty. It got downright bloody, but you fought your ass off for him. You're not a magnet for trouble. You're a goddamn superhero. Superheroes need a personal life too, though. Make time for yours."

"I'll get right on that."

"Kelsey," Bridget called, opening the slider door. "Charlie's on the phone."

Shipwreck laughed. "Have Bridget pencil it in on your calendar." He got up and followed the route that Wild Card had taken.

"What am I supposed to put on your calendar?" Bridget asked as I walked toward her.

"Time to fix my personal life," I said as I took the phone.

Bridget bit her lip. "Maybe I can squeeze in a half an hour after dinner."

I rolled my eyes. "Hey, Kid."

"You in the middle of something?"

"Always."

"You okay?"

"Did you know Wild Card was still in love with me?"

"Everybody knows that."

"Shit."

"Do we have to talk about boys? I mean, I'm here if you need me, but I'm drowning in this quality cuddle-time crap. I've been secretly thinking of ways to set Kierson's house on fire—preferably while he's sleeping."

"I'm really glad I know you well enough to know that you'd never actually murder him."

"Okay. Maybe set the house on fire when he's at work."

"That sounds probable," I said, laughing lightly. "Speaking of Kierson, why were you two fighting about coffee creamer?"

"Don't get me started! How was I supposed to know that caramel vanilla creamer was the only kind he likes? The container said *coffee creamer*! And when he wouldn't let me throw it away because it was a waste of money—I showed him. *I drank it!*"

I laughed. "How sick did it make you?"

"Worst diarrhea of my life. My ass is still burning."

When I stopped laughing, I asked, "Any updates on our cocaine slinging cartel?"

"Lots. Did you read what I sent earlier?"

"Been trying to get to it, but I keep getting interrupted."

"Let's start with the brother: Miguel Remirez. He was the middle son out of three. He went to college in California and earned a Master's degree in Business Administration. He has extensive investments outside of the family's umbrella that are almost as lucrative as their illegal business."

"Interesting. What happened to the older brother?"

"The older brother died in a car bomb four years ago. His wife and child were in the car with him."

"Sucks. What about ma and pa Remirez?"

"Papa Bear died when Miguel was a teenager. Shot outside a village. Not many details were available except that two women were also killed. Both were reported to have been raped and tortured."

"Papa Bear was up to no good and someone put an end to him."

"That's the picture I was getting, yes."

"Mama Bear?"

"Committed suicide six months after Papa Bear died."

"Who raised them after their parents died?"

"Their uncle."

There was a long pause while I waited for her to say more but she was silent. "If you're going to make me beg, I'm hanging up."

"You're bitchy today." She paused again, likely waiting for me to laugh. When I didn't, she sighed and continued, "The uncle became their guardian. Rumor has it that he was even more brutal than his deceased brother, but when Miguel returned from college, suddenly the uncle disappeared. Shortly thereafter, Miguel started the legit businesses. He appointed Santiago as the face of the family cartel, but Miguel is still in charge. Santiago handles the daily activities of the cartel while Miguel grows the legitimate businesses. He's good, too. The way Miguel conquers one business after another reminds me of you ten years ago."

"I'm still in the game. I haven't retired."

"You're slowing down."

"I'm rich. I made *you* rich. I made your future unborn children rich. I'm allowed to slow down. You have nothing to bitch about."

She laughed. "As far as the uncle—"

"Yeah, yeah," I said, cutting her off. "One of the boys killed him. It doesn't take a profiler to figure that out. Which one of them did the deed, though?"

"Either one of them is capable. Santiago is almost textbook cartel crazy. Miguel is a calculating entrepreneur who'll do anything to succeed."

"When did Santiago and Miguel get married compared to the uncle's disappearance?"

"Ooh, let's see..." I could hear Charlie flipping through paper. "Says here that Santiago married a woman after he got her knocked up. It was a few months after the uncle disappeared. Miguel married..." I heard more pages being shuffled. "... a year to the day after his uncle disappeared."

"How much money did Miguel make that first year after his uncle disappeared?"

"Enough. He turned a hundred grand into a million in assets that first year. I doubt he slept."

"Bingo. Miguel was the one motivated to get his uncle out of the way."

"Does that help us?"

"It might. It depends on what the real story is between Sebrina and Santiago."

"If Tebbs manages to get his hands on Sebrina's file, it will be classified. They won't share it with me."

"Okay. Well, the information you dug up helps. I mean it. Good work."

"You're acting odd. Since when do we thank each other?"

"I'm not acting odd. You helped me. I said thank you. It's called being respectful."

"What's really going on?"

"I recently realized I'm an insensitive ass who needs to fix her personal life."

"Why? What's wrong with your personal life?"

"Rumor has it that Grady dumped me to get back together with his ex-wife Sebrina."

"I wouldn't believe whoever told you that rumor."

"It's kind of hard when the rumor came from Grady himself."

"What?"

"Yeah, I know. I'm dealing with it. He should actually be at Headquarters soon. I need to take care of a few things before he arrives."

"Do you need me? I can fly to Michigan."

"You're just trying to run from Kierson. You can't use me as an excuse to bail."

"You suck." She hung up on me as expected.

Chapter Twenty-One

I walked inside and looked at Nicholas. "I need you to read the book on your nightstand for a little while. I should be back in less than an hour."

"I don't like that book."

"You don't like *the cover* of the book. You'll like the story once you start reading it."

"Ah, man," he whined as he stomped toward his bedroom.

I whistled at the top of the basement stairs. Three Devil's Players appeared. "I need a volunteer to babysit for me. One hour, tops."

A guy named Farmer climbed the stairs and looked around. I hadn't spent a lot of time with Farmer, but he was a friend of Whiskey's.

"My son occasionally has exploding temper tantrums. They're rare, but if you can hang out in here until I get back, I'd appreciate it."

"Where is he?"

"In his room reading *Treasure Island*," I said, pointing down the hall.

"Great book," Farmer said as he moved over to the couch and sat.

I looked at Alex and then at Hattie.

"We'll be fine, sunshine. Farmer and I are acquainted. We share an interest in botany."

"That's plants, right?"

"Yes."

"Like ferns?" I said, trying to figure out the shared interest.

"Sure, dear."

I shook my head. "Come on, Bridget. I need your special set of skills."

"Happy to be of service. This body wasn't made to sit behind a computer all day."

I grabbed the keys from the kitchen hook and handed them to Bridget. We both knew she was a better driver than me. She walked around the SUV as I slid into the passenger seat.

"Do you know where Tech keeps all his spy craft toys?" I asked.

"He thinks I don't, but yeah, bottom drawer of the file cabinet has the good stuff." She backed out of the garage. "What's the plan?"

"I need both Grady and Sebrina's rooms bugged. The problem is, I don't which rooms were assigned to them and we can't ask or they'll figure out what we're doing. I hate putting everyone in a position of betraying Grady."

Bridget had backed out into the road but hadn't changed the SUV gear out of reverse. "I have an idea. Call Lisa."

"Shit. I was supposed to call her hours ago about Abigail."

As I called Lisa, Bridget reversed further down the road and then pulled into Lisa's driveway.

Lisa answered her phone.

"Hey. I forgot to call you earlier. We moved Abigail to my house. The nanny, too."

"Alex called and told me. He said you had a lot going on and would likely forget."

"Sorry."

"All good. Covering for each other is what we do. As long as my daughter is safe, I'm happy."

"Great. Now I need to hand the phone to Bridget."

Bridget took the phone, placing it up to her ear. "Hey, Lisa. I'm going to run inside your house and steal a few sets of new sheets. They're for a project Kelsey's working on."

She *uh-huh*'d a few times, paused for a long moment while she listened to Lisa, then *uh-huh*'d a few more times.

"Cool thanks." She ended the call and handed me back my phone.

"What are we doing?"

"The guys all bitch about the cheap sheets Jerry bought for the apartments. Lisa has a stockpile of new sheets. We'll say we're putting better sheets in Grady and Sebrina's rooms."

"Everyone will think I'm nuts if I put nicer sheets in Grady and Sebrina's room. I'm more likely to leave spiders in their sheets."

"I know," she said, climbing out of the car. "I'll be back in a minute."

I watched Bridget pick the lock on Lisa's door, followed by entering the code into the alarm panel. A few minutes later, she jogged out carrying a pile of nicely folded sheets. She pulled a set of keys from her pocket and relocked the door.

"If you had the key, why did you pick the lock?" I asked her when she got back into the SUV.

"Practice."

I shook my head, refocusing my thoughts. "We need to work on this story before we go over to Headquarters."

"No, we don't. It's a good story." She reversed the SUV back onto the road. "You just can't participate."

I narrowed my eyes at her. "Where exactly will I be?"

"You'll be covering for Lisa in the Bridal Room. Tech is prepping the equipment we need. Lisa will storm into Jerry's office, insist he let us into the apartments, and then help me set the spy equipment. It will work because everyone knows Lisa's crazy when it comes to things being *just so*."

"How do Lisa and Tech already know what we're up to?"

"As soon as you moved the kids out of Headquarters, everyone was waiting to see what you'd do next. Lisa guessed that you wanted the rooms bugged and asked if she should have Tech get the equipment ready. After I said uh-huh, she told me I had to be the one to tell you that she'd be going in your place."

"It's a good plan," I admitted, turning in my seat to grin at Bridget. "But Anne will need to go with Lisa. I'll cover Menswear for Anne while you cover Bridalwear."

"Why is that better?" she asked as she pulled into the parking lot of The Changing Room.

"Everyone knows you're my devious sidekick. No way would you help put nice sheets on Grady's bed."

"Damn it." She pulled into the handicapped spot in front of the store, leaving the SUV running. "I was really looking forward to being devious."

"Sorry. But if I can't go, you can't go."

"Rock, paper, scissors for Menswear," she said, turning in her seat and holding her hands out.

We counted out to three and looked at our hands. I had paper. She had scissors.

"Two out of three," I said, ready to go again.

"Hell no!" she laughed, climbing out of the SUV.

"Damn it. I hate bridezillas!" I yelled as I jogged toward Bridalwear.

Inside, Lisa gave me the thirty second update on the customers. I gave her the ten second update that Anne was going in Bridget's place. Lisa ran out of the store as I greeted the bride who was standing in front of the mirrors.

"This is it. This is the dress!" she squealed.

"Really?" I asked.

Five heads swiveled almost demonically in my directions, piercing me with glares.

"Yes, I see it now," I said, taking a step back, then another. "You look lovely." I quickly walked around the counter and stood behind it for my own safety. Maxine, Lisa's sales assistant, smirked as she helped the bride back to the dressing room.

"Do you have this dress in a size six?" a woman asked from the other side of the room.

"We might have something similar, but this is a resale store, so no."

"Could you order a size six?"

I looked at her, then looked at her friends and family who were all eagerly awaiting my reply. "Uh, no."

"The people here are so rude," the bride said, putting the dress back on the rack and storming out.

The bride from earlier marched out of the dressing room and stopped in front of me. "What did you mean when you said *really*?"

Her friends and family shook their heads back and forth so fast I thought they'd injure themselves. I looked back at the bride. "I cannot lie. You look horrible in that dress. Your boobs are too small and your ass is too big for an A-frame dress. Anything but an A-frame would look good, but you picked the one design that makes you look like a white fluffy triangle."

The bride's mouth dropped open as she stared back at me. A moment later she ran toward the dressing room, stripping the gown off before she made it to the curtained area. In less than thirty seconds, she ran past her friends and family and out the door while still carrying her shirt and shoes.

"Who's next?" I called out.

"That dress really did look horrible on her," a mother of another bride whispered loud enough for everyone in the store to hear. "Oh, darling, you look beautiful!" she said as her daughter exited the dressing room.

"Really?" I asked.

"*Out!*" Maxine yelled, pointing toward the door. "*Lisa is going to have my head.* Just leave!"

"I can go?" I asked, grinning.

"OUT!"

"I'm going. I'm going." I ran out the door, past the main store entrance, and into the Menswear department. "Ah, ha!" I said, jumping into the store.

Several men turned to look at me like I was crazy.

"Why aren't you in Bridalwear?" Bridget asked with a fist on her hips.

Katie walked through the side entrance that connected the front of the stores.

"Maxine kicked me out!" I couldn't contain my smile.

"Wouldn't have anything to do with multiple brides crying in the parking lot, would it?" Katie asked.

"Maybe."

Katie and Bridget continued to stare at me.

"It's not my fault! She had no boobs, a big ass, and picked an A-frame dress!"

"Oh, that's different," Bridget said as she took the clothes away from one guy and replaced them with the ones she was holding. "Good call on stopping that mistake."

"And the other bride?" Katie asked.

I took the purple shirt the guy next to me was holding and handed it to the guy behind me. Then I took his silver shirt and handed it to the first guy. "She asked if we carried the dress she liked in a size six. If you're a size six, you should shop the rack that's clearly marked size six. You can even go to the higher sizes and have alterations. What you don't do, is shop the rack that says size four." At the tie rack, I selected ties for each of the men, handing them over. "Am I right, guys?"

"Makes sense to me," the one guy said.

"I don't get it," the other guy said.

I pointed out the window to the size six bridal group. "You must be related to them."

He looked out the window and smiled. "Yes. My daughter's the bride. How'd you know?"

"That's wonderful," Katie said as she steered the man out of the room. "We have a special today for fathers-of-the-bride only. *Yay, for you!*"

"I kind of get why you were kicked out of the Bridalwear," one of the men said, grinning. "Will they fire you?"

"Nope. I own the place," I said as I picked out two more shirts for him and a pair of pants.

His smile widened as he looked around. "Maybe we should make plans to meet up for a few drinks when you're done today."

"That's very brave of you," Wild Card said from behind me. "You'd have to get in line, though." He walked around me, closer to the man as he crossed his arms over his chest. "It's a long line, too."

"Not funny," I said, walking over to straighten out another customer who had all the wrong merchandise picked out. "Why are you here?" I asked Wild Card.

"I was looking for the two of you. Figured you were here covering for Lisa and Anne while they were doing your dirty work. Are you aware that several women are crying in the parking lot?"

"They're still out there?" I asked, walking over to the window. "Damn it. I need to get rid of them before Lisa gets back."

"You can't shoot them," Wild Card said as he followed me out the door.

"Both of you!" I yelled at the brides, pointing at them. "Come back inside."

They both glared.

"*Now*!"

They both scurried back inside the store. I looked at the first girl and then at the size six rack. I flipped through the dresses and found one that would work.

"Take your shirt off," I said as I unzipped the dress.

"What?"

"*Shirt. Off. Now.* I don't have all day."

She pulled her shirt over her head and I dropped the dress in its place before zipping it up.

"Turn."

"What?"

"*Turn*!" the bridal party yelled at her.

"Now listen to me. I don't bullshit people. That dress looks great on you. If you want to spend the next three months shopping for a dress—whatever—but don't bitch at us later when you realize you missed out."

She looked at herself in the mirror, her eyes starting to water. "I'll buy it."

"Great. Maxine, can you help her box it?" I didn't wait for Maxine to answer. I turned to the other bride instead. "Having a big ass can be a good thing. Your husband to-be wouldn't be marrying you if he didn't like your body. Let's find something more 'fit and flare' to show off that golden rump. Take off your shirt."

She removed her shirt and leaned over for me to drop a dress over her. I held the front in place while her friend zipped her in.

"Damn, girl. She's right. Your ass looks great in this dress," her friend said.

"The lace detail in the bodice is beautiful, too," her mother said.

"Go to the mirror and take a look," I said.

"Maybe if you go to spin class a few more times a week, it will look good," another woman said.

"Mother of the groom?" I asked the bride to be.

Tears pooled in the girl's eyes as she nodded.

"Does your groom share her opinion? That you need to take more spin classes?"

She nodded again.

"Here's my advice."

"Oh, boy," Wild Card said from where he was leaning against the far wall. Maxine inhaled sharply, her head swiveling my direction as she handed the first bride a receipt.

I ignored them and focused on the bride. "Buy the dress, dump the guy, and find a man who will love that ass."

"And there it is," Wild Card said, laughing.

The bride looked over at him. "Is she crazy?"

"Definitely," Wild Card said. "Doesn't mean I don't agree with her. You have a great ass. If your guy can't appreciate it, find someone who does."

"I agree," her friend said.

"Me too," her mother said. "The dress is perfect for you. Roger is not."

"You should be grateful my son even wants to marry you," the mother of the groom scolded.

The bride looked at her, threw her shoulders back and raised her chin to the woman. "If the choice is Roger or this dress, the dress wins."

Her friends cheered and her mother clapped. The mother of the groom pivoted and walked out of the store, fuming.

"My work here is done," I said to Wild Card.

Lisa was almost to the door when I walked out of the store. "How'd it go?"

"Great! I sold two dresses!"

"Really?" Lisa asked with a raised eyebrow.

I decided it was best to change the subject. "How'd the sheet changing mission go?"

"It was a snap. Jerry practically ran to let me inside their rooms. Let me know if you need anything else."

Wild Card laughed, taking the keys from Lisa. As he got behind the wheel of the SUV, I climbed into the backseat.

Bridget came out of Menswear and jumped into the front passenger seat. "Did they say *Yes to the Dress*?" she sing-sang.

"Yup. Both of them."

"One of them is no longer getting married, but she's still buying the dress," Wild Card said, laughing.

"You broke up an engagement?" Bridget asked, turning in her seat to face me. "How is that even possible in such a short amount of time?"

"Roger and his mother want the bride to lose weight for the wedding."

"Oh. Well, then, good riddance, Roger."

"Exactly. I'm all for losing weight to be healthy, but not for a man."

Wild Card had an odd expression, a slow grin appearing.

"Whatever you're thinking, just stop thinking it."

His smile widened.

"Good grief. What time is it?"

"Almost time to confront Grady," Wild Card said. "Jackson is at the airport picking them up. Sebrina's awake. Grady's starting to stir. Jackson plans on driving fast."

"I promised Farmer I'd be back in less than an hour."

"Which one is Farmer?" Wild Card asked.

"The one with the marijuana tattoo on his bicep," Bridget said.

"Yeah, I know which one now," Wild Card said, nodding. "The big guy with the black hair. He's a nice guy. Kind of quiet." Wild Card looked at me in the rearview mirror. "I'll keep Nicholas at the house while you deal with Grady. Best if I keep my distance since I still want to punch Grady for the shit he pulled with Nick."

"Do you know what you're going to say?" Bridget asked, looking back at me again.

"No clue. My big plan was to wing it and hope they don't have me arrested for kidnapping."

Wild Card laughed.

Chapter Twenty-Two

When we pulled in front of the house Wild Card got out and Tyler claimed the driver's seat. The back doors of the SUV opened and Shipwreck climbed in on my right and Tech on my left.

"I don't need an escort."

"Team Kelsey, remember?" Bridget said, giggling.

"I'm not Team Kelsey nor Team Grady on this one," Shipwreck said. "I just thought it would be fun."

I looked at Tech, waiting to hear his excuse.

"What?" Tech said, grinning. "Katie kicked me out of the store. She said I was annoying her."

"Everything annoys Katie."

"What's the plan?" Tech asked.

"I'll calmly explain to Grady and Sebrina that they need to stay at Silver Aces until the situation with Santiago is resolved. That's it. Nothing more."

Tyler and Bridget laughed from the front seat. Shipwreck started humming. Tech shook his head.

Outside Headquarters, Shipwreck left us, heading toward the building entrance. Donovan was already outside, making a beeline for us, but paused to do some kind of hand-clap-shake-shoulder-bump maneuver with Shipwreck before he continued our way.

"You should've warned me," Donovan said, shaking his head. "He's pissed."

"I figured it would be easier if you had plausible deniability."

Donovan nodded in agreement as he looked back at the building's doors. "Bones isn't faring as well. Grady's ready to tear his head off."

"I can handle Grady. What's Sebrina's mood?"

"Drama is sort-of her forte. She's enjoying the scene."

"I can work with that."

Donovan cringed. "I'm sorry I didn't tell you about Sebrina."

"I know you, Donovan. You would've pestered Grady to tell me about her. You would've predicted it biting him in the ass."

"If I would've guessed he'd get back together with the bitch, I never would've kept his secret."

"That's the least of my worries at the moment. First task, convince them to stay."

"And then?"

"We deal with Santiago and end the threat," I said, walking toward the doors.

"You make it sound simple. Mechanical," Donovan said, holding the door open.

"It's not, but one task at a time."

We heard the yelling when we entered the building. Walking into the gym, I was happy to see almost everyone at Aces had gathered to witness the showdown. I wasn't sure who was on which side, or if there were more than just two sides, but the more public this conversation was, the greater my chances were of getting Grady to stay.

Grady was standing in Bones' personal space, screaming up at him and shoving him with his one good arm. His other arm was in a sling with heavy bandages around his shoulder. Trigger, Pops, Jackson, and Whiskey had been standing by the gym doors and joined my pack as I walked to the center of the room.

"Enough! Bones didn't order this—I did."

"I'm well aware they were following *your orders*!" Grady yelled in my face.

Sebrina stood off to the side. Her smile ticked up a notch as she chuckled silently.

"Your discharge papers said you needed plenty of rest," I said to Grady, shrugging. "I was making sure you followed doctor's orders."

"And then what? Are you going to have them lock me in the basement?"

"Don't be silly," I said, rolling my eyes.

"*I'm leaving*! I told you, we're *done*! Jealous, *psycho bitch* isn't a good look on you, Kelsey."

"Jealous? Of her?" I asked as I looked at Sebrina openly.

Her black silky hair accented her almond skin. Her figure was slim and sensual, and her clothes accented her curves. In almost all accounts, she was a classic beauty. The tiny lines around her mouth from pursing her lips and her narrowed eyes piled full of hate were too obvious to be ignored, though.

"I'm not jealous, Grady," I said, shaking my head. "I'm sure you wish it were that simple, but you should know by now that I'm not that girl."

I stepped away from him, looking around the gym and focusing to keep my emotions under control.

"What I am—is *pissed*. Maybe a dash of confused and hurt as well, but *pissed* is the emotion beating the others by a long shot."

Grady growled, taking a step away from the pack, closer to me. "You have no right to be pissed at me. You're the one who refused to get married."

"You think I'm pissed because you dumped me? Do you know me at all? Do you not get that the first priority in my life *is* and *will always be—my son*?"

Whiskey stepped closer to me and placed a hand on my shoulder. I knew he was cautioning me to calm down. I nodded, stepping away again and breathing through my anger. When I felt I had it bottled again, I walked back to Grady, standing directly in front of him.

"You hurt Nicholas. Abandoning him over the phone like you did sent him over the edge. It was bad. I didn't even recognize him, he was so angry. I had to pull him from school for Sara and Beth's safety. He has to be guarded—*to keep other people safe*. My son. My sweet little boy is a danger to others." I took off my leather jacket and passed it to Bridget. Taking a step closer to Grady, I held up my swollen and bruised arm. "He threw a chair at me, Grady. My nine-year-old son threw a fucking chair across the room at me."

Grady went to reach for my arm, but I stepped away.

"You tore his heart out and then hung up on him like he meant nothing to you."

Grady sighed, looking down at the floor. "I didn't mean to hurt Nick. I'll talk to him. Explain it better."

"No," Pops said, stepping beside me. "You won't."

"Pops is right," I said, placing a hand on Pops' arm to keep him at bay. "You won't go near my son, Grady. Or Sara or Abigail. You lost my trust. They've been moved out of Headquarters, and you're no longer welcome in my home."

Grady stepped away, continuing the physical dance between us. "You have a funny way of kicking me out. You drugged me and flew me across the country against my will. What was the point? To collect my things? To tell me what a horrible person I am?"

I held up my index finger, indicating for Grady to wait. "Pops, head to the house. Hattie's awake, and I know she's anxious to see you."

"You sure, baby girl?" Pops asked, not looking at me as he glared at Grady. "She'll understand if you need me to stay."

"I'm sure."

Pops kissed the top of my head before jogging out of the gym.

I turned back to Grady. "You may continue your rant now."

"What the hell was that about?" Grady asked, waving a hand toward the doors.

"You ended our relationship, remember? My family business is no longer your concern."

"If that's the case, then why the hell am I here? What the hell were you thinking having me drugged and shipped back to Michigan?"

"I seem to recall you drugged me against my will not too long ago."

"That was different. I did that to protect you from yourself."

"Which is exactly what I did today. Even if you can't put that together yet." I pulled a set of keys from my pocket and tossed them to him. "Your belongings were already moved into one of the apartments. A room was arranged for Sebrina as well. Sort the sleeping arrangements as you please. I don't give a shit. What I do care about, is the men and women in this building and those across the street."

Grady looked at the keys in his hand, then looked back at me. There was a hint of something in his eyes. Pain? Regret? I wasn't sure. "Why am I here?"

"To keep your promise. You used to be a man of your word. Are you still that man? Or has Sebrina stripped you of your honor, too?"

"Leave Sebrina out of this," he snapped, stepping into my space again. "This is between you and me."

"No, Grady. You're wrong. You and your team made choices that impact everyone." I walked toward the men of Aces, standing in front of them. "We have a cartel coming after us because of those choices. Four of us were kidnapped yesterday. Tweedle had a Glock pointed at her head." I turned toward the side, looking back at Ryan and Tweedle. "Are you going to stand here in front of Ryan and tell him he's on his own to protect his wife?" I walked over to Donovan and motioned with my thumb at him. "What if they get to Donovan's daughter? Is that his problem to deal with too?"

Grady looked to Ryan then to Donovan. I could see the indecision.

"I had you drugged and dragged home for one reason—to ask if you were man enough to stay and help us protect everyone until I can eliminate the threat." I walked back to Grady. "It's your decision, though. I can't make you do the right thing."

I walked away, dry eyed and calm. What I didn't expect was that everyone would follow me. Not just Tech, Bridget, Trigger—those known as being Team Kelsey—but all the men of Aces as well. I'm not sure if they even knew why they were following me or what it meant. What it would mean to Grady.

"Will he stay?" Wayne asked when we reached the parking lot.

"I think so."

"Sebrina?" Donovan asked.

"She'll stay if he stays."

"What's the plan?" Ryan asked, snaking an arm around Tweedle. "I need my wife kept safe."

"I have people digging into the cartel," I said as I watched the front doors open and Grady walk out holding Sebrina's hand. I didn't say anything else, waiting instead until they crossed the lot.

"We'll stay," Grady said, stopping to stand beside Bones. "Only until the threat with Santiago is over, but we'll stay until then."

"Good. We could use your help. I have one rule, though, and it's nonnegotiable. You and Sebrina are not to cross that highway," I said, pointing to the busy road. "Aces will continue to secure this side of the highway. Tyler will continue to lead the security for the store and houses."

Tyler walked over and stood beside me, directly across from Grady.

"Tyler?" I said.

"Yeah," he said without looking away from Grady.

"If Sebrina or Grady cross over onto my property—for any reason—your orders are to shoot them."

"Understood," he said between clenched teeth.

Sebrina laughed lightly, turning her eyes to me. "What did I do to earn such disregard?"

"Why is Santiago obsessed with you?" I asked, stepping in front of her to study her reaction. "Why does he want you so badly?"

"I'm a DEA agent building a case against him. We're natural enemies."

"That's funny. His men had a different story."

I watched a flicker of something cross her face, but it vanished too quickly for me to identify the emotion.

She leaned into Grady, rubbing her breast against his arm. "I have no idea what crazy stories Santiago has told his men. I only hope that we can put him in the ground before he gets to me again."

Grady raised a hand and caressed her cheek. It was an action he'd done a million times with me. Sebrina spotted my unease and watched me as she turned her face into his hand to kiss his palm.

"Kelsey?" Donovan called out. "What do we know about the cartel?"

I turned away, walking out of the circle, feeling the need to gain some personal space.

"Santiago *is crazy*. My sources confirmed that. He also has a network of drug smugglers across the country who he calls upon to complete tasks such as the kidnapping that occurred yesterday."

"Are the kidnappers dead?" Sebrina asked.

I ignored her question. "Santiago has a daughter in Arizona. She broke ties with her father, but if we push the wrong buttons, he may have her dragged against her will across the border. I've assigned some guys to keep an eye on her for her safety. We won't use her against Santiago, though. She's innocent."

"Should I ask the FBI to put her in a safe house?" Donovan asked.

"No. If we have to move her, she'll go to one of *my* safe houses. I might be being paranoid, but I sure as hell didn't like how fast Santiago's men found Shipwreck's place in Mexico. Shipwreck had operated under the radar for years with no issues. Someone tipped him off."

Several men glanced at Sebrina.

"Why would I have tipped Santiago off?" she asked, looking at the men. "He held me hostage and had me beaten."

"I don't see any bruises," Ryan said, moving Tweedle to stand behind him.

Sebrina lifted her shirt and showed a single bruise the size of a fist under her right ribcage. Turning her head upward, we could see a fading bruise on her neck. No one said anything, but I was sure we were all thinking the same thing: the bruises looked staged. Why though? What was her objective?

"Sebrina was kept in a shed—*chained to a wall*!" Grady yelled. "She was starved of food and water and forced to watch two women beaten to death."

"If you say so," I said, sighing dramatically.

Several of the guys chuckled quietly.

Wayne cleared his throat. "Does Santiago ever travel to the States, or will we have to take him out in Mexico?"

"Take him out?" Tweedle whispered to Ryan. "He means, kill him, right?"

Ryan shrugged, but didn't say anything, waiting for me to answer Wayne's question.

"He seldom comes to the States, but he might this time. He wants Sebrina. He's obsessed with her. If his men keep disappearing, he might make the trip to supervise the situation himself."

"How many men were involved in the kidnapping yesterday?" Grady asked.

"Eight."

"And were all of them..." he looked at Sebrina and then back at me, "punished? Or did some of them escape?"

"All eight were *punished*," I answered.

Grady knew if I was unwilling to tell Sebrina what happened to the men, then I had a reason. He played along so he could get at least a few answers to his questions.

"What else do you know?" Sebrina asked.

"Nothing else I'm willing to share. Those who need to know, will be updated as needed. You're not on that list."

"I'm a DEA agent."

"You're a guest of Silver Aces until I say otherwise."

"You're not in charge of Silver Aces," Grady hissed.

"No," Donovan said to Grady. "If it comes to it though, she'll have my vote to have you both removed. Kelsey won't risk the safety of her family, including my wife and daughter. If she feels either of you are a threat, I'll back her decision."

"Some brother you turned out to be," Grady said.

"What would you have him do?" Bones asked. "Risk his men and his family because you're in *love*? It's not that simple, man, and you know it. We've all got people we need to protect."

"Maybe it's best if we leave then?" Grady said.

"Are we really back to you abandoning us all to clean up your shit?" Wayne asked. "Damn, man. That woman has you fucked in the head."

Grady charged at Wayne, but Donovan, Ryan, and Bones blocked his path with a wall of solid muscles. Even if Grady wasn't injured, he'd never be able to take them all on.

"*This is bullshit*," he growled, moving away and pacing.

Sebrina walked over to him and rubbed her hands up and down his chest, calming him. He looped an arm around her, tucking her into his body.

"What about the tournament?" Donovan asked me.

"Cancel it," Grady answered.

"The tournament is still a go," I said. "All the festivities are a go unless something else happens. We can't live the job twenty-four seven and expect to stay sane. Most of us need the tournament weekend to regain our sanity. I'm not taking that away from anyone unless it becomes a safety concern."

"We have a few guys bringing clients," Wayne said. "What about them? We can't put clients in danger."

"Get the files of the clients. You, Donovan, and I will decide together what to do."

"I'm still a partner!" Grady yelled.

"*I don't give a fuck*!" I yelled back.

Donovan walked over, placing his hands on my shoulders and walking me backward away from Grady. "Breathe, little dragon."

"We have another issue that needs to be settled for security purposes," Bridget said.

Donovan wrapped an arm around my shoulders while we looked back at Bridget.

She looked about the crowd of men and women. "Donovan, Wayne, Ryan, Jackson, and Bones, we need to talk about whether you'll be allowed on the other side of the street. Everyone else, stay on this side. Our security team will be closed for visitors."

"I'm not allowed to cross?" Shipwreck asked.

"Sorry, but no," Bridget answered. "No offense, but we only met you yesterday."

"Kelsey trusts me enough to build me a bar."

Bridget laughed. "That's just money. She's got a lot of it to spare."

Jackson crossed his arms over his chest, glaring between Bridget and me. "Don't sweat it, Shipwreck. The rest of us are practically family, but we're on the *maybe* list?"

"Did you hear Kelsey's orders?" Donovan asked Jackson. "She ordered Tyler to *shoot* Grady or Sebrina if they cross onto her property." He looked around at the men. "How many of you are willing to pull the trigger if it comes to that? That's the question being asked of you if you want permission to cross the road."

The men looked away, almost tormented by the thought. Bones reached out and grabbed Bridget's hand, kissing her knuckles before intertwining their fingers as he led her over to stand behind me. "Don't cross the highway, Grady. I don't want to shoot you, brother, but I will."

Donovan crossed his arms over his chest and nodded at Grady. "I will, too. I'll hate myself, but I'll do it."

"I can't believe this is happening," Grady said, running his free hand through his hair.

Wayne stepped forward, standing beside Grady. "Kelsey, I'd give my life for you or your family. Most of us would. I don't have it in me to shoot Grady, though. Not even if he held a gun to my head. I'll honor your wishes and stay on this side of the highway."

"Your honesty is appreciated. No hard feelings," I said.

Tweedle walked over, leaving Ryan and standing beside me.

"Babe," Ryan said, slowly shaking his head. "What are you doing?"

Tweedle shrugged. "While you were gone, Kelsey saved me from being shot and also stopped me from being decapitated. If the price to pay is shooting two people I don't know, I'll pay it."

"Do you even know how to shoot?" I asked her.

"My uncle's a cop. He taught me how to shoot and makes me go to the firing range twice a year," she answered, nodding. "He just doesn't let me walk with a loaded gun."

Ryan sighed, placing his hands on his hips and looking at the parking lot.

"When Tweedle visits, we'll protect her like she's one of our own," I said to Ryan. "Donovan or Bones will escort her back and forth as needed. There's no reason for you to commit to something we both know you can't do."

"Grady saved my life more than once overseas. I can't do it. I can't agree to shooting him."

"He did?" Tweedle asked, looking over at Grady with appreciation. "I didn't know that."

"Relax, Tweedle," Bridget said, grinning. "No one is dumb enough to hand you a loaded gun. You'd never be put in a position to shoot Grady."

She giggled. "Whew. That's a relief."

"Wait—" Ryan said. "How were you almost decapitated? And why don't I know about this?"

"Ryan, dude, you don't want that mental image," Bridget said before looking over at Jackson. "Jackson? Where do you stand?"

Jackson glared at me. "What about Reggie?"

"Reggie doesn't get a vote," I said, shaking my head. "He goes where you go. Even if he fired a gun, it's likely he'd miss."

Several of the guys chuckled.

"Are you really making me decide?" Jackson walked within a few feet of me. The veins in his biceps threatened to break through the skin as he gripped his fists in tight knots. "You've called me your *brother* for years, and this is what it comes down to? *Fuck you, Kelsey!*" Jackson stormed toward Headquarters, followed by Wayne and several others.

"What about me?" Trigger asked.

"You're on this side of the highway," I answered. "Sorry, Trigger. We haven't worked together long enough for me to allow you to cross."

"I've shot three people with tranquilizer guns on this side! I did it because you *ordered* me to!"

"Are you worried about retaliation, my friend?" Casey asked, throwing an arm over his shoulder. "Relax. We've all done shit because of orders. No one will hold it against you."

"Wanna bet?" Grady said, glaring over at Trigger.

"He's off limits, Grady," Donovan ordered. "He's still an employee."

Grady shrugged, not committing to anything.

I doubted Grady would actually go after Trigger. He preferred intimidation over beat-downs. This new Grady was a stranger to me, though.

"Donovan, I need a private word," I said, walking away from those who remained.

Donovan followed me away from the crowd until I was sure we wouldn't be overheard.

"Shit. That was intense," Donovan whispered. "I hope you have a plan to fix this mess."

"I have several. We can discuss in more detail later. We'll meet at your house after dinner."

"Why not your house?"

"The seams of my house are ready to burst. It's now the school, the nursery, and my office. Your house is better. Fewer ears. We'll meet in your basement."

"What do you need until then?"

"Go through the client files with Wayne and turn everyone away except for a minor actress by the name of Daphne Davenport. We'll keep her safe, but I plan on exposing her lies this weekend."

"What is she lying about?"

"I think she invented her stalker for the attention."

Donovan shook his head, perplexed by the concept. "What the hell. I'll play along."

"Deal. I best get going before Grady starts round three."

"Pops took your car, so take mine. I'll walk or get a ride." He handed me his keys.

"Watch out for vans filled with armed men if you walk."

Donovan looked over his shoulder at the road. "Oh, hell, yeah. I'll definitely walk home."

I made my way toward Donovan's SUV and whistled, getting Bridget, Tech, and Tyler's attention and nodding toward Donovan's ride.

"Kelsey," Grady called out. "Can you give me a minute?"

He motioned for Sebrina to wait before he jogged over to me. I secretly hoped he'd tell me it was all a lie or that I'd misunderstood. The hard set of his jaw and cold glare of his eyes told me that wasn't the case.

"Make it quick. I need to get home."

"I want to see Nicholas."

"No."

"Just let me talk to him."

"No."

I climbed inside Donovan's SUV and closed the door, turning over the engine. Grady started yelling at me through the closed window. Bridget got into the front passenger seat and turned the radio to the highest level. Tyler and Tech slid into the backseat. I pulled out, leaving Grady in the parking lot still screaming.

Chapter Twenty-Three

"What day is it?" I asked as I pulled into the garage.

"Thursday," Tyler answered. "And, no, you didn't forget to make dinner. I asked Lisa to cover for you tonight."

"See what I mean about us being a good team?" I said, grinning at him in the mirror.

Tyler smirked back at me. "Figured you had enough on your plate."

"Which reminds me," I said, sighing. "I might've caved about Nicholas getting a dog. Can you talk to Beth about buying a guard dog? Seeing Storm in action the last few days has swayed my vote."

"Agreed," Bridget said. "Watching Storm sink his teeth into the guy who tried to take Beth was—*awesome*!"

"I'll talk to Beth," Tyler said. "And Nightcrawler. He mentioned he's worked with guard dogs before."

"Sounds good, but let's keep it quiet until we find out the details. Nicholas can't handle any more disappointment right now. I also don't want him to think I'm replacing Grady with a dog."

"Even if you are?" Bridget asked.

"I'm not," I said, shaking my head. "It's about protection, companionship, and teaching Nicholas responsibility by caring for a pet."

Reggie opened the kitchen door and looked out at us. "Are you guys getting out of the car?"

I climbed out. "Reg, we need to talk."

"What's up?" he asked as he walked out and closed the door behind him.

"If you have any belongings here, you need to get them. You're being relocated to Headquarters. Only

Bones, Donovan, Wild Card, and Tweedle will be allowed on this side of the highway until we sort out the current cartel threat."

"I don't understand. You think I might be a mole?"

"No, but the decision was made that only those who are willing to shoot Grady or Sebrina can stay on our side. Jackson refused to agree, and the two of you are a package deal."

"*You're kicking me out?*" Reggie asked, his voice escalating three notches higher than normal.

"Yes."

"Is this about charging the plane to go to Indiana?"

"No. This is about the security of my family," I said, stepping closer to him and placing my hands on his shoulders. "This doesn't change how I feel about you."

"I don't understand."

"You just need to trust me, Reggie. Can you do that?"

His eyes showed how betrayed he felt, but he nodded.

"Do you need to grab anything?" Tyler asked him. "I can give you a lift back across the highway."

"No. My stuff's in Jackson's apartment," Reggie answered, taking Bridget's place in the front seat.

I passed the keys to Tyler before walking into the house. I couldn't wait for this day to be over.

Entering, my spirits brightened on hearing the kids laughing. I followed the noise past Lisa and Beth, who were in the kitchen making dinner, and leaned against the wall in the living room. Anne rolled the dice and groaned as the kids laughed again. They were playing Monopoly. Hattie and Anne sat on the floor, leaning against the couch. Whiskey and Pops sat on the couch behind them, laughing. Wild Card sat on the floor on an oversized pillow at the end of the rectangular coffee table, reaching over to snag the dice. The kids sat on the floor across from Anne and Hattie, cheering Wild Card on as he dropped the dice onto the board.

"*Yes*," Wild Card said as he moved the shoe around the board and landed on the community chest square. He drew his card and flashed it around to show everyone. "Collect a hundred dollars!"

Pops checked the card and then, serving as the banker, paid Wild Card. Wild Card glanced over at me and winked before handing the dice to Nicholas.

Nicholas didn't fare as well, landing on one of Anne's properties, but he was laughing as he paid her. Looking at the measly few fake dollars she had in front of her, she'd likely be out of the game soon. I smiled before turning back toward the kitchen and then down the basement stairs, sneaking out of sight before the kids saw me.

At the bottom of the stairs, I checked to see if anyone was sleeping on the bunk beds but the room was empty. I walked to the far corner and stepped behind the bar, pulling out several bottles before deciding on an expensive cognac that Mickey McNabe had sent me as a gift. I turned, selecting a brandy snifter glass from the hanging rack on the wall.

"Grab a glass for me, too," Katie said as she walked through the patio sliding door.

"I didn't know you drank cognac," I said, pulling another glass and pouring us both a drink.

"Never tried it." She slid onto a barstool and smelled the alcohol before taking a sip. "Damn. That's smooth."

I walked around the bar and slid on top of my own barstool. "How'd you know I was down here?"

"Tech texted me to check in with you," Katie said. "Want to talk about it?"

"About what?"

"Whatever horrible thing is weighing you down, making you feel the need to hide in the basement."

"Who says I'm hiding?"

"Aren't you?"

I took another small sip before shaking my head. "I have everything I can't control properly locked away in my head. My focus is on figuring out my next move on the things I can control."

"*Our* next move," Katie said, setting her glass down. "Grady might've bailed, but the rest of us are still here. Don't revert back to the old Kelsey who carried the weight of the world on her shoulders and wouldn't rely on anyone for help."

"Yeah," Bridget said, snickering as she walked across the gym. "What she said. Ooh, cognac. Yum."

"Here, take mine," Katie said. "I think I prefer beer." Katie slid her glass to Bridget and pulled a beer from the basement refrigerator. "What's the plan? What's next?"

"There's a meeting tonight at Donovan's after dinner. You both should be there, along with Wild Card, Tyler, Tech, and Bones. I'll go over everything then."

"Sounds good," Katie said, looking toward the stairs. "I know you're juggling a lot, but Anne and Lisa are hoping to talk to you about the prostitution case. I think they found a lead."

"What kind of lead?"

She shook her head. "I don't want to steal their thunder. They've been working hard trying to solve the mystery."

"Fair enough. I'll make some time for them tonight."

Bridget snapped her fingers, shaking her head. "There goes that half an hour I scheduled for you to have a personal life."

"We both knew it was never going to happen," I said, grinning.

"What are you two talking about?" Katie asked.

"Shipwreck said I needed to schedule time to sort out my feelings and shit."

"Yuck. It's bad enough to have emotions, but he expected you to think about them on purpose?"

"Yes, Katie," Donovan said, coming down the stairs. "Emotionally stable people actually do that from time to time."

Katie stuck her tongue out at him.

He walked over and checked the bottle of cognac before grabbing a glass. "We're drinking the good stuff tonight. What's the occasion?"

I smirked, shrugging.

Donovan poured his drink. "This is one of those female *fuck you*'s to Grady, isn't it?"

I couldn't help the smirk. "We might've been saving the bottle for a weekend getaway."

Donovan lifted his glass, saluting me, before taking a sip. "Hmm. You and Grady need to break up more often. This is good."

"At three thousand a bottle, it better be," Bridget said.

Donovan and I looked at each other, then looked at Bridget.

"Seriously?" I asked.

"You didn't know?"

"No. It was a present from Mickey."

"I really need to meet this guy," Katie said, laughing.

Donovan's eyes narrowed. "Did you and Mickey ever..."

"I'm not a slut!"

"Who said anything about being a slut?" Donovan asked.

Bridget poured more cognac into my glass. "Shipwreck put his foot in his mouth earlier about the whole Bones, Wild Card, and Grady thing. Kelsey didn't react well."

"How angry was she?" Katie asked, leaning toward Bridget.

"Steam was hissing between her eyelids. It was epic."

"I'm right here," I grumbled.

"Our little dragon." Donovan chuckled, shaking his head. "You're not the first one to sleep with all of them. Hell, most of us spent time with Sebrina before she and Grady got hitched."

"Including you?" Lisa asked from the bottom of the stairs.

"Uh," Donovan answered, eyes wide with surprise to find Lisa standing there.

"Dinner's ready," Lisa snapped as she raised her chin, jaw set in anger, and climbed the stairs.

Donovan scrubbed a hand down his face. "Oh, shit."

"Relax," I said, picking up my glass and walking toward the stairs. "Lisa will get over it in a month or two."

Bridget and Katie laughed as they followed me up the stairs.

~*~*~

Dinner was divine. It wasn't fancy, but the table was filled with all my favorite comfort foods: meatloaf, mashed potatoes, scalloped corn, dinner rolls, and even cheesecake for dessert.

"The boys and kids are in charge of cleanup tonight," I said, standing and carrying my plate into the kitchen. "The girls and I need to go over a case I have in Miami. Rumor has it they found a clue."

"It might be nothing," Anne said, doubting herself.

"Yeah," Lisa chimed in. "It's not like we know what we're doing. Maybe we're imagining it."

"You're not," Tech said, clearing his plate. "You both should be proud of yourselves. You found a needle in a haystack."

"Now I'm really curious," I said. "Let's meet in the atrium. Team Kelsey only."

"Team Kelsey?" Donovan asked, raising an eyebrow.

"It's a thing now," Bridget said. "I even had shirts made."

"Are they pink?" Bones asked, smirking.

"Of course not. They're for the paintball tournament this weekend. They're camo green with pink glitter."

I walked down the hall to my bedroom before the guys saw the smile on my face.

Tech carried his computer, following me. "Bridget is an extraordinary liar."

"The trick is to keep part of the lie true, so you can focus your mind on the truth part, which was that she really did have shirts made."

"I can't wait for the paintball war on Sunday. Team Kelsey's going to own that trophy."

The atrium, now functioning as Abigail's nursery during the day, was cluttered with toys, books, diapers, and other baby essentials. Tech and I scooped everything up from the couches, dumping it into a play pen.

"Are you sure you don't want Abigail and her nanny to be at my house during the day?" Lisa asked as she and Anne walked into the atrium.

"It's safer to keep the kids under one roof," I answered, tossing Abigail's baby blanket to the side as I sat on a couch. "It's fine. It's only until we straighten out the cartel mess."

"You make it sound like an audit," Bridget said, walking in with my laptop. "Just show a few documents and the death threat will be over."

I tilted my head, focusing on the coffee table. Was it that simple? Charlie described Miguel as a cold-hearted businessman. Would he go so far as giving up his own brother to protect his companies? "Tech, I need everything you can access on Miguel's companies. Financial reports. Tax filings. Employee lists. Focus on the companies in the U.S."

Lisa, Anne, Bridget, and Tech grinned at me.

"Sit! We need to go over the Miami case. What did you find?"

"It might not be anything," Anne said, sitting beside me as she handed me a folder.

"What might not be anything? Talk to me."

Katie walked in and set my cognac on the table before cracking another beer and dropping onto the other couch.

"Okay," Lisa said, sitting beside Katie. "We gathered the list of possible abduction sites like liquor stores, churches, pawn shops, hair salons and at first none of them seemed likely."

"How did you sort the lists?"

"First we narrowed by their neighborhoods," Anne said as she pulled a list from another folder and read from it. "When you look at most of the businesses, though, either the neighborhoods had multiple options, like liquor stores on every block, or the locations were too big, like the local community college."

"The larger places like the courthouse, college, YMCA, and social services all seemed unlikely locations to pull off abductions without witnesses," Lisa said. "Other companies didn't fit the profile of attracting prostitutes, like the limo company and a few nice restaurants."

"You'd be surprised, but keep going," I said, nodding. "That left…"

"A dental clinic," Anne said. "They do discount dental work for pennies on the dollar for low-income patients."

"It also made sense that the women wouldn't be addicts," Lisa added. "Junkies might target the clinic for drugs, but not for routine cleanings."

"Did you run a background on the clinic?"

Anne pointed to the folder I was still holding. "They looked legit until last year when they lost their federal funding. The clinic was scheduled to close until they received a donation to keep the doors open."

"A private donation?"

Tech nodded. "They filed the paperwork as an anonymous donation."

I opened the file and flipped through the tax statements, quarterly financial report, a list of employees, and random news articles. The next twenty or more pages were patient names. On several pages, I saw the highlighted names of the girls who'd disappeared.

"Are all the girls on this list?"

"They all went to that clinic, yes," Lisa said. "We can't figure out who at the clinic is behind the kidnappings, though." She handed me another folder. "We ran backgrounds on everyone. No one sparked an interest."

"Who had the most to lose if the clinic closed?"

"Everyone," Anne answered. "We originally thought only those in charge would care."

"But it's tough finding a good job these days," Lisa added. "If someone was worried about paying their bills, they might've started the abductions."

"What if the person responsible isn't an employee, but scouts the clinic for girls?" Bridget asked.

"I don't think so," Anne said. "We had Sara hack the clinic's appointment system. Each of the women had some type of dental work done on their last appointment."

"They were drugged," I said, standing up. "Damn, that makes perfect sense. It would make it easier to have them leave without making a scene as long as the dosage was under control."

"They'd have to slip them something stronger than nitrous oxide," Katie said.

"Or give them just enough nitrous so they were woozy," I said, starting to pace. "They're trying to stay under the radar, right? What if there's an inside person who kicks up the gas a notch or two, or even slips the women something else that still leaves them able to walk and talk, but off their game? Then another person offers them assistance when they aren't feeling well. It could be as simple as the girls feel dizzy or queasy. They'd be appreciative of anyone offering to sit with them or helping them home."

"They're not likely to accept a ride from a stranger," Bridget said. "These are street girls. They'd know better."

"Maybe they'd accept cab fare, though," I said.

"*That—*" Bridget said as she stood, "*—would work*! The girls come out of the clinic, but they feel dizzy. A good Samaritan offers to get them a cab, paying it forward bullshit." She waved her hands about as she thought out the con. "Then the cab driver, who was waiting down the street, pulls up and takes the victim to another location. *Poof*! They're gone. It would explain why there weren't any witnesses."

"Now we're up to three people involved," Katie said. "The person who dosed them, the good Samaritan, and now a cab driver."

"That's exactly how a big fish would play the game," I said. "Human trafficking is built on networking. Everyone involved has a role to play."

"How do we find out who the actors are?" Anne asked.

"Surveillance," I said, sighing and throwing myself onto the couch. "But they'd spot law enforcement a mile away, and I can't get down there with everything else going on."

"You already banned me from going, and it's too big of a case to send Trigger alone," Bridget said.

"What I need is time..." I drummed my fingers on the arm of the couch. "I need to stop the abductions until I get shit here sorted."

Katie laughed, looking up at me with a devious smile. "What about a small kitchen fire?"

"It's a dental office," Tech said, looking at Katie with a raised eyebrow. "Not a soup kitchen."

"Not her point," I said, standing again. "A small fire would work. They'd have to make repairs and have re-inspections. Appointments would be rescheduled. If the fire was controlled, it would buy us a week at least."

"It's fire," Lisa said. "How the hell are you going to control it from spreading?"

"Does the building have a sprinkler system?" I asked Tech.

He looked to his laptop and started typing. A few minutes later he nodded.

I pulled my phone and called Mickey.

"How's my favorite cop?" Mickey asked when he answered.

"Ex-cop. You need a new line."

Mickey chuckled.

"Is your phone clean?" He knew I'd mean if there was a wiretap.

"Phone is. The room I'm standing in isn't."

"That'll work. I need a small fire to take place at a dental clinic. It's related to that prostitution case I told you about. I just need the clinic to be closed for a few days, nothing more. The building has a sprinkler system."

"Sounds intriguing. Send me the details."

"Just like that?"

"I'm not in a position to ask questions, and we both know I can't tell you no. There's just something about you, Harrison."

"My easy-breezy personality?"

"Not likely."

"I cracked open that cognac, finally. It's delicious. Thanks."

"My pleasure. Did Grady like it?"

"He wasn't invited to the taste testing."

"Lover's quarrel?"

"More like hurricane season."

"Need me to handle that as well?"

"No. I hate to think of what your solution would be."

Mickey chuckled and disconnected.

I set the phone on the coffee table and threw myself back on the couch, grinning.

"You always have this evil gleam after you talk to Mickey," Bridget said.

Wild Card laughed from the entrance of the atrium. Donovan and Bones stood next to him, smiling.

"She had that same look the first night I met her," Wild Card said, walking further into the room. "It's her good-girl gone bad vibe."

"At least I'm not an adrenaline junky like you," I said, picking up my phone again and standing. "Class dismissed. Those attending the Destruction-of-the-Cartel meeting, regroup at Donovan's. Those staying here, be on guard and protect the family in our absence."

"We've got it handled," Anne said, gathering the files. "Whiskey, Farmer, and James are staying inside with us. Tyler's leading the troops outside. I'll put Nicholas to bed if the meeting runs late."

"One of us will swing back to say goodnight to him if the meeting runs late," Wild Card said. "I set an alarm on my phone."

Something about Wild Card setting an alarm for Nicholas' bedtime sat uneasy with me. Was it because I should have done the same? Was it because the relationship between Wild Card, myself, and my son was beyond complicated? Or was it because I liked the thought of him caring enough?

"Don't overthink it, sweetheart," Wild Card said, watching me.

"Who? Me?" I asked as I carried my glass of cognac out of the room.

Chapter Twenty-Four

Regrouping in Donovan's basement family room, each of us found a place on either the couch or one of the four club chairs. I sat in one of the club chairs with Bones and Bridget sharing a chair to my right. Wild Card was on my left with his feet stretched out, crossed at the ankles, and his fingers laced behind his head. Tech had the last chair and moved an end table over to use as a workstation for his laptop.

Tyler entered through the sliding door, nodding to me before leaning against the wall so he could watch outside and still listen in on the meeting.

Donovan looked around the room, realizing he had the couch to himself. He turned sideways and stretched out, taking up all three cushions. "I'm not used to having so few people attend these meetings."

"I still can't believe you made Jackson choose," Bones said, shaking his head.

"I didn't," I said as I dragged the coffee table over to prop my feet on. "Jackson volunteered to be my spy."

Donovan sat up, swinging his feet to the floor. "*What?*"

I shrugged. "I needed moles."

"Jackson and Trigger," Bridget said, grinning. "You have two spies, though I'm not sure how long Trigger will survive if you keep pitting him against the guys."

"That shit with Jackson was fake?" Bones asked. "He was pissed. I thought he was going to take a swing at you."

"He's a hell of an actor," Wild Card said, looking over at me and grinning. "Jackson took acting classes with Reggie and played Henry Higgins from *My Fair Lady* in the annual county musical."

"His English accent was perfection, but man, can he sing," I said, grinning at Wild Card.

"You're shitting me?" Donovan said. "Jackson? One of the biggest bad asses of jungle warfare?"

"We don't have a lot of time," Tyler said in a serious tone, drawing our attention. "Can we stay on task? How will Jackson and Trigger communicate if they can't cross the highway? If they use their phones, they risk being overheard."

"Tweedle," I answered. "She agreed to be the messenger. No one will expect her to be complicit, and her baked goods make her approachable."

"Does Ryan know?" Bridget asked.

"No. We agreed Ryan wouldn't like her being involved, so we aren't providing him with the details until the situation is resolved or the weekend ends, whichever happens first."

Bones laughed, tucking his forehead against Bridget's shoulder. "You guys really did corrupt Tweedle while we were away."

"Nightcrawler's approaching," Tyler said, opening the slider door. "Maggie's with him."

"Did we know Maggie was coming?" Bridget asked.

"No. But she was gathering intel on Sebrina," I answered as Maggie and Nightcrawler stepped into the room.

"Security around here is over the top, Tyler," Maggie said as she entered and pinched Tyler's cheek.

Tyler grinned back at her until Nightcrawler threw an elbow into his stomach.

"Tell me you brought me something," I said to Maggie.

Maggie walked over and sat next to Donovan on the couch. Nightcrawler sat next to her, but there was a distance between them. "I wasn't allowed to print Sebrina's file, but I was allowed to peek at it."

"And what did we see?"

"Smart. Beautiful. Competitive."

"I knew all that."

"Did you know she's never been assigned to work the Remirez cartel?" Maggie asked.

"Now we're getting somewhere," Bridget said, leaning forward and clasping her hands.

"The DEA knows she's taken six trips to Mexico over the last year and that on three of those trips she met with Santiago. She also met with Santiago twice in the States. She reported the trips to Mexico as vacations or related to other cases, and claims Santiago sought her out."

"What about payouts?" Tech asked. "Is there a financial trail we can follow?"

"Business as usual in her personal finances," Maggie said, shaking her head.

"She's too smart to get caught holding the money," Donovan said. "She knows her way around the system. If she was involved—and I'm not convinced yet—she'd have Santiago fund a foreign bank account under a false ID."

"Why do you think she's innocent?" I asked Donovan.

"I don't, but that doesn't make her guilty either. You want her to be guilty. I get that, but as Maggie said, Sebrina's competitive. Just because she wasn't assigned the Remirez case, doesn't mean she's not working it."

"He's right," Bones agreed. "Taking the Remirez family down single handedly would be right up her alley. She likes to be in the spotlight and doesn't play well with others."

"Tell me more about her," I said, watching them. "How is it that so many of you ended up sleeping with her?"

Maggie and Nightcrawler looked back and forth at Bones and Donovan.

Bones sighed, rubbing his jaw. "Really, Donovan? You felt the need to share that?"

"What?" Bridget asked, looking over her shoulder at Bones. "It's not like either of us were virgins when we hooked up."

"It's different," Bones said, shaking his head. "We were in the military still. Things were..."

"Less emotional and more physical?" I asked.

"Exactly," Donovan said. "It was sex, not love."

"Until Grady fell for her," Bones said.

"What was everyone's relationship like before Grady and Sebrina got serious?"

"Convenient," Bones answered with a shrug. "If one of us—or two of us—landed in the same place as Sebrina with time available, we'd spend it between the sheets."

"Or... in the back of a Humvee. Or... against a tree in the rainforest." Donovan raised an eyebrow as he looked at me. "If any of this gets back to Lisa, there'll be hell to pay."

I waved off his concern. "Was it just sex for Sebrina?"

"She enjoyed sex, but it was more of a power trip for her," Bones said.

"She liked being the center of attention," Maggie said, nodding. "She was turned on by it. I can see that based on her profile."

"Exactly," Bones said. "None of us thought anything about sharing her because it was something she wanted, and we already respected her for the work she did with the army."

"Why was Grady different?" I asked.

"At first he wasn't," Bones said.

"His first encounter with her was a group event," Donovan said. "Bones and Grady spent time with Sebrina while Ryan watched."

"What changed?"

"Grady changed," Bones said. "It was after a mission that had gone bad. We all tried to help him shake off the mission, but we weren't having any luck. We arranged to meet Sebrina in Germany for a long weekend."

"Grady didn't participate. He just watched," Donovan said, looking at me to see if I wanted him to continue.

I nodded.

"Sebrina had been watched plenty of times before, but that night, she couldn't take her eyes off Grady. It was the same for him. It was like they suddenly saw each other."

"The rest of the weekend, it was just the two of them," Bones said. "Two weeks later, we were out on a mission when he finally admitted that they'd gotten hitched."

"Just like that? They got married and reported back to work?" Katie asked.

"Sebrina was in the field a lot for counterintelligence missions. We ran into her every few weeks while we worked missions of our own," Donovan explained.

"During the rare breaks between missions, everyone met up in Germany," Bones said. "It wasn't as far to travel as the U.S. so it became our off-duty destination. Sebrina included."

"You could've traveled to Italy, Greece, or went to Paris," Bridget said. "Why Germany?"

Bones laughed, rubbing her shoulder. "We weren't looking for romantic getaways. We wanted to get drunk, get laid, and relax in a country where we were less likely to be shot."

"Our stomping ground was also close to the Army hospital," Donovan said. "It made it easier to visit each other anytime one of us got shot." Donovan pointed to Bones.

"I was only shot twice. Grady spent more time at Landstuhl than I did."

I shook my head at Bones and Donovan. They were having fun reminiscing. Lifting my glass, I took a slow sip of my cognac and closed my eyes.

"Where do I get one of those?" Maggie asked.

I opened my eyes and saw she was pointing at my drink. "My basement bar."

Maggie hurried toward the tunnels.

"Bring a couple of glasses and the bottle," Donovan called out. "I'm already in the doghouse with Lisa. I might as well enjoy the downtime."

"Dangerous words, brother," Bones said, grinning.

"What were Grady and Sebrina like after they married?" I asked.

"At first, nothing changed," Donovan said. "Other than Sebrina was no longer part of our sexual experiences."

"Eventually things got weird, though," Bones said, shaking his head. "Sebrina enjoyed group sex, but Grady wasn't having any part of it. Not as his wife. Being watched during sex was enough for Grady. He didn't need anyone else in the bed with them."

"This is way too much fucking information," Nightcrawler said.

"Agreed," Tyler said, still leaning against the wall while he watched out the window. "How's this relevant?"

"It's uncomfortable, I'll admit," I said, rubbing my neck. "But understanding what makes Sebrina tick will help us unravel her faster. I'm not willing to let this situation with the cartel drag on for the next six months. One way or another, *that bitch has got to go*."

"Amen, sister," Bridget said, reaching over to tap our brandy glasses.

Maggie returned with several glasses and the cognac. I helped her set the glasses down and then filled a few before topping off Bridget's glass and mine.

"Damn. This is good," Maggie said after taking a sip.

"It's three thousand a bottle," Donovan said.

"Must be nice to be rich," Maggie said, taking another drink.

"It was a present from Mickey," I said.

Maggie choked on her drink, leaning forward and coughing after it went down the wrong way. Donovan beat on her back a few times while laughing.

"That fucker," Maggie said. "I can't believe he did that."

"Sent me an expensive bottle of booze?"

Maggie coughed again as she shook her head. "The shipping company you sold him is being monitored by the Feds. Mickey and Lisa's brother Phillip are the prime suspects for the increase in high-end black-market merchandise coming into the U.S. from Spain, France, and Italy."

"So much for them going legit," I said, grinning at my glass of cognac. "Feds closing in on them?"

"Hell, no. Mickey and Phillip are way smarter than the team trying to nail them."

"Tick-tock," Tyler said, reminding me to stay on task.

"Thank you, Tyler," I said, turning back to Bones. "When did the marriage fall apart?"

"After they returned to the States. Grady came back first to arrange their housing. Sebrina came back a month or two later and played house for a bit, but then she took off and started her DEA career. Grady started the security company with Donovan, taking point on the cases, while Donovan ran the business side of the company."

"They stayed married for another six months or so," Donovan said. "It wasn't until Grady went to pay her a surprise visit in California that he came back saying they were getting a divorce. I got the impression that Sebrina cheated on him."

"Oh, she cheated all right," Bones said. "With Grady's brother Mitch."

"Wait—" I paused him while trying to imagine the scenario where Mitch would sleep with Grady's wife. "Nope. This doesn't make sense. Explain."

"Can't. Whenever I brought it up to Grady, he'd say it was water under the bridge. If I asked Mitch, he'd rant that Sebrina was a duplicitous bitch. Never got the full story out of either of them."

"Grady just forgave Mitch?"

"I guess," Bones said, shrugging. "Grady seems fine with Mitch when he's around. Maybe a bit distant, but most men would've beat the hell out of their brother for sleeping with their wife."

"Let me ask this... Did Mitch actually know Sebrina? Had he ever met her as Grady's wife?"

"I don't know," Bones admitted.

"We didn't spend much time with Mitch," Donovan said. "He was stationed at a base camp for most of his tour, whereas we moved around a lot."

"You're thinking Sebrina purposely set Mitch up, aren't you?" Maggie asked me.

"She likes drama. Earlier today, she was in her element watching the showdown between Grady and me. She could've tracked Mitch down and given him a fake name, hoping Grady would discover them."

"But if Grady was surprising her, how would she know he'd be there?" Katie asked.

"She worked counterintelligence. She was capable of manipulating situations, but she also might've planned to keep the affair going until the eventual day when Grady walked through the door. It would be more suspenseful for her that way."

Donovan and Bones looked at each other. They'd known Sebrina for years and would know if she was capable of something so deceitful.

"Yeah, I can see it," Bones said.

"Damn. Me too," Donovan agreed.

Bridget's phone chirped, and she read the screen. "Kemp needs my help at Headquarters accessing one of the background apps. I'll be back in five."

"I'll escort you," Bones said.

"I don't need a bodyguard."

Wild Card looked over at her with a raised eyebrow. "Are you forgetting you were kidnapped yesterday?"

"Oh," Bridget said, giggling. "It was so much fun, I actually did forget."

I turned my attention to Tech. "Well, partner, what have you been working on?"

"Miguel's American companies," Tech said as he continued to type. "I've got six so far, ranging from a small bakery to a global health food manufacturing company."

"I'm sick of baked goods, but the health food company is a maybe. What else you got?"

"A retail mall."

"Pass."

"A trucking company."

"Interesting. It's likely to be tangled with their illegal business, though, so pass."

"A pharmaceutical company."

"Again, interesting, but pass."

"Last on the list... a textile mill."

"Ooh. I like fabrics. Give me everything you've got so far. Where's it located?"

"Texas."

"Bonus. Start printing. I need to run home and get my son ready for bed." I pointed to Maggie and Donovan. "Don't drink all my booze while I'm gone."

Wild Card stood, planning to follow.

"Oh, no you don't. Since you were the one who had the bright idea to give the prisoner's ex-lax, it's your turn to empty the buckets."

"What prisoners?" Maggie asked.

"Pretend you didn't hear that," Nightcrawler said, before turning to Wild Card. "Lisa set aside food for them. I'll meet you over there."

Wild Card watched Nightcrawler leave through the tunnel and then looked back at me. "You seriously expect me to dump their *shit*?"

"Yup. There're gloves under the kitchen sink."

"You should've left them for the rats," he mumbled as he walked into the tunnel that led to Alex's.

I looked over at Donovan.

"Yeah," Donovan said as he stood and followed Wild Card. "I'll make sure the prisoners are still breathing when he's done."

Katie snickered, going over to get another beer from Donovan's basement refrigerator. Maggie refilled her glass of cognac. Tech was still typing on his laptop. I nodded to Tyler before taking the tunnel back to the main house.

Chapter Twenty-Five

Thirty minutes later, I shared a pillow with Nicholas as he read *Treasure Island* to me. I started to drift off until he shook my arm.

"Mom, you missed the best part!" Nicholas said.

"I'm sorry. I only missed a minute of it," I said, rolling to my side so I could watch him. "It's a good book, isn't it?"

"The cover still sucks," Nicholas said, grinning.

"I'm thinking kids shouldn't say the word sucks, but I can't remember why. I'm a terrible mother."

Nicholas giggled, handing me the book.

"Tomorrow you can make a new cover for the book, and we'll tape over the old one."

"I'm too old to color pictures."

"Who said anything about crayons? You can paint a picture or do a charcoal sketch. You could even design a cover on your computer."

"I don't know how to do any of that."

"Then you should ask someone to teach you."

"Can you teach me?"

"I can't sketch or paint, but Bridget can. I can do a few things with computer graphics, but Aunt Charlie is better at it."

"Can you teach me how to do it on the computer, and then if I get good at it, then I can call Aunt Charlie to teach me more?"

"Sure," I said, tweaking his nose. "Now... it's time to sleep."

I rolled out of his bed, setting the book on the nightstand before leaning over to smother him with kisses.

"*Mommmm*! Stop!" he said, giggling and burying himself under the blankets for protection.

"Goodnight, Nicholas." I walked over to the door and shut off the light.

"Mom?"

"Yes?"

"Do you promise you'll never move away and leave me?"

"You and me are forever, Nicholas. You couldn't get rid of me if you tried."

He pulled his blanket up to his chin. "Okay."

"I love you." I closed the door and released the breath I'd been holding. I waited until I felt less shaky before making my way down the hall.

In the living room, Pops, Hattie, Lisa, Anne, and Whiskey were watching a movie. Hattie was sitting on the end of the couch closest to me.

I leaned over and whispered, "How are you feeling?"

"I'm about ready to head upstairs. I'm getting tired, truth be told."

Pops heard our conversation and wiggled back and forth until he was at the edge of the couch to stand. He reached out with both arms to pull Hattie up as I assisted from my side.

"Do you need help getting up the stairs or dressing for bed?"

"I've got her, baby girl. I'll take good care of her," Pops said.

Hattie was smiling up at Pops. "Pops can take care of me from here. No need to worry."

"It's my job to worry about everyone, remember?"

"I'll make a cup of tea and bring it up for you," Anne said, hitting pause on the movie and standing. "Pops? Would you like a cup too?"

"That'd be mighty nice of you," Pops said as he led Hattie to the stairs with one arm snug around her waist.

"I'm going to follow you guys upstairs," Whiskey said, standing to stretch. "I want to peek in on Sara and make sure she's asleep."

"Or you don't trust an old man to catch his wife if she falls?" Pops asked as he glanced back at Whiskey with narrowed eyes.

"I'm just walking up the stairs, man," Whiskey said. "Don't read too much into it."

Hattie giggled. Pops mumbled something under his breath. Whiskey winked at me.

Since they seemed to have everything under control, I returned to Donovan's basement through the tunnels.

Tech glanced up from his laptop when he sensed me enter the room. "How's the captain?" Tech asked, referring to a character in Nicholas' book.

"Very dead."

Tech nodded. "Too much rum will do that."

"Someone dies from drinking alcohol in a children's book?" Katie asked.

"It's an old pirate story," I said, shrugging.

I sat in my chair as Maggie leaned forward to refill her glass. Her thick brown hair slid forward and with an unconscious flip, she tucked it behind her shoulder as she leaned back again. I always saw Maggie for her intelligence, but I'd been around the guys enough to know they drooled over her natural beauty.

A thought struck me, and I couldn't help but to smile. "What's the status between you and Nightcrawler?"

She raised an eyebrow, wondering at my question, but after a brief pause, she answered. "It fizzled. No hard feelings on either side. Why?"

"Are you staying for the weekend?"

Her eyes danced with humor as she answered. "I figured I'd play it by ear. Why are you smiling like that? It's creeping me out."

Katie and Tech were watching me, waiting for an answer, too.

"Daphne Davenport," I said.

Tech laughed as he turned his attention back to his laptop.

Maggie had a quizzical look on her face. "That crappy actress with the pitchy voice?"

"That's the one. She's a client. Supposedly she has a stalker, but I'm not buying it. Are you willing to play pretend girlfriend to her security guard so I can see how she reacts?"

"With everything else going on, how is this anywhere near the top of your to-do list?"

"It's not, but it's on my to-do list, and you're conveniently here."

Maggie's eyes narrowed as she considered. "What's my new boyfriend look like?"

"I have no idea. I've never met him."

Tech turned his laptop to show us a picture. "Meet Billy Hobbs."

"Ooh, la, la," Maggie said as she ogled his picture. "Is he single in real life?"

"He's not married," Tech said.

"Gay?"

Tech shrugged. "Not that I'm aware of, but it's not something we keep in our files."

"What don't we keep in our files," Donovan asked, returning with Wild Card and Nightcrawler.

"Sexual preference," I answered as I leaned forward to get a better look at Billy's picture.

Donovan saw what we were looking at. "Hobbs isn't gay."

Donovan's reply sealed the deal for Maggie, and she started bouncing up and down on the couch. "*I'll do it*! This is going to be the best undercover assignment *ever*."

"What are you doing?" Nightcrawler asked.

"Pretending to be that stud muffin's girlfriend to make a client jealous."

Nightcrawler laughed.

I looked at Katie, and we both exhaled.

"You didn't believe me when I said Nightcrawler and I were over?" Maggie asked me.

"I believed that's how *you* felt. I just wasn't sure Nightcrawler agreed."

Nightcrawler grinned. "You thought I'd be jealous?"

"Jealousy is a common trait amongst the men in my life."

"I have my eye on someone else. It's all good."

"Who?" Maggie asked, nudging him with her elbow. "Tell me. Tell me."

"No."

Tyler laughed, looking over at Nightcrawler and shaking his head.

Bridget and Bones came down the stairs. Bridget was carrying a stack of papers.

"What's all that?" I asked.

"Tech was too lazy to walk upstairs to get the pages he printed," Bridget said, dumping the stack on the coffee table in front of me. "He texted me to pick them up on our way back."

"That's pathetic, Tech," I said, shaking my head.

Tech continued working on his computer. "I'm not lazy. It was more efficient for Bridget to get the papers on her way through so I could keep working."

"Efficiency isn't heart healthy," Maggie said, moving to the floor and starting to sort the papers.

Katie and I moved to the floor as well.

"What are we doing?" Wild Card asked, sitting in the chair behind me and leaning over my shoulder.

"We need to get Miguel's attention. I figure the best way to do that is to attack one of his companies in some way."

"How does that help?" Bones asked, sitting on the couch as Bridget sat on the floor in front of him.

"Based on what Charlie was able to dig up, I'm betting Miguel Remirez cares more about his companies than whether his baby brother, Santiago, is dead or alive."

"You're kidding," Wild Card said from behind me.

"Nope. I already suspect Miguel was the one who killed his older brother and his uncle. He needed them out of the way so he could focus on his legal businesses."

"What if he wants Santiago to still run the cartel?" Maggie asked. "Seems Miguel has never wanted the figurehead role."

"He'll have to decide which he wants more—the convenience of having his brother handle the drug trade or me not destroying everything he's built in the last decade."

"How hard are you planning to go after him?" Donovan asked, the worry lines appearing on his forehead.

"I'll start small. A disruption of some kind. If he doesn't play ball, then I'll strike again. I'll keep going until he has nothing left on this side of the border if that's what it takes."

"But you don't think it will go that far," Maggie said, reading my mind.

"I don't. I think one very strategic plan could convince him to green light any action we take against his brother. Miguel's ruthless, but he's a businessman. The last thing he wants is someone like me to come after him."

Maggie tapped a finger to her temple. "You want him to know you're an ex-cop with contacts extending from a mafia family to a crime boss in Miami and even to the FBI."

"I sound scary on Google."

"Not just on Google," Wild Card mumbled behind me.

I turned to the side and slapped his calf.

He laughed as he shoved my shoulder. "Put us to work. What do you need?"

"Everyone except for Donovan, grab a pile and start taking notes. I need a cheat sheet on everything important."

"What's my assignment?" Donovan asked.

"You are going to go check on Lisa and Abigail. If Lisa sees you changing a diaper or two, maybe she'll thaw some about the whole sleeping with Sebrina thing."

"That's actually a good plan," Donovan said, heading for the tunnel.

"Tyler and I are going to make the rounds," Nightcrawler said, leaving the basement with Tyler.

"I can only work for a couple of hours," Maggie said. "I need to get my beauty sleep tonight so I look fresh when my man hunk gets here tomorrow."

I laughed as I grabbed a tax report and started reading.

"I sent Billy an email explaining the grand plan and printed a bio for you to read," Tech said to Maggie. "It's on the printer upstairs."

"Get off your ass and go get it!" Katie ordered him, pointing toward the stairs.

Tech sighed but set his laptop on the coffee table and walked off to get the papers.

"Maybe we should get both Tech and Genie Fitbits," Maggie said, referring to her analyst at the FBI. "She spends too much time behind a monitor, too."

"Maybe Carl can link them so they get alerts when the other one reaches a new goal," I said.

"That would require Carl coming out of hiding," Bones said. "You really did a number on him."

"He didn't leave me much of a choice."

"Agreed," Katie said. "We all understand why you had to scare him, but he can't live the rest of his life in his bedroom. This weekend is just as much about Carl as it is about the guards at Aces."

I narrowed my eyes at Katie. "He bought *chemicals* used to make *bombs!*"

"And you haven't spoken to him in *over twenty-four hours!*" Katie snapped back. "In Carl's world, that's an eternity."

I sighed, throwing the tax report onto the table, before I stood and walked away. I walked through the tunnel, down the hall, up the stairs to the main floor, hollered at Haley and Alex who were making out on the couch, and then walked down the hall to Carl's room. I knocked twice. Carl mumbled something incoherent, so I entered.

"Aren't you done pouting yet?" I asked Carl as I walked over and sat on the bed next to him.

"I was bad."

"Yes, you were." I tipped my head back and sighed. "We all screw up, though. It's time to move on."

"Are you still mad at me?"

I shook my head. "I'm not mad at you, but if you do something like that again, we'll have to find somewhere else for you to live. I have to protect the kids and keep them safe."

"I wasn't going to make a bomb. I swear."

"Remember Hattie's oven? You didn't mean to blow that up, either."

"I know," he said, leaning his head on my shoulder.

"Did you eat dinner?"

He nodded.

"Are you still hungry?"

He nodded again.

"Why don't you go raid the kitchen at the main house and then meet us in Donovan's basement. We're working a case."

"Really?" he asked as he lifted his head and looked at me.

"Yes, really."

Carl threw his arms around me and squeezed me too hard before abruptly releasing me and running out of the bedroom.

I followed at a slower pace.

"I take it Katie guilted you into talking to him?" Alex called over the back of the couch.

"Bite me."

I heard Haley giggle as I walked down the stairs.

Chapter Twenty-Six

It was a long night. After several hours of research, Maggie was asleep on the couch with a quilt draped over her and an accent pillow tucked under her head. Bones had taken Bridget back to his apartment an hour ago. Tech and Katie had left a few minutes later. Carl was sleeping on the floor, snoring.

"Time for bed," Wild Card said, pulling me up from the floor by my armpits.

"I have too much work to do."

"It's mental work at this point, and your brain is fried. Time to get a few hours of sleep."

I nodded, too tired to argue as he led me down the tunnel. Before I knew it, I was in my bedroom.

"Are you heading over to Headquarters?" I asked between yawns.

"I'm sleeping in the atrium."

I thought about how Nicholas had asked if Wild Card would be sleeping in my room. "I'm not sure that's a good idea."

"Lucky for me, you're too tired to fight me about it," Wild Card said, pulling a pillow and blanket out of the far closet.

I nodded to myself, agreeing to his logic as I stripped off my boots, jeans, and took my bra off without removing my shirt. I started to crawl into bed when I noticed the bedroom door was closed. I opened it before returning to bed and crawling under the covers.

Wild Card laughed. "What was that about?"

"Closed doors send the wrong message."

"Are you worried Nicholas would get the wrong idea, or are you worried you'll be tempted to fool around?"

"Nicholas, of course. *Geesh*. What kind of girl do you think I am?" I curled onto my side with my back toward the atrium.

It was quiet except for the rustling of the blanket as Wild Card made up a bed on the atrium couch. "I shouldn't have said all that I-love-you shit this afternoon. For the record, I'm not going to do anything to jeopardize your chance to fix things with Grady. And, even then, I refuse to be your second choice. If there ever comes a day when I'm your first choice…" He sighed. I heard him settle onto the couch. "Never mind. Not the point. *We're friends*. That's it."

"I'm glad you told me how you feel. I never meant to hurt you."

"I know that."

I rolled over to face the atrium but could only make out his general shape on the couch. "You're the best damn ex-husband in the world. You know that, right?"

"I'm also good in bed," Wild Card said in the darkness. "Get some sleep."

The day's events drifted from my mind, and I fell asleep with a smile on my face.

~*~*~

Nicholas' screams woke me in the dead of night. I ran from my room and into his bedroom before I'd even opened my eyes. He was covered in sweat, throwing punches into the air, as he continued to scream.

I threw myself onto his bed, wrapping my arms around him to pin his arms to his sides. "*Nicholas*! Wake up! Wake up, baby!"

Wild Card turned on the light as he entered the room. "Nick! Wake Up!" Wild Card yelled as he grabbed a blanket and wrapped it around Nicholas' legs to prevent him from kicking out.

"Please, baby," I said in his ear. "Mom's here. You're safe."

I repeated the words, over and over, before I felt him gradually settle in my arms. I couldn't see his face, but I could feel his breathing slow to a steady rhythm.

"That's it, sweetheart. Mom's here. You're safe."

"Mommmm," he cried, trying to reach his hands toward me.

I released my hold and pulled him onto my lap, rocking him side to side. Through blurry eyes, I glanced over at Wild Card and saw his anxious expression. I stroked Nicholas' hair. "It's okay, sweetheart. I've got you. It's going to be okay."

"What can we do?" Anne whispered from the doorway. Whiskey stood beside her in his boxers, holding her hand.

"He'll be all right," Wild Card said while tucking the blanket around Nick. "A cup of warm cocoa might help him go back to sleep when he's ready, though."

"You got it," Whiskey said, steering Anne down the hall.

"You're safe, sweetheart," I whispered as I continued to rock him. "I've got you. I'm right here. Always."

It took twenty minutes to settle Nicholas down. He wouldn't tell me about his nightmare, but I could guess it was either about Grady or Nola. It sickened me that Grady was now someone who could haunt my son's dreams.

I continued to hold him, rocking him from side to side, as I leaned against his headboard with him on my lap. Wild Card moved to the floor, one arm stretched over my leg and his hand rubbing Nicholas' knee. I'm not sure how long we sat like that before I fell asleep.

~*~*~

When I woke a few hours later, I found myself still sitting with Nicholas' upper body on top of his pillow and his lower half stretched across my lap. Wild Card was on the floor with his head tilted back against the bed, eyes closed, and an arm stretched toward us. The bedroom light, which was still on, glared brightly. I closed my eyes, taking a mental moment, before shifting Nicholas onto the bed and adjusting his blanket around him. Wild Card woke startled, but relaxed when he realized it was me. Dropping his arm, he rotated his shoulders and his neck.

As I climbed out of the bed, careful not to wake Nicholas, Wild Card stood. We walked out together and I turned the light off, waiting a minute to see if Nicholas woke. When I was sure he was sound asleep, I closed the door.

Turning to Wild Card, I lifted onto my toes and kissed his cheek. "Thank you."

"No need to thank me," he said, resting a hand on my shoulder.

I stared up at the man who was always there for me when it counted. Even when we couldn't be in the same room together for more than five minutes without screaming at each other—or worse, when we'd gone months without speaking—he always came through when I needed him.

Without thinking, I raised on my toes again and kissed him. Really kissed him. His firm, warm lips wrapped with mine as his arms folded around me and pressed me against him. My hands wandered into his hair, tugging him closer as I felt the heat of his tongue meet mine.

He moaned as he turned us and moved me backward into my bedroom. As he fumbled to close the bedroom door, I scrambled frantically to unbutton his shirt. I expected when he started moving us again that we'd land in my bed, but he walked us into the bathroom instead. Holding my ass with one hand, he used the other to start the shower. I moaned as my body reacted to his touch, his strong hands, his warm mouth, his heated chest rubbing against mine. Without taking our clothes off, Wild Card lifted me and stepped into the tub, placing us both under the stream of *freezing cold water*.

He covered my mouth with his hand so I wouldn't scream. Leaning his head against my shoulder, he laughed. I shoved his hand away and pushed past him to get out. He continued to laugh as he shut the water off.

"What the hell?" I said, grabbing a towel to wrap around me. My teeth chattered as I tried to dry off.

"Sorry," he said, stepping out and sloshing water all over the floor. He chuckled again, placing his hands alongside my face and tilting my head up. "Friends, remember?" He grabbed a second towel and wrapped it around me. "We tried being each other's comfort buddies back when we were married. The result was you not speaking to me for over a year. I'm not willing to risk that happening again."

"You could've just turned me down for sex," I said, shivering.

Wild Card smacked his lips against mine in a quick kiss. "You weren't the only one who got carried away with that kiss. We both needed a dash of cold water. Besides, at least you have clothes to change into." He looked down at his soaked shirt and jeans. "Mine are in my duffle in your war room at Headquarters."

"Why is your duffle in my war room and not in your apartment?"

"Jerry ran out of apartments so I gave up mine for Grady."

"You should've said something. I didn't mean for you to give up your place."

"I usually sleep on one of the couches here when I'm in town, anyway." He shrugged as he looked down at me and moved a lock of hair out of my face. "Food is better on this side of the highway."

I tossed him a clean towel from the cabinet. "Do you want me to send Tyler to Headquarters to get your clothes?"

Wild Card started to unbutton his jeans. "Better to wait until daylight when the guards can see who's who."

I turned my back as he pulled his wet jeans off. "I'll see if I can find you something to wear."

I slipped out of the bathroom and dressed in yoga pants and a thick sweatshirt that came to the top of my thighs. I dug around in the drawers and then the closet, but failed to find anything large enough for Wild Card.

"Any luck?" Wild Card asked as he stepped out of the bathroom wearing only a towel.

"Nope. Do you want me to wake Whiskey?"

Wild Card shook his head. "It's four in the morning. Let him sleep."

"You can crash in my bed. Whiskey will be up in another hour, and I'll bring you some clothes then."

"Where are you going?"

"I'm wide awake and freezing. I need coffee."

"Coffee sounds good," he said, walking over to the door and opening it for me.

I looked down at him in his towel. "You're going to wander the house in only a towel?"

He shoved me out the door and down the hall as he followed, chuckling.

I went to the kitchen and started the coffee pot, which someone had prepped the night before. As the pot brewed, I leaned on the breakfast bar to wait. Wild Card settled at the table, tucking his low-riding towel as he sat.

I caught his smirk before I forced my eyes away to stare at anything but him. "This isn't going to work. I can't relax with you sitting there naked."

"I'm not naked."

"Close enough," I said, going into the living room and partially opening the blinds. I turned the porch light on and off three times and a minute later unlocked the door for Tyler.

"What's up?" Tyler asked.

"Do you have any clothes Wild Card can borrow? His got wet."

Tyler glanced into the dining room. Wild Card was still sitting there in his towel, grinning. Tyler shook his head and stepped through the door. "I've got a bag in the basement. Let me see what I can find."

By the time the coffee was ready, Wild Card was dressed in a Harley t-shirt that was several sizes too small for him and a pair of black sweats that were a few inches too short and looked as tight as yoga pants in the thighs and butt. At least it covered more than the towel had.

I set three cups of coffee on the table and sat down to join the boys.

"Heard about the commotion last night," Tyler said. "Whiskey filled me in. How's Nick doing?"

"He'll be okay," Wild Card said. "This shit with Grady just threw him."

"It's my fault," I said. "I shouldn't have let Grady move in. I shouldn't have let Nick get so attached."

"Bullshit," Wild Card said, setting his coffee cup down. "Kids need to connect with people. It's not like Grady was a one-night stand you brought home."

"Agreed," Tyler said. "We all trusted Grady to do right by Nicholas. That failure is on Grady, not you."

I sighed dramatically. "If only I had a crystal ball and could see into the future."

Wild Card snorted. "With your life? It's hard enough keeping up with the crap we already know about."

Tyler nodded. "I don't even want to remember the shit that happened over the last three days. The kidnapping. Carl ordering chemicals to blow us up. Grady losing his mind. Hattie getting sick."

"Wait! That's it!" I said, getting up to grab the files off the credenza where we had dumped them the night before.

"What's it?" Wild Card said. "What's going on in that head of yours?"

"Just a minute," I said, rearranging the papers, taking up enough space that they both had to pick up their coffee cups. "Shit, I need Tech."

I ran into the bedroom and grabbed my phone from the nightstand. My gun and harness were sitting next to it so I grabbed them as well. Back in the dining room I put the phone on speaker and called Tech while I strapped on my shoulder harness. Out of habit, I checked my gun, ensuring I had a full clip before snapping it into place.

"Are you insane?" Tech said, answering the phone. "It's four-thirty in the morning."

"Tell her I hate her," I heard Katie say in the background.

"Grab your laptop. I need your help."

"It can't wait?"

"I'll make you cocoa?"

Silence.

"And blueberry pancakes?"

"Fine. But I want whipped cream on both."

I hit the end-call button and went to the kitchen to heat a cup of milk. While it heated, I dug around in the refrigerator and was happy when I found we still had a half quart of blueberries left.

Tyler stood, looking at his phone. "Ryan is parked at the end of the road, asking me to pick up Tweedle. I'll be back in a minute."

I got flour out and then dug around for Hattie's pancake recipe.

"Go," Wild Card said to me, turning me out of the kitchen. "I'll make breakfast. You focus on stopping the cartel."

I went back to the dining room and grabbed my laptop, starting it up.

"What the hell, Kelsey?" Tech said as he stumbled in through the garage door. "I'm a delicate creature. I need sleep."

"I need you to hack the trucking company and find out the schedule for their shipments from the textile mill. Search to see if any of their trucks will be hauling stock from the textile mill to the East coast. If they do, we can likely sabotage it en route. One stone, two companies."

"Could work," Wild Card said. "Easier than breaking into the mill, too."

"And less time consuming to plan than some of my other ideas," I said.

Tweedle entered through the garage wearing a bright yellow dress with large pink flowers. "Good morning, everyone." She set her purse on the counter and took off her coat. "Did everyone have a good night last night?"

"No," everyone answered back.

"That's a shame. Maybe some chocolate muffins will cheer up everyone." She walked over and looked in the bowl that Wild Card was stirring. "Can I help you first?"

"Sure," Wild Card said. "You can add cocoa to the milk and pour Tech a cup with whipped cream on top while I chop some vegetables for omelets."

"Sounds like an excellent plan. Teamwork. That's what it's all about."

I pressed my lips together and looked over at Tech. He smirked, but started typing on his laptop.

Bridget and Bones entered through the front door, stripping off their coats.

I turned back to Tech. "After you get the trucking schedule, is there a way to find out if the bakery has any big orders at the mill today or tomorrow?"

"I can try. What are you thinking?"

"Ex-lax in their baked goods. If we can make their employees or clients have to go home sick, that's another double strike."

"You'd be too late for today," Tweedle said, bringing Tech his cocoa and filling up my coffee cup. "Any decent baker starts filling catering orders before sunrise."

"What about switching the order with a contaminated order?" Bridget asked.

Tweedle shrugged. "I can bake anything you need. Won't be the first time I drugged someone."

I looked at my coffee. Tech looked at his cocoa.

Tweedle shook her head. "I wouldn't drug you guys."

"I'm sure that's what Ryan thought before you drugged him, too," Bridget said.

Tweedle rolled her eyes. "Oh, I almost forgot." She hurried into the kitchen and back, handing me two sheets of paper.

I opened the first one and recognized Jackson's handwriting: *I got nothing. Everyone's talking about the tournament.* Crumpling the waste of paper, I tossed it to the floor before opening the second one. Trigger: *I'm bored. Do you have a job for me?* I crumbled the second one and tossed it on the floor too.

"What good are spies if they don't gather intel?"

Bones laughed as he went into the kitchen.

Bridget sat next to me at the dining room table. "You know, the pharmaceutical company that Miguel owns sells a sleep aid."

I looked back at Bridget, thinking it over. "They might not realize they're drugged and do something dangerous."

"I thought of that. We could make an anonymous call and warn them after ten minutes or so."

"Still too risky," I said, shaking my head. "Someone could get hurt. Does the pharmaceutical company sell anything other than sleep aids?"

She shook her head. "It's a small company. They have a lot of drug trials in progress, waiting for approvals, but the sleep aid is the only one on the market at this point."

"Lie," Wild Card said.

"Explain," I said, following his one-word language.

"Don't bother switching the catering order. Do the anonymous-call thing and say the drug was in the food. People will still panic. Hell, some of them will probably get diarrhea worrying about it, but you don't actually need to drug anyone."

"We still can't control the narrative. What if the receptionist who takes the message runs out the door before sharing the information?"

"Email alert," Bones said, walking over with a cup of coffee for Bridget and himself. "Email the employees warning them that the baked goods were exposed to the sleeping aid."

"Ooh," Bridget said. "That's good. Everyone who works there with a computer will be talking about it. It will spread through the rumor mill to the textile mill in no time."

I nodded, liking the idea. "And mass employee panic will cause at least half the employees to go home sick."

"See? Teamwork!" Tweedle said, clapping.

I shook my head at her. "You are way too perky in the morning."

"Eat your fruit and play nice," Wild Card said as he set a plate of fruit between Bridget and me.

"Ignore her, Tweedle," Bones said. "She's a bitch when she hasn't gotten enough sleep."

"Only then?" Tech mumbled.

"Cut her some slack guys," Wild Card said. "Nicholas had a rough night. It wasn't pretty."

"He okay?" Tech asked.

"He will be," I said, repeating Wild Card's line from earlier.

Maggie appeared at the top of the basement stairs. "Someone needs to find me coffee. Donovan's couch is horrible. I woke with the worst kink in my neck."

Maggie's hair was standing in every direction possible. Yesterday's makeup was smeared an inch under her eyes. And her once nicely pressed blouse and skirt were wrinkled beyond recognition.

"So much for that beauty sleep, aye, Maggie?" I said.

"Bite me," she said as Wild Card handed her a cup of coffee.

I smiled back at Maggie. "Now that's the attitude I can appreciate in the morning."

Maggie started to walk into the dining room but stopped, turned, and openly inspected Wild Card from head to toe. "Did you become gay overnight or were you always gay?" she asked him.

Wild Card smirked but didn't say anything as he flipped pancakes.

I laughed into my coffee cup. "He looks like a ballet dancer, right? Those sweats are practically eating his ass."

"It's a nice ass, no matter which way he's swinging this morning," Maggie said as she walked in and sat down.

Tyler walked into the kitchen through the garage door and dropped a duffle bag. Without saying anything, he turned and left out the same door.

Wild Card walked over and opened the door. "Thank you, Tyler."

"No sweat, man. Keep the clothes you borrowed, though. I know you're riding commando."

Wild Card closed the door and grabbed the duffle. "Tweedle, watch the pancakes, will you?"

"You betcha," she said as he ducked into the guest bathroom.

"Why was he wearing Tyler's clothes?" Bones asked.

I couldn't help my cheeks heating as I tried to focus on starting my laptop. "Because it covered more of him than the towel he was wearing before that."

Maggie leaned back and closed her eyes. "I have this amazing image in my head."

"Me too," Tweedle said, giggling as she set a plate of pancakes beside Tech.

"Shipping records are printing." Tech nodded to the printer, moving the plate of pancakes out of range from Bones and cutting a huge chunk which he folded and stuffed into his mouth.

Whiskey walked halfway down the stairs before stopping and looking around. He turned to me and sighed.

"I know." I nodded back at him. "This is supposed to be *our* quiet time."

"It's the only time of the day that isn't crazy," he said, pouting.

Tweedle met him at the bottom of the stairs like a housewife from a fifty's sitcom, wearing an apron and handing him a cup of coffee, a bright smile plastered on her face. "Good morning, Whiskey."

Whiskey glanced at me again.

"Just go with it," I said, holding my cup up as Tweedle made the rounds with the coffee pot.

"What are we doing this morning?" Maggie asked, looking at the papers scattered about.

"We're finalizing a plan of attack. We've narrowed it down to sabotaging a semi filled with textiles and emailing the employees at the mill that their morning bakery treats were exposed to the pharmaceutical company's sleep aid. We're hoping it will cause a mass panic."

Maggie took a drink of her coffee before looking over at me. "Can I be honest?"

I looked toward the ceiling and thought about it. On one hand, I appreciated Maggie's candor. On the other, I wasn't sure I was fueled with enough caffeine for her honesty. Either way, she was going to tell me, so I might as well get it over with.

"Hit me with it."

"I've always respected you, Harrison, but you've finally let me down. That's the most juvenile plan I've ever heard. Sabotaging a truck? Planting a fake rumor? You are *hoping* people panic?" Maggie rolled her eyes. "You can do better."

"*But I'm tired!*" I whined, dropping my head to the table.

"She's right, though," Tech said. "It's kind of a cobbled plan. You started off saying we were disabling a semi full of fabric and somehow landed on emailing employees that they may or may not be sick. You're all over the place."

"It's her fault," I said, pointing to Tweedle. "All this teamwork crap before I've even had a full cup of coffee."

"Don't blame, Tweedle," Wild Card said, throwing a blueberry across the room at me.

I caught the blueberry and passed it to Bridget to eat. I wasn't a fan.

"You've got too much shit in your head which is why you can't think straight," Wild Card continued. "Now start over. What's your objective?"

I sat up straight and answered as if I was a student talking to a professor. "To financially impact Miguel in a way that results in no physical injuries and no long-term financial damage."

"You also said the plan has to be savvy and intelligent, though," Maggie said. "You need Miguel to view you as a threat to his legacy, remember?"

She had a point. Causing a semi to break down or a few employees to worry about being drugged wouldn't earn Miguel's respect as a rival.

Bridget shoved me, almost making me fall.

"What are you doing?"

"You need to get up." She shoved me again.

"Why?"

"You think better when you pace."

I glared at her, but got up, taking my coffee with me. I wandered into the living room and started to pace. *What could I do to get Miguel's attention*? If I could somehow shut down production for a day, without anyone getting hurt, that would be ideal. But how? I could take out the electrical system but they'd have emergency generators. Starting a fire would be a bad idea. The email notice had merit, but it would cause more confusion than anything. I'm sure Tech, Carl, or Sara could send a virus to their computer network and really screw some shit up, but I wasn't sure if they could control the virus before it caused long term damage. Miguel wouldn't negotiate a peace deal if we accidentally disabled his IT networks.

Think, Kelsey. *What can we do to shut down business for only a day*? Hell, even a half of a day would be enough. *Email. Fire. Sick. Poisoned. Electrical. Email... Great, now I'm repeating myself.* "Wait..." I said aloud, turning to face everyone. "Not email!"

"She's got something," Bridget said. "I just have no idea what the hell she's saying."

"What if instead of emailing, we *texted* the employees? We can tell them not to report to work until

Monday. We can exclude management who might question why they didn't already know."

"Tomorrow's Saturday," Tyler said.

"It could still work," Maggie said. "The retail mall, bakery, and the trucking company will definitely have employees working over the weekend."

"The textile mill has a weekend shift from seven to three," I said. "I remember seeing the shift schedules on one of the hundreds of documents I read last night."

Bridget nodded. "The pharmaceutical company has so many drug trials going, I'm sure they have employees working this weekend. They do animal testing though, so we'll want the message to be worded so the animal caregivers still go in."

"That leaves the health food company," I said, looking at Tech.

He nodded as he typed. "Looks like they run two shifts on Saturdays."

"Maggie?" I said, bracing myself for her honesty. "Is the plan *savvy* enough to get Miguel's attention?"

"It's perfect, actually. Having his employees not show up to work at all six of his companies will cause his head to spin. I like it."

"Tech, is it doable? I don't know anything about texting mass alerts."

"I can create a dummy account no problem. I'll need help to enter the employees' phone numbers into the app and separating the companies, but yeah, it's perfectly doable."

I set my coffee cup on the end table and did a little dance, excited to have a plan.

"What the hell is wrong with you?" Katie said.

I turned to see her standing in the doorway of the back slider.

"I was just stretching," I said, grabbing my coffee cup and returning to the table.

Chapter Twenty-Seven

Hours later, we were nearing the end. The bakery's message said there was an issue with contaminated flour. The pharmaceutical company's message was that overtime was being discontinued until further notice and that only the animal caregivers were to report in as needed. Both the trucking company and the health food company's messages stated there was a change in management and that all employees would receive more information on Monday. The textile mill's message said that there was a gas leak that would require repair before anyone was allowed into the buildings.

My favorite message was for the retail mall, though: *Due to deteriorating sales caused by the increase of shoppers looking for quality second-hand apparel, the mall will be closed on weekends, effective immediately.*

I knew most employees would predict it was a hoax, but it was too funny to pass up. I was also banking on many of those same employees using the text as an excuse to play hooky.

Tech completed uploading all non-management staff for each company to a different dummy alert account about the same time I narrowed down the delivery times for each message. We both leaned back in our chairs, sighing when we were done.

Sara giggled. Everyone else sitting around the table eating breakfast looked at us with grins.

"How are you going to let Miguel know it was you?" Maggie asked.

"I'm not sure. Which country is he in this week?"

Maggie picked up her phone and made a call. "Hey, Genie. I'm with Kelsey and we need to know what country

Miguel Remirez is currently in. This is off the record, by the way." Maggie bopped her head up and down, listening. "Yes, that means don't tell Kierson." A few minutes lapsed before she said, "Perfect. Thanks." She smiled at something Genie was saying. "Hang on." She hit a button on her phone and turned the phone toward the table. "You're on speaker, Genie. Gang's all here."

"Hello, my wonderful Michigan friends!" Genie sing-sang over the speaker.

"*Hi, Genie!*" everyone shouted back.

"Oh, it's lovely to hear everyone!"

I leaned closer to the phone. "If you're not doing anything this weekend, you're welcome to come visit."

"Maybe next time. You know, after the cartel thing."

"Understand completely. Enjoy your weekend."

"You too. Bye, everybody!"

"*Bye, Genie!*" everyone shouted back.

Maggie disconnected the phone as Tweedle filled our coffee cups again. "Why aren't you cranky about her being happy in the morning?"

"Because Genie doesn't poke the bear," Wild Card said, taking the coffee pot and nudging Tweedle back to the kitchen. "Genie runs the other way when Kelsey's having her mood swings."

"I don't have mood swings."

The room became quiet, and everyone conveniently found somewhere else to look than my direction.

Maggie was the first to speak. "Genie said Miguel is in Mexico and isn't expected in the States over the next few days."

"He's likely to cross the border once the text alerts go out," I said. "I'll have to think about our introduction."

"What's the agenda for the rest of the day?" Wild Card asked as he walked around the table, filling coffee cups.

"What time is it?" I asked.

"A little after eight."

"Damn," I said, realizing Hattie and Pops should have been down by now.

I went into the kitchen and filled two coffee cups before climbing the stairs. After knocking twice on Hattie's door, Pops called out to enter. Hattie was curled up on the bed, half asleep. Pops had moved the rocking chair over next to the bed and was reading to her.

I handed Pops a cup of coffee and set Hattie's on her nightstand before sitting on the edge of the bed. "I was hoping you'd be feeling better today."

"I don't feel sick, just tired." She shuffled back, trying to sit up.

"Stop. No reason for you to sit. What sounds good for breakfast?"

"Something light will do," she said. "I'm not very hungry."

"I'll bring you up a few things and you can eat what you want. Pops? What would you like?"

"Anything will do," he said, watching Hattie as her eyes drifted closed again.

I leaned over, kissing Hattie's cheek, before I left.

At the bottom of the stairs, everyone stood waiting for me. "Hattie wants a light breakfast. Maybe some fruit, scrambled eggs, and toast?"

"Sure thing," Wild Card said. "Pops?"

"He said anything is fine."

"How is she?" Lisa asked.

"Worse," I answered, walking into the other room and picking up my phone. I called Doc, wandering into the living room as the phone rang.

"Sorry, Kelsey," Doc said when he answered. "I meant to call the lab first thing. How's Hattie doing?"

"Doc, she's bad. It's a struggle for her to even sit up."

"Give me five minutes. I'll call you right back." Doc disconnected.

I looked up to find Sara and Nicholas staring at me with worried faces.

"Come, here," I said, calling them over as I sat in the chair in the living room.

"Hattie doesn't have a virus, does she?" Sara asked as she climbed onto my lap.

"We don't know. Doc came over yesterday and took a blood sample. We're waiting to see what the results say."

"Is she going to die?" Nicholas asked.

"No," Wild Card said, scooping up Nicholas and sitting on the arm of the chair. "Hattie's going to get better as soon as we figure out what's making her tired. If she needs a doctor in Switzerland, we'll take her to Switzerland. If she needs a week on the beach, we'll fly her to Jamaica. Until we know what will make her feel better, we have to be patient."

Nicholas looked back at me, waiting for me to say something. He knew I wouldn't lie to him about something so important.

"Right now, Hattie's tired, and we don't know why. If we find out it's something bad, I'll tell you."

"Promise?" Sara asked.

"Promise. For now, though, there's nothing for you guys to worry about. Scout's honor."

"Mom!" Nicholas said, rolling his eyes. "You can't be a scout. You're a *girl*."

"There are girl scouts," Sara said, gearing up to argue.

"Go get dressed and brush your teeth," I said, interrupting their anticipated argument. "After Hattie's had a chance to eat some breakfast, I'll take you up to see her. Vamoose!"

The kids were barely out of the room when my cell phone rang.

"It's Kelsey," I answered.

"I'm on my way over. I got the results, and I'll explain when I get there."

"Explain now."

"I can't. Doctor patient confidentiality."

"Hattie won't care."

"Doesn't make it legal. I'm on my way." Doc hung up.

"He says he's on his way over."

"I'll stay at home today," Katie said. "I can work on the books from here."

I shook my head. "One of us has to be at the store while we're on red alert. And if I go, I'll have to take Nicholas."

"I'll stay at the house," Anne said, placing an arm around Katie's shoulder. "I'll text you every hour with updates."

Wild Card stood. "I'll take breakfast upstairs and let them know Doc is on his way."

Lisa wrapped her arms around me. "I know you're worried, but you called Doc instead of taking her to a hospital because you trust him."

"Maybe she has mono," Alex said, wrapping his arms around both Lisa and me, squeezing us together.

"Wouldn't that be funny? Hattie would blush for a year knowing she caught the kissing disease."

Lisa and I laughed as we broke out of Alex's hold and stepped back.

"Why does everyone look so freaked out?" Maggie asked, walking into the dining room. Maggie had showered and changed. Her make-up and hair were done to her normal perfection.

"Is that my dress?" I asked, looking at her outfit.

Maggie did a slow spin, swinging her hips back and forth. "I raided your closet. I needed something fabulous to wear to impress my new fake boyfriend."

"Nailed it," Bones said, earning himself a whap in the gut from Bridget.

Lisa pointed at Donovan. "Eyes anywhere but Maggie's ass, Donovan!"

Donovan leaned back in his chair and stared up at the ceiling.

"Well?" Maggie asked. "What did I walk in on that looked so serious?"

"Alex can explain. Lisa, send Doc upstairs when he gets here. Anne, can you stall the kids?"

"We'll handle it," Anne answered before I started climbing the private stairs.

~*~*~

The door to the bedroom was open, and I heard Pops and Hattie laughing as Wild Card told some story in his slow-drawling cowboy voice. "I honestly don't know if Kelsey can take anymore of Tweedle's rainbows and sunshine shit. She was grinding her teeth so bad I thought she'd break a molar."

I leaned against the wall and listened.

Hattie giggled. "Someone needs to warn Tweedle."

"We've all tried," Wild Card said. "She's convinced she'll win Kelsey over to her perky side."

"Not my baby girl," Pops said, chuckling. "She's a fighter, not a cheerleader."

"She's definitely scrappy." Wild Card laughed. "I don't know how she keeps everything going. On top of everything else, she arranged for a client to come this weekend so she can prove the woman is faking her stalker. Maggie's going to pretend to be the security guard's girlfriend so Kelsey can see how the woman reacts."

"Oh, I want to see that," Hattie said.

"No can do," Wild Card said, shaking his head. "Even if you were feeling well, Kelsey's drawn a line at the highway. Only a handful of us are allowed to cross back and forth."

"How did Jackson and Reggie end up on the other side?" Pops asked.

"Can't say. It's classified."

"You can tell them," I said, climbing the last two stairs and joining Wild Card on the other side of the bed. "I trust them not to say the wrong thing to the wrong person."

"Good. Because I really wanted to tell them," he said, laughing.

Wild Card explained how Jackson was pretending to be mad at me, but how he was really faking it to spy on Grady and Sebrina.

Hattie rolled her eyes. "Who else stayed on that side of the line?"

"Most weren't given an option," I answered. "Wayne chose to stay at Headquarters, which I expected."

"I'm assuming Mr. Tyler made sure the security on this side understands that the order was *not* to shoot to kill?" Hattie asked.

"Yeah," I said, laughing. "Tyler explained to everyone that the order to shoot Sebrina or Grady if they crossed meant to use a tranquilizer gun or wound them, not to *shoot-shoot* them."

"Good." Hattie nodded. "I'm surprised Wayne didn't figure that out."

"I'm glad he didn't. Grady would've thought it suspicious if Wayne chose my side."

"Am I interrupting?" Doc asked from the top of the stairs.

"Not if you've got answers for us," Pops said, standing to shake Doc's hand.

"I do, but first," Doc said, turning to Hattie. "Do you want to talk in private?"

"Not necessary," Hattie said, shaking her head.

"All right then," Doc said, pulling a chair over from the small table. "I got the blood test results back."

Wild Card laid his hand on top of mine. Pops was already holding Hattie's.

"You have hypothyroidism by the looks of it. It's perfectly treatable. In a nutshell, your thyroid isn't getting the right amounts of hormones to the rest of your body."

"How is it treated?" Pops asked.

"A simple pill. It might take a few weeks before she's back in the swing of things. We'll retest her blood every few weeks to make sure we have the dosage right, then after that we'll test every six months." Doc patted Hattie's arm. "You'll have to take the medication every day, likely for the rest of your life, but I assure you that once you're feeling better, you won't care. I already called the prescription into the pharmacy."

"And next time," I said, fake glaring at Hattie, "you won't wait so long to tell us you're feeling poorly."

Hattie smiled at me. "Yes, sunshine."

I shifted onto my hands and knees, leaning over to hug Hattie. "Don't scare me like this ever again. I can take a lot of things, but worrying about something happening to you is too much."

"I'll do my best," she said, patting my cheek.

I crawled over to the far edge of the bed to get up. "Do you feel up to having a few visitors while I go pick up your pills?"

"If everyone's not too busy that would be nice. Should I go downstairs?"

"Nope," Wild Card said, walking over to the top of the stairs. He whistled loudly and a dozen people, including the kids, ran up. "She needs to take a pill. That's it. She'll be back to her normal self in a few weeks."

Everyone cheered as they converged on Hattie and Pops, climbing on top of the bed or taking their turns leaning over to hug her. I snuck out and down the stairs.

"I didn't want to intrude," Maggie said from the bottom of the stairs. "Seemed like a family moment."

"She's going to be fine. I'm heading to the pharmacy for the pills she needs."

"Do you think it would be okay if I snuck upstairs?"

"Hattie would get a kick out of seeing you in that dress. Wild Card told her about your undercover assignment. She seemed disappointed she wouldn't be able to witness it. Can you talk to Tech about sending the video highlights to her? She could use the laugh."

"I'll take care of it," Maggie said, heading up the stairs.

I went to my bedroom to put on my boots. They didn't exactly coordinate with my yoga pants and sweatshirt, but I didn't care. The only thing that mattered was getting Hattie's pills so she would feel better. When I returned to the kitchen, Tweedle stood looking toward the stairs.

"Go on," I said. "You can go say hi, too."

Tweedle hurried around the kitchen, stacking a tray of baked goods before climbing the stairs. I grabbed my handbag and was reaching for the door when I heard a loud ruckus above me.

"I'm okay," Tweedle said. "Just a little rug burn."

I shook my head as I walked out.

Chapter Twenty-Eight

Doc must have warned the pharmacy to have the prescription ready to go, because I breezed in, paid, and breezed out. I was crossing the parking lot, digging my keys out of my handbag, when someone grabbed me from behind, covering my face with a rag.

Reflexively, I tried to breathe, realizing my mistake too late as I smelled the chloroform. Knowing I only had seconds, I threw an elbow into my assailant's ribs, kicked his kneecap hard enough to hear it crack, and felt his weight drop to the side and his hands loosen their grip. Turning, I managed a throat punch as my head spun with dizziness.

As the world tilted, I staggered toward the pharmacy. The electronic glass doors swooshed open, and I fell to the floor. Dragging my handbag in front of me, I pulled my phone as I was surrounded by customers and employees asking if I needed help. I managed to hit the call and speaker buttons, calling Tyler, before my vision blurred again.

"What's up?" Tyler answered.

"Help! Send help!"

"Where are you?" Tyler yelled.

"She's at the pharmacy on the corner of ninth street," one of the customers answered for me. "She seems dizzy. Should we call an ambulance?"

"I'm on my way, Kelsey! Hang on!"

"Chloro—" I'm not sure if I finished speaking before I passed out.

~*~*~

When I woke, my head was propped on Dave's thigh as he smiled down at me. I blinked a few times, trying to clear my vision. He was wearing his uniform, meaning someone had called 911.

"Blood pressure is coming back down," Doc said from my left, removing a cuff. "Heartbeat is still a bit fast."

Renato stood at my feet, watching the crowd.

"How long have I been out?" I asked, trying to sit up.

"Easy there," Doc said, pushing me back. "Do you know what happened?"

"Chloroform."

"That's what Tyler thought you were trying to say," Doc said, nodding. "We should take you to the hospital for observation."

"No."

"That's what *I thought* you'd say." Doc chuckled, moving a stethoscope to my chest. "Give me a few deep breaths."

I did as he asked, but as soon as he moved away, I grabbed Dave's arm and pulled myself into a sitting position. My head spun a few times, but my vision settled after a few seconds. I reached a hand out to Renato for him to help me stand. "Where's Tyler?"

Renato grasped my hand and extended his other arm behind my back as he helped to lift me. Once I was upright, the ground tilted. He held me steady.

"Tyler's with Steve," Dave answered. "They're watching the security footage."

"Take me to them."

Dave walked beside me holding one arm as Renato held the other and braced my back. The distance from the front of the store to the backroom seemed never ending.

"Hurry up!" Steve barked at someone as I walked into a small office.

Tyler saw me and reached out a hand to guide me into a chair. "What can you tell us?"

"I wasn't paying attention. Hattie—" I looked over at Doc, "—damn it. Where did Hattie's pills go?"

"They were scattered in the parking lot. The pharmacist is filling another order. We'll get her pills to her."

"They'll worry." I shook my head. "If I'm not back with the pills, they'll worry something happened."

"Something did happen," Steve said, glaring over at me.

"She's right," Tyler said, digging into my handbag which was strapped over his shoulder. "Hattie and the kids can't take any more stress." He pulled out one of my cash envelopes. "Doc? Can you take the new order of pills to Hattie? Tell her there was a mess up at the pharmacy and you offered to bring them back while Kelsey runs an errand for Father Eric at the mission. Hattie and the kids know Father Eric ropes Kelsey into doing favors all the time. They won't think anything of it."

"I'll handle it, but only if you promise to make sure Kelsey doesn't drive for the next twenty-four hours and will be closely monitored."

"Deal," Tyler agreed. "What should we be watching for?"

"She'll likely be dizzy for a while, maybe nauseous too. I'm most concerned about her heart, though. If she loses consciousness or starts having heart palpitations, call an ambulance, then call me."

Renato nodded. "We'll keep a close eye on her."

Doc shook Renato's hand and left. I tried to roll my eyes, but I think they went more cross-eyed than anything.

"*How in the hell did someone get the jump on you?*" Steve yelled at me.

"I wasn't paying attention," I admitted with a shrug. "I was thinking about getting home and getting the pills to Hattie. She's been sick, and I'm worried about her. I was digging my keys out when someone came up behind me."

"Did you get a look at him?" Tyler asked.

"Not really. About your height. Good muscle strength, but lean. The rest is a blur."

"I have the footage," the store employee who was sitting in front of the computer said.

Tyler reached over and turned the monitor so we could watch the video. It wasn't easy to focus, but there wasn't much to see. My attacker wore a beanie, pulled low over his forehead and ears, and kept his back to the camera.

"Damn," Dave said. "He'll be limping for a few weeks, that's for sure."

"I would've done more damage if it weren't for the damn chloroform."

"This is a problem," Renato said, nodding toward the monitor. "He's not a part-time smuggler picking up a side job."

"I know," I said, running a hand through my hair. "Santiago sent a professional this time. I got lucky."

"Email that video to me," Steve ordered the employee, dropping a business card on the desk.

Tyler helped me stand and took one side as Dave took the other. Renato walked out first, scanning the store, then the parking lot, as they half dragged me to my SUV and loaded me into the passenger seat. Tyler got behind the wheel. Renato and two of his men rode their bikes in front of us as Tyler drove us home. One of our security SUVs followed behind us.

"What do you need?" Tyler asked.

"For my head to clear. Shit. I can't let Nicholas see me like this."

"Headquarters?" Tyler asked.

"No way. I don't need the men at Aces to grill me with questions. Besides, I'm not up to dealing with Grady or Sebrina either. Take me to the store. Katie can babysit my ass until my head clears."

Tyler turned on his com and radioed Renato and whoever was behind us that we were making a detour. A few minutes later, Tyler pulled up to the back of the store and jogged around to my side of the SUV to help me inside. Farmer was one of the men in the other SUV. He helped Tyler get me in the building, across the inventory room, and into the breakroom.

"Thanks," I said as they settled me onto a barstool.

Alex walked into the room with his hands pressed to his leather-clad hips. "I would totally be giving you shit for wearing sweatpants and a baggy sweatshirt in public if you didn't look like you'd just lost the war."

"Just one battle. The war is just beginning."

"Anything the non-fighter of the family can do to help?"

"Water and a wet rag for my forehead."

Alex pulled a bottle of water from the refrigerator and handed it to Tyler before walking out of the room. He returned a few minutes later with a warm wet rag for my forehead. "Did she see Doc?" he asked Tyler.

Tyler nodded, but he had worry lines creasing his forehead. "Said she's to be monitored. No driving either."

"I'm guessing we're hiding her from Hattie and the kids until she looks less like death warmed over?"

"That's the plan," Tyler said, sighing. "I need to make a few phone calls. Can you watch her?"

"Go. I got her." Alex pulled out the stool next to me and wrapped an arm around me. "Do you need to cry?"

"I'm too pissed to cry. I screwed up."

"There's always a first time," Alex said, chuckling. "Just don't make a habit of it."

Despite my headache, I smiled. Then my stomach rolled. "Shit," I said as I leapt off the chair to the trash can.

Alex held an arm around my waist and used his other hand to hold my hair as I puked. When I nodded that I thought I was done, he helped lower me to the floor. He handed me my water and wash cloth before getting me a paper cup to spit into.

Farmer walked in and wordlessly pulled the plastic bag from the trash can, carrying it out. Alex put a new bag in its place.

"Feel better or worse?" Tyler asked as he leaned against the door frame.

"Not sure yet," I answered honestly.

"I've got Doc on the phone and he's not surprised you puked, but he wants to know your pulse."

Alex reached down for my wrist and counted it out as he watched the wall clock. "One ten."

Tyler relayed the message. "Doc's sending Haley over to help watch her."

Alex took my washcloth and rinsed it before warming it in the microwave. When he handed it back, it felt like heaven on my forehead.

"Alex?"

"Yeah, luv," he said, crouching behind me and rubbing my back.

"I puked on my sweatshirt. I need something else to wear, but I'm not wearing a bra, so it has to be something baggy."

"Go find her something to wear," Katie said, walking into the breakroom. "I'll watch her." Katie squatted in front of me. "You going to live?"

"Yup. Not ready to get up, though."

"Let's slide you back so you can lean against the cabinets."

Katie half dragged me as I tried to scooch back. It was exhausting moving just those few feet, but the reward was that I could lean against the cupboards without worrying I was going to topple over.

"Explain why the rest of us have guards twenty-four seven, but you thought you were invincible enough to run around town on your own?"

"I fucked up."

"As long as you know it," she said, nudging me in the shoulder.

"Careful," I said, sighing. "I might fall over."

"If you do, I'm not catching you. You smell like vomit."

Alex returned with a pair of jeans, a tight Henley, and a loose cardigan. As embarrassing as it was, Katie helped me dress while Alex stood guard outside the door. When I was decent, Alex helped me to my feet and over to the sink, handing me a new toothbrush and some toothpaste.

From there, I was moved into a chair so Katie could apply foundation to my face.

Haley arrived and took my blood pressure and pulse again. She said it was improving, but she was ordered to shadow me until it was back to normal. I tested my feet, first standing and then walking a bit in the small room, before I ventured out to the docks. Goat was there, finishing a drop off.

"I need a smoke."

"You sure that's a good idea?"

I gave him a look, and he pulled his pack.

"Come on. We can sit at the top of the stairs, just outside the door."

He helped me down one stair, and I sat on the step. "The cold air feels good."

"You won't be saying that in another month. You'll be champing at the bit to get to Texas so you can warm up."

"I hate winter."

"I know you do," Goat said, laughing. "Personally, it's my favorite season."

"Why's that?"

"Women everywhere with their nipples poking out. Keeps me smiling all day."

I checked my cardigan, and sure enough, it was open, displaying my braless undershirt in all its perkiness. I wrapped both sides of the sweater around me as Goat laughed again.

Chapter Twenty-Nine

It was almost ten o'clock by the time I felt steady enough to return home. Wild Card was in the kitchen, wearing one of Hattie's aprons. Nicholas was sitting at the dining room table reading while Beth worked with Sara at the far end on something having to do with sentence mapping.

Tyler took my handbag and coat, hanging them on the hook beside the door. I walked into the dining room and grabbed my laptop, starting it up.

Sitting beside Nicholas, I said to him, "Time to make a book cover."

"You're not too busy?" he asked, looking up at me.

"Too busy to spend time with my favorite guy?" I said, opening a familiar online program. "Never."

"What if it takes me too long to learn?" Nicholas asked, closing his book.

"No such thing."

"But I'm not as smart as Sara."

"Your brain is different from Sara's. Doesn't make her better or worse than you."

He set his book aside and moved over to my lap. I showed him the basic icons and their functions, before pulling in a few graphic files for him to manipulate. When he had the basics down, I opened a new window on the computer and went to a site where graphics could be bought. Giving him a budget, I left him searching for pirate ships as I walked into the kitchen.

"He's having fun," Wild Card said, nodding at Nicholas.

"I hope so. I hate seeing him worried all the time."

"Me too." Wild Card handed me a chocolate muffin, before whispering to me, "You going to explain what happened to you this morning?"

"Do I have to?" I tore off a chunk of chocolate muffin and ate it.

"Yes."

"What's the difference between a chocolate muffin and a cupcake?"

"One's breakfast and the other's dessert." Wild Card took the muffin and set it on the counter. "Talk."

I eyed the chocolate muffin, surprised my stomach had settled enough to tolerate it. "I was caught off guard outside the pharmacy. I handled it, but not before I inhaled some chloroform. Bad guy got away."

"You puke yet?"

"I take it you're familiar with the side effects?"

"Self-inflicted test," he said, shrugging and handing my muffin back. "I felt better after I puked, but I was still shaky for a day or two."

"Why would you intentionally drug yourself with chloroform?"

Wild Card grinned as he picked up a pan from the dish rack and started drying it. "I was teaching a self-defense class, and a woman asked me if they'd have time to react if they were drugged. I decided to test a few drugs to determine the reaction time."

"You're crazy."

"That's why they call me Wild Card."

"They call you Wild Card because of a poker reference. The best card a person could hope to draw is a wild card."

A noise erupted in the dining room, drawing our attention. Nicholas threw the laptop to the floor before running down the hallway toward his bedroom. Wild Card shot after him. I checked on Sara and Beth, before picking the laptop up. On the screen was Nicholas' email account showing an email from Grady.

"Damn him!" I said to myself as I read the email.

Grady apologized to Nicholas for how he handled the situation, explaining that his relationship with me was complicated, but how he never meant to hurt Nick. Grady added that he thought it was best if he moved away for a while.

I set the laptop on the table and walked down the hall. I found Nicholas and Wild Card sitting on the floor, leaning against the bed. Both of them were quiet.

"I'm sorry Grady emailed you," I said, sitting beside Nicholas. "He had no right to do that."

Nicholas shrugged, staring at the floor.

"I wish I knew how to make this better for you," I said, wrapping an arm around him.

He tucked his head into my shoulder but remained quiet.

"I'll give you guys some privacy," Wild Card said, getting up and walking out.

"Mom?" Nicholas asked.

"Yeah, buddy?" I caressed his hair from his face.

"Grady's not going to stay, is he?"

"I don't have any answers yet."

"You have to talk to him. You have to make him listen."

"That's a tough ask, buddy. You can't force someone to listen."

"You can. I know you can."

"And if he still doesn't want to be in our lives?"

Nicholas sighed. "Then he doesn't get to be my dad anymore."

"Aww, Nick. My heart's breaking for you right now." I wrapped my arms around him and held him.

~*~*~

It took a while, but I eventually convinced Nicholas to leave his room and return to his book cover project. Farmer stood leaning against the wall at the end of the hall in the dining room. I looked around, not seeing Wild Card. "Did Wild Card ask you to watch Nicholas?"

Farmer nodded.

"Did he say where he was going?"

Farmer shrugged.

"Said he was going for a run," Beth answered.

"In jeans?" I asked, gathering my coat and handbag.

Haley appeared beside me, taking my keys as she grabbed her coat and followed me out of the house.

"Where are we going?" she asked as she slid behind the wheel.

"Headquarters. Wild Card went to confront Grady."

"Oh, shit," Haley said, throwing the SUV in reverse and hitting the gas.

Haley wasn't on the guest list at Headquarters, and the guards refused to let her inside. When I rounded the corner, turning into the gym, I stumbled, surprised by the sight in front of me. Grady and Wild Card were on the far mat. Both were panting hard, covered in sweat, and bleeding from facial wounds. They must've been at it for a few rounds, because they both sagged from exhaustion. I placed a hand on the wall to steady myself before making my way across the gym.

Donovan stepped in front of me, blocking my path, but Bones grabbed him by the shoulder and shook his head. "It needs to end."

Donovan nodded and stepped aside.

Walking onto the mat, I lightly kicked the back of Grady's legs, throwing him forward to his knees. If he wasn't so physically spent, he could've easily avoided the amateur move. I shook my head and moved in front of Wild Card. I pushed him by his chest, forcing him to stumble backward until he was off the mat and standing on the hardwood floor.

"This isn't about you," Wild Card said, exhaling a deep breath as he wiped a streak of blood away from his eye with his forearm.

"I know, Cooper."

"Cooper, huh?" Grady said, chuckling as he sat back on his ankles. He wheezed, trying to catch his breath. "How cozy. Knew it was only a matter of time."

I walked back to Grady. Crouching in front of him, I inspected his wounds. The bandage around his shoulder was bleeding through. "Say anything you want about me, Grady," I tilted my head to the side, watching him, "but if you contact my son again, it will be me, not Wild Card, coming after you. And I'll do more than hurt you. *I'll end you.*" I stood and stepped back. "Promise."

I walked off the mat, only to come face to face with Sebrina.

"You make a lot of threats for such a little thing." Being a good six inches taller than me, she looked down her nose at me.

"Look around, honey," I said, stepping closer. "Do you think everyone would be so quiet if they thought it was an empty threat?"

Sebrina glanced around, seeing everyone was indeed quiet. "You wouldn't actually *kill* Grady."

"I've killed many times to protect my family. What makes you think Grady would be exempt? Because I've slept with him? Honey," I said, shaking my head, "unlike you, my pussy doesn't run my life."

Wild Card laughed before groaning and leaning over to hold his gut.

"Come on, slugger," I called to Wild Card over my shoulder. "Let's get you cleaned up."

I started for the exit, but stopped halfway there. A large white board displayed the randomly drawn teams for the weekend tournament. I grabbed the eraser and cleared the board. No way in hell was I teaming up with Grady.

At the top of the board I wrote *Team Kelsey* and added my name, Bridget, Trigger, Tech, Katie, Anne, and Wild Card, completing our seven-person team. Donovan took the marker, adding Team Alpha with his name underneath. Bones wrote his name under Donovan's. Wayne started another team name for Team Bravo. I left as everyone silently lined up.

In the parking lot, Donovan jogged over to me as Haley helped Wild Card into the SUV. "We were supposed to kick off the team competition with the relay race in the woodlands tonight."

"And?"

"My guys aren't allowed to cross the highway."

I glanced toward the road, considering the security risks. "We'll open the border a half hour before the event and close it a half an hour after. No one is to be within fifty feet of the houses or store. They also have to walk across so my security team doesn't need to worry about searching vehicles. Clear?"

"I'll make it work," Donovan said. "I heard about the pharmacy incident. You okay?"

"I'm good, but the guy was a pro. Stay alert."

"You got it. Take care of Wild Card."

"You *betcha*," I said, grinning as I mimicked Tweedle. "It's all about teamwork."

"Yeah, sure. Then why aren't you staying to help clean the blood off the mats?" Donovan said as he jogged backwards toward the building.

~*~*~

Once again, we ended up at the store. Alex offered to help clean Wild Card's wounds and find him a change of clothes. I decided to track Katie down, finding her in the office we used to share.

"Looks different in here," I said as I walked in.

"I only changed a few pictures and painted the walls," Katie said, leaning back in her chair behind the desk. "You like?"

"It's nice. Not as fun as my war room, but it works."

"I'm not sure axes and crossbows mounted to the walls is the best impression for a retail store office. Otherwise, I'd be cool with it."

I laughed, sitting in the guest chair. "I signed you and Anne up to be on Team Kelsey for the tournament."

"*Yes!*" Katie said, making a fist in the air. "Anne and I were hoping we could compete. Are you sure it's okay since we don't work for Silver Aces?"

"It's a done deal, whether people like it or not."

"This is going to be epic," Katie said, laughing. "Oh! Bridget and I ordered t-shirts." Katie jumped out of her chair and grabbed a box from the floor. Opening it, she tossed me a grey t-shirt with silver glitter lettering: *Kelsey's Crew*.

"Did you get a variety of sizes?"

"I got one for everyone in the family, including Grady, and one for Tyler, Bridget, Tech, and Trigger."

"Wild Card can have Grady's shirt, though I'm not sure how much help he'll be after going six rounds on the matt with Grady. They both look like hell."

Katie's eyes narrowed as she leaned against the desk. "They've been keeping their distance from each other. Did something else happen?"

"Grady emailed Nicholas."

Katie threw the shirt she was holding at the empty guest chair. "That bastard. Maybe it's time for you to send Grady packing."

"I might have to, when it's safe. I'm not willing to risk Grady's life until then. Despite the threat I just made, Grady's funeral would be a lot harder for Nicholas to handle than an apology email."

My phone beeped, alerting me to a text. I dug it out of my purse and checked the screen. It was from Mickey McNabe. Opening the message, I saw a picture of the dental clinic with flames shooting out the window. The message under the picture said the fire was bigger than anticipated and ETA on repairs would be two to three weeks.

I texted back a thumbs up before calling Uncle Hank.

"You still coming to Florida next week?" Uncle Hank asked when he answered.

"My schedule has changed, but my girls figured out how the prostitutes were disappearing and I had the operation shut down for a few weeks. It wasn't exactly by legal methods, so don't ask questions. I have a few problems at home to take care of before I make the trip south."

"That sounds ominous."

"I've got it handled at the moment."

Uncle Hank chuckled. "I keep hoping you and Grady will settle down into a nice quiet life, get married and pop out a few brothers and sisters for Nicholas. I'm dreaming, aren't I?"

"Grady's sleeping with his ex-wife these days. Nicholas is having King Kong-sized anger issues. And a Mexican cartel keeps trying to kidnap me. So, *no*, I don't think the quiet family life is on the agenda in my immediate future."

Uncle Hank was silent for a beat. "Do I need to come beat the shit out of Grady?"

I couldn't help but laugh. "Wild Card got to him first."

"Always liked that boy. I wouldn't be opposed if the two of you got back together. Your Aunt Suzanne likes him, too. Says he's a good eater."

I threw my free hand into the air as I rolled my eyes. "Because *that's* the quality every girl looks for in a man." I started moving toward the inventory room. "I have to go, but I should be in Miami in two weeks. I might need to bring Nicholas with me."

"Your aunt and I will take him to the beach while you work the case. It will be fun."

"Oh, sure. I see how it is. Sand and sunshine for you guys—prostitutes and human traffickers for me?"

"Sounds about right. See you in a few weeks. And... I'd tell you to be safe, but I know better. So instead—stay alive."

"I can do that... I think."

Uncle Hank hung up as he laughed.

"You ready?" I asked Wild Card, finding him at the loading dock talking to Goat. Wild Card had butterfly strips holding the cut above his eyebrow together, and his right hand was wrapped in gauze.

"Ready enough, but we've got a security problem. Goat says some employees were planning on watching the relay tonight."

"Shit." I ran a hand through my hair. "They'll be safe enough from the cartel, but it could get messy keeping the border rules intact."

"I'll talk to Tyler," Wild Card said. "If we keep friends and family close to the house, we can have Tyler's security team protect them. Donovan can keep his guys off the front lawn."

I nodded. "Tyler finally crashed. He's barely slept the last few days, so I don't want to wake him. You, Goat, Whiskey, and Renato arrange whatever you need. Fill Tyler in when he wakes."

"You sure he won't get mad? I don't want to step on his toes."

I grinned at Wild Card. "Are you afraid of Tyler?"

"No, but he does a hell of a job protecting your family, so I don't want to do something that pisses him off and has him quitting."

"Tyler's not like that," Goat said, standing to pull out his phone. "His first priority is what's best for the family. His second priority is fucking with Donovan and James because their egos can't handle it." Goat looked up a number on his phone. "I'll call Whiskey. You can talk to Renato."

Haley drove me back to the house so I could help Nicholas finish his book cover while the boys worked out the security details. Upon entering through the garage, I saw that the kitchen and dining room were empty. Hearing laughter, I followed Hattie's private staircase and found Nicholas, Sara, Beth, Tweedle, Hattie, Pops, and Tech upstairs watching something on her television. Farmer stood in the corner of the room with his eyes on Nicholas and his hands clasped in front of him. He nodded once to me before turning toward the stairs.

"Tech, rewind the video so Kelsey and Haley can see that," Hattie said.

"Yeah. I want to watch it again too," Nicholas said, giggling. "Maggie's crazy."

"What did Maggie do?" I asked as I walked over and lifted Sara, setting her on my lap after I sat on the bed.

"She's pretending to be GI Joe's girlfriend," Tweedle said.

"GI Joe?"

"Billy Hobbs," Tech said. "He's a little..."

"Stuffy," Hattie said, giggling.

Tech restarted the video, and it all made sense. Maggie walked across the gym and practically shoved her tongue down Billy Hobbs' throat. He stood rigid with surprised eyes as he patted her back awkwardly. When she broke the kiss, she ran her fingers into his short-cropped hair as she shoved his face into her ample chest. His hands moved to her waist in an effort not to lose his balance, but it was enough bodily contact to cause Daphne Davenport to storm across the gym and exit toward the apartments in a jealous rage. Maggie released Billy as soon as the door closed. She turned, winked at the camera, and walked off in the other direction. Billy stood there, dumbstruck.

"How does a man that handsome not know how to make out with a woman?" Hattie asked.

"I have no idea, but we'll need to catch Daphne before Maggie gets bored. She didn't sign up to school a grown man on..." I turned to see the kids listening intently. "Um..."

"Kissing is the word you're looking for," Beth said with a smirk.

"Yes. Kissing. Sorry, drew a blank."

Hattie and Tweedle giggled again.

"Are you ready to finish your book cover?" I asked Nicholas.

"It's already done," he said, scrambling off the bed and running over to the table. He ran back, handing me the book.

"Nick, this is great!" I said, turning the book over. He had found an old pirate ship picture which he had turned on an angle and had it floating from the back cover to the front. A boy stood at the front of the ship; his sword pointed out into an oncoming storm. "How did you do this?"

"It was easy. I had to watch a few videos to figure out how to get the picture of the boy on the ship, but after that, it was *smooth sailing*." He laughed at his own joke.

"The title looks good too," Beth said, admiring the cover. "I'm impressed. It looks professional."

"Except I had to tape it onto the book," Nicholas said, shrugging.

"Have you showed this to your Aunt Katie, yet?" Haley asked, taking the book from my hands as she flipped it over.

"Uh-uh. Why?"

"She's designing a flyer for the year-end sale. Maybe you can help her."

"Can I call her?" Nicholas asked, lighting up with a big grin.

"I think she'd like that," I said, ruffling his hair before he ran downstairs. "Thank you, Haley. He needed that."

"You're welcome, but I wasn't kidding. He's good." Haley handed the book back to me. "He has an eye for it. After he helps Katie with her year-end sale, maybe he can fix the graphics on the store's website." She pulled her blood pressure kit and wrapped a cuff around my arm, pumping it tight.

"Why is Haley checking your blood pressure, sunshine?" Hattie asked.

"Because Doc was worried about some chemicals I inhaled. How are you feeling?"

"Alert enough to know you're not telling the whole story."

"Do you want to hear the whole story?"

"No," she said, sighing. "Not really."

Sara giggled.

Hearing activity in the front yard, Pops walked over to the window. "Why is Whiskey parking a flatbed trailer in the front yard?"

"Likely that will be the spectator's area for the relay race tonight. We have visitors coming to watch."

Sara ran over to look out the window with Pops. "Can we decorate it?"

"As long as you help clean up later, sure."

"Come on, Beth. We have decorations in the basement," Sara said as she ran over and pulled Beth by the hand toward the stairs.

I fell back onto Hattie's bed, closing my eyes.

"We have a few things we need to chat about," Tech said, nudging my shoulder. "You can take a nap afterward."

"But I'm so comfortable."

"You woke me at four-thirty this morning. I have a right to mess with your mid-day nap."

"Fine!" I whined, mimicking Nicholas when he was throwing a fit. I rolled off the bed and stomped my way dramatically down the stairs. I could hear Pops and Hattie laughing behind me.

Tech followed me with his laptop. At the bottom of the stairs, I stopped to figure out the best place to have a private conversation. Nicholas was in the dining room, talking to Katie on speaker phone while he worked on his computer. In the living room Bridget was working on her computer while her head bounced wildly to whatever was playing through her earphones. Abigail and her nanny would be in my atrium, so that wouldn't work either.

Going to the basement, we walked through the gym quietly, hoping not to wake the security shift who were napping. We passed Beth and Sara who were pulling out decorations for the trailer before Tech and I turned into the furnace room to follow the tunnel down to Donovan's.

"This is getting a little out of hand," Tech said as we entered Donovan's basement family room.

"Agreed. Now what has you acting so secretive?"

"When I was pulling the video for Hattie, I saw something odd," Tech said, opening a video file on his computer and hitting play.

I moved closer, leaning over to see better. "What am I looking for?" The video was a wide-angle view of the gym at Headquarters.

"Watch Grady."

Grady was leaning against the far wall, fiddling with his phone. His head was bent like he was watching the screen, but I knew him well enough to know he was scouting the room. "Who's he watching?"

"Sebrina," Tech said, pointing to the other side of the room where Sebrina and Shipwreck were talking next to one of the makeshift buffet tables.

Shipwreck stormed off and Sebrina wandered over to sit next to Donovan. She whispered something to him, leaning a little too close. Donovan stood, glaring at her as he walked over and sat beside Wayne. Sebrina winked at Donovan before she left to join another group of guys. Bones walked by, shaking his head at her as he passed. Grady shifted, turning to lean his good shoulder against the wall so Sebrina remained in view.

"Odd, right? If Grady's so in love with Sebrina, why's he watching her like that?"

"Do you have video from inside the apartment building?"

"There's a camera at the entrance and one in each hallway."

"Pull up last night's video."

"I don't have to," Tech said, leaning back in his chair. "Grady and Sebrina shared his room last night. They went inside around eleven and didn't come out until seven this morning."

I wrinkled my nose but didn't say anything.

"What's he doing, Kelsey?"

"I don't know. There are several reasons he could be watching Sebrina. Maybe he loves her but doesn't trust her not to cheat on him. Maybe he's not sure if she's involved with Santiago. Maybe he's faking the whole relationship. It doesn't matter."

"What if he's faking it? What if this is all some misguided attempt to keep the family safe? Can you forgive him?"

I thought about the question before shaking my head. "I don't think so. Maybe I could find a way to forgive him for cheating on me, but how could I ever forgive him for hurting Nick? He broke his heart."

"We both know Grady wouldn't intentionally hurt Nicholas. He loves that kid."

"Like he loves me?" I asked, pointing toward the video. "Damn it, Tech. I can't trust him."

Tech nodded. "Sorry. I guess I'm feeling betrayed by Grady, too. I just want him to be innocent of all this. I want to believe he was the man we all thought he was."

"You're not the only one," Donovan said, entering the room. "He's been my best friend for nearly a decade. I keep searching for an excuse that would make his behavior somehow excusable."

"Why are you home so early?" I asked, wiping a stray tear away.

"Tyler assigned me the task of feeding the prisoners lunch," Donovan said, holding up a brown paper bag.

"I'll go with you." I looked at Tech. "Anything else I need to know?"

"No. I'm screening all the videos for Sebrina and Daphne, but so far everything has been as expected."

Donovan looked at Tech. "One of these days, you'll burn out working these crazy hours with Kelsey. If you worked for me, you'd have steady hours."

"I'd die of boredom," Tech said, smirking as he turned his attention back to his laptop.

Chapter Thirty

I practically ran from my thoughts of Grady as I followed the tunnel to Alex's. Exiting the other side, I looked around the room. I walked toward the small kitchenette, peeking around the corner, but no one was there. A closet spanned the other end of the room. I walked over and opened all the doors.

"What are you looking for?" Donovan asked.

"No one. Nothing."

"No one? As in someone?"

"I feel like someone's been in here," I said, turning around in a circle, looking about.

"You mean other than Alex, Carl, Bridget, Haley, and Tyler?"

"Ignore me. I'm not making any sense." I walked down the short hall and unlocked the deadbolt. After opening the door, I stepped back and held my sleeve over my face. "Oh, holy. That stinks. I'll get the gloves so I can empty the buckets."

"Damn. What are you feeding them?" Donovan asked, stepping away from the room.

"Wild Card likely gave them ex-lax again."

Donovan took a deep breath and entered the room. I went to the kitchenette to get a pair of gloves. When I returned, Donovan was relocking the door.

"What are you doing?"

"We have a problem," Donovan said, leading me by the elbow back into the family room. "They're dead."

"What?"

"Their throats were slit."

"Are you messing with me?"

"Not in the slightest. Who knew they were here?"

"Shit," I said, sitting on the love seat. "I don't know. Tyler, a few of the Devil's Players, Nightcrawler, Shipwreck, Wild Card, you, Alex, the girls…"

"Too many people. Anyone could have talked about it and been overheard."

"We're practically stacked on top of each other lately. It's not easy to find somewhere private to talk."

"Tyler checked on them this morning," Donovan said. "That means in the last five or six hours, in the middle of the day, someone snuck in here and killed them while we had guards posted everywhere."

"Head back to the main house. Call Katie and tell her to close the store. Keep everyone safe until I get back."

"What are you going to do with seven dead bodies?"

"Seven?" I asked. I didn't wait for an answer. I followed the short hall to the room and unlocked the door. Stepping inside, I counted seven bodies. "Son of a bitch."

"What?"

"There were eight of them."

"I'm heading to the main house!" Donovan said as he jogged toward the tunnels. "You armed?"

I pulled my gun as I shut the door. "Go! I'll be there when I can."

Wild Card and Bones walked through the tunnel as Donovan was running toward it.

"Where's the fire?" Bones asked, but Donovan didn't stop to explain.

Wild Card watched me and slowly pulled his gun. "What do I need to know?"

"The same guy who escaped last time is missing."

"He knew about the tunnel to Donovan's."

"Go! Search Donovan's. I'll search the rest of Alex's house."

A scream sounded from upstairs, followed by a loud thump and glass breaking. Bones led the charge up the stairs. We found Bridget standing in Alex's dining room over the body of our missing guy. He was knocked out cold from the vase that lay shattered around him.

"He hurt you?" Bones asked as he moved to Bridget's side.

"He came out of nowhere and tried to grab me. Alex is going to be so pissed when I tell him I broke his vase."

"I'll buy him another vase," Bones said, pulling her into his body.

Wild Card checked the man for a pulse and nodded that he was alive.

"Roll him over," I said, keeping my gun pointed at the man.

Wild Card rolled him over, and sure enough, he was covered in enough blood to convince me he had killed the others. Still gripped in his hand was a long-handled hunting knife.

"*I stripped him of his clothes,*" I said, holstering my gun. "How did he get out of his cuffs again? Where did the knife come from?"

"The better question is, how'd he escape from the storage room?" Bridget asked. "The new lock has a plated cover on the inside of the room. It can only be unlocked from the hallway side."

"Are you guys saying he had help?" Wild Card asked.

I dragged a hand through my hair. "Bones, find Whiskey and have him send his contractors home. Wild Card, get this asshole downstairs and tie him up for me. We'll have to move him somewhere secure. Bridget, I need you to clean upstairs."

"What are you going to do?" Bones asked.

"Clean the mess downstairs."

Bones rubbed a hand down his face. "What kind of mess is down there?"

"The kind of mess you're thinking is down there."

"Fuck," Wild Card said.

~*~*~

I called Goat and asked him to bring one of the freight trucks through the field to Alex's house.

Goat laughed. "Should I throw in the large rolls of the plastic wrap we bundle the clothes with?"

"That would be handy," I answered. "I could also use a dolly, a dozen extra-large totes, and some bungee straps, too."

Goat was silent for a few moments, but when he spoke his voice was low and serious. "Call off the security team surrounding the houses. The fewer witnesses the better."

I tucked my phone into my pocket and turned toward Wild Card who was just finishing tying up our remaining bad guy. "Pull security for a meeting in my garage. Keep them busy going over the plan for tonight. I need at least an hour."

"What are you going to do?"

I took off my cardigan and tossed it onto the couch before sliding the couch and recliner toward the far wall. "I'm going to get the bodies out of here before whoever's working against us calls the cops and has us all arrested."

I heard someone coming through the tunnel and held my finger up to stop Wild Card from responding. Haley stepped out, followed by Tyler.

"Bridget called me," Haley explained as she tossed me a set of coveralls, then tossed a set to Tyler. "Wild Card, you should go. Do as Kelsey said and keep the guards' attention away from us." She opened a package and started stepping into a pair of bibs.

"Haley—" I started to say as I quickly pulled the coveralls on over my clothes.

"Do you have a plan to get the bodies out of here?" she asked, interrupting me.

"Out, yes, but I'm not sure where to take them."

"*I sleep for less than two hours,*" Tyler grumbled, "and all hell breaks loose."

"If only we could clone you, Tyler." Haley grinned as she slid on a pair of elbow-length gloves and looked at me. "We need to hurry. I told everyone you were taking a nap at Lisa's house."

I stretched a pair of gloves over the sleeves of my coveralls, heading to the storage room. All three of us stepped back and tried not to gag when I opened the door. After a minute, Haley raised her head and pushed past us into the room. Tyler and I cringed, following her inside.

By the time we bagged the bedding, unchained the corpses from the wall, and emptied and cleaned the shit buckets, Goat was pulling the freight truck up behind Alex's house. We wrapped the men with the long rolls of plastic, then lifted them one at a time into the rolling laundry bins that Goat had thought to grab. From there, we rolled each bin up the ramp and into the back of the freight truck.

Bridget came downstairs after the last bin was loaded. "I'll help Haley clean the storage room."

"Sounds good," I said. "Tyler, move our remaining prisoner somewhere safe, but don't tell anyone his new location."

"You sure you don't need me with you?" Tyler asked.

"She's sure," Goat answered as he looked over at me. "Come on. We'd best clear out."

"Goat, I can handle it from here."

"Get your ass in the truck," Goat ordered, pointing to the passenger side.

I hurried around the truck and climbed inside.

"I'm guessing you don't have a clue how to get rid of a body, let alone seven," Goat said as he started the truck.

"I'm hoping as we drive down the road a brilliant idea will pop into my head. If I was in Texas or Florida, the wildlife would help me get rid of a body or two. But seven?"

"We can't take a chance these men will ever show up on an autopsy table. That means we're heading somewhere no one else knows about. I need your word it will stay that way."

I thought about Goat's wife Marcy who disappeared, never to be seen again, after I assaulted her in a storage room at the store. "You have my word."

"Good enough. Find us some music to listen to. It's an hour drive."

I did as I was told, pulling the long gloves off and fiddling with the radio until Goat started to sing along to a song. I leaned back into my seat and closed my eyes, wondering how my life had become so insane.

~*~*~

"Wake up! We're here," Goat said, startling me awake.

I opened my eyes, looking around. An old cabin with its roof half caved in sat to the far right of the property. Between the truck and the cabin, an assortment of old furniture and appliances were scattered about, rotting and rusting.

"Welcome to my weekend getaway," Goat said, grinning.

"You don't live here, do you?"

Goat laughed. "No."

"Is the property titled in your name?" I asked as I climbed out and met Goat in front of the truck.

"Nope. Belongs to my uncle."

"And where's your uncle?"

"About twelve feet under that old refrigerator," Goat answered, pointing to a refrigerator about forty feet away.

I raised an eyebrow at Goat. "I'm guessing the State of Michigan doesn't know he's deceased?"

"Miraculously, his taxes are paid by money order every year." Goat steered me toward the back of the truck. "Come on. We've got work to do."

"What if someone sees us?"

"There's not another neighbor for almost a mile, but I leave this place looking like a horror movie to keep snoops away." He opened the back of the freight truck and motioned for me to climb up as he pulled the ramps out.

It didn't take me long to realize that Goat was a little too experienced at getting rid of bodies. He drove a front-end loader out of a rickety looking barn. After a closer look, I saw the inside of the barn had another support structure built to protect and hide the front-end loader. Goat drove behind the barn and dug a large, deep hole before returning and moving the bucket to the back of the freight truck. We emptied four bodies into the bucket before he drove them behind the barn. He returned a few minutes later, and we dumped the last three bodies into the bucket. While he drove off, I took the bottle of bleach from the back of the truck and started wiping everything clean.

Goat returned and motioned for me to follow him. He grabbed two white buckets and nodded to a third. I picked it up, grunting at its weight, carrying it barely two inches from the ground as I tried to keep up.

"Glad you still got your gloves on," Goat said, stopping at the edge of the hole.

"Why's that?"

"We need the plastic off them," he said, nodding at the bodies in the bottom.

"You want me to climb down there?"

"Is that a problem?"

I ground my teeth together to keep from saying any of the four-letter words rambling around in my head. Sitting on the ground next to the hole, I slid off the edge, trying to control the descent as much as possible. Once at the bottom, I took a moment to find solid footing before I started unrolling the guy on top. I was making progress until the body became wedged between the dirt wall and another body. Goat laughed as he watched me struggle.

"If you think you can do better, come on down!"

"If I come down, who's going to pull us back out of the hole?"

I looked up, then around the sides. "I can't believe I didn't figure that out."

"You're tired. Which is why you haven't realized yet that if you use the knife in your boot to cut the plastic off, it would be a lot easier. We just need enough plastic peeled away to expose them to the chemicals."

"Shit. Why didn't you say something?"

"It was too funny watching you try to unroll the fat bastard."

I flipped Goat off after I removed my gloves. It took some wiggling to retrieve the knife from inside my coveralls, but I managed eventually. Once I had my gloves back on, I found it much faster to cut the plastic off each man, tugging what I could away from them and leaving the rest.

I looked up at Goat a few minutes later. "Good?"

"Yup. Hang on. I'll lower the bucket down to pick you up."

I briefly thought about the bodies having been carried in the bucket, but then looked down at myself. I was covered in dirt and other bodily substances that I didn't want to dwell on. When the bucket of the front-end loader reached me, I didn't hesitate to step in and sit down. Goat ran the controls above, lifting me out and onto the ground. I climbed out and walked over to help him pour the chemicals into the hole.

"Go get the water hose by the cabin. It should reach this far, but you'll need to make sure you don't drag it across anything sharp."

"Sounds challenging," I muttered as I went to get the hose.

I managed to drag the hose over the top of two refrigerators, using their height to keep it from snagging on most of the yard ornaments. From there, I stretched the remaining hose to where Goat waited behind the barn. Unfortunately, I forgot to turn it on so I had to run back to the shack. By the time I returned to the hole, white fumes clouded the air above where Goat sprayed the water.

"Don't breathe this shit," Goat said as he covered his face with his arm and kept his head turned away.

"I'll just stay back here."

"You're learning."

Ten minutes later, curiosity got the best of me and I inched toward the hole and peeked in. It wasn't pretty. My stomach lurched, and I hurried back to the truck to breathe in fresh air. I heard Goat laughing as I ran.

I spotted a jug of lighter fluid in the barn and carried it out to an old burn barrel. Stripping off my coveralls and gloves, I tossed them in the barrel and covered them with fluid. I heard the front-end loader start up and what sounded like Goat moving the dirt back into the hole. I walked over to the truck, climbing up to pull Goat's cigarettes and lighter.

I was standing beside the burn barrel smoking my third cigarette when Goat returned. He tossed his coveralls and gloves into the flaming barrel.

"I hate this place," he said, looking around. "Only happy memory I have out here was the day my uncle died. Until today that is."

"Today was a happy day?"

Goat chuckled. "Watching you roll a fat naked guy without touching his private bits was funny as shit."

I couldn't help the laugh that barked out, nor the snort that followed.

Goat lit a cigarette before wrapping an arm around me and walking me back to the truck. "You did good, Kel. You protected your family. I know you didn't want it to go down like this, but you can't always control how things turn out."

"I can't wait to get my hands on the bastard who killed them. He has some explaining to do."

Goat helped me up into the truck. "Are you going to lose sleep over this?" he asked, nodding toward the barn.

"No," I answered, looking back at the barn. "It somehow fits within my rules."

"What rules are those?"

"I didn't kill them," I said, shrugging. "I told myself a long time ago that bad guys killing other bad guys was not my problem."

"And burying the bodies?"

I shrugged. "We both know I've done worse."

Goat laughed as he closed my door and walked to the driver's side to climb in.

I waited until he backed the truck up, giving myself time to think out my question.

"Whatever you're thinking so hard on, just spit it out," Goat said.

"Is Marcy..." I started to ask, pointing at the yard.

"Nope. As much as I wanted to, I couldn't do it," Goat said. "Marcy's an evil bitch, but she's still Amanda's mother. She's allowed to write to Amanda, but that's the only contact she's allowed. She's living in El Paso and knows if she ever crosses the Texas border, she forfeits her life."

"Marcy's not that bright. You sure she'll stick to the rules?"

"Dumb or not, her missing ring finger should help her remember."

I looked down at my hand, specifically my right hand that held the diamond and sapphire ring. "That's one hell of a reminder."

"You judging?"

"*Me*?" I laughed. "I nearly killed her with my bare hands, remember? I'm just happy I don't have to worry about her filing charges."

"It's all good. We held her until her bruises healed so she should couldn't prove the assault. Then Wild Card took her to Texas and got her settled. Between me cutting off her finger and Wild Card promising to check on her every few months, she's harmless."

"Wild Card? But he was shot and then went to Florida with me to take down Pasco."

"After the shit with Pasco, Wild Card flew back to deal with Marcy."

"Why didn't he tell me?"

"I suppose for the same reason you don't tell him a lot of things. It's just how you two work. It's not a matter of keeping secrets, it's just automatic that you two have each other's backs. Like how he stayed with Nicholas when Nola kidnapped you. Not searching for you nearly destroyed him, but Nicholas was his priority. He said he'd protect your son until his last breath because that's what you'd want him to do. The rest of us followed every lead we could find, but Wild Card stayed on that ranch close to Nick."

"I thought Charlie was there?"

"She was, but she wasn't handling things too well. She tried, but she didn't snap out of her despair until you called to say you were safe. Then it was like a light flipped on, and Wild Card knew it was okay to fly out to meet you and leave Nick with her."

"What about Grady?"

"Grady, Jackson, and Eric fanned out in different directions as soon as we got the call you were missing. Nothing was keeping them from traveling the world to find you."

I looked out the side window as we passed empty fields. "Why didn't anyone tell me any of this?"

"Tell you what? That we all love you? That the months you were missing were hell?" Goat leaned forward, turning down the radio. "Remember how messed up you were when you came home? You didn't need anyone adding to your burdens. By the time you healed, so had everyone else."

I looked down at my hand, realizing I was twisting the ring around in circles. "I'm glad Nicholas had Wild Card. I worried when we left Texas how Nicholas would handle being away from him."

"Wild Card calls him," Goat said, shrugging. "Last I knew, they talk every Saturday."

I looked over at Goat, eyebrow raised. "That's who Nick calls? I thought he was calling Pops."

"I know." Goat laughed. "Nicholas is a smart kid. He knows that Grady and Wild Card are friends, but that there's tension there. He told you he was calling Pops because he didn't want to hurt Grady's feelings."

"Why are you telling me all this, Goat? Why now?"

"I think you know why," Goat said, looking at me sideways. "There's no shame in being in love with two men. But ignoring it? Pretending the feelings don't exist? That's not healthy for anyone involved."

"I love Grady," I said, shaking my head. "We're likely over, but that doesn't change how I feel about him."

"I know you love Grady. Got no problem with that. But you also love Wild Card." Goat flicked the blinker on before turning left onto the interstate ramp.

Chapter Thirty-One

I snuck in through Alex's basement, then followed the tunnels to the main house furnace room. From there, I climbed the ladder to my room, peeking out of the closet to make sure the nanny wasn't around before I slipped into my bathroom and started the shower. Ten minutes later, I was dressed in a sports bra, shorts, and workout shoes as I walked down the hallway, pulling my wet hair into a ponytail.

"Where's my shirt?" I called out to the loud, packed dining room.

"Got it," Katie answered, tossing me a t-shirt.

Haley and Tyler were both watching me.

I nodded slightly as I pulled the shirt over my head. "Is everything ready for the relay?"

Before anyone could answer, Hattie laughed from the top of the stairs. Whiskey carried her down while she gripped him tightly, both of them wearing their *Kelsey's Crew* t-shirts. Pops carried Hattie's favorite rocking chair down the stairs behind them.

"Let's do this," Wild Card said as he walked up behind me, carrying an afghan and a cooler. He had cut the sleeves off his shirt and added another slit in the collar for his sunglasses to hang from. The lettering on the front of the men's shirts was the simple black lettering, not glittered like the women's shirts. It wasn't until everyone shuffled toward the door that I read the back of the shirts: *Kelsey's Bitches*.

I laughed, reaching over to cover the kids' eyes.

"We already saw it, Mom. We made everyone do pushups."

"Except Hattie. Wild Card did her pushups for her," Sara said.

Walking outside with the kids, I admired the decorations on the flatbed trailer which served as a spectator's stage. The trailer was surrounded with white Christmas lights and red garland and had *Team Kelsey* handmade signs attached all the way around it. Hattie was carried onto the trailer and settled in her rocking chair. The kids and the other spectators unfolded lawn chairs, setting them on the trailer or around it.

"You sure you're up to this?" Bridget asked. "Haley says you might not be able to run because of the chloroform."

I led the way across the street. "I can't take the lead position like we planned, but I can run." I turned as our group circled up. "Running order is as follows: Bridget, Katie, Kelsey, Wild Card, Trigger, Anne, and Tech takes the tail. Bridget, remember to tag the next person before you grab the next flag." Bridget nodded, so I continued. "All of us need to cross the finish line before they call time. We'll need to finish in at least second place to have any chance of snagging the trophy."

"Why second place?" Tech asked.

"She's expecting a loss of one of the competitions," Katie said, crossing her arms. "You think we can't win the tournament?"

"Look around," I said, nodding toward the other teams that consisted of mostly oversized men. "Now look at us. Who honestly thinks we can beat any of these teams in the rope pulling competition?"

"You have a point," Bridget said as she admired Bones' body in the group beside us.

"Maybe we could win if we bent the rules a little," Wild Card said, scratching his chin.

"What are you thinking?" Bridget asked.

"I have an idea, but it depends on what the rules say."

"You and Bridget can scheme later. Let's still shoot for at least second place tonight, though. Understood, Tech?"

"It's not my fault if we lose. I told you Tyler would be better at this," Tech said.

"Tyler's busy protecting the family. Besides, who's more Team Kelsey than you?"

"If I get hurt, I'll never forgive you."

Katie wrapped her arms around Tech and whispered something in his ear. He smiled wildly down at her as she playfully bit his chin.

"All right," Tech said as he released Katie and started jogging in place. "Let's do this."

"Kelsey," Wild Card said, pulling me to the side. "If you take third spot, that's still four laps in the woods. I know you're faster than the rest of us, but Doc warned for you not to overdo it."

"On a good day, I can run fifteen laps, so yeah, I think I've got it."

"Ladies and Gents," Donovan called out. "Remember the rules. Each runner has a designated number of flags at their table. The first runner will tag the next runner in, but all runners have to complete their laps, returning their flags to their team's basket. Everyone on your team must be at the table and have all flags accounted for in order for your team to have completed the relay. Pops, Jerry, and Whiskey have agreed to be judges and will disqualify anyone caught cheating. Any questions?"

"Is this full contact?" Ryan asked.

"No. You'd know that if you read the rules. The trails are not wide enough for six people, let alone forty-some of us. Runners can pass by cutting to the *outside* perimeter of the trail only."

"Simple enough," Ryan said, crossing his arms and appearing impatient.

"First runners, line up!" Donovan called before he moved over to the starting line.

Jerry passed out the first round of flags and then stepped aside. Pops lifted a shotgun, aiming away from the group. When the loud boom sounded, the first runners took off into the woods. Bridget immediately moved to the outside and ran parallel to the men in the woods.

Bones laughed. "If she wins this damn thing, I'll never hear the end of it."

"Just be glad she put on ivy protection," Katie said, holding up a green and white bottle. "The woods are ripe with poison ivy and poison oak this time of year."

"Shit. Can I have some of that?" Bones asked.

Katie tossed him the bottle, and he smothered it on his legs, arms, and face. Someone else asked for the bottle and it was quickly passed around. Katie tossed another two bottles out to those who were asking for some.

I stepped over to Katie and turned my back to the crowd. "Weren't you the one who asked Nicholas to have a pail of soapy water ready for us to wash off with after the race?"

"I have to get ready," Katie said, grinning back at me. "Bridget will be here any minute."

I moved over between Tech and Wild Card who were silently laughing. "What's in the bottles?"

"Lilac, itching powder, and honey," Tech said. "She's going to get our asses kicked."

"Crap. They're going to be pissed when they get eaten alive by mosquitoes."

"What the fuck, Katie?" Bones yelled as he started scratching his legs.

Just then Bridget and Donovan came out of the woods and tagged their next runners. Katie shot out ahead of Bones like her life depended on it. Bridget and Donovan both looked surprised but ran over for their next flags and back into the woods as more runners came out.

"What the hell is this crap?" Jackson yelled as he scratched his arms.

"I'm innocent!" I said, holding up my hands. "I had nothing to do with it, but she didn't break a single rule."

"This is bullshit, Kelsey," Wayne said, slapping at a mosquito. "This is a competition to see who's the best at Aces."

"Best what, Wayne? *Strongest*? Most *manly*? Does intelligence not fit into your line of work?"

"She has a point," Casey said, slapping at his arm.

"Quit kissing her ass," another guy yelled. "She and her misfits shouldn't even be allowed to compete."

"Misfits, huh?" I moved over to the starting line. "We'll see about that, asshole."

Katie came flying out of the woods, tossed her flag in the basket and grabbed the next. Bridget came tearing out seconds later and tapped my shoulder to tag me in. I was off, flag in hand. I focused on my breathing and watching the trail ahead. I knew these woods better than anyone else, having run my frustrations out under the giant trees' canopies on nearly a daily basis. Seeing Katie ahead, I called to her that I was approaching on her right. She moved inward without slowing down. As I caught up with her, we rounded the bend and three men were ahead of us. "Follow my lead," I said as I turned to the outside trail, jumping over two fallen trees until my feet hit a deer trail I knew well.

"Sweet," Katie said as she ran hard behind me.

"You're three runners deep but the boys are coming," Bridget called from behind us.

I kicked it up another notch, giving it everything I had as we passed parallel to six runners before I veered hard to the left and back on the main trail.

"Donovan and Bones will have to power around the others, but we need to make this lead count," Bridget said as she passed us and ran faster than I knew was possible.

"Shit," Katie heaved behind me. "Go. Go. She's making us look bad."

"You're just worried Bones will catch you. He's pissed."

Katie passed me on the left and kept going, glancing behind her quickly before leaving me behind. I didn't blame her. I could already feel my lungs burning as I made the last turn before exiting the woods and exchanging my flag.

"You okay, boss?" Trigger called out.

I didn't have the lung capacity to answer him as I looped back into the woods. By now there were too many runners on the trails and I jumped off the path again. Weaving around trees and over fallen branches, I kept going. When I made it to the deer trail on the back stretch, I wasn't surprised to hear Bones and Donovan coming up behind me, following the same trail.

"You okay?" Donovan called out. "Trigger said you didn't look good."

"I'll make it," I said, jumping to the left at the last minute, diving under a branch and back onto the main trail.

I heard Donovan thrashing behind me, but Bones must've missed the jump. Twigs and branches snapped as he cursed loudly. Donovan laughed as he passed me and kept going. The next group of runners were moving at a good clip and I didn't have enough energy to pass them. I stayed in pace with them rounding the next corner and out of the woods again. I slapped my flag onto the table and grabbed for the next flag, but I swayed.

"Kelsey?" Tech called out, grabbing me to steady me. "You need to stop. You're not well."

I took a deep breath, focused my eyes and grabbed the flag. "I'm halfway there."

"Kelsey—" Anne started to say as I jogged into the woods.

I made it down the straightway before I started to sway again.

Wild Card caught me and turned me away from the tree directly in my path. "What the hell?"

"I'm just winded," I said, squeezing my eyes shut and then opening them, trying to focus my vision.

"Wild Card?" Katie called, coming up behind us.

"I got her. Go."

I tried to run faster but swayed again.

"Stubborn woman," Wild Card said, running ahead of me and pulling me by my arms onto his back.

I wrapped my legs around him and held on, trying to slow my breathing. "Just winded." I heaved another deep breath. "The rules."

"I read the rules. Doesn't say anything about the runner actually running the lap. Says each runner has to make it around each lap."

"Shortcut... Seven feet after next tree..." I panted, trying to get the words out. "Veer right."

Wild Card cut to the right and found the deer trail. "Damn."

"At the end... log, jump, duck... leap to left."

"Log. Jump. Duck. Leap left. Got it. Concentrate on your breathing."

I tucked my forehead into his shoulder and tried to steady my breaths. They were ragged and burned with each inhale. I felt Wild Card tense and held on for the jump, duck, left leap. His feet hit the hard-packed trail, and I felt him laugh as it reverberated against my body.

"She okay?" Bridget asked, coming up alongside us.

"I'll get her there."

Bridget nodded and took off ahead of us. She was drenched in sweat and breathing hard.

"Another group ahead of us," Wild Card said.

"Not worth... brush and prickers. We're almost to the last turn." I inhaled again, filling my lungs. "Go ahead and drop me. I've got my breath back."

Wild Card slowed enough to lower me but grabbed my arm, running alongside me.

"You don't need to hang back."

He laughed. "How come you're always trying to get rid of me?"

Our pathetic pace was greeted with cheers as we ran out of the woods and exchanged our flags for fresh ones. Trigger ran up behind us and grabbed a new flag too. Wild Card and I stepped aside for him to run ahead of us before we jogged back into the woods.

"This is last lap... right?"

"No talking. Focus on your breathing," he said as he gripped my arm harder.

I focused on taking slow deep breaths into my diaphragm and out just as slow, while keeping my feet stretched out ahead of me as I ran. My vision blurred a few times, but Wild Card kept me on the trail. I nodded as we neared the back turn and I veered to the right to follow the deer trail.

"Why isn't everyone else following this trail yet?"

"Probably... saw... Bones," I said between heaved breaths. "Wiped... out... hard."

"Quit talking. Breathe."

"Quit... asking... questions..." At the log I jumped, ducked, and veered left but my body kept going. I would've toppled over if it weren't for Wild Card grabbing hold of me in time to pull me back on course.

He jogged next to me holding my arm. "There's at least twenty runners ahead of us. Any ideas?"

I nodded, too short of breath to talk. Making a hard right again, I jogged fifteen feet to the south, straight into the woods, before jumping down into a shallow creek and turning to the east. The creek held less than an inch of water, splashing us as we ran toward the road. I heard more splashes behind us.

"Just Katie and I," Bridget called out. "Take us to the finish line, boss!"

I ran as hard as my legs would take me. Wild Card stayed close behind me as the creek turned slightly to the left and ended. I ran at full speed toward the inclined slope, but my two leaping steps failed to propel me over and I felt my weight shift backward. Wild Card wrapped an arm around my waist, dragging me upward, as Bridget ran up beside me on my right and pulled me by my arm. I felt hands against my back, pushing me onward. Somehow, with everyone's help, we made it up the bank and onto the side of the road. I pointed toward the end of the trail as I staggered in that direction.

"You did good," Wild Card said, pulling me onto his back.

Once again, I hung on as Wild Card ran with me on his back. I could hear the cheers, but my vision was too blurry to see anyone. My arms gave out, and I felt myself falling backward.

"Got her!" Tech's voice called out behind me. "Go!"

Tech was carrying me by the arms and Wild Card carried my legs. Together they got me to our table and lifted me up to drop my flag into the basket.

"Second place!" Pops called to our team.

When they lowered me to the grass, I rolled into a sitting position—and puked on my shoes.

Chapter Thirty-Two

I'm not sure who was the angriest with me. Everyone seemed to be competing to yell the loudest. Sara and Nicholas were the only ones being nice. They brought me several bottles of water to drink and rinse off with as Haley and Doc took turns checking my pulse and listening to my heart. I wasn't sure where in the medical journals it said yelling at the patient who was having heart palpitations was a good idea—but they must've read it somewhere.

Wild Card stripped off my puke covered shoes before carrying me over to the flatbed trailer and setting me in a lawn chair next to Hattie.

Hattie giggled. "Welcome to the infirmary."

"Do they serve beer here?"

Bridget opened a cooler and passed me a cold bottle. I didn't have the strength to open it so I held it against my forehead.

"Kelsey!" Grady called out, jogging over.

"*Stay away from my mother!*" Nicholas yelled, charging into the yard to stop Grady.

Several guards moved over, pointing guns at Grady.

Wild Card and Donovan walked toward them. Wild Card picked up Nicholas, carrying him back to the trailer. Donovan exchanged quick words with Grady before they started walking toward the highway. I scanned the crowd, noting that Sebrina was watching me. I nodded in acknowledgment. She smirked before turning to follow Grady.

I looked back to my team. "I'll hang with the kids and Hattie so everyone else can go across the street to celebrate."

"And have them glare at us all night for that stunt Katie pulled?" Tech asked as he got out his phone and made a call. "You can come out of hiding now. Everyone's leaving."

Katie ran out of Lisa's house and leapt onto the trailer. "That was so much fun."

"Running in the race? Or running for your life?" I asked.

Katie walked over and uncapped my beer, handing it back. "Both. What's the next competition?"

"Scavenger hunt in the morning," Trigger answered. "It starts at nine, though. You and Anne will be working at the store."

"No, they won't," Hattie said. "Alex and I arranged extra staffing so the girls can compete."

"Are you sure?" Anne asked, looking between Alex and Hattie.

"Lisa and I will be there," Alex said, nodding. "And Haley, Pepper, and a couple other girls offered to work for old-time's sake. If you two get done early, though, you know where to find us."

"What about security?" I asked.

"Whiskey's taking lead at the store, and I've got the house," Tyler answered.

"The kids?"

"They're going on the scavenger hunt with us," Wild Card said. "I already cleared it with Donovan."

"Yes!" Nicholas exclaimed, jumping up and down.

"Do you know what a scavenger hunt is?" I asked him.

"No, but I'm sick of being home," he said, leaning against my shoulder.

Wild Card laughed and turned back to Alex. "We'll need Katie and Anne for the three o'clock rope pulling contest too." Wild Card pulled a beer from one of the coolers. "It should be quick. We'll take at least third place."

I raised an eyebrow. "How do you figure?"

"Rules say the winner is the last group holding the rope. Doesn't say anything about wearing fireman's gear and lighting the rope on fire. Since the competition is single elimination, that means after one bout there'll be three winning teams and three losing teams. Thus, we take third place if we lose the next two."

"If my husband asks, I knew nothing about this," Lisa said, sitting in the yard chair next to me. "But just so you know, there's extra lighter fluid in our garage."

"Uh, I might need to steal some of that," I said. "I have some bags that need to be burned."

"I can take care of it," Nightcrawler said, dumping an empty beer bottle into a box and pulling a new one.

"No need," Tyler said, taking Nightcrawler's beer from him. "I lit the burn barrel during the race. We're all set."

"We really do need to clone you, Tyler," I said. "You did good tonight."

"Right back at you, boss," Tyler said, clinking my beer bottle.

"Am I the only one who doesn't know what you guys are talking about?" Katie asked.

"Consider yourself lucky," I said, leaning my head back and closing my eyes.

"Aunt Kelsey?" Sara said, giggling. "Remember that guy who called you misfits?"

"Yeah," I said, opening my eyes and looking over at Sara. She was watching her laptop.

Tech moved behind her, looking over her shoulder at her computer. "Casey's beating the crap out of him in the parking lot at Headquarters."

I grinned, pulling my phone. "Tyler, let security know that Casey's been invited back for a beer."

As Tyler jogged off, I texted Casey and extended the invite. Twenty minutes later, Donovan, Bones, and Casey walked across the highway and joined us for drinks. All three of them were slapping mosquitoes away. We all looked at Katie.

"I'll get a fresh bucket of soapy water," she said as she jogged into the garage, giggling.

My attention turned to the end of the street. Six cop cars drove down the street with their lights on and parked alongside the road. I glanced over at Bridget.

"I swear," Bridget said, not turning her attention away from the cops as she talked to me. "That storage room is so spotless, I'd willingly lick the walls."

"We used a sprayer to soak the walls, ceiling, and floor in bleach. They won't find any DNA," Tyler said.

"Then we washed everything in Lysol so it didn't smell bleachy," Bridget added. "But then it smelled like Lysol, so we washed it again with dish soap. Just smells clean now, but not too clean."

"I think you're getting the point," Tyler said. "Bridget went overboard again."

"This time, I'm grateful," I said, standing and drawing the attention of the officers who were gathering. "What can we do for the police officers of Kalamazoo this evening?"

"Sorry to bother you, Kelsey," Steve said. "We got an anonymous tip that there were bodies in the basement of Alex's house. I'm afraid we need to check it out."

"Bodies?" I laughed, looking at Wild Card who laughed with me. "How odd someone would call and say we had bodies in the basement. I'll be glad to open the house and allow you access."

"You sit and rest," Wild Card said to me. "She hasn't been feeling well," he explained to the group of cops. "Donovan and I can let you inside to look around."

They shuffled as a group across the front yards toward Alex's house.

"They're not going to find any bodies, are they?" Dave asked as he and Steve walked over alone.

"Nope," I said, leaning my head back and closing my eyes again.

~*~*~

I woke with a start, sitting up to find myself fully clothed in bed. I looked at the clock, discovering it was almost five in the morning. I couldn't remember anything past sitting in the lawn chair on the trailer the night before.

I heard someone stir and turned to find Wild Card sleeping on the other side of the bed. He was fully dressed, including his running shoes. I slid out of bed and into the bathroom, shutting the door before I turned on the light. Making quick work of a shower, I grinned when I stepped out and saw a cup of coffee sitting next to the sink. Wrapped in my robe, I walked into the bedroom with my coffee to an empty room. I dressed in jeans, a tailored button-up blouse, and my favorite pair of boots. I checked my gun and secured it in a belt harness. Grabbing my coffee and phone, I walked out to the dining room, surprised to find Tech already up.

"First text messages went out to the bakery employees. So far, eleven of the fourteen have read the text."

"Who's next? The mill employees?"

Tech nodded, not taking his eyes off his computer. Wild Card set a cup of cocoa next to Tech, before sitting beside me.

"Why are you up so early?" I asked Tech. "I thought you had the messages programmed to go out automatically."

"They are automatic, but you weren't the only one who went to bed early last night. Most of us drank a beer or two before calling it a night. I think I was asleep before ten, which means I woke up before dawn."

"A good night's sleep works in our favor," Wild Card said.

"How so?"

"Scavenger hunt this morning. Half the guys at Headquarters will be hung over."

I laughed, sipping my coffee.

The garage door opened and Tyler walked in, stopping to look at me. "What's your mood like this morning?"

I grinned at Tyler. "I'm good. It's safe to let Tweedle inside."

Tyler smirked, stepping back to let Tweedle pass.

"Good morning, everyone. How was your night?" Tweedle asked as she breezed through the doorway and set her purse on the counter.

We all mumbled various replies.

"Okay, then. I'll just get started on breakfast. I promised Ryan I'd go on the scavenger hunt later. I'm so excited. I just hope I don't do anything embarrassing."

"Why do you care?" I asked.

"What do you mean?" Tweedle asked.

"Why do you care what anyone else thinks?"

"They're all so impressive, of course. I don't want to embarrass Ryan in front of his friends."

"Ryan doesn't keep those type of friends," Wild Card said. "He'd never hang out with anyone who would judge you for being you."

Maggie walked through the garage door, wearing the same clothes as the night before.

I shook my head. "Talk about no judgment," I said, grinning.

She winked at me as she filled a cup of coffee.

"Tyler, can you call Ryan and invite him over for morning coffee?" I asked. "There's no reason he can't have breakfast with his wife for at least one morning."

Tyler nodded, pulling his phone and sending a text.

"And Tyler?"

He looked up at me.

"I expect you to assign someone else to be in charge for a few hours while you sleep. You look like hell."

Tyler smirked before walking out.

"I just don't get it," Donovan said, shaking his head. "You run your team ragged, working all hours of the day and night, and they still won't quit and come work for me."

"Maybe someday I'll tell you my secret," I whispered to Donovan.

"Enough about them," Maggie said, sitting on the other side of me. "You haven't asked me about my night yet."

"Based on your walk of shame, I figured your night ended in bed with Billy."

"I'm never ashamed," Maggie said, grinning. "However, you are also way off base. I thought it would be more authentic if I slept in Hobbs' apartment, but *Billy-boy* freaked out."

Wild Card and Donovan looked at Maggie with puzzled expressions.

"Freaked out how?" I asked.

"He handed me clothes to sleep in—and left. He never came back."

I turned to Tech. "Can you pull the footage and see where he went?"

"I thought we were spying on Daphne, not my guards?" Donovan asked.

"Are you telling me you don't want to know?"

"Doesn't matter what Donovan wants," Lisa said, standing and moving behind Tech. "I want to know. I can't imagine any man turning down—" she waved a hand toward Maggie's body, "—all that."

"Why, thank you, Lisa," Maggie said.

"You're welcome, but if you ever make a move on my husband—"

"*Lisa!*" I snapped. "A little less bat-shit crazy this morning, please. It's too early."

Lisa huffed but her attention moved to the computer monitor. "Well, that's weird."

"What's weird?" Ryan asked as he entered through the garage door.

I walked around the table to join everyone else looking over Tech's screen.

"Why is Hobbs sleeping in the hallway outside his apartment?" Ryan asked, looking at the video. "And why do we care?"

I started laughing when I saw the apartment number. "That's not his apartment. It's Daphne's. I'll be damned. Billy's her stalker."

"Excuse me?" Donovan asked.

My mind raced to put the pieces together. "When Maggie kissed Billy yesterday, no one could figure out why a man like him was so clueless. What if he reacted like that, though, because he didn't want Daphne to see him kissing another woman?"

"That's a stretch," Wild Card said. "I'm not saying he doesn't have feelings for her, because it happens, but that doesn't make him a stalker."

Tech looked over his shoulder at me.

I nodded. "You know the drill." I moved back to my chair.

Tech started typing, pulling data.

"Shit," Donovan said, rubbing his forehead. "Daphne started as a security job for a red-carpet event. She hired us a few times for special gigs—*before she had a stalker*."

I couldn't stop grinning. "The notes that accompanied the flower deliveries were also non-threatening. More like X-rated love letters from someone with no social skills."

"Kelsey's right again," Tech said, shaking his head. "I've identified three of the gifts on Billy's personal credit card. He's our guy. He didn't even try to hide the expenses."

Wild Card and Ryan started laughing.

"*This isn't funny!*" Donovan yelled.

"Donovan," Hattie said, coming down the main stairs. "Inside voice, please."

Wild Card hurried over, offering Hattie his arm. Lisa went to the kitchen to get her a cup of coffee.

"Sorry, Hattie," Donovan said as he got up and walked toward the garage, grabbing my SUV keys on his way out.

"Why is Donovan upset?" Hattie asked as she sat in the end chair.

"He just found out one of his bodyguards is a stalker. He's having a bad morning," I said, glancing up at the clock. "It's not even six, yet."

"He'll get over it," Lisa said, placing a cup of coffee on the table by Hattie. Lisa rested her hand on top of Hattie's. "I'm glad to see you're doing better."

"Me too, dear," Hattie said. "I feel better than I have in weeks."

"Just take it easy," I said, pointing at Hattie. "If I hear you're overdoing it, there'll be hell to pay."

"Like that time when you ran in a race after being exposed to chloroform?" Hattie asked, grinning over her coffee cup.

"That's different," I said. "Everyone knows I'm an idiot."

Tech looked up from his computer at me. "Three thousand texts were just sent to the trucking company and the textile mill. Looks like everything's going according to plan."

"Was the package delivered for Miguel?" I asked.

"Last night," Tech said, nodding. "If he heads to the airport, he'll find it sitting on his private jet in his favorite leather seat."

"What's the package?" Maggie asked.

"A peace lily," I answered, grinning. "The card has my burner phone number and says: *We can do this the hard way or the easy way—you decide.*" I nodded to the burner phone on top of the credenza.

"What the hell is a peace lily?" Ryan asked.

"It's the big, dark green plant with the white flower shoots that's in our living room at home," Tweedle said, elbowing him. She turned to look back at me. "I can't believe you sent a flowering plant to the cartel."

"It's a *peace* plant," I said, smirking. "I couldn't resist."

"You have the wickedest sense of humor," Wild Card said, shaking his head.

Chapter Thirty-Three

Getting the kids ready was harder than normal. Based on their level of excitement, you'd think they were going to Disneyland, not being herded into a ten-seat passenger van for a local scavenger hunt.

"Nicholas, I'm reaching my limit with you this morning. *Go!*" I said, pointing down the hall.

Wild Card chuckled as we watched Nicholas stomp down the hall. "Man, that kid hates brushing his teeth."

"You were the same way," Pops said from the breakfast bar. "Always too busy for hygiene at that age. Your mother had the patience of a saint. Then one day, the arguments ended. Just like that"— Pops snapped his fingers—"you started showering and brushing your teeth. You were near obsessed with it."

Wild Card turned to me, grinning. "I remember what my mom did, too." He walked down the hall and into the bathroom.

I didn't want to know why Wild Card looked so devious. I was agreeable to any plan that ended the twice a day argument. I turned to check on Sara and sighed. I'd sent her to her room three times to change into something sensible. The last change resulted in substituting her patent leather shoes for her running shoes. She was still wearing a pink party dress, though.

Beth held up her hand, stopping me from saying anything, as she turned Sara back toward the stairs.

~*~*~

Donovan stood on a chair, holding six sealed white envelopes above his head. "I hired the local police department to write the scavenger hunt list so there'd be no accusations of cheating. I was told there's one item on the list that they will be actively working to prevent us from acquiring. That's all they told me. And, no, Kelsey, your pals Steve and Dave were not allowed to contribute to or look at the list—so you can't use them to your advantage."

I grinned. "But according to the rules, we can call *anyone* other than the local cops as a resource, right?"

"Any online resource or anyone *other than* a Kalamazoo police officer can be used as a resource, yes," Donovan answered with a grin.

"So…" I crossed my arms as I looked around smiling. "The hundred or more *other resources* I have in this town will have to do?"

"Feeling cocky, are we?" Donovan asked.

"Oh, I'm all over this competition," I said, grinning back as the kids giggled beside me.

Bridget laughed, shoulder bumping Tech who looked bored.

"Yeah, yeah, yeah," Wayne yelled. "Let's get on with it."

Donovan grinned. "The vans all have a full tank of gas, and the keys are in the ignition."

"Bridget drives," I whispered to our group. "Katie, get ready to run for that list and the rest of us will get the kids loaded in the van."

Wild Card took the kids' backpacks and handed them to Trigger.

Jerry walked over and took the envelopes so Donovan could join his team.

"One, two, three, go," Jerry said without much fanfare.

Wild Card lifted a kid in each arm as everyone in our group except Katie started running for the vans.

"The middle van!" I called out. "It's a straight shot out of the parking lot!"

"You're taking this a little too seriously," Anne said, running beside me.

"Do you want Bones and Donovan to hold a win over our heads for the next year?"

Everyone ran faster to the van, throwing the doors open and climbing inside. The kids climbed in and scurried to the back. Wild Card and I took the middle seats while Anne, Trigger, and Tech took the second row. Bridget jumped behind the wheel and started the van as Katie jumped into the passenger seat.

"I only read a few lines," she said, passing the list back. "A stripper outfit, Coney Dutch dogs, a chicken, and a garden gnome."

Bridget was already squealing tires out of the parking lot, turning toward town.

"Go to Dallas' house!" I called out as I read the list and called Dallas.

"I thought you had that scavenger hunt this morning?" Dallas said, answering.

"We'll be at your house in three minutes. I need you to pull your stripper outfits and meet us in the front yard."

"Regular stripper or dominatrix?" Dallas asked.

I took the phone off speaker. "Regular will be fine. Hurry!" I hung up and continued reading the list.

"Mom? What's dominatrix?" Nicholas asked.

"Do you two have your seatbelts tight?" Wild Card asked, turning around in his seat to check their belts and make sure they were latched.

"Sara, did you start your computer?" I asked.

"It's booting up now," she said.

"Good," I said, looking over the list. "I need you to find the architectural plans for the city's art museum. That must be the warning the police gave Donovan. We'll have to find a way into the building and around the police to take a picture of the painting on loan to the museum."

"Thirty seconds to Dallas' house," Bridget called out.

"Trigger, get ready to jump out and grab the outfits."

Trigger didn't need to jump out of the van. Dallas was standing next to the mailbox with an armful of sparkling tops and bottoms. A few had dropped in her yard, leaving a trail of unmentionables from her door to her mailbox. Trigger opened the side door, and Dallas climbed in with her loot.

"I wasn't sure what color you wanted, so I grabbed everything in the third drawer," Dallas said as she sat next to me in the middle seat.

"What's in the other drawers?" Wild Card asked, picking up a sequined bikini top that had fallen on my lap.

"Don't answer that!" I said to Dallas, nodding to the kids in the back seat.

Dallas glanced over her shoulder before pressing her lips together, trying to hide her laughter.

Katie turned in her seat and looked at Dallas. "You realize you're stuck with us until after the competition now, right?"

Bridget whipped the van in a sharp U-turn, and I grabbed Dallas before she fell to the floor.

Dallas laughed as she sat up straight. "Beats sitting at home, cleaning. Besides, I might prove to be a valuable team member."

I looked down at the pile of stripper outfits in Dallas' arms, and an idea popped into my head. "Tech. Can you look up what the indecent exposure law in Michigan is? Find out what the penalty is if a senior citizen were to wear a stripper outfit outside a public museum."

"Dave's going to kill you," Wild Card said, laughing beside me.

"Where to?" Bridget called out.

"Head towards town," I called back.

"Katie, call Madge Grenner. Ask her if we can borrow her gnomes for the day. Tell her I especially want the one flipping the bird."

"Trigger, call the hot dog place on West Main and have them prepare two dozen Coney Dutch dogs and charge them to the company card. Tell them we don't care if they get cold, but to have them ready for us."

"Anne, call Mayor Henderson and have him meet us ASAP at the mission. Tell him there'll be a photo op, but only if he hurries. We need a team picture with him in it."

"Dallas, call Father Eric and tell him we need six purple shirts. With all the clothes we donate, I'm sure he can find at least six that no one wants. I don't want to bother Alex on a Saturday. And we can take the picture with the Mayor while we're there."

Dallas called Father Eric and proceeded to talk to him in a flirty voice. I rolled my eyes.

Trigger turned in his seat to look at me. "I've got the owner of the hot dog place on the phone. He says they don't open until eleven, and it will take an hour to get the steamers and grills going."

"We don't have to eat them," I said, rolling my eyes. "We just need two dozen to take back with us."

Trigger nodded.

"Head to Pine Street," Katie said, hanging up her phone. "Madge is packaging a few gnomes and will meet us at the end of the driveway."

"What else is on the list?" Wild Card asked.

"A comical sign, four flamingos, and a beach umbrella."

"They have flamingo drink decorations at the dance club downtown," Bridget said. "I know a bouncer there. Katie, pull my phone and call Elvis."

"Elvis?" Katie asked.

"Nickname," Bridget said, listening to her phone when Katie put it on speaker.

"Is this the beautiful Bridget?" a deep male voice answered.

"You're so lucky Bones isn't with me right now," Bridget said, laughing. "I need a favor. We're on a scavenger hunt and in desperate need of pink flamingos. Can you get your hands on those cocktail decorations from the club?"

"I happen to have a box in my kitchen. Don't tell the owner. I live on Pacific Street. Can you make it this way or should I meet you somewhere?"

"We can meet you," Wild Card called out as he looked at a map on this phone. "We need to stop at Calvin's gym, which is only two streets away."

"I'll have them ready."

Katie pointed at the upcoming road. "Take a right. Blue house on the left."

Bridget took a sharp right turn before pulling to the left side of the road and stopping the van illegally. As Bridget finished talking with Elvis, Katie jumped out of the van and met Madge mid yard to take the box of gnomes. Trigger opened the side door and took the box when Katie returned, passing it back to set on the floor out of the way.

"Why are we going to Calvin's gym?" I asked Wild Card.

"Comical sign," Wild Card said, pointing to the list. "He has a sign in his office that says: *Due to the rising cost of bullets, there will be no warning shot.*"

"He also has a sign in the bathroom that says: *Weed - Next 3 Exits*," Trigger said.

"Doesn't he have more scattered in the gym too?" Anne asked. "I remember a road construction sign that was supposed to say drive slowly, but was a misprint and says: *Caution - slow drively.*"

I called Calvin's personal cell.

"No," Calvin said when he answered. "You can't have them all, but I'll let you borrow *one* sign."

"I take it Bones called already?"

"Called and showed up five minutes later. He's still here, taking down the bathroom sign. They wanted all of them, but I refused. I'll take a few more down and have one waiting for you."

"I'll send Trigger in when we get there, but we have another stop to make before your place."

"I was Bones' first stop. How far are you on the list?" Calvin asked.

"We're about five minutes from our third item, then you'll be our fourth. We already have people working on the rest of the list."

Calvin laughed. "You're smokin' their asses. Power to you, sweetheart, but I want to see your scrawny ass in my gym next week."

"Deal. I'll bring the girls with me and you can put us through the wringer. Thanks, Calvin." I hung up. "All right, Calvin's going to save us a sign. Bones is there now and they're getting their *first* item."

Everyone cheered except for Bridget who was leaned forward and used both hands to grip the oversized steering wheel as she made the next tight turn. Dallas landed on the floor, half wedged between the door and the seat. She laughed as she worked at pulling herself up.

"Did you hear Kelsey, Bridget?" Wild Card asked. "We're winning. You don't need to drive like a maniac."

"Which means it's our opportunity to clock the best time," Bridget said, making another tight turn to the right a little too fast. "I want Silver Aces guards trying for years to beat our record. We'll be legends."

"*I'd rather the kids lived through the day, Bridget*!" I yelled as I grabbed the ceiling grip bar.

"Shit. Sorry," Bridget said. "I forgot we had fragile cargo."

"Pushups!" Nicholas called out.

Bridget looked back at Nicholas in the rearview mirror and sighed. She took the next turn closer to the legal speed, before calling out the next stop. "Elvis' place is down on the right."

I looked at the cluttered yard and an old RV sitting in the driveway. "I'll go with you," I said to Bridget. "Wild Card, take the driver's seat."

As soon as the van stopped, I jumped out and ran across the yard beside Bridget. Elvis met us at the door, handing Bridget a plastic sack. She checked inside and nodded to me.

I looked back at Elvis. "Do you have an old boom box we can borrow? And music someone could dance to?"

"Sure," Elvis nodded, holding the door open and letting us in. "It's dusty. I haven't used it in years. My CDs are mostly heavy metal music, though." He waved a hand at an oversized entertainment stand that displayed a stack of CDs and an old boombox.

"Anything will do," I said, grabbing the top three CD's that sat on a shelf and the boombox. "Does this take batteries?"

"Yeah sure. Let me get you a fresh pack." He returned less than a minute later with a new pack of D batteries. "Anything else?"

"That's it. We'll get everything back to you today or tomorrow."

"No problem. I trust Bridget."

Bridget and I took off running toward the van.

"That's a *lot* of marijuana," I said to Bridget as I ran.

"You noticed that, huh?" Bridget said, laughing as we both dove through the van door.

"Kind of hard to miss," I said as I handed my goods over to Anne so I could close the door.

"Calvin's?" Wild Card asked as he pulled away from the curb.

"Yup," I answered. "Anyone know where we can find a beach umbrella in October?"

"What about the rooftop bar?" Anne asked. "Or the bar attached to the big hotel downtown? Both of them have patio furniture."

"They've already closed their patios for the season," Katie said.

"Can we buy one?" Nicholas asked. "Or is that against the rules?"

I looked at Wild Card. "Is that allowed?"

"The rules didn't say we couldn't," he answered, shrugging. "Calvin's gym, up ahead. Get ready, Trigger." Wild Card pulled up alongside the gym's front entrance.

After Trigger jumped out, Wild Card looked over his shoulder at me. "Where would you even buy a beach umbrella this time of year?"

I shrugged. "Anne and Nicholas, find us a beach umbrella!"

Their thumbs started working their phones.

I pulled the list from my pocket. "A chicken. We need a chicken."

"Where the hell are you going to find chickens?" Dallas asked.

"We'll have to head out of town," I said, shrugging. "I don't know anyone who has chickens, but we're likely to find a farm with a chicken coop if we drive west into farm country."

"We can't just drive around looking for a chicken coop," Bridget said. "That'll take too long."

Not knowing the area west of town, I called Renato.

"You in trouble?" he asked when he answered.

"Only as far as clocking the best time for the scavenger hunt. Any clue where we can find a chicken?"

There was a long pause before he answered, "The grocery store?"

I remained silent, completely dumbfounded. I glanced at the list, and sure enough, it said nothing about the chicken being alive. When I could close my mouth, I mumbled a *thank you* and hung up.

"Well?" Bridget said.

"We're idiots. The grocery store."

"Wow." Katie laughed. "We were overthinking that one just a smidge."

"The Harding's on Drake has two beach umbrellas still," Nicholas called out.

"I betcha they have chickens, too," Wild Card said, laughing.

After Trigger returned with the sign, we picked up the Coney Dutch dogs and then went to the grocery store. Anne, Wild Card, and the kids tracked down the beach umbrellas as the rest of us grabbed every fresh and frozen chicken they had, including the ones they had in the backroom. At the checkout counter, I was surprised to see Wild Card had his arms filled with coolers, folding lawn chairs, and tiki torches. I raised an eyebrow at him.

He stacked everything on a conveyor belt. "What? Their seasonal crap is fifty percent off. It's a steal."

I shook my head at him as Bridget encouraged the cashier to hurry.

We were back in the van in less than ten minutes and at the mission five minutes after that. We posed for a picture as the Mayor shook Father Eric's hand and the rest of us held up our donated chickens in the background. We collected the six purple shirts from Father Eric, and once again, we were on the road with two more items on our list crossed off.

The final scavenger hunt item was a picture of two team members in front of a painting at the museum. Everyone stood outside the van, leaning over Sara's laptop as we reviewed the architectural plans.

"I only see three ways in," Sara said. "The loading docks, the employee entrance in the back, and the front doors."

"I can shut down their alarm system remotely," Tech said, starting up his laptop. "It's a locally monitored system."

"The police are everywhere," Trigger said. "I counted eight cops at the front and side entrances."

Wild Card sighed. "They've got cops stationed at the back doors and loading docks, too."

I studied the museum down the street. "We can distract most of the cops," I said, biting my lower lip. "Dallas, go ahead and change into one of your costumes."

Tech pointed at her with his serious face. "Make sure you pick a costume that covers *everything*. The law is clear that *all* of your private bits have to be covered."

"We can call in a fake 911 call," Katie suggested.

"Not allowed," I said. "Whoever wrote the list put a notation that they'll arrest *everyone* at Aces if a false alarm is called in during the scavenger hunt."

"I don't blame them," Wild Card said, grinning.

"Is this like the chicken?" Anne asked. "Can't we just walk in there and take a picture? It's open to the public, right?"

"They're normally open on Saturdays by eleven, but they don't open today until two o'clock for some reason," I answered. "We need to get in there now if we're going to win this thing."

"Then we need to know why they're opening late," Bridget said.

"They have some fancy party this afternoon," Nicholas said, reading from his phone. "It's a fund raiser."

"Which means they'll have party decorators and caterers," Bridget said. "We can enter as staff."

"Most of the cops know us," Anne said. "A chef's coat or a pair of coveralls won't get us past the doors."

"There's no time to plan an operation like that anyway," I said, rolling my head around on my neck, trying to work the kinks out from Bridget's driving. "We need something quick and easy."

"Hello, my name is Nicholas Harrison," Nicholas said into his phone. "I understand you are having a fundraiser tonight?"

We all watched Nicholas as he talked on his cellphone.

"Yeah, we know it starts at two. Problem is, we need a picture of one of your paintings, *now*, not later. How big of a donation will it take to make that happen?"

He looked up at me. "Five hundred per person?"

I gave him a thumbs up.

"We accept," he said, smiling broadly. "We'll meet you at the side entrance. I assume you can order the police to let us in?" he nodded a few times. "Yeah, that's what I thought. The FBI?" Nicholas listened for a few minutes and then giggled. "It's okay. She's part of the scavenger hunt, too."

He disconnected the call and tucked his phone into his pocket.

"You are your mother's son," Wild Card said, shaking his head as he mussed Nicholas' hair. "Good job, buddy."

"What was that about the FBI?" Anne asked.

"Maggie used her badge to get inside," Nicholas said. "She told the woman she was investigating a stolen art ring. She's still there."

"So, we can walk right through the door?" Anne asked. "Hand them the money and take a picture with the painting?"

Nicholas nodded. "Yup."

"Dave and Steve were definitely involved in the making of this list," I said as I dug into my bag for a cash envelope. "They planned on us donating to the museum to gain access. They know how much the guys at Aces make and knew everyone could afford it."

"Dave's on the community fundraiser committee," Dallas said, walking over wearing a bright blue sequined bikini set.

It was mid-morning, and we were standing next to a park. Katie peeled off her coat and draped it around Dallas. It didn't cover everything, but it helped.

Dallas shrugged. "They were talking last night that donations were down at all the local events, but they were hoping things would change this weekend."

Tech looked at Dallas and then looked at me. "You thinking what I'm thinking?"

I smiled as I grabbed the boombox. "That we no longer need Dallas as a distraction, but it would be a fun way to get back at Dave, anyway?"

Chapter Thirty-Four

Our official time was clocked at fifty-seven minutes. We sat in folding chairs at Headquarters drinking coffee when Dave and Steve arrived.

"Really?" Dave said, dragging Dallas by her elbows into the room. "Every cop in the district now has a video of my mother, in a stripper outfit, dancing to AC/DC's "You Shook Me All Night Long"!"

"You're the one who planned a thousand-dollar entry fee to the museum," Tech said, not looking up from his laptop.

"It was for a good cause!"

Wild Card laughed. "What? More sidewalk art?"

"They're raising money for the *public schools*. The art programs suffered from the last round of budget cuts, so the museum is raising money earmarked for art education."

We all looked at each other, feeling guilty, before we pulled our purses and wallets. Dave was less angry when they left with a pile of cash, but he said he was leaving Dallas behind as punishment.

"Who's the hussy?" Dallas asked, her hands on her bare hips and her sequined boobs jiggling as she nodded across the room.

Sebrina was standing beside Jerry, near the offices, smiling up at him as she rested a hand on his arm. Jerry smiled shyly back at her, his cheeks turning pink from embarrassment.

"That's Grady's ex-wife. Why is she a hussy?"

"She's working Jerry like a pro. She's after something."

"Jerry's in charge of the scavenger hunt," Anne said. "Maybe it has something to do with that."

"Why didn't she go on the hunt?" I asked. "Friends and family were invited to participate. That's why we rented the large passenger vans."

"I heard her tell everyone this morning that she was too hungover to go," Trigger said, watching Sebrina in his peripheral vision. "Grady offered to stay behind, but she said she'd be sleeping, so there was no point."

"Who else didn't go?" I asked as I glanced again at Sebrina, who didn't appear in the least bit hungover.

"Not sure," Trigger said. "Not everyone is participating in the team competitions. Some of those who weren't on a team rode along with other teams and some stayed back to sleep, work out, or relax."

I tilted my head and looked at Tech.

He grinned, sensing my unasked question. "I'm on it. Give me a minute to review the security video."

I turned in my chair, openly watching Sebrina as I drank my coffee. Jerry shook his head at whatever Sebrina was saying and abruptly walked away. Sebrina seemed pissed, clenching her jaw and fisting her hands. When she saw me watching, though, her body relaxed and she smiled a false all-white smile at me before sauntering across the gym toward a group of guys at the food table. I watched Shipwreck nod at her before turning into the breakroom with his plate. She followed him inside after grabbing an apple from the table.

I jumped over and sat in the empty chair next to Tech, digging in my shoulder bag for earbuds. "Did you get the breakroom wired? I need to know what they're saying."

Tech switched over to the live feeds and clicked a few screens before his screen showed Shipwreck and Sebrina huddled together, talking in the corner of the room. I plugged my earbuds into the laptop and handed one end to Tech as I put the other up against my ear.

"Where the hell is he?" Sebrina hissed. "We've searched everywhere."

"I'm thinking one of the biker clubs has him," Shipwreck said, leaning against the wall and appearing on camera like he was ignoring her. "I'm keeping an eye on that Tyler guy. If anyone knows where he is, it'll be him."

"If your guy talks, we're in deep shit," Sebrina said. "He knows too much."

"He won't talk. He's too afraid of Santiago."

"Until he's being tortured."

"Kelsey won't let anyone torture him," Shipwreck said, snorting. "We'll find him. Meet me tonight in the field and we'll compare notes. That is..." he said, turning to look at Sebrina, "if you're not too busy fucking your ex."

"You know I don't have a choice," she said, putting her hand on his arm. "We'll only be here for a few days. Once we prove to Santiago that we're allies again, we can both go back to Mexico and resume our lives."

"And Grady?"

"What about him? He can rekindle his relationship with that mousy little thing who likely enjoys meatloaf dinners and having missionary-style sex."

"*Mousy*. I'm not mousy!" I said, getting mad.

"You do like meatloaf," Tech said, grinning at me sideways. "I'm not going to ask about the missionary sex."

"I feel so left out," Katie said from the other side of Tech.

I looked up to see everyone from our team was watching and listening to us. Wild Card shook his head, laughing, as he got up and walked away.

Looking back at the monitor, a couple of guys entered the breakroom and Sebrina and Shipwreck distanced themselves from each other. I handed my side of the earbud to Tech and walked off. Climbing the stairs, I went to my war room and pulled my phone to call Tyler.

"What's up, boss?" Tyler said, answering. "Did you guys really finish in fifty-seven minutes?"

"Did you doubt us?"

"Only when I heard about the *chicken* question."

"Yeah, that was embarrassing. Anyway... Shipwreck's dirty. He's going to get close to you later to squeeze information from you about our special guest, the one you have tucked away somewhere."

"Damn. I was looking forward to the bar you were going to build for him."

"I can still build the bar. I'll put you in charge of finding a new bartender."

"How do you want to play it with Shipwreck?"

"Did you get any information out of our guest last night?"

"Nope. Thanks to Nightcrawler, our guest has been in and out of consciousness since his relocation, but I'll pay him a visit this afternoon and see if his head has cleared any. Hopefully, he'll be more alert."

"He's not a priority. Drop a hint to Shipwreck this afternoon that you're holding our guest at the empty warehouse where they held us girls. We'll see what shakes out when he shows."

"The warehouse?" Tyler asked.

"Is that a problem?"

"Not really, I guess, but what made you think of that location?"

"Nobody would ever guess we'd take him back to where he held us."

Tyler was silent.

"That's where you stashed him, isn't it?" I sat in my chair as I laughed.

"I think we're spending too much time together," Tyler said. "I'm reading your mind. It's freaking the shit out of me."

The burner phone in my handbag started to ring. "I gotta go, but we can still use the warehouse. I'm not too worried about our guest accidentally getting shot."

I hung up on Tyler and switched over to the burner phone. "*Hola.*"

"Who is this?" a man asked.

"That depends. Am I speaking to Miguel or one of his henchmen?"

"What do you want?" Miguel demanded.

"I want your brother to *back off*," I said, strolling over to the window to look into the field below. "He's targeting my friends and family because of Sebrina. It's pissing me off and ruining a perfectly nice weekend."

"Then you should discuss the issue with Santiago."

"We both know you're the one in charge. Either you handle the problem, or I start a war you can't win."

"You're threatening me?"

"I'm warning you. Having your employees not show up for work was child's play. You have no idea what I'm capable of. If I can take down a gubernatorial candidate like Jonathan Vaughn, I can demolish your U.S. based companies with a few phone calls. *Call Santiago off.* Do whatever you have to do to handle this shit." I hung up the phone, setting it on the conference room table as I sat again.

A minute later, Tech walked in followed by Wild Card and Bridget.

"Did you listen to the call?" I asked.

Wild Card nodded, taking a seat on the other side of the table. "Nice touch dropping Jonathan's name. Miguel will spend the next twenty minutes reading the news articles online of how you financially and politically ruined Vaughn before you killed him."

"He'll know you're an ex-cop, wealthy, and connected," Bridget said, leaning against the door. "Just like you planned."

My personal cell rang, and I looked at the screen and saw Genie's smiling face. I pressed the accept button. "Where's he heading?"

Genie giggled. "He was heading to Texas, but he just changed his flight plan to Chicago."

"Interesting."

"Is this good or bad?"

"I don't know. I'll have to think about it. What's his ETA?"

"He'll be in Chicago in less than five hours."

I looked up at the clock. "That might work."

"What might work? *Wait*. Do I even want to know?" Genie asked.

"Probably not." In the background on Genie's side of the call, I could hear arguing. One particular voice stood out. "Are you with Charlie?"

"Yeah." Genie sighed. "I was invited for breakfast, but Kierson and Charlie haven't stopped fighting long enough for us to eat."

"Can you put Charlie on the phone?"

A minute later, Charlie was on the line. "What's up?"

"Jump on a plane. I need you here, but when you arrive, don't let anyone see you."

"Whatever. I'll be there. Anything's better than this," Charlie said before hanging up.

I laughed, looking at my phone. Definitely trouble in paradise.

I returned to the window to process my thoughts. Miguel was either heading this way to confront me, or else Santiago was already here and Miguel was coming to stop him. Either way, I could use the information to my advantage. "Tech, can you go through the security videos and see if Sebrina and Shipwreck had any other, not so private, conversations?"

"That's a lot of video. I'll need a few people to help."

"We'll handle it," Wild Card said, nodding for Bridget and Tech to follow him to the door. "We'll work at the house, though. Fewer ears."

When the door closed, I paced the room, thinking. It wasn't until my third pass by the window that I noticed Nicholas and Sara playing with Storm in the field. Looking around, I didn't see any of their security guards with them, but I saw Sebrina who was walking their way.

I ran from the room, down the stairs, and across the gym toward the back doors, cursing the entire way that the building didn't have a side door exit. I heard several sets of feet pounding the floor behind me as I threw open the door and ran around the outside corner of the building. Sebrina stood in the middle of the field with the kids, smiling toward them, but she was prevented from getting closer to them by the snarling and snapping of Storm's teeth. Behind Storm, Nicholas stood protectively in front of Sara, holding his arms out and glaring at

Sebrina. I slowed to a jog, happy to see that Storm had it handled and my son was showing no fear.

When I reached the kids, I leaned over and whispered to them. "You guys okay?"

"Yup," Nicholas said in a short-clipped voice that reminded me of Grady. His eyes never swayed from his focus on Sebrina.

"Where's your security team?"

"My fault," Nightcrawler said, jogging over. "I told them I brought Storm over, but to give me a few minutes and then I'd bring them out to play with him. I was talking to Wild Card about something."

I looked back at the kids. "You two were told to wait, and you came outside by yourselves, anyway?"

"Sorry," Sara sighed, looking down at the ground.

Nicholas didn't answer, but glanced at me quickly to gauge my anger before looking back at Sebrina.

"Storm, stand down," I ordered.

Storm stopped growling and sat.

"Nightcrawler, take the kids and Storm back to the house. I want eyes on them until I get there. I should only be a few minutes."

"No fair," Sara whined. "We wanted to wait until everyone came back from the scavenger hunt."

"You should've thought of that before you broke the rules and came outside alone," Anne said, walking up behind me. "You heard Aunt Kelsey," she said, steering them by the shoulders toward the parking lot. "Both of you, let's go."

Nicholas reached for Sara's hand, pulling her with him as he whistled for Storm to follow. Storm barked once, then took off ahead of them.

Anne and Nightcrawler followed close behind them.

I wasn't surprised to see Katie, Jerry, and several of the less familiar guards standing around, waiting and watching. An audience wasn't going to stop me, though.

I turned as if to walk away and threw a sidekick into Sebrina's lower ribcage. The force of my kick, fueled with rage, tossed her on her ass about five feet back. I slid a switchblade from my boot and hit the release, walking toward her.

"*That's enough!*" Donovan yelled, jogging toward me.

I ignored him, leaning over Sebrina, my blade ready if needed. "That was for approaching my kids. You go near them again, and I'll carve that pretty little face of yours to bits." I spit at her, stepped back, and closed my blade. As I slid the blade into my boot, Sebrina kicked out, hitting me in the shoulder. The impact knocked me back a few steps, giving her time to stand.

"Now we're talking," I said, grinning as we circled each other.

"Sebrina," Donovan said, now standing at the perimeter of our fight ring. "You don't want to fight Kelsey."

"I'm not afraid of this mousy little bitch," Sebrina hissed before she struck out with a right punch.

I easily deflected her arm to the outside, landed my own right to her jaw, a left fist to her abs, and then pulled her head down to meet my upward knee. She stumbled before her legs folded underneath her, dropping her to the ground as she sagged forward onto her hands. *Game over.* "I'm a lot of things, but there's nothing mousy about me." I left her there and turned toward the parking lot.

Katie walked up beside me. "I'm heading to the store to help out. You need anything before I go?"

I loved how Katie was immune to me assaulting someone. "I'm all set until the rope pulling contest."

We rounded the corner of the building, into the parking lot, and stopped abruptly. Grady and Bones were struggling as they tried to hold chickens. *Live chickens.* As they grasped their clawed feet with one hand, they used their other arm to protect their faces as the chickens wildly flapped their wings and tried to peck them. Feathers floated everywhere.

"I'm so glad that's not us," Katie said, laughing and getting out her phone and recording them.

"Damn things," Donovan muttered as he walked up beside me. "How do you control them?"

"I have no idea."

"How'd you get yours back then?"

I started toward the front doors, calling over my shoulder, "A grocery sack."

Katie had turned her phone for a close-up of Donovan's face when the light bulb came on. I smiled and opened the door to go inside.

"*You're kidding me?!*" Donovan yelled. "*Do you know how long it's going to take us to clean the inside of the rental van?*"

"Not my problem!" I yelled as the door closed behind me.

I was still smiling as I climbed the stairs to the war room to retrieve my phone, the burner phone, and my shoulder bag. I was picturing how much madder Donovan was going to be when he heard Team Kelsey beat him by almost an hour. After grabbing my stuff, I was walking down the stairs when Bones and Grady ran into the gym, still holding their chickens away from them, to get to the check-in table before Maggie, who was running with a grocery bag, a very large patio umbrella, and a stuffed pink flamingo toy. Bones made it to the table first, but not before all hell broke loose. Grady's chicken managed to free himself, and in an effort to make a fast escape, took off running toward Maggie. Tripping over the chicken, Maggie went down, and a frozen chicken slid out of her grocery bag, skating across the floor like a bowling ball into Grady who went down, face first. The room erupted in laughter.

I shook my head, walking toward the front exit.

Looking around the parking lot, I didn't see my SUV. Likely it was used to take the kids back to the house. I flipped my handbag strap over my head and tucked the bag under one arm as I walked toward the road. As I passed between a row of the rental vans, a side door opened and a man lunged toward me with a knife.

Startled, I jumped back—but not fast enough. The knife sliced my skin, setting fire to my nerves just below my ribs. Spinning to the side, I kicked out, bouncing my attacker into the side of the van. Before he had time to go on offense, I grabbed his wrist, twisting it inward as I threw my weight forward, pushing the knife into his chest.

We stood face to face as he realized he'd been stabbed.

"Where's Santiago?" I asked him.

He staggered to the side. "Fuck you."

I maneuvered his slack body toward the interior of the van before he fell. When he took his last breath, his upper body was sprawled on the van floor between a row of seats. His legs hung out at an odd angle.

I gripped my side, looking down at my shirt. It was soaked with blood. I pulled up the edge of my shirt to inspect the wound. The cut was long, but less than a half-inch deep. I'd need stitches, but thanks to a healthy layer of body fat and muscle, I wouldn't need surgery.

"Fucker," I whispered. I leaned over, whimpering slightly at the pain, as I picked up the man's legs, rolling them and tucked them inside the van. I stood for a moment, recounting my actions and staring at the knife, still lodged in the man's chest. I'd grabbed his wrist, not the knife, then forced my body weight against his own arm. My prints wouldn't be on the knife, but my DNA would be on the body. Being it was the same guy who was caught on video attacking me at the pharmacy the day before, I could explain the DNA away. I nodded to myself, sliding the side door closed with a loud slam.

"Kelsey?" Bones called from the front entrance of Headquarters, halfway across the parking lot.

I moved my handbag to cover up the blood stain on my shirt before stepping away from the van to yell back. "Yeah?"

"Do you need a ride to the house? I'm heading that way."

"I'm good. I'm going to take this van. I might need it later."

Bones nodded and left in the other direction.

I walked around the van and climbed behind the wheel, turning the keys in the ignition. "A normal person would call the cops," I said to myself as I pulled my phone and called Wild Card.

"Hey," Wild Card answered.

"Can you grab my medical kit and meet me at Alex's house without being seen?"

"Doc's here checking on Hattie. Should I bring him?"

"I'm not sure that's a good idea. Doc tends to overreact."

"How hurt are you?"

"Just a scratch."

Wild Card snorted. "I've heard that story before."

Chapter Thirty-Five

"Either throw some damn stitches in it, or I'll do it myself!" I yelled, interrupting Doc and Wild Card from their argument of whether I should go to the hospital.

Wild Card grabbed the suture needle and thread, loading the needle.

"Don't even think about it," Doc said, pushing Wild Card out of the way. "The wound needs to be cleaned first." Doc sanitized my side with a saline solution and added an antibacterial cream, before taking the needle and thread. "This is going to hurt."

"She can handle it," Wild Card said, crossing his arms over his chest and focusing on me. "What happened?"

"The same asshole who was at the pharmacy hid in one of the rental vans and jumped me when I walked by."

"*At Headquarters*? In front of everyone?"

I hissed between my teeth as Doc pulled a long length of thread through my skin. "We were between the vans. No one saw us."

Wild Card used his index finger and thumb to pinch the bridge of his nose. "Do you know what direction the guy ran?"

"I know where he is. It's under control."

He released a long breath, relaxing his shoulders.

The front door of Alex's house opened and Bridget walked inside. "Why are you lying on Alex's kitchen floor, bleeding?"

I hissed again at the pain. "I figured it would be easier to clean the blood off the vinyl floor."

"That looks painful," Bridget said, leaning over to watch Doc. "What happened?"

"I'll explain later. Keep the family distracted until I get myself straightened out."

"I was just going to grab a sweatshirt," Bridget said as she walked toward the hallway. "I'll grab you one, too." She returned a minute later and tossed a spare sweatshirt to Wild Card. "You going to keep an eye on her?" Bridget asked him.

"I'll babysit Kelsey if you watch the kids," Wild Card said, nodding.

She walked toward the door. "A group of us are taking the kids into the field to play with Storm. Give us five minutes, and the house will be clear."

Doc clipped the excess thread as the door closed behind Bridget. "That should do it. Should I even bother to give you care instructions?"

"Waste of time," Wild Card said, leaning over and helping me up. "She already knows them, and we both know she's not likely to follow them."

As Wild Card grabbed some paper towels to clean the floor, I threw my shirt in the trash and grabbed a package of bandages from my med kit. I used a wet paper towel to wipe off the worst of the blood on my side and hip, before loosely taping a bandage over the wound to prevent staining the next outfit. Doc helped me put on Bridget's zip-up sweatshirt.

"Now what?" Wild Card asked, throwing the bloody paper towels he'd used into the trash and pulling the trash bag.

I ignored his question and turned to Doc. "Thanks for the house call. I'll send a check next week to the clinic."

Doc waved a hand dismissively as he walked toward the door. "Donations are welcome, but we're doing fine these days thanks to your support."

I looked over at Wild Card. "I need to grab some clothes for later. Can you pull the van into the garage and lock the garage down?"

"You sure? I can make the van disappear."

"No. I might need the van and its cargo." I walked down the hall.

It was obvious when I opened the door to the spare bedroom that Bridget was staying in this room. Her clothes were scattered on every piece of furniture in piles. When I walked across the room to the closet, it made more sense. Packed full of designer fashion labels, the closet didn't have an inch of space to spare. Alex had always squirreled away clothes for me, but I would've never guessed he'd become this obsessed with it. From ballgowns to sundresses to business suits, there was an outfit for every occasion. I had to dig around for a good five minutes before I found a navy suit and white blouse. I started to bend to find shoes, but I winced when my stitches tugged tight.

"Don't be a fool," Wild Card said, pulling me gently away from the closet. "What am I looking for?"

"Navy high heels."

Wild Card flipped the lid off several shoe boxes before he held up a pair of shoes.

I shook my head. "Those are royal blue, not navy." I pointed to another box at the end. "What's in the Valentino box?"

Wild Card lifted the navy and white shoes out of the box, holding them up for me to see.

"*Purdy*," I drawled as I took the shoes.

"I don't get why women wear heels. Looks painful to me."

The thought of how much Grady would enjoy me in the heels—without a stitch of clothing—crossed my mind. I turned toward the door as my cheeks pinked. "Let's go."

"Where?" Wild Card asked as he followed.

"I'm hungry. Let's see if anyone made lunch," I answered, walking toward the front door.

"And just leave the van and the dead guy?"

"Yup."

"What on earth are you scheming?"

"Still working out the details," I said as I pointed to my head.

~*~*~

Wild Card took the bag of trash to the burn barrel, while I went to the house. I used my keys to unlock the atrium side door. Abigail's nanny was peeking around the corner to see who was entering my bedroom, while holding Abigail.

"It's good to be cautious, but next time if you're not sure who's entering, take Abby and run."

"I thought it was you, but with the sweatshirt's hood up, I couldn't be sure."

"It's fine. I should've used the front door, but I keep forgetting you guys are in here." I threw the clothes on my bed before reaching over and tickling Abigail's feet. She squealed and drooled, kicking her chubby little legs.

"Will you take her for a minute while I use the restroom?" the nanny asked, holding Abigail out for me.

"No way," I said, taking a step back. "Last time I held her, she puked on me."

"I haven't fed her yet. You'll be fine," the nanny said before forcing Abigail into my arms and turning toward the door.

Holding Abby out away from me pulled at my stitches. I moved her to my good side, carrying her on my hip. I walked into the nursery. "I heard you're crawling these days, but I don't believe it," I whispered to her as I sat on the carpet. "Let's see what you've got."

I laid her on her belly and scooched away. Abigail fussed a bit but got her arms under her and started rocking her body back and forth as she watched me.

"That's it. Build your momentum," I said as I held my hands out and wiggled my fingers. "Now come here."

She launched forward a little too fast, landing on her face. Without crying out, she lifted herself again and moved an arm forward, then the other. Her legs weren't as fast as her arms, but eventually she reached me and I lifted her up, holding her in a standing position as she squealed and bounced her legs underneath her.

"That was good stuff, Miss Abby. We just need to strengthen those legs. Maybe register you for a kick boxing class." I moved her back and only partially held her weight, letting her test her legs and practice standing.

"Better not let Lisa see you," the nanny said as she entered and sat on the couch. "She insists babies don't walk or crawl at this age."

I scooched back again, still holding Abigail but increasing the distance between us. She squealed, stepping forward before teetering sideways. I kept her upright, and she watched me intently as she placed her fist halfway into her mouth and covering it with drool.

"I'll take care of Lisa," I said, looking at the nanny. "In the future, if you think there's an issue that would negatively impact Abby's developmental years, let me know. I'm a pro at manipulating Lisa."

The nanny laughed. "I'll be sure to do that."

I sat Abigail down and moved to the side to roll myself onto all fours to stand. My side pinched a bit, but it wasn't too bad. "I need to go hunt down some food. You need anything?"

"We're all set. Thank you."

Abigail saw I was leaving and started to cry. I hurried toward the door.

Entering the dining room, Hattie greeted me with a plate of food. "You read my mind, but you should be resting."

Pops chuckled from the breakfast bar where he sat reading a newspaper.

"Nonsense. I've been resting all morning, sunshine," Hattie said. "Is Wild Card coming back? He hasn't eaten yet either."

"He'll be here any minute."

"He's here," Wild Card said, closing the front door. He hung my handbag from the hook by the garage door. "I was distracted by Abigail's aunt teaching her to walk."

"I always knew you were a rat," I said, giggling.

I took a bite of my ham and cheese sandwich. Wild Card washed his hands at the kitchen sink while Hattie prepared a plate for him.

"Are you going to explain why Wild Card took Doc with him to Alex's house to see you," Hattie asked as she set a plate on the table for Wild Card.

"You hurt?" Pops asked, lowering his newspaper.

"Just a scratch," I said, shaking my head.

"What kind of scratch?" Pops asked, raising an eyebrow and looking at Wild Card.

"The kind that needed stitches," Wild Card answered as he joined me at the table. "We need to keep it quiet, though, *for some reason.*"

"Is she safe?" Pops asked Wild Card.

"I'm sitting right here. You can ask me."

Wild Card chuckled as he answered Pops. "She took down the bad guy, but that's also a secret *for some reason.*"

"Good enough," Pops said, lifting his paper back in front of him.

"You're not curious as to why she's keeping it a secret?" Wild Card asked.

"Would be a waste of mental energy," Pops said behind his paper. "She's always got something cooking in that brain of hers. Whatever it is, it will work. That's all I need to know."

I took another big bite of my sandwich before setting it down and walking over to pull my phone from my handbag. I texted Jackson and walked back to the table. Before I took another bite, Jackson replied. I grinned to myself as I chewed and texted Charlie. It took a few more bites of my sandwich before her reply came through. I nodded to myself and texted Donovan. By the time I finished my sandwich, Donovan walked through the front door with Jackson.

"Aren't you worried someone will see him here?" Donovan asked, pointing a thumb over his shoulder at Jackson as he stole some chips from my plate.

"Not really. You can tell anyone who asks that you needed help to prepare for the rope pulling contest."

"There's not much work involved in a rope pulling contest."

"Whatever. Make up an excuse."

"What do you need?" Jackson asked, stealing a chip from Wild Card's plate.

"First," I said, turning to Donovan. "Charlie will be here soon. According to the rules, substitutes are allowed for the rope pulling contest as long as they are comparable in size. Do you agree Charlie's my approximate height and weight?"

"I'm fine with her being your substitute. Why do you need someone to cover your spot?"

"I have a meeting that I can't reschedule."

"I'll let Jerry know," Donovan said, stealing another chip. "With a bullet wound in Grady's shoulder, he's out as well."

I slid my plate in front of Donovan, offering up the last of my chips. "I also want the rope pulling event moved to the field behind the house. The kids can watch with their guards from the back deck. I don't want any of the family at Headquarters while I'm gone."

"Easy enough to arrange. Is Tyler okay with it?"

"He will be when I tell him. All three houses will be on lockdown. If anyone needs a bathroom, they'll need to use the woods."

"Sunshine," Hattie said, pointing a finger at me. "Your *manners*."

I sighed, turning back to Donovan. "Can you have a porta potty delivered?"

Donovan pulled his phone, walking into the living room.

"Jackson, follow me," I said, leading the way down the hallway. "How's Reggie?"

"He's still sulking about you kicking him to the other side of the highway. He's on season three of Dawson's Creek."

"He's seen that show a hundred times."

"Yet, he still cries in every episode," Jackson said, shaking his head.

Entering the bedroom, I crossed into the atrium and asked the nanny to take Abigail out to see Donovan and the rest of the family. She smiled, seeming excited to escape her isolation as she gathered Abigail and left. I nodded for Jackson to close the bedroom door as I opened the closet door and then the hidden compartment in the back of the closet.

"What's the mission?" Jackson asked as I passed him bullets.

"I need a sniper to watch my back this afternoon."

Jackson tossed the bullets onto the bed and took both sniper rifles I handed him. "What's the exposure?" he asked as he inspected the rifles and handed back the one he didn't want.

"An empty warehouse. It's huge, with lots of open support beams. I'm planning on meeting at least two, possibly as many as ten, non-friendlies for a little chit-chat."

"Who else will be there for protection?"

"No one. I can't risk Sebrina or Shipwreck noticing a bunch of the guys missing from the team competition."

"You've confirmed Shipwreck's dirty, then?"

"Yeah. He's Team Sebrina, all the way."

"Bastard." Jackson set the rifle down, leaning it against the wall. "We need at least one more guy. What about Nightcrawler or Tyler?"

"I don't want either of them involved. The cartel could retaliate against their clubs. Both clubs have chapters in other states. It's bad enough that all of Silver Aces is on their radar. We don't need to endanger the clubs, too."

"Fine. What about using Casey then? He didn't sign up for the team competitions either."

"Would he be willing? This isn't going down on the right side of the law. I'm planning on giving the cartel a few bodies to take with them."

A slow smile stretched across his face. "Sounds right up his alley."

Jackson sat on the bed, and I started explaining my plan. As we were finishing up, Charlie entered the bedroom.

She looked at the two rifles Jackson was holding and rubbed her hands together. "I want to play."

"Sorry, Kid. I have another assignment for you," I said, rummaging in my closet and pulling out a ball cap. I walked over and tugged it onto her head. "I need you to pretend to be me for as long as you can get away with it this afternoon."

"That doesn't sound as fun," she said, wrinkling her nose.

"Don't be so sure. Wild Card's going to light the rope on fire during the rope pulling contest."

"Casey's here," Jackson said, nodding toward the atrium. "Play it smart this afternoon. If anything goes sideways, hit the ground. Casey and I will deal with it."

"Yes, dad," I said, rolling my eyes.

Jackson kissed my cheek before strolling into the atrium, carrying the guns and bullets.

"I need to shower and change," I said to Charlie. "Find something in my closet or dresser that looks less like you and more like me. Don't forget to put your hair up too, unless you want Dallas to dye it?"

"She could do that?" Charlie asked, raising an eyebrow.

"She's at Headquarters," I said, nodding. "I can ask Maggie to bring her over. We have all the supplies here."

"Then—hell yes."

I lifted my phone from the bed and texted Maggie. She replied with a thumbs up.

I walked into the bathroom and turned on the shower. Carefully removing my sweatshirt, I peeled off the loose bandage. I didn't have a choice but to get the stitches wet. Someone knocked on the door and I used the sweatshirt to cover the front of me as I cracked it open. Wild Card pushed his way inside. Taking the sweatshirt, he tossed it to the floor before unwrapping a waterproof bandage.

"Are you going to tell me what's going on?" he asked as he placed the new bandage over my wound.

"It would only make you worry, and I need you to be here for the rope competition. Sebrina needs to think everything is normal while I sneak out."

Wild Card's jaw tightened. "Does Jackson have your back?"

"Jackson and Casey both will have my back."

Wild Card's hand slid upward over an older scar. "Don't come home with another scar," he said, lifting his head to stare at me.

I smiled up at him, laying a hand against his cheek. "I won't."

"I'm not kidding, Kelsey." He slid his arms around my back. "I'm not stupid. You're meeting with either Miguel or Santiago. Neither of them will be traveling alone."

"I'll be as careful as I can, but we both know everyone is in danger until this is handled."

"It doesn't always have to be you, though, who puts their life on the line."

"Miguel's a businessman. This will be a business meeting."

Wild Card leaned his forehead against mine. "And if the meeting becomes hostile?"

"I'll be ready. Jackson and Casey will be ready."

He closed his eyes. "Things go wrong. You know that. What if you don't make it out?"

"Then help my son survive it," I whispered.

"Who's going to help *me* survive it," he whispered back, pulling me into a hug.

He held me for a long time as the steam filled the bathroom. When he released me, he hurried from the room, turning on the fan on his way out.

"Shit," I said to myself as I stripped the rest of my clothes and stepped into the shower.

Chapter Thirty-Six

It wasn't easy being stealthy in three-inch heels. I waited until both Santiago's guards had their backs turned before moving from the office where I had hidden to a spot behind a wide support column. I waited again for my next opportunity before crossing to the center of the room and placing my gun to the back of Santiago's head. He stopped yelling at the half-conscious prisoner who we'd left strapped to a chair. At the immediate silence, his guards pivoted toward us, pulling their weapons.

"Nice and slow, boys. Lower your weapons, or I blow his brains out."

"You shoot me, then they shoot you," Santiago said, holding his hands out to his sides.

"Are you sure about that?" I asked as I raised a hand signal into the air.

The rifle fire sounded in the warehouse, the warning shots landing in the ceiling.

Santiago startled at the sound. "Who else is here?"

"Just a few ex-military buddies, spoiling to get some sniper practice in this weekend."

Santiago motioned for his men to lower their weapons. "Someone might have called the gunshots into the police. They're likely to arrive at any moment."

"Don't you worry your pretty little head over it. I have friends keeping everyone out of my way." I looked over at Santiago's goons, sliding my shoulder bag off and tossing it toward them. "You two, grab the flex cuffs out of the bag. Strap them on with your hands behind your back." I reached forward with my free hand and removed the gun from Santiago's back.

"If anything happens to me, my brother will kill you," Santiago said.

"We shall see." I kicked the back of his knees, forcing him to the floor. Keeping my gun on Santiago, I stepped behind the other men. I kicked my bag away from them, tossing Santiago's gun on top before I tightened their cuffs. The original prisoner still had his hands bound behind his back and his ankles zip tied to the chair.

"Kelsey?" Tyler called from the doorway.

"I thought I told you to stay home?" I called out as I stepped back a few paces and retrieved my shoulder bag.

"I decided to follow Shipwreck," Tyler said as he urged Shipwreck through the door with a shotgun pointed at his back. At least Tyler hadn't worn his club jacket, advertising the Devil's Players.

"I could've handled it."

"You've already got four prisoners," Tyler said, grinning. "That's a few too many, even for you. What's the plan?"

"Since you volunteered your services," I said, grinning back as I passed him flex cuffs from my bag, "Santiago and I need to step outside for a moment. If any of his men try anything, just raise a hand and the guys in the rafters will take them out."

Tyler glanced around but didn't see anyone. "*O—kay.*"

I grabbed Santiago by the back of the shirt, jerking him upward. I felt my stitches pull and was glad I left the waterproof bandage on so I wouldn't bleed on my white blouse. It was a nice blouse.

I turned Santiago toward the door and forced him outside. I didn't have backup outside, so the quicker I could get us back inside, the better. I walked him to the van, holding him against the front quarter panel while I slipped on a pair of black driving gloves, one at a time, so I could keep my gun trained on Santiago. When I had both of them on, I moved him to the side door. "Open the van."

"Why?"

"*Do it*," I ordered, holding the gun to the back of his head and distancing my stance, preparing to fight.

Santiago opened the van and unconsciously stepped back when he saw the body. I holstered my weapon and shoved Santiago—*hard*—on top of the dead man. I stepped back, readying myself, as Santiago braced his hands on the body to lift himself off the corpse. As expected, he pulled the large-handled knife and turned, swinging it in an arc toward me.

Anticipating the move, I easily kicked the knife free. Grabbing his wrist, I held it firmly as I ducked under his arm and behind him, pivoting him toward the van and slamming his chest into the front passenger's door with his arm now wrenched at a painful angle behind his back.

"Thank you," I said as I pulled a flex cuff out and secured first one, then the other, wrist behind his back. "You made that too easy."

He coughed and wheezed, trying to fill his lungs with air. "What the hell was that all about?"

"I needed someone else's prints on the knife." I forced him to his knees, pulled my gun again, and held it to his head as I reached out with the other gloved hand to pick up the knife. I tried not to think about it as I slid the knife back into its original hole in the dead man's body. "Who is he, anyway?" I asked as I stepped away from the van.

"A loser. I paid the bastard ten grand to kill you. If he wasn't already dead, I'd kill him all over again." He spat, impressively hitting the body from five feet away.

"Thanks for the extra DNA." I pulled Santiago up from the ground. "Damn. I can't believe you hired someone for only ten grand. I used to be worth a lot more than that."

"I had trouble finding someone who would take the job," Santiago admitted, shrugging. "Three guys turned me down when they heard the hit was for you. They called you the Death Demon."

"Yeah, I've heard that before." I shook my head, laughing. "The nicknames people come up with these days." I closed the van door. "Back inside. Let's go."

"Are you going to kill me?" Santiago asked, standing tall.

"Only if I have to," I said, shoving him forward.

"Not so fast," Sebrina said from behind me. I felt a gun to the side of my head and froze.

"Sebrina," I said without turning. "I'd say I was surprised you're here, but truthfully, I expected you to make an appearance at some point."

"I won't be staying long. Let Santiago go and we'll be on our way."

"Shipwreck's inside. Do you want him too?"

"No thanks. Shipwreck's served his purpose. You can keep him."

"And Grady?"

"Been there. Done that. Now quit stalling. Let Santiago go."

"I can't do that. His brother is expecting him."

"Miguel?" Her voice pitched higher. "He's coming here?"

"What's wrong, Sebrina?" I asked. "Are you scared of Miguel? Why?"

"He's not someone you want to mess with, is all. Why's he coming here?"

"To pick up Santiago, of course, and he won't be happy if he flew all this way for nothing."

"Shit," she said as she took a step back. "This wasn't part of the plan."

"What was the plan? Ride off into the sunset with the cartel boss?"

"You'll never know. I'm afraid I'll have to kill you both. It will distract Miguel long enough to get away."

"Oh, you're not going anywhere," I said, turning my head to grin at her. "Good night, Sebrina," I said as I nodded to Grady who was standing behind her.

She started to turn, aiming the gun away from me as Grady's arm slipped around her neck in a choke hold. Within seconds, she was passed out on the ground. Bones, Donovan, and Wild Card moved out from behind the van. I passed a set of flex cuffs to Donovan, and he secured her hands.

"Unless you want to turn her over to Miguel to disappear, I suggest you get her out of here. Take Shipwreck, too. He's inside."

Grady lifted her into his arms and without a word, carried her across the parking lot. Donovan nodded to Bones to follow them. I nudged Santiago with the gun to head inside.

"Took you long enough," Tyler said as I walked in.

"Sorry. I had visitors," I said as Donovan and Wild Card followed me inside.

"Is my brother really coming here?" Santiago asked. "Or did you say that to scare Sebrina?"

"Oh, he's definitely on his way," I said, shoving him to the center of the room. I swiped my leg low against the back of his calves as I threw an arm across his chest. He landed hard on his ass. "Didn't he tell you he was flying in for a visit?" I stepped a few paces away and circled him. "It wasn't hard to get his attention. Seems losing money is a big deal to him."

"What did you do?" Santiago asked as he rolled to his side and looked up at me. Beads of sweat started to rise on his forehead.

"It doesn't matter what I did. What matters is that Miguel wants his businesses protected, and that's not going to happen until my family is safe."

"Give me Sebrina," Santiago said, nearly begging me as he sat up. "Give me Sebrina, and we'll leave. You'll never see either of us again."

"You want me to hand over a dirty DEA agent *to you*? The head of the cartel? *Get real*."

"*She belongs to me*! You can't keep her from me!"

"You are insane. Sebrina was going to leave you out there to die as soon as she heard your brother was coming."

"She would've come back. She would've found another way. We're destined for each other."

"Sebrina's not in a position to save anyone. I have her and Shipwreck on video plotting against both sides. They're done. *Finito*."

"You'll regret this. One of us will find you. We'll destroy you."

"I'm not too concerned," I said as I took the butt of my gun and slammed it against the back of his head.

He slumped to the side, unconscious.

"*Finito* is Italian," Tyler said, pushing Santiago over with his foot.

"Damn, I really need to learn Spanish. What's the word for finished?"

"*Terminado*," Shipwreck said, chuckling as he leaned to one side, then the other, moving his legs out from under him to sit flat legged on the floor.

"Thank you," I said, turning my gun on him. "You know, for a jackass, you're still a fun guy to hang with. Everyone's going to be super disappointed to hear you're a traitor. You'd likely have gotten away with it too, if you didn't continuously underestimate me. I mean, how many times are you going to fail before you figure it out?" I asked, squatting down two arm-lengths distance away from him and holding my gun pointed at his head. "Tyler?"

"Yeah?"

"Relieve Shipwreck of his knife and re-secure his hands."

"Where the hell did he get a knife?" Tyler asked, moving behind Shipwreck and kicking the small blade out of his hand.

"Did you search him?" I asked, grinning at Tyler as he pulled another flex cuff from his back pocket.

"No," Tyler admitted, reluctantly.

"Think maybe next time you will?"

Tyler pulled Shipwreck's hands into the cuffs. Tyler's face scrunched in anger, but I knew he was angry with himself, not me. He patted down Shipwreck, relieving him of his phone, keys, sandals, and socks. Tyler wasn't taking any chances. He even pulled Shipwreck's necklace with a jerk, breaking the chain.

"Did you search the other guys?" Tyler asked.

"*Nah*. Wasn't worth my time. They know the snipers will shoot them if they try anything."

Shipwreck shook his head. "Everyone's at the rope pulling competition. Your scare tactics won't work. You're not fooling anyone."

The sound of a bolt-action rifle, ejecting their cartridges, echoed in the empty warehouse. Shipwreck visibly gulped.

"Yeah. That's how dumb you were," I said, grinning at Shipwreck. "Face it, I'm smarter than you." I squatted in front of him, tilting my head to the side as I studied him. "I'll give you credit, though. You surprised me by getting past security to release your guy from the storage room. How'd you do it? We had the houses covered from every angle."

"Construction site," Shipwreck said, shrugging. "Figured you'd extend the tunnel to the next house. My guess paid off when I found the access."

"Why kill the other men?"

"They knew I worked for Santiago. I couldn't chance them talking."

I stood and shook my head. Those men didn't need to die. They didn't care that Shipwreck worked for Santiago. They only wanted to live. I sighed, looking over at Wild Card. "I don't like Shipwreck knowing about the tunnels."

"Maybe I should help him forget," Wild Card said as he walked over and punched Shipwreck.

Tyler stomped on Shipwreck's leg. Donovan grabbed Shipwreck by the shirt and pulled him up from the floor to hold him as Wild Card punched him a few more times.

It didn't take long before Donovan tossed Shipwreck's battered body to the floor. He then grabbed Shipwreck by the belt and started dragging him toward the back of the warehouse. "I'll take him out the back door to our vehicle and send Bones inside."

"No. You might need Bones' help if Grady changes his mind about Sebrina."

"It's no longer up to Grady," Donovan said as he pulled Shipwreck through the door.

Wild Card stood with his arms crossed over his chest. He glanced at each of the prisoners before glancing with only his eyes into the rafters, nodding briefly at Jackson, then Casey. I winked at Wild Card before strolling in a circle around the prisoners.

"We thought Santiago was crazy," one of Santiago's goons muttered to the other.

"Do I need to worry about you guys overhearing anything you shouldn't have?" I asked them.

"No," they both said at once, shaking their heads.

My phone buzzed, and I pulled it from my bag to read the screen. Jackson was texting me that two black SUVs with tinted windows pulled into the parking lot. I tucked the phone into my handbag and exchanged it with the burner phone, calling Miguel.

"Ms. Harrison," Miguel answered.

"I'm inside with your brother and his men. Come in slowly and let's discuss the situations like professionals."

"How do I know it's not a trap?"

"If it was a trap, I wouldn't have warned you I was inside." I hung up and tossed the phone into my bag. "He'll likely to debate whether to enter or not for at least five minutes," I said to Tyler. "That gives us time to work on your training. Close your eyes."

"Umm," Tyler said, pointing his gun at the prisoners. "We're kind of in the middle of something."

"It's fine. Close your eyes."

Tyler exhaled in frustration but closed his eyes.

"Now with your senses, I want you to feel, not see or hear, but *feel* your surroundings."

"I don't get it."

"You do, you just don't recognize it. Search for that creepy feeling you get when the hair on the back of your neck stands up for no logical reason. The one you get when you tell me to tighten security or to keep the kids in the house. Find that sensation."

"Okay," Tyler said. "It's not the same feeling, but I've got this tingle. Like..."

"Like you're being watched through the scope of a rifle?" Wild Card asked.

"Holy shit," Tyler said, opening his eyes and looking directly at Jackson's location in the rafters. He turned halfway around and zoomed in immediately on Casey's location. Casey's laugh echoed across the warehouse. "How'd I know where they were?"

"Sixth sense. I always knew you had it," I said, slapping him on the shoulder. "Nice job."

"Is there a way to practice? Hone the skill?"

"I don't know. As a kid, I was always in some kind of danger and had to use my senses to stay aware of my surroundings. Later when I became a cop, it helped keep me alive." I made another circle around the prisoners. "What you felt was the sensation of being watched. Take that same vibe and mix in a dash of danger, and you'll know when to duck, *fast*."

Tyler laughed.

"You're a good teacher," one of Santiago's men said.

"Yeah," another one agreed. "You're good for him. Teaching him the right way. You let him know when he screws up, but then you move on, teaching him something else."

"Awe, shucks, guys," I said, strolling around the group again. "You're going to make me blush."

The warehouse door opened, and a guard walked inside, holding a gun but keeping it lowered.

I waved him inside. "You can keep your gun, but if you raise your weapon, you'll leave this warehouse in a body bag."

The guard looked around the room before speaking in rapid Spanish behind him. Another guard entered, followed by Miguel. Both guards kept their focus on Tyler and Wild Card as they walked forward. Miguel glanced at everyone, then focused on me. He walked halfway to us, then stopped and glanced up at Jackson before turning his head and spotting Casey. He looked back at me.

"They're protective. It's a safety measure only," I said, shrugging.

"Damn, he's got the sense," Tyler whispered.

"I'm perfectly capable of hearing, too," Miguel said as he holstered his weapon behind his back. "I wasn't expecting you, Ms. Harrison."

"I knew your brother would be here." I wandered over and stood next to Tyler. "How'd you find Santiago so quickly? Your plane landed less than ten minutes ago."

"His men work for me. They told me where he was going. Did you arrange a meeting with him?"

"I didn't have to. I tipped off one of his spies to this location," I said, nudging Santiago's head with my gun. "He wanted to have a word with this guy," I said, pointing my gun to the half-unconscious guy still strapped to the chair. "He works for Santiago."

"I don't recognize him."

One of the bodyguards stepped forward and leaned closer to whisper to Miguel.

"I stand corrected. It seems he does work for Santiago." Miguel nodded to the man in the chair. "What happened to Alfie's face?"

"Well, first he kidnapped me and my friends, which is a big no-no. Then, *after* we agreed to provide him and his coworkers with a safe place to stay while we sorted this mess, he up and decided to kill his own men and leave a huge mess for me to clean up. I'm sorry to say that one of my guys no longer felt the need to play nice and beat the crap out of him."

Tyler and Wild Card smiled proudly.

Miguel nodded, trying to keep a straight face. "It happens to the best of us."

"I have a good faith present for you," I said, taking a piece of paper out of my suit jacket pocket and passing it to one of Miguel's guards.

The guard passed it to Miguel. "What's this?" Miguel asked as he looked at the slip of paper.

"The website address and login information for the texting app service we used to text your employees. It's a handy service. Worked much more efficiently than I'd planned."

Miguel slid the note along with his hand into his pocket. "What exactly do you want from me, Ms. Harrison?"

"Peace. To achieve that peace though, you'll need to control your brother and ensure the safety of my friends and family."

Miguel glared at his brother who was still sitting on the floor. "And if I can't control him?"

I shook my head side to side. "I'll tear your world to pieces, starting with your U.S. businesses. Then I'll come after you and your brother." I walked over and stood in front of him. "I won't stop. And there won't be another opportunity to negotiate. I'm ruthless like that. A dog with a bone you might say." I looked at Miguel's guards, measuring them up, before turning back to Miguel. "Next time we meet face to face—one of us will die."

His guards stiffened, taking a step forward. Miguel raised a hand, a silent order to stop. "If I end this war between you and my brother, it's over?"

"Yes. We'll go on with our lives as if we'd never met."

Miguel studied me for a long moment before nodding in agreement.

I walked over to Tyler who stood at ready, watching the guards. "Help everyone to their feet."

Tyler holstered his weapon and started cutting the flex cuffs from the prisoners. Wild Card walked over and stood beside me with his arms still crossed over his chest.

"Leave my brother's hands bound," Miguel ordered his men. "Get everyone loaded. I'll be there in a moment."

When the prisoners and Miguel's guards stepped outside, Miguel turned back to me. "There's one remaining issue. I'll deal with it, but I need more time."

"And that issue is?"

"Santiago hired a hitman to kill you. I haven't been able to make contact yet to stop the orders."

I looked up at Jackson and pointed toward the window. He stepped away from the thick vertical column and walked the few feet to the window, pushing it open to reposition his gun.

"Follow me," I said to Miguel as I walked toward the door.

"Your men have skill," Miguel said.

I glanced back and followed his line of sight to where Casey stood, balancing on a beam, holding his rifle pointed at Miguel while he walked sideways toward the window on his side of the warehouse. "All the men at Ace's are top notch. Fighting, shooting, explosives, you name it, they're trained." I walked out the door of the warehouse and down the stairs.

Miguel offered me his arm, but I ignored it. Wild Card chuckled behind us.

"I've done my homework, Ms. Harrison. You don't have to keep warning me. I know what's at stake. I'll handle my brother. I just don't know how to contact the hitman he hired."

"You mean, this guy?" I asked as I opened the side door of the van.

I stepped aside so he could see the dead guy lying inside the van.

Tyler leaned over Miguel's shoulder, looking inside. "Where the hell did *he* come from?"

"He tried to kill me this morning," I said, wrinkling my nose at the smell. "I've had him in the van ever since. He's starting to smell."

"Damn it." Tyler stepped back and looked at me. "Why does the fun shit always have to happen when I'm sleeping?"

"Maybe it's because you do such a good job keeping me safe when you're awake," I teased Tyler, pinching his cheek.

Miguel looked at me, then at Tyler. He glanced over his shoulder at Wild Card who was smiling a big toothy smile. Miguel sighed and turned back to his own men, speaking in rapid Spanish. One of Santiago's guards jogged over. He looked inside the van and nodded to Miguel, speaking in rapid Spanish.

"I really need to learn the language," I said to Tyler. "Do you know how to speak Spanish?"

Tyler nodded. "Miguel asked if this was the hitman. The guard confirmed it was. That's it. The end."

Miguel's mouth turned up at the corners into an almost smirk. "What now?" Miguel asked, nodding to the dead man.

"He needs to go with you. I'm tired of burying bodies this week." I stepped over to the passenger door, opening it. "But before you move him, you should know that I tricked Santiago into handling the knife and exchanging DNA with the body."

Miguel's eyebrow rose as he looked back at the body. "Is any of your DNA on the body or the knife?"

"I wouldn't be surprised if there was a stray hair or two, but he was video recorded trying to abduct me yesterday, so any DNA could be explained," I answered as I lifted a bag from the passenger seat and handed it to Miguel.

Miguel looked into the bag, and this time, he did smile. "Thank you for providing me with an alternative, Ms. Harrison. I'll remember you fondly."

"No offense, Mr. Ramirez, but I'd prefer to forget you existed completely. Good day." I walked back toward the warehouse with Tyler and Wild Card following.

"What was in the bag?" Tyler asked as he opened the door for me.

"Packages of plastic coveralls and gloves, so they can move the body without transferring DNA." I called up to Jackson and Casey, "We're clear. It's safe to come down."

I walked around the room, picking up the ropes and flex cuffs. Tyler dragged the chair to the corner office. Wild Card watched out the front window while we worked. When we regrouped in the center of the room, I knew Tyler was still trying to figure out what had transpired.

"Miguel promised to control Santiago, but Santiago's obsessive, which makes him near impossible to deal with. Miguel also can't outright kill Santiago because the cartel business could capsize. But if Santiago was arrested..."

"Then Miguel has full control and no one would doubt his place at the head of the cartel," Tyler said finally seeing the full picture.

"Damn," Casey said, looking at me. "That's absolutely fucking brilliant."

"Your talents were wasted as a cop, Sis," Jackson said as he wrapped an arm around my neck and pulled me closer to kiss the top of my head.

"What happens to Shipwreck and Sebrina?" Wild Card asked.

"That's not up to me. You, Donovan and the rest of your team will have to decide their fate, but as you already know, there's video evidence you can use to turn them in to the DEA if that's what's decided."

"Is that what you want us to do?"

"I'm fine with it," I said, nodding as I walked toward the back door. "There's been too much blood spilled already."

Chapter Thirty-Seven

Tyler drove my SUV, following me, as I drove the van to Chops' shop. Both Chops and his lifetime girlfriend Candi were waiting as planned. They'd strip the interior of the van, acid wash the interior frame, before putting it all back together, including installing new carpet. I trusted them to do the job right and to keep me out of prison.

When we were almost home, I saw the Devil's Players were closing down the store and the cars clearing out. It was a little after four, so they must've sold out of inventory early. I directed Tyler to drop me off at the entrance. Walking inside, I nodded to several familiar faces and helped start shutting down lights and cashing out registers.

"Well, don't you look fancy for a rope pulling competition," Lisa said as she walked over. "What brings you to the store?"

"I just finished a meeting and saw you were closing. Any problems?"

"Normal Saturday craziness. We had two shoppers arrested for fighting over a tank top, an insane bride-to-be who threw a chair at my head when I told her there was no way to alter a size two dress into a size sixteen, and Alex," she paused while she rolled her eyes, "attempted to use a scooter in the store to move racks from the inventory room. He crashed into the wall. Luckily no one was hurt, and Katie wasn't here to see it."

"And the wall?" I asked, grinning.

"Goat says he can fix it."

"Come on," Alex called, running over to us and grabbing our hands. "We've missed all the best parts of the rope pulling. Let's go."

"We still need to lock down the store," Lisa said.

Alex shoved us toward the back door. "Goat and Carol said they'd handle it."

"Wait," I said, stopping to take off my shoes. "These look fabulous, but they're killing my feet."

We walked out the back door, across the lot, and into the field. The stiff grass felt somewhat comfortable under my aching feet. I waved to Hattie, Pops, and the kids who were watching us from the main house balcony. Six guards stood either on the balcony or in the surrounding area.

Turning my attention to the group ahead of me, all eyes turned to me as I walked their way. Several people snapped their heads from me to Charlie, then back to me again.

Wild Card and Donovan stood on the sidelines, waiting for me. "Sebrina and Shipwreck?"

"Bones and Grady are watching them until the DEA agents get here," Donovan said.

"Why am I getting the feeling you were at more than just a meeting?" Lisa asked.

Several of the men, circled around us to listen.

"It *was* a meeting. Only it was with Miguel and Santiago Remirez."

"*Shit*," Wayne said, raising both hands into his hair as he stared at me in shock. "You met with the cartel and didn't tell us?"

"I didn't want anyone to worry."

"That wasn't your call," Donovan said, wrapping an arm around Lisa, "but I get why you felt the need to handle it the way you did. We didn't think much of Shipwreck missing, but when Sebrina slipped away, Grady asked us to postpone the competition and send a team with him. He knew something was going on, especially with Charlie pretending—very poorly—to be you."

"Hey," Charlie said, fisting her hands onto her hips. "It's not easy pretending to be Kelsey without speaking or lifting my face to anyone."

"You did good," Tech said. "Sebrina never noticed, so that's all that mattered."

"Why didn't we set a net to arrest Miguel and his men?" Donovan asked.

"And spend the rest of our lives hiding our children in fear of retaliation?" I asked, shaking my head. "My family—" I pointed toward the balcony "—matters more to me than any cocaine slinging cartel. Miguel can do as he pleases as long as he leaves us out of it."

"And the rest of us?" one of the men of Aces asked. "All's well as long as you and yours are safe?"

I stepped forward, wanting nothing more than to deck the guy, but Wild Card threw an arm around my chest, pulling me back. "Easy, darlin'. Breath through the rage, little dragon."

Tech chuckled, looking at the guy. "She's a sister to the men of Aces, dickhead. She's not the type to leave anyone behind."

"My peace deal was with Miguel. Everyone is safe from the cartel, including Shipwreck and Sebrina, though they don't deserve it," I said, gritting my teeth. "Santiago will probably to be arrested for murder either today or tomorrow."

"Who did he kill?" Donovan asked.

"I can't discuss the details," I said as I stepped out of Wild Card's hold. "I can say, the dead guy wasn't a good guy, so it doesn't matter."

A slow grin spread across Donovan's face. "You're brilliant."

"I know," I said, winking at him.

"Anything else we need to know?" Wayne asked.

"That's it. Other shit has happened the last couple of days, but it's all been handled. How did the rope pulling contest go?" I asked the group at large.

Everyone started yelling and talking over each other.

"One at a time!" I yelled.

"Your team cheats," Wayne said, glancing over at Katie and Bridget with narrowed eyes.

"What do you think I did today, Wayne?" I asked him. "We are clear of the mess with the cartel because I cheated. I hacked and defrauded Miguel's companies, causing chaos before breakfast. Before lunch, I purposely didn't report a felony to the authorities. This afternoon, I did even more shit like—*maybe, possibly, somewhat*—planted DNA evidence."

"I didn't hear that," Maggie said, grinning.

"The point being, we cheat all the time. We don't work for the military or for law enforcement because we don't like to be hogtied by the rules. Our jobs at Aces require us to think outside the box for the good of the world, so why would we run an Aces competition by any other standard?"

Casey grinned, nodding to me. "Well said."

"Technically," Tech smirked, "we didn't break a single one of the competition rules."

"We just applied a little creativity to make them work in our favor," Bridget added.

"They're right," Jerry said, holding up the rules sheet. "Doesn't say anything about setting a rope on fire, or pretending everyone dropped the rope while Anne hid in the back holding it until everyone let go."

I turned to look at my team, proud of them.

"It was so much fun," Anne whispered, grabbing my arm and bouncing in excitement.

"We won two of the bouts?" I asked.

"Three." Katie shook her head at Trigger. "Dumbass here convinced Nightcrawler to sneak into the woods and fire a gun. Everyone, except for Trigger, dropped the rope and started running toward the woods shooting."

"I didn't drop the rope," Trigger said, raising his arms and flexing his muscles. "I pulled that sucker across the line all on my own. Single handedly got us a first-place win."

"How in the hell did Nightcrawler survive?" I asked, turning to look back toward the house and confirming he was unharmed.

"Bulletproof vest, fast running, and a getaway car on the other side of the woods," Bridget said.

I stepped over to Trigger, gripping his shirt in a wad. "You pull something like that again, and you'll have to settle with me on the mats. Understood?"

His happy grin fell as he turned white and gulped. He nodded slowly.

"From now on," I said, stepping away, "if I'm not available to consult, you run your ideas past Bridget or Tech."

"Yes, boss. For the record though, I did warn Hattie. I didn't want her and the kids to worry."

"I appreciate that, but you could've gotten Nightcrawler killed. Most of these men have sniper training.

"Told you she'd be pissed," Charlie said as she walked over and took off the baseball cap. Her hair streamed down in choppy layers, dyed at the tips in silver and black. It was a little unnerving seeing how alike we looked. "Now, cuz, are you going to explain the blood staining your shirt?"

I looked down at my shirt, and sure enough, a patch of blood had leaked through. "I must've pulled a stitch. Sorry."

Alex lifted the edge of the shirt to look at it closer. "I can get the blood out, but what stitches?"

"I accidentally bumped into a guy at Headquarters while he was swinging a knife at me. Security over there's not so good."

Wayne ran a hand down the front of his face as he sighed and looked at my stitches.

"Damn," Lisa said, resting a hand on my shoulder. "You had one hell of a day, didn't you?"

"I need booze," I said, nodding. "A lot of it."

"Should the rest of us head back across the highway?" Wayne asked.

"No. Not tonight. Come on," I said, waving for everyone to follow as we walked toward the main house. "Drinks are on me tonight."

Chapter Thirty-Eight

"Did you hear about Billy Hobbs?" Wayne asked.

"That he was fired?" I said as Hattie set a drink on the table in front of me.

"No. That him and Daphne are getting married."

I choked on my drink. "You're shitting me! He was stalking her!"

"Apparently, she knew the whole time it was him. She liked the attention."

"Damn," Maggie said, sitting next to me. "Did not see that one coming."

"Kelsey?" Jerry said, walking into the dining room, looking nervous.

"What's up?" I asked, turning to face him from my chair.

"Um. There was this weird thing with Sebrina this morning. I'm not sure if I should tell Donovan about it."

"I saw her trying to weasel info from you this morning. What was she after?"

"I didn't help her, I swear it. She wanted the architectural plans of Headquarters and the other buildings."

"No worries. She was looking for someone we were hiding." I looked over at Tyler. I had ordered him to take the rest of the night off, leaving Renato in charge of security. "We would've never been that obvious by hiding our guy at Headquarters, would we, Tyler?"

"That would've been a prospect's move," Tyler said, laughing. "Of which," he turned, showing me the back of his cut, "I am not." The back of his leather club jacket no longer held the bold word *Prospect* across the back.

"When the hell did that happen?" I asked, walking over to hug him.

"Bones told me I was voted in two nights ago, but they were waiting to throw a party for me until the dust settled."

"You earned this," I said, tugging on his leather vest. "It's about time they recognized you're no one's prospect."

"Except yours?" Tyler asked, raising an eyebrow.

"You still have a few things to learn, but I trust you with my family, Tyler. You're not my prospect. You're the head of my security."

"Which says a hell of a lot," Wild Card said, walking across the room to clap Tyler on the back. "Kelsey could hire almost anyone at Aces to run her security, but you're the one she trusts. I'd be honored to work with you on any job."

Several other men from Aces and both clubs agreed and took turns congratulating Tyler on being voted into the Devil's Players as a full member. I gave him some space, walking into the kitchen. Hattie was fussing with a platter.

"You're tired. You need to quit," I said as I placed my hand over hers.

"It would be rude to go to bed when we have company."

"I'll kick everyone out then," I said, turning to do just that.

"Kelsey Harrison, don't you dare," Hattie scolded, grabbing my arm to stop me.

I laughed. "Go to bed. Everyone will understand."

"Are you sure?" she asked, wringing her hands.

"She's sure," Pops said, walking up behind us and taking Hattie's hands in his. "And if it gets too noisy for you to sleep, I'll come down and kick everyone out."

Hattie looked adoringly up at Pops. "Well, all right then, but I can get myself to bed. You two stay up and have fun."

"I'll be up to check on you in a few minutes," Pops said, kissing her forehead and turning her toward the private stairs. When Hattie disappeared out of sight, Pops turned back to me. "Let's step outside. I'd like to talk to you for a moment."

This didn't sound good. If Pops wanted to talk to me in private, he was likely going to tell me something I didn't want to hear.

"Is this about Hattie?" I asked as we walked out to the driveway.

"No. This is about you. And the decisions you make." Pops placed his hands on his hips, looking uncomfortable. "I try not to meddle, but the way I see it, you have an opportunity in front of you, baby girl. I don't want you to blow it and miss your chance."

"What are you talking about, Pops?" I laughed, shaking my head, trying to figure out why he looked so darn uncomfortable. "If you've got something to say, just say it."

"You have choices, Kelsey," Pops said, placing his hands on my shoulders. "You tend to jump into relationships as a reaction to whatever drama you're facing at the moment and finding comfort where you can. I understand that, and I'm not judging. Right now, though, you have an opportunity to think through what you want. To decide who makes you happy."

"You're giving me dating advice?" I asked, with an eyebrow raised.

"No. I'm not telling you who to date, only that you have time to figure things out the right way this time. You keep crashing into relationships based on who's nearby when shit hits the fan. It's good to pick someone who'll stand beside you when you need them—but did you ever consider who makes you the happiest when you don't need anyone? Who makes you laugh? Who brings you the most joy?"

"My life's not that simple. I need someone strong who can handle the dangers and not run for the hills when things go sideways."

"Look around, baby girl," Pops said, waving his hand to the security guards gathered in the side yard, then waving his hand toward the packed house. "Everyone who knows you is there for you. Do you need a strong man who can handle being both alpha and beta—*yeah*. Don't limit yourself though to proximity. You need to take the time to decide who you enjoy spending time with when you're not out chasing bad guys. Because the day will come when you're not in the game anymore. Then what?"

For the first time in my life, I imagined myself getting older with grey hair and a few *moderate* wrinkles. The thought jarred me enough to cause me to take a step back. I'd never imagined that long into the future. If I was being honest, my whole life never focused on more than the next year because I always expected to die young. Every business and property I owned was immediately added to my estate plan. The day I adopted Nicholas, I signed a new will so guardianship was clear when I died. I'd faced down deadly situations since I was a child and expecting my death to happen at any moment was ingrained in most of my decisions—including the men in my life. Eric had been a fling while we were partnered on a case together. Bones had been a comfort when I felt lost and alone. Wild Card had been an escape from danger. Grady had been a friend by my side, who shared my goals and held me up long enough for me to keep fighting. I'd loved all of them, though in different ways, but... *would I have chosen any of them if I was planning on living a long life*? Was that why I couldn't commit to Grady when he asked me to marry him? Could I see any of the men in my life drinking coffee with me on the back porch when we were old and grey? I didn't know the answer, which I suppose was Pops' point. I looked up at Pops.

He must have seen the confusion on my face because he folded me into his arms and sighed. "Yes, baby girl. That's the life you deserve. The one you just pictured in your head. That's the life you've always deserved."

He held me, rubbing my back, while I sniffled. It wasn't until Wild Card ran past us, stopping when he saw I was crying, that I pulled away and wiped my eyes.

"Everything okay?" he asked, stepping closer and cupping my face as he looked down at me.

"Pops and his wise words," I said, nodding. "All is well."

"Good," Wild Card said, grinning down at me. "Because I have a surprise for Nicholas."

He turned, running across the yard to a white van that was parked down the side road. A few minutes later, it all made sense as he led a young dog out of the van on a leash.

"*Oh, no, he did not*," I said, laughing.

"He got Hattie's permission," Pops said, throwing an arm around my shoulders. "He also arranged for a dog trainer to come to the house twice a week to work with Nicholas and the dog. Nightcrawler and Beth offered to help as well. The dog has almost two years of training as a protection companion dog. He'll keep Nick safe, and..." Pops looked down at me grinning. "Nicholas agreed to brush his teeth without argument if Wild Card bought him a dog."

I laughed harder. Nicholas ran out of the house and across the yard. He dropped to his knees in front of the dog and started hugging him. The dog looked up at Wild Card who was grinning down at them. Nightcrawler walked by and winked as he carried a large bag of dog food and two oversized paper tote bags, likely filled with dog supplies.

"Well, I guess we have a dog then," I said, shaking my head and turning into the house. "Is that how Wild Card's mother convinced him to brush his teeth?" I asked Pops.

"Nope," Pops said, opening the door and holding it open as I walked through. "She bought him a horse."

"Damn. I'm getting off easy on this bribery thing," I said, grinning. I turned to step into the kitchen and came face to face with Grady.

"Nicholas isn't ready for a dog," Grady said, seeming annoyed.

"Not your decision to make."

Grady sighed, looking down at the floor. "Can we talk?" he asked, looking up at me then at Pops who stood behind me.

"Remember what I said, baby girl," Pops said, kissing the top of my head before he turned up the private stairs to Hattie's room.

"What was that about?" Grady asked.

"Life, death, and old age," I answered. I pointed to the other side of the house and led the way to my bedroom. Lisa had cleared Abigail's spare crib, toys, and supplies earlier, so the atrium was once again my quiet place. "What do you want, Grady?"

"Can we sit?" Grady asked, motioning for me to join him on the couch.

"No. I don't think so." I walked over to the window where I could still see Wild Card and Nicholas with the dog. Nicholas looked happy. Happier than I'd seen him in a long while.

"I'm sorry," Grady said.

I turned to watch him. He was sitting on the couch, leaned forward with his elbows on his knees and running his fingers through his hair. He looked almost lost.

"When I suspected Sebrina was responsible for the shit in Mexico, I tried to pull her in the other direction, to keep the mess away from the family. That plan took a nosedive though when you drugged us and dragged us here."

I leaned against the cool glass of one of the windows. "I couldn't leave you out there, alone, unprotected. That wasn't something I could accept. Your death would've hurt the whole family. Nicholas might be angry with you right now, but he loves you. He couldn't have handled losing you. Not like this."

Grady nodded, not looking up. "I hurt him. I hurt *you*. I'm sorry."

"You did," I admitted, wiping a tear away. "You broke my heart, Grady. In my head, I understand it. I understand you still being in love with Sebrina. I understand you wanting her to be a different person.

Someone worth saving. Understanding, though, is miles away from forgiveness."

"I love you. You have to know that. I thought my feelings for Sebrina were over. I would never have started a relationship with you if I didn't, but in Mexico…"

Neither of us needed him to finish that sentence. We both knew how emotions were heightened in life and death situations. Hell, it was the foundation of our entire relationship.

"I need you to leave," I whispered.

"Leave Michigan?" he asked, without looking up.

"That's up to you. Right now, Nicholas and I both need some space. We need to know our home is a safe place to think and figure things out."

"What if I stayed at Headquarters? Can we work things out if I give you some space?"

"I don't know," I said, walking over and sitting on the couch across from him. "If nothing else, I hope we find a way to be friends. I care about you—deeply." I took the diamond and sapphire ring off, setting it on the coffee table. My hand felt naked without it. "There's something else you should know. I made a promise to Pops earlier. He asked me to take the time to figure out who I wanted to spend my life with. Not who made me feel safe, or who I worked well with, but who I wanted to grow old with."

"Like Wild Card?" Grady asked, gritting his teeth.

"Pops didn't weigh in favor of either of you. In fact, he made a point that it could be anyone, including someone I haven't met yet. He wants me to stop building relationships for the short term, and figure out what I want long term."

"Marriage and kids?"

"Marriage, kids, retirement, dying from something normal like a heart attack or a car accident. I've never taken the time to think about it because I honestly never planned on living long enough."

Grady looked up at me with deep creases in his forehead. "You've never thought about getting old?"

"You've only been in my life for a little over a year, but how many times have I faced death in that time? It's like a shadow that follows me. It's part of who I am. Planning a future seemed irrelevant if I wasn't going to be around to live it."

Grady looked away, thinking. "But, Nicholas," he said, shaking his head. "You adopted him. You committed to him."

"He had *no one*," I said, wiping another round of tears away. "No one was there to love and protect him. No one was there to hold him, clothe him, feed him. I knew I could give him a better life, and when I died, Charlie would keep him safe."

Grady whispered back my words like an echo, "*When you died.*"

"*When,*" I said, nodding. "I can picture Nicholas graduating college, getting married, having children. I just can't picture myself being around when those things happen. I need to figure out what that looks like, what I want that to look like, inside my own head."

"Is it possible that I'm in that future?" Grady asked.

"I don't know. First, I'm angry and hurt for what you did. In my head, I understand your actions. In my heart, you cheated on me. You lied to me. You turned your back on me and my son. And worst of all, you devastated Nicholas."

"Most of what I did was to protect both of you."

"Sleeping with Sebrina had nothing to do with us," I said, standing to walk toward the atrium door. "Take the ring with you when you leave."

The cool air felt good on my hot skin. Instead of walking toward the driveway, I turned to the right, walking around the house and into the back yard. I called out to warn the security team as I walked down the short hill to the patio area below.

"Why are you wandering around by yourself?" Bones asked.

"I think it's about time I walk alone for a while, don't you?" I said, grinning at how cute Bridget and Bones looked together as he held her so her back was snug against his chest.

"Am I supposed to understand that?" Bones asked, raising an eyebrow.

"No," Wild Card said, walking out of the basement gym onto the patio. "But I do." He walked toward me. "I got a call from a buddy who needs my help on a job. You going to be okay for a week or two if I leave?"

"You're not staying for the rest of the tournament?"

He shook his head. "This job can't wait. Jackson said he'd take my place in the paintball competition. As for The Circle of Hell, I'm betting the winners will be local." Wild Card tilted his head at Bones. Bones smiled proudly. "I can challenge them for their titles another time. Besides, Tech promised to send me the video highlights."

"You'll be missed, but I get it."

"You're good then?"

I hugged him. "I got this."

"I know you do," he said, kissing my cheek. "I'm going to say goodbye to Nick and Jager before I take off. Call me if either of you need me."

"Jager?"

"The *dog*," Wild Card answered as he jogged backwards into the field. "By the way, I've secured a promise from Nicholas to brush his teeth without argument."

I smiled at Wild Card as he continued to jog backwards. "You mean bribed?"

Wild Card shrugged. "Do you care?"

I shook my head. "Be safe, Mr. Wesley."

"What fun would that be?" he asked before turning and jogging away.

"What was that all about?" Bones asked.

I didn't answer. I watched Wild Card throw the ball for the dog and then steer Nicholas away from everyone so they could talk. Nicholas nodded several times before something Wild Card said made him laugh. Nicholas looked over at me and waved. I smiled and waved back.

"You okay?" Bridget asked, stepping away from Bones and looping her arm through mine. "You're crying."

"They're happy tears, Bridget. Happy tears."

THE END

Thank you for reading the Kelsey's Burden: *Hearts and Aces*.

If you enjoyed this book, would you honor me by leaving a review? Reviews communicate to other readers whether a book is worthy of their time. I hope this book met that mark, and you'll leave your honest opinion for the next reader to consider.

What's next? Sign up for my newsletter to keep in touch with the latest release dates and book gossip: www.BooksByKaylie.com.

BOOKS BY KAYLIE

<u>Kelsey's Burden Series</u>
Layered Lies
Past Haunts
Friends and Foes
Blood and Tears
Love and Rage
Day and Night
Hearts and Aces

<u>Standalone Novels</u>
Slightly Off-Balance
Diamond's Edge

For a complete and up-to-date list of novels, visit www.BooksByKaylie.com

Special Thanks:

Special thanks to the following individuals for helping me get this book across the finish line and into the hands of readers:

Judy G., and Kathie Z. for your beta reading and proofreading assistance. Your feedback is appreciated beyond words! Thank you. Favorite writing blooper caught: "...*I could imagine him on the other end of the phone, shanking his head.*"

Editing and proofreading services by Sheryl Lee via BooksGoSocial.

Contact the Author

My readers are welcome to stalk me at any of the below listed sites to keep up-to-date on future book releases and other news. Because I prefer to hide in my girl cave writing new novels, I'm terrible about posting regularly to my social media accounts, but when I do show up—I read everything.

Twitter: @BooksByKaylie
Facebook: BooksByKaylie
Amazon Author Page: Kaylie Hunter
Website and Newsletter sign-up: www.BooksByKaylie.com

Kaylie Hunter resides in lower Michigan in the same city she moved to for college. It was the perfect distance from her family—close enough to visit, far enough that it wouldn't become a daily habit.

Feeling uninspired after several semi-successful careers, in 2014 she picked up a pen and an empty notebook and began to write. And while she had dabbled with writing before, starting and stopping multiple novels, this time she was driven to find out if she had what it took. Two years later, she published her first three books in the Kelsey's Burden series and hasn't quit writing since. Her search for what was missing in her life was over.

www.BooksByKaylie.com

Printed by Amazon Italia Logistica S.r.l.
Torrazza Piemonte (TO), Italy